COROMANDEL

ALSO BY PAT BARR

Non-Fiction

THE COMING OF THE BARBARIANS
THE DEER CRY PAVILION
A CURIOUS LIFE FOR A LADY
TO CHINA WITH LOVE
THE MEMSAHIBS
TAMING THE JUNGLE

Fiction

CHINESE ALICE
UNCUT JADE
JADE
KENJIRO

COROMANDEL

by

PAT BARR

HAMISH HAMILTON LONDON

HAMISH HAMILTON LTD

Published by the Penguin Group
27 Wrights Lane, London w8 5tz, England
Viking Penguin Inc, 40 West 23rd Street, New York, New York 10010, USA
Penguin Books Australia Ltd, Ringwood, Victoria, Australia
Penguin Books Canada Ltd, 2801 John Street, Markham, Ontario, Canada l3r 1b4
Penguin Books (NZ) Ltd, 182–190 Wairau Road, Auckland 10, New Zealand

Penguin Books Ltd, Registered Offices: Harmondsworth, Middlesex, England

First published in Great Britain 1988 by Hamish Hamilton

British Library Cataloguing in Publication Data

Barr, Pat, *1934*–
Coromandel
I. Title
823′.914 [F]

ISBN 0-241-12195-7

Typeset by CentraCet, Cambridge
Printed by Richard Clay Ltd, Bungay Suffolk

FOR MY DEAR FRIEND
'Gwyneth of Lewes'

COROMANDEL

The name is in fact *Chôromandala*, the Realm of *Chôra*; this being the Tamil form of the very ancient title of the Tamil Kings who reigned at Tanjore.

And the name occurs in the forms *Cholamandalam* or *Sola-mandalam* on the great Temple inscription of Tanjore (11th century), and in an inscription of AD 1101 at a temple dedicated to Varāhasvāmi near the Seven Pagodas.

From *Hobson-Jobson*

The question now before us is simply whether . . . when we can patronise sound philosophy and true history, we shall countenance, at the public expense, medical doctrines which would disgrace an English farrier – astronomy which would move laughter in girls in an English boarding school – history abounding with kings thirty feet high and reigns thirty thousand years long, and geography made up of seas of treacle and rivers of butter . . .

Thomas Macaulay, *Minute of Education on India (1834)*

AUTHOR'S NOTE

In writing this book, I've tended to avoid the familiar, clichéd vocabulary of the 'British Raj' because it is not really appropriate to the context. That vocabulary, much of which originated from the languages of north India, became common currency throughout British India during Queen Victoria's long reign; but, as far as I can gather, was not so in the Madras Presidency during the 1830s. Europeans living there then seem to have retained a number of customs and speech usages which developed during the previous century. These were often peculiar to the region and stemmed from the south Indian vernaculars. Many of them are quoted in the invaluable *Hobson-Jobson*, but would need explanation today because they fell into disuse when the growing ascendancy of the north and the improvement of internal communications lessened regional variations of this kind.

I am fully aware that the custom of suttee is usually associated with north India, especially Bengal and Rajasthan, but it is well documented by the Portuguese that the rite was also practised in the south, especially during the time of the Vijayanagars, and cases of it occurred there in the nineteenth century. In other respects, too, I have striven for historical accuracy, and all my references to such 'off-stage' personages as Sir Thomas Munro, Miss Emily Eden and Bishop Heber can be verified in the history books – where truth is assumed to reside. The only 'real-life' figure to appear 'on stage' is Raja Sevaji of Tanjore. According to the sources I consulted (admittedly all in English), his character was very much as I've described it; indeed Company records paint a darker picture of a man bordering on religious mania. This view is suspect, but the facts of his life indicate that he certainly did not possess the strong character and outward-looking intelligence of his predecessor.

Pat Barr
Norwich 1988

CHAPTER ONE

From the verandah of Spring's Gardens Marguerite Hervey waved languidly to Theophilus as he stepped into her second-best carriage. He failed to notice, of course. He'd been totally preoccupied since hearing of the *Minerva*'s safe arrival in the roadstead the previous evening. She could not blame him for this because, among the ship's passengers who'd left Portsmouth 120 days earlier, were his wife and the baby son he'd not yet seen.

Marguerite wandered into the drawing-room and settled in her usual chair, beside which, as usual, the day's copy of the *Madras Herald* and her morning cup of chocolate had been placed. She read and sipped, half-attentive to the slow rhythm of everyday household sounds: a servant beating inside dust from the dining-room punkah; a garden-boy scraping outside dust into piles with a broom; raised voices from the kitchen compound where fruit and vegetable vendors were enjoying the daily bargaining with the cook. Yes, there it was in the Vessels Arrived column – the *Minerva* with eighty passengers aboard including a judge, a visiting Director of the East India Company and a bishop; Mrs Theophilus Lang did not, naturally, merit any special mention.

She put down the paper and closed her eyes, unresistingly transported back to that day about fifty years ago when she herself had first set foot on the warm Indian sands. Exhilarated, excited, frightened, she had come dipping and plunging through the roaring Madras surf in one of the massalah boats that ferried passengers ashore from their ocean-going ships. Dark-skinned natives had lifted her over the high-sided boat and carried her to dry land where, damp with spray, laughing with joy, she had rushed into Roger's arms and proudly presented him with their son, born during the voyage out. Today, Theophilus's wife would present him with her first-born and they, in their turn, would cling to each other in grateful celebration of her safe arrival.

Imagining the scene, Marguerite thought wearily of the hundreds of buoyant young Europeans who had come bounding into India, and how many of them had never returned to their homelands. Roger – a cavalry officer – had been killed in the Third Mysore War against Tippu Sultan, leaving her with that ship-born baby and a younger one to face the first of her three widowhoods.

She reached for a cologne-drenched handkerchief, dabbed her temples and wandered to the window, looking vaguely towards the ever-pounding sea. Overnight rain had perked up the bushes and grassy tufts in the garden which, undoubtedly, would still look a dusty desert to Mrs Lang. A farmer's daughter apparently but, in the way of young husbands, Theophilus had not been very forthcoming about her. Theo's father, her late friend Bayard Lang, had been a splendidly unorthodox orientalist of the old school, as pickled in India as a mango in a jar. Theo had shown promise of similar development and Marguerite had encouraged him, for there were precious few originals among the young these days. But this conventional-seeming marriage to an ordinary-sounding Englishwoman, contracted during his last visit Home, disappointed her, and she was not disposed to think highly of the arriving bride.

'Have they come, madam?'

Kamba, the old ayah, stood in the doorway, eyes unusually bright and eager.

'Not yet. And it's no use getting excited about the baby. Mr and Mrs Lang won't be staying here long. I told you.'

Kamba shook her head and lowered her eyes, drawing her white cotton shawl tightly over her ears, for she'd long mastered the art of hearing only what she wanted to.

'They're going south – to Tanjore. I told you,' Marguerite added irritably. 'The Raja has offered Mr Lang a job there.'

'But why should he want to go off to such an out-of-the-way jungle hole when he had work here already?' Kamba mumbled. Her withered arms ached for one more white baby to croon over. All the mistress's grandchildren lived in distant places and seldom came to Spring's Gardens; in any case, they'd grown too big to cuddle.

'Just make sure there are no holes in the mosquito-netting of the cot. It hasn't been used for years.'

Kamba turned to leave, then paused. 'Adviser to a raja, hey? And baby will live in a rich palace with servants to fan him and rings on his fingers and toes?'

'Oh fiddle-de-dee! Nothing near so grand. Mr Lang is to work in the library and tutor His Highness a little, that's all.'

Marguerite shook her head in annoyance, more at herself than the ayah, for she was aware of becoming over-familiar with the servants and losing control of them in consequence. It came of living too long alone without a man in the house. She'd suggested that Theo and his new family share her home; but that wretched letter from Tanjore had put paid to her plans. Couched in the flowery language of the court, Raja Sevaji's missive had dwelt at length on the friendship that had once existed between his father and Theo's, and the hope that Theo, in his turn, would provide His Highness with 'good advice and protection from crafty rogues of all kinds'. To Marguerite it all sounded very fishy and insubstantial, in the usual Indian way, but Theophilus could not be persuaded to reject the offer. He was as impulsive, impractical and hot-blooded as his father – keen scholars both, but certainly not dried-up, over-cautious pedagogues. She laughed suddenly, remembering her first encounter with the thirteen-year-old Theophilus, who'd stayed with her in Madras before being bundled off Home to school in disgrace, following a little misdemeanour in Tanjore.

Well, that was many moons ago. Theo had been an anxious, shy and skinny boy. Now he was married, and she must put on her best face to meet his wife who might, just possibly, be a raving beauty – as Marguerite herself had once been. Hearing the crunch of wheels outside, she hurried to watch the carriage's return. A servant opened its door and a young woman with a baby in her arms stepped out, looking round curiously. Marguerite reached for her spy-glass and focused it; then she smiled and, without further ado, went to welcome the new arrivals.

Amelia Lang found herself before a two-storey, flat-roofed house with bungalow-like extension wings curving away on either side. Pillars and walls were sun-blistered yellow, rolls of dusty-green Venetian blinds hung askew on frayed cords; the main portico was flanked by shuttered arches at ground level, so that the front looked imposing only because of a row of high windows and a long balcony on the floor above. The general impression was of faded-pastel, tropical grandeur such as she'd seen in books of 'Pictures of the East', though she was surprised that the garden was only a stretch of dusty tufts enclosed by prickly pear bushes and dotted with spindly palms.

A servant held a parasol over her head and hurried her inside as if from a snowstorm. On the sweep of stairs stood a tall, stately, silver-haired woman.

'Mrs Lang – welcome to India and Spring's Gardens.'

As Theophilus introduced her, Amelia felt almost inclined to curtsey, but then Mrs Hervey swooped for the baby, cooing at him in quite an ordinary manner.

'Allow me to present him properly – Roland Theophilus Lang,' announced Theo triumphantly, 'usually called Rolly and just ten months old.'

'Delightful – utterly scrumptious! Mrs Lang you are to be congratulated for bringing him and yourself safely to us. You can't imagine how Theo has been huffing and puffing about you – braving all the perils of the deep without his protection. I trust you had a bearable voyage?'

'As bearable as is customary, thank you, Mrs Hervey. We had our share of gales round the Cape, three shipboard deaths, and Father Neptune shaved the gentlemen as we crossed the Line . . . Nothing untoward.'

Her tones were low-pitched and collected, with a slight rural burr that was pleasing though not fashionable.

'Then you were more fortunate than many. But come – I'm sure you'd like to refresh yourself in your bedroom before tiffin. So pray let my old ayah Kamba take Rolly from you. She's simply dying to hold a real live baby again.'

As Amelia handed Rolly over he squealed loudly, and little wonder, she thought, for Kamba looked so very wrinkled and ancient, and as dark-skinned as the native who'd carried her off the massalah boat and through the shallows to the shore. His strong, wet arm had glistened across her body much more blackly than she'd imagined Indian skin to be. And, just for a second, she'd felt panic-stricken, held in the grip of that darkness which also lurked in the beautiful land she'd reached. Then he'd released her on to the sand, still clutching baby, her shoes and skirt-hem soaked, her eyes a-shine, her straw bonnet dangling by a single yellow ribbon – which was how Theo first saw her. He rushed up, closing them in the circle of his joyous, grateful embrace.

'He's a little frightened by so many strangers, I think,' she now apologised.

'Then I'll stay with him.' Theo stroked his cheek. 'Because I'm not a stranger, Rolly my boy, I'm your father.'

A servant conducted Amelia along a wide passage to a spacious bedroom where her hand-baggage had already been deposited. It looked rather sordid in these orderly surroundings – hessian bags stuffed with last-minute dirty linen, shawls, scent bottles, handkerchiefs, a prayer book, remaining quantities of camphor pills, arrowroot and chloroform that had stood her in good stead during the long voyage.

She had shared a cabin with one Mrs Constance Green, also India-bound for the first time. For days on end their cramped quarters had reeked of sweat and vomit, the floor awash with water spillage, and they had lain in their heaving berths, their respective baby sons dozing fretfully in swinging cots, talking wistfully of families at Home and the husbands they were to join. They had shared confidences, and misery and fear when the vessel bucked in the Cape gales and the babies howled in tune with the storms and the lamp-glass shattered, leaving them in the topsy-turvy and terrifying dark. But their mutual ordeals had not made them friends, for Constance was, in Amelia's opinion, a timorous, fretful creature who'd often been more trouble than both babies put together. Now, sitting on the bed, Amelia grinned happily in the knowledge that, on the morrow's morn, she would wake to neither the piper's calling up the crew nor Constance's dreary whine, but in the company of her beloved husband.

'That's to keep the white ants at bay,' Amelia announced to herself, seeing the little saucers of water in which each leg of furniture stood. It filled her with a satisfying sense of arrival and accomplishment actually to see with her own eyes this odd phenomenon about which she'd read. No vast quantity of saucers was required however, for the room contained only two rattan chairs, a cot in an alcove and, in the centre, the large, high, square bed draped in green-gauze mosquito-netting. In the adjoining dressing-room stood a wash-stand and a chest of drawers, atop which she laid her hairbrush, comb and face cream, taking great pleasure in seeing them stay put instead of sliding about all over the place as they had for the past four months. She also intended to stay on terra firma, and consciously enjoyed the brief walk across a solid tiled floor and out on to the balcony.

A gardener's boy and three hens were dozing in the shade of a bush; a few sheep, goats and two bony bullocks were cropping the sparse green clumps. How amazed her relatives would have been to see these farmyard creatures almost on the house doorstep! Her grandfather had been a successful farmer and, as proud evidence of his success, had built a six-bedroomed house, its main rooms facing away from his farm at two fields' distance. Amelia and her three brothers had grown up there, and the only animals allowed near were two pet spaniels and the carriage horses. Mamma, daughter of a lawyer, used to wrinkle her nose at the smell of manure.

'Amelia!' Theo came hurrying to the balcony, dragging her inside. 'You mustn't go out in the heat of the day without a bonnet, dear. You're not used to the sun.'

'But it's supposed to be the cool season, isn't it? And everything's so strange outside. Fancy letting those animals . . .'

Theo began kissing her fervently, thrusting his tongue insistently and deeply into her mouth and she, having had no such attention since he had left her in England over a year ago, had to remind herself that this was something husbands enjoyed doing. Indeed it was very pleasant once one got used to it again.

He drew away from her. 'Oh my dearest, I wish it was already night-time and we could . . .' He looked longingly at the bed.

'Theo, you've quite mussed me up! And I don't think Mrs Hervey would approve.'

He grinned. 'She'd probably be jealous! I've come to fetch you for tiffin.'

Huge dishes of odorous food were spread over a long table and served by a number of turbanned servants fussily supervised by a spindly Indian with white hair and moustache. His name, Marguerite said, as she speared a few morsels, was Dashwood, which seemed increasingly inappropriate as time went by. She and her third husband, Clifford, had inherited him with the house. They'd bought Spring's Gardens twenty years before when Dashwood had been quite dashing and frisky, and for some reason she could no longer remember he'd been named after her favourite hound.

'And it's Spring's Gardens, not "Spring"?' ventured Amelia, trying to distract attention from Rolly who was getting fractious.

'Oh nothing whatever to do with primroses and daffodils. The house was named after one Reverend Spring, a chaplain at Saint George's Fort some fifty years ago who made his fortune out of funerals, I daresay. Most of these so-called "garden houses" are named after their early owners. This land was once part of the extensive Moubray's Gardens, George Moubray being the first Accountant-General of Madras, who probably made *his* fortune fiddling the books! Ah, such characters were here in days gone by, Mrs Lang. And a few still with us. It's a great pity you have to move on so soon. I suppose Theophilus has told you he's determined to whisk you off to Tanjore where you'll be absolutely starved of civilised society?'

'Oh but I shan't mind that in the least, Mrs Hervey. So long as I have Theo and Rolly with me.'

Marguerite rolled her large blue eyes in amused disbelief. 'Ah – the words of the romantic young griffin-wife. A "griffin" means a new arrival, by the way.'

Amelia nodded politely, distracted by Rolly who seemed increasingly upset. 'May I take him to his cot, Mrs Hervey? Honestly, I'm far too excited to eat much.'

She carried the child to their bedroom, soothing him while Kamba stood close behind, longing to take over. At length, rather reluctantly, she left him in the ayah's care and was conducted to an immense drawing-room that looked somewhat austere, owing to the absence of homely items like mantelpieces, curtains or carpets, such furniture as there was being formally arranged on a tiled floor away from the white walls. Mrs Hervey, her eyes closed, was reclining on an ottoman, while Theo sprawled in a low chair, smoking.

Amelia stared. 'Why! That's a hookah, isn't it?'

He withdrew the mouthpiece. 'It certainly is. What a sweet little griffin you are.'

'But I'd no idea you smoked one!'

'Well it's hardly the thing in England anymore. But here gentlemen of the old-fashioned school like myself frequently indulge.'

She felt inclined to laugh at the quaintness of it, but there was also something disquietingly alien about this husband of hers, lounging there in his loose white trousers and jacket, puffing at that strange, twisted contraption.

Marguerite was amused. 'Oh you'll soon grow to love that hubbly-bubbly sound and exotic aroma, Mrs Lang! And it gives one the pleasant sense of having a gentleman around.'

With that she resumed her doze and Theo his smoking, while Amelia fidgeted on one of the several sofas, irritable as a child at this enforced inactivity.

'You promised me a little tour of Madras, Theo. Shall I go and get ready?'

'My dear Mrs Lang, you can't possibly venture out till after four o'clock. One doesn't, even in this cool season . . . Boy . . .'

Marguerite's voice, though not above a whisper, summoned the wizened servant crouched in the doorway, who shuffled up and, on instruction, fetched Amelia a book.

'The latest *Madras Almanac*, Mrs Lang. Now you can find out about the city without moving an inch. Too much activity ruins the constitution, as you'll discover.'

Amelia opened the book, feeling rebuffed. Constance Green had been told that, in India, enthusiasm among ladies was considered improper and this was apparently correct. But she couldn't contain herself long.

'My, there are over a thousand four-wheeled carriages in use here, did you know, Theo? And – oh listen! – "rates of hire for good, medium or common tank-diggers, stone-cutters and chucklers". Should we hire a common chuckler in case we ever feel melancholy?'

Theo laughed. 'He mightn't be much help. Chucklers are shoemakers of a low caste, almost pariahs. Not a very happy breed of men, I fancy.'

He came to sit close beside her, wishing they could retire to the bedroom for a while. If only Amelia would droop a little – but she was relentlessly lively.

'And here's a list of the resident bigwigs: "Covenanted Civil Servants to the Honourable East India Company. Lord Elphinstone, Governor of the Madras Council; Lt-General Sir Peregrine Maitland, KCB, C.-in-C."'

Marguerite yawned. She had forgone her habitual bed-nap in deference to Amelia's arrival, and was regretting it. 'He's about to resign in a huff, did you know, Theo?'

'Oh what grounds?'

'Oh, another religious rumpus.' She turned to Amelia. 'Such a row when the last monsoon began! The natives like to welcome the rains with a pretty little ceremony. They break coconuts on the beaches, say a few prayers and throw them out to sea with wreaths of flowers.'

'An invocatory chant, Amelia,' interrupted Theo, 'that goes something like this: "Oh Goddess, daughter of the sun, wife of the sea, pardon all our sins! As the waves follow each other, so let happiness follow us. In our labour and trade bless us, send us a flood of prospects and preserve us."'

'Anyway,' Marguerite said, 'it's long been the custom among our Company officials to attend and make small donations towards the festivities. But "Oh no," thunders Sir

Peregrine in the columns of the *Herald*, "we can't have this anymore! Christians actually giving money towards pagan rites . . . Tut tut!" "Stuff and nonsense, it's no more than dancing round the maypole to welcome the spring," pipes up Mr Disgusted in the same paper. "And even Sir Lickpenny Peregrine would shell out for that!" "Not on your life," roars Sir P. "And worshipping deities with coconuts and flowers is downright sacrilegious. Instead of contributing, we should be telling the natives about the one divine God who brings the rains and . . ." Oh, you can imagine the rest . . .' She faded away, yawning again.

'What the deuce has it to do with him? He's head of the army, not the Church.' Theo wandered to the balcony to feel how hot it was.

'That's why the matter has come to a pretty boil. An infantry sergeant in Vellore, infected with Sir Peregrine's zeal, refused on religious grounds to march in the escort of some Hindu deity. His officer reprimanded him, but Sir P. heard of it and reprimanded the officer, and the upshot is Sir P.'s sent in his resignation to the Governor-General.'

'And which side will the G.G. come down on, think you?'

'Lord Auckland is always for whichever is easier. But he's no missionary either, so Sir Peregrine may go.'

'And good riddance! Damn these enthusiasts! Isn't the Company supposed to remain neutral in religious matters? At least the old Company men were wise enough to steer clear and put their money on all the horses.'

'But that was before our busybody Evangelicals started popping up all over the place. And I warrant this is but the beginning of their trouble-making.' She turned to Amelia. 'I trust you're not a fervid Evangelical, Mrs Lang?'

'Er . . . no, but my father certainly supported Wilberforce over the abolition of slavery, Mrs Hervey . . . as every right-thinking person did, surely?'

'Ah, the abolitionists!' she waved a jewelled hand. 'Well, slavery still exists here in India, I do assure you. And suttee, too, even though a few years ago that tedious old Dutchman Bentinck declared it to be illegal forever and ever amen. And we still have female infanticide . . .' She yawned again. 'These busy white men can't change the blacks of the beauteous East with a few strokes of the pen. And just as well too, hey Theo? Boy . . .' She whispered further instructions to the servant. 'I've ordered tea, and then it will be cool enough for you to venture on your sight-see, Mrs Lang.'

'Thank you.'

Amelia, taking refuge in the *Almanac* again, was reassured to learn that St George's Cathedral had its archdeacon, its chaplains, clerks and even organist, all complete. Organists, she then discovered, were among the list of lesser mortals designated as 'English, Americans and East Indians not in the Honourable Company's Covenanted Service', which included attorneys, makers of watches and coaches, dentists, undertakers, schoolmasters – and there was Theophilus Lang. What a beautiful mellifluous sound the two words made! Often, on the long voyage out, she had whispered them over and over just for the pleasure of it.

She turned the pages and giggled. 'Oh, here's a list of Remarkable Days – John the Baptist lost his head on August 29th, no year given, and Lady Jane Grey lost hers on February 12th 1555, and Lord Cornwallis defeated Tippu Sultan in the Third Mysorean War on February 6th 1792.'

Theo leaned over to stroke her neck. 'And next year there'll certainly be an entry as follows, "On December 1st 1838, Mrs Theophilus Lang and her infant son landed safely at Madras after a voyage of 4,687 miles." What could be more remarkable and wonderful than that, I ask you, Marguerite?'

But she, supervising the serving of tea, felt her mouth stretch into a smile that was slightly painful, though she couldn't at first trace the pain's root. Of course, the tender adoration in Theo's eyes as he gazed on his wife reminded her again of Roger. Roger had often looked at her like that, but so long ago that she could no longer summon the memory of what it felt like either to receive or to give such wholehearted messages of love.

Marguerite honestly hoped that Theophilus and Amelia would have longer together than she and Roger had, even while she coolly assessed Mrs Lang's attractions should she need to resort to them again one day, as ladies in India often did. Amelia's chances were reasonable, but not unlimited. She was of medium build, hair of medium brown, satisfactorily thick and lustrous; the eyes were good – large, grey-green, candid rather than alluring perhaps, but with a lively sparkle. The shoulders were well sloped for a ball-gown, but the extremities too large for real grace, and there was a distinctly rural ruddiness about the complexion. Still, better than the gawky blue-stocking Theo might have married.

Amelia, becoming aware of the scrutiny, glanced at Marguerite, who smiled disarmingly. 'Another cake, Mrs Lang? I was just admiring your splendid colour. After months spent at sea, most ladies arrive looking as pale as the drowned.'

Amelia touched her cheek. 'Oh dear, I always seem to carry it!'

Theo took her hand from her face gently, 'And it's splendid, as Marguerite says. Ladies in India usually have to rely on the paint-box for their pink, but not you!'

Marguerite's eyes flashed. 'It must be your country upbringing, Mrs Lang. Where was it now? Theo did mention.'

'Thaxted, Essex, Mrs Hervey. My family owns land there.'

Marguerite flung out her arms. 'Oh Theo, did you come upon her by chance? On a golden summer's day, skipping through the meadows, a wreath of wild flowers in her hair; or was she perhaps sitting beside a brook, dreaming of a dark-haired young man who would . . .?'

'What an incorrigible romantic you are, Marguerite! Did I never tell you? Amelia's brother Roland took me to his home to stay for the school holidays years and years ago – and there she was. Just nine years' old with tight ringlets, in a pinny, and the first time I saw her she'd been down to the farm dairy stealing cream and her little fingers were all sticky when I took her hand!'

Amelia blushed. 'And he looked so grown-up, Mrs Hervey. Seventeen whole years old.'

'Well, well, a pretty story.' Marguerite gulped down another yawn. Pretty, but rather commonplace. Should she tell them how she met Roger? Her very first masked ball in a grand house in Kew with gardens running down to the river.

She sighed: they couldn't possibly envisage that this wizened old crow with a painted face had once danced across a garden terrace where the lines of flambeaux reflected in the water had so lit up her beauty that all heads had turned – including Roger's.

She shook herself, feeling it an inauspicious occasion for brooding over the long-dead Roger, whom she seldom remembered these days. The Langs' happiness was the cause of it – their bubbly, loving, young happiness in each other. She moved to the door.

'I'll have the small open carriage brought round for your first Indian sight-see, Mrs Lang.'

They drove along Mount Road, lined with acacias and areca palms, and on to the wide Esplanade, where the glittering surf roared and pounded. Landward ranged a number of public buildings much admired for their Italianate style, and indeed the grand pillared façades covered with a fine white plaster shining lustrous as marble in the late-afternoon sun did suggest a Mediterranean setting. The way was busy with buggies and carriages, most of whose occupants had taken this same drive at the same hour too many times before and were thus interested only in its variables: who was out with whom, and why those not out had stayed in. For Theo, also, this was the main diversion, though at Amelia's prompting he pointed out the spire of St Andrew's Church and the Customs building where bales, barrels and sea-chests were being unloaded from horse-drawn carts. At the north end of the Esplanade stood famous Fort George, the British colours flying from its flagstaff, and on the nearby sands blue-jacketed ensigns from the Horse Artillery were galloping about and shouting like schoolboys.

'There's a regular little town inside the Fort,' Theo explained. 'European shops, a school and St Mary's, the oldest church in India, where Robert Clive was married. We'll go inside another day,' he added, quenching her eager look.

On a patch of ground beside the Fort's sea-gate was pitched a cluster of army tents, with foodstalls nearby from which

drifted the pungent odour of coconut oil, curry spices, vege-
tables and fish which Amelia smelled there for the very first
time, not guessing how familiar it would become. Passing the
tents, she had her first sight of an Indian sepoy dressed for
guard duty in regulation red jacket, white trousers, musket
over his shoulder and, on his head, a bulging black hat like
an upturned coal bucket that was called, Theo said, a chaco.

Beyond the Fort the way grew narrower and smellier, and
Theo ordered the driver to turn back.

'But can't we go on to Black Town where you used to
lodge?' Amelia pleaded.

'No, dear. Today you shall see only the grandest sights of
Madras, and my poor old lodgings are not among them.'

She glanced at him timidly, for he didn't discuss financial
matters with her. 'I suppose you weren't earning very much
teaching? But did you think it wise to leave, Theo? It was a
regular salary, after all.'

'So I thought. But when I left you in England I didn't
realise how rapidly the tide had turned here. Poor father – as
well he died when he did, just as Lord Bentinck passed those
wretched decrees making English the official language of
government. Funds from colleges of oriental studies have been
diverted to seminaries for the teaching of English now, and
many of our students have left us to study the tongue of their
conquerors.' He snorted angrily. 'Following the call of reformers like Macaulay who consider Sanskrit, Persian and the like
so many dead letters, "useless treadmills for the inculcation
of crude error, puerile fable and gross immorality". I quote.
Enough to make father turn in his grave . . .' He grinned.
'Luckily he was cremated!'

'Was he? How very odd!'

'Well, he was more Hindu than Christian.'

She was silent. Theo had never talked much about his
father, who'd worked for years at the famous Tanjore school
of Sanskrit studies. He'd been a greatly respected scholar and
Amelia had imagined him as a retiring, venerable, bearded
English pedagogue. How could he be a Hindu? She glanced
at her husband, realising again how little she really knew
about him; then she sighed and gazed away towards the sea.
The sands looked chill and bleak after the day's bright heat

and, in a little hollow, a skinny woman and her skinny children were clustered round a driftwood fire.

'Are they cooking a meal, Theo? But why outside?'

'Oh, they're just beach people – that's probably their home; hardly room for a fire inside.' He pointed to what looked like a derelict rabbit-hutch propped against the Esplanade wall. She set her jaw to say nothing; he had warned her against being shocked by Indian poverty.

'And will you be drawing a regular salary in Tanjore, Theo?'

He hugged her. 'Don't worry your head, Amy. The Raja will make things right for us, I'm sure. Remember what I told you – things just slide into place here, one doesn't push them.'

She nestled against his shoulder, feeling tired at last and very happy – for was she not safely landed in India and in her husband's arms?

And that night, when he had at last made his long-pent-up love to her, Theo was certainly unworried. For had she not survived unscathed the long perils of the deep with their new-born child? As she lay cradled asleep in his arms he could trace in her relaxed features a faint likeness to the sticky-fingered little girl he'd first met running from the farm dairy eighteen years before. I shall give her the cream of India, he thought, nestling his nose in her thick hair. Only that is good enough for my love.

CHAPTER TWO

The high arcs of surf that swept seafarers to damp and bumpy landings on the shores of India boomed close against the walls of historic Fort St George where the first important settlement of the East India Company had been founded nearly 200 years before. Inside the Fort's Council Chamber, within earshot of the surf's pounding, members of the Madras Council dispensed letters of advice, information, command and reprimand to every British outpost in the southern Presidency. These documents, decisive to the lives of many, were based on directives received from the Company's head office in Leadenhall Street, London, which in 1835 had been declared responsible for British possessions in India. No longer holding a monopoly of trade, 'John Company' was now the official agent of the British Government, acting as landlord, revenue-collector, keeper of law and order. Its senior officers wielded authority over vast tracts of Indian territory; its Governor-Generals, based in Calcutta, travelled through their domains with as much pomp and ceremony as the great Moghul emperors of an earlier age. Many British residents liked to imagine themselves the new Moghuls – masterful empire builders, cultural conquerors of a subject and degenerate people.

Theophilus Lang was contemptuous of such men, knowing how little they understood the stubborn durability, the hidden quality of Indian life; but because of his contempt he underestimated his compatriots' tenacity, their capacity to produce change and, in some cases, the worthiness of their endeavours. Far removed from the circles of power, he usually ignored them and the degree of ascendancy they had attained in the land. But he was reminded of all this the following day, when his wife stood gazing at the official portraits of past British rulers that hung in the Fort's banqueting hall: Robert Clive, Warren Hastings, round-faced Lord William Bentinck. Theo, to whom they were familiar, took pleasure in watching her dutiful scrutiny as she followed the guide from one to the next.

At the end of the row she exclaimed, 'Why – a woman! Who is she, Theo?'

'That's Lady Munro, wife of Sir Thomas, best governor Madras ever had.' He joined her. 'He's next to her – see. He died here in '25 just before his term of office ended. What a man! Now he's really worth telling about. Sit down a minute.' He dusted a chair with his sleeve. The guide, resigned to a discourse, squatted in a corner.

'Munro saw the need to preserve what is good as well as change what is rotten in this country. None of this hasty pushing on, pulling down and pouring scorn for him. He understood the British as few before and fewer after. "We proceed in a country of which we know little or nothing as if we knew everything," he wrote. "As if everything must be done now and nothing could be done hereafter," whereas we should remember that "the period of our ascendancy is a little nothing in the existence of the Indian people."' He banged his fist against her chair. 'Munro knew that the only way to initiate reform properly is through the participation and consent of the people, Amelia. But already his wise counsels are disregarded. Now we have men like Macaulay, Bentinck and their ilk who understand nothing of this country and even vaunt their ignorance, trumpeting their "we know what's best for you" to the benighted natives. Munro warned that it's not "the arbitrary power of a national sovereign but subjugation to a foreign one" that destroys national character – but that's what the British are set to do.'

Drained by his own oratory, Theo leaned against the wall. 'Oh, would I had the capacity of a Munro, Amelia! But I lack the driving force, the dedication to a single cause that's needed for public life. Is this "little nothing" of British power worth spending one's life on, I wonder?' He looked up. 'Sir Thomas thought so and I revere him for it. But look what happened – he was cut off in an instant and the fruits of his labour turned sour from neglect and wrongheadedness.'

She got up to touch his sleeve. 'But what you do *is* worthwhile, Theo. You teach and translate – isn't that of more lasting value than the temporary rule of office which can soon be overturned and contradicted?'

He hugged her. 'How sweetly you say the very thing with which I reassure myself, dear! You, just yourself, are certainly of more lasting value.'

She swung her bonnet from its ribbons, glancing at the portraits. 'But I can't do anything – neither interpret nor teach nor rule. Now my friend Joanna . . .'

'Ah the terrible Joanna.' He tweaked her ringlets. 'I thought you might forget your female dragon out here.'

'Of course not, she's my dearest friend and I promised to write to her every week. If she was here now, she'd say . . .'

'Heaven forbid that that blue-stocking should ever . . .'

She cut him short. 'Well, all I'm saying is that no women are commemorated in this hall, nor anywhere else much, and if we're supposed to be of such great value . . .'

'Oh tush, look at Lady Munro!'

'But she's only there because of her husband, which doesn't count – and she looks more miserable than anyone.'

'Because that was painted soon after her husband's death and they were apparently a devoted couple.'

'What happened?'

'He was on a final tour of the south, in camp near Trichy, when he suddenly felt unwell after breakfast and was dead by nightfall. Cholera, naturally.' He followed her gaze to the picture. 'Lady Munro had left a few months before and was back in England by then. I remember meeting one of his ADC's who told me how dreadful they felt about sending off the packet of letters with the news. Like firing a cannon at someone you liked, he said, which wouldn't actually reach its target for a hundred days, but you couldn't not fire, nor move her out of the way of it. They concocted a black-bordered note for her to read first, warning that news isn't always good and hoping she was feeling strong that day.'

26

He took her arm. 'But come, enough of this – let's get our supplies ordered.'

Outside, Amelia's spirits were lifted immediately by the shining light. Laden carts and porters were shoving through the crowds towards the Customs house, followed by a grand official in an escorted palanquin. A juggler, who'd been trying in vain to attract his attention, darted to Amelia and began throwing coloured sticks and balls in the air, while also managing to hold out his hand for money; beside him a ragged urchin banged a tiny drum.

She watched in fascination, half her mind still dwelling on those stiff white men in the hall who had wielded great power here, and whose descendants continued to do so. In the dramatic contrast between that orderly, sombre room behind her and this colourful, haphazard street-life she sensed for the first time the mystery of the European presence in India, which was more precariously poised than any juggling trick. She would never understand the mystery and often forgot its existence but, whenever she was reminded of its amazing riskiness, she remembered those stately indoor portraits and the juggler outside throwing sticks and balls and grinning at her.

In the oilman's stores round the corner – its shelves packed with dusty jumbles of gingham umbrellas, Jews' beef, Milroy's hunting whips, Twankey's tea, Yarmouth bloaters, straw bonnets, tin kettles, jujube lozenges as well as oil – Theo and Amelia had their first quarrel, over the subject of strawberry jam. Even a small jar, Amelia found to her dismay, cost more than a dozen pots at Home.

'But we must buy some for Rolly,' she told her husband. 'His appetite has been so poor since we landed and it might tempt him.'

Theo shook his head. 'He mustn't be allowed to get used to expensive luxuries, Amelia. He's in India now . . . And look at me – I managed perfectly well without it as a child.'

'But Rolly's already learned to like it.'

'Then he must learn to prefer the mango variety as I do.'

'Oh come – I'm sure when you first tasted strawberry jam in England you loved it!'

'I loathed it,' he retorted, going to a shelf of second-hand books. It was true: he had loathed everything about cold, grey, bland England. After two lonely years at boarding school, he'd been sent to Haileybury College where John Company trained young men for service in India. That, too, he had loathed: the cold baths and cold rowing on the grey river. He'd been one of the 'steady men' who'd studied hard and late enough sometimes to hear the gay blades returning in dog-carts from some drunken spree. But he'd been isolated from them by his unusual sympathy for the country they were all expected to serve, his spirits invigorated only by his academic achievements in the oriental tongues and his friend-ship with the equally studious Roland Carter through whom he'd met Amelia.

Wiping mildew from a copy of Shelley's poems, he had a chilly vision of Haileybury's dining-hall: pallid, scrawny youths scooping up grey sago pudding with dollops of jammy red. He'd eaten it all right, for he'd been constantly hungry and constantly cold. But he'd loathed it and everything else – the goose pimples and buttoned-up uniforms, the snobberies and arcane jests of an alien land. Three months before his final exams he had walked out, not because he couldn't pass them but because he could never become a covenanted servant of the Company.

Theo bought the poems, for he never grudged money on books; Amelia, who had surreptitiously purchased and stowed in her bag two jars of strawberry jam, handed him a leaflet with a beguiling smile.

'Look – an inventory of newly-arrived toys. Let's buy Rolly something to cheer him up. You didn't go toy-less as well as jam-less, I hope?'

'*Strawberry* jam-less,' he corrected, willing to placate. 'I had a painted wooden elephant once. I'll get one made for him in Tanjore.'

'But he must have one of these – look. "Rabbits with moving ears on wheels." How exciting! And it'll help him learn to walk.'

He frowned. 'Well . . . all right.' He wasn't a curmudgeon, but Amelia must learn that their son was to be brought up in

28

proper Indian fashion – neither as a pampered princeling nor as most Anglo-Indian children, who were grossly over-indulged during their infancy and then sent to England to suffer what he could only view as years of deprivation and misery. On the way back to Marguerite's he tried to explain this to his wife, but she wasn't receptive: Rolly had an entirely English constitution, he was entitled to some cossetting, and she wasn't about to feed him on curry and rice.

'I'm not suggesting you do. Anyway, he isn't old enough for it,' Theo replied curtly. 'Nevertheless, luxuries like straw-berry jam are unnecessary.'

They lapsed into silence; the jars weighed heavily in Amelia's bag and on her conscience, for this was the first time she'd deceived her husband. In England such problems had not arisen; the months following their marriage had been like a prolonged honeymoon. Then Theo had returned to India while she had waited to bear her baby at home instead of on the high seas. Since his birth Rolly had been the focus of her life, and was it not natural to spoil him a little considering the shocks and upheavals he'd already experienced? But Theo was claiming all her love and attention now, protesting he'd been bereft of her for so long, and she remembered with joy his passionate protestations in bed the previous night. Still, Rolly too had his claims, and when they reached the house she held tight to her bag and hurried to him.

He was lying awake in his cot staring up with puzzled blue eyes at the drapery of the mosquito net that looked so much like a shroud, she thought, pulling it aside and touching his hot forehead. Kamba, emerging from nowhere as usual, assured her all was well, but Amelia wasn't convinced. Raising the child's head, she fed him a spoonful of jam and he sucked noisily, opening his mouth for more.

'Oh good little Rollikins! Isn't that just scrumptious?'

'May I come in?' asked Marguerite from the doorway, and was beside Amelia before she could contemplate concealment.

'Strawberry jam! Lucky little fellow! That will buck him up!' They watched him gulp another spoonful, then Amelia stood up, looking uncertainly at Marguerite.

'I bought it at the oilman's stores with my own money – Theo considers it too luxurious for him.'

'Oh tush!'

'He says Rolly must get accustomed to Indian ways from the start.'

Marguerite chuckled. 'He would, but what's good for father isn't always so for son. And wasn't entirely good for Theo, either.'

She instructed Kamba, who took the jar from Amelia. 'I told her to give him a spoonful now and then – on the quiet.'

Amelia smiled gratefully. 'You mean – not good for Theo to have been brought up in Indian ways? That was his father's doing I suppose? Theo's not told me much about him and rather shocked me yesterday by saying he was almost a Hindu. Was that so?'

'Oh . . . Bayard Lang.' Marguerite drifted towards the balcony and peeped out. 'There – I knew the carriage would be left. The servants get quite beyond me sometimes.'

'But you liked Theo's father?' Amelia persisted.

'Very much. Rather a man of the last century in his thinking and habits. A disciple of the great orientalist William Jones, you know, and somewhat . . . Hinduised. I expect that's what Theo meant.' That and rather more, Marguerite could have said, but why should she make a stir? Amelia would discover certain things for herself in time.

Meanwhile Amelia was still watching her, expecting further explanation, and Marguerite added, 'Bayard was very wrapped up in his study of the Hindu classics and history – dynasties of Pallavas, Cholas, Vijayanagars, and so on. Clifford used to call them his "jolly palavers". Perhaps you'll be good for Theo – bring him down to earth. But come, let's see if we can find something for baby in my little dispensary.'

A servant with a large bunch of keys led the way along the wide passage. From locked doors on either side came a variety of long-trapped smells: beeswax, ginger, cardamon, soap, nutmeg, garlic, gum. The servant unlocked a room from which came medicinal odours of oils, herbs and ointments. On its shelves stood rows of tin boxes with labels, which Marguerite adjusted her spectacles to read.

'For bruises, cuts, etc.; for headaches, toothaches, etc.; for fevers, chills, etc.; for diarrohea, colic, etc. . . . That'll be the one.' She gestured to the servant.

'The last box is for dying, etc.,' announced a sepulchral voice behind them.

Amelia jumped. 'Theo . . . Don't creep up like that. And what a thing to say!'

'True – isn't it, Marguerite?' He winked, but she was advancing on an odd-shaped dust-sheet in the corner.

'Why I do believe it's . . . I quite forgot . . . But I seldom come here: too tough these days to need any remedies except for those in the last box, hey Theo?' She whisked off the sheet to reveal a mangy-maned rocking-horse dotted with red and yellow paint that flaked off as she gave it a sad, creaky little rock. 'It was Peter's.'

'Your son's?' Amelia queried.

'My youngest – Clifford's and mine. He died when he was six, but an imperious little man already. "Go and fetch the bruises box at once, ayah," he would command when he fell over. The very sight of it stopped him crying.' She chuckled, rocking the horse with her fingertips. 'Then one day his toes touched the floor when he was on it. "I'm going to ride a proper pony now, mamma," he announced, and wouldn't look at poor old Dobbin anymore. But then he became ill so . . .'

'I'm very sorry,' Amelia murmured. 'What was . . .?'

'Oh fevers, chills, etc. . . . Too many of them. Well open it, silly man!'

The servant cut the seal on the box he was holding.

'You must be careful with Rolly, his constitution isn't made for this climate, remember.'

Amelia said feelingly, 'Oh Mrs Hervey, I think of the dangers every day.'

'No point in that, either. Just build up his stamina with roly-polys, egg custards, rice puddings and jam – that sort of thing. Anglo-Indian children often lack stamina. I'll give you some receipts.'

Amelia glanced triumphantly at her husband, who shrugged. 'You two will have him grow up a namby-pamby.'

'I just want to make sure he *does* grow up.' Amelia stared at the horse that Marguerite was still idly rocking.

'Would you like Dobbin for Rolly? A lick of paint and he'd be good as new.'

'Oh no, thank you, Mrs Hervey. We've just bought him a rabbit on wheels and . . .'

Marguerite smiled, tweaking the toy's grey mane. 'Never mind, Dobbin, you stay here and when I come for the last box – which is empty, isn't it, Theo? – you can rock me away to join all the other children on the further shore. In the meanwhile . . .' She rummaged in the box and brought out a phial of clear fluid, 'Give baby this – omum water, made from oman seeds, excellent for upset tummies or over-indulgence. "Oh ma'am, give me some omum," Clifford used to groan after a late night at the mess. He drank it down like claret, but just give Rolly three drops every four hours.'

'Oh, thank you, I'll start at once.' Amelia almost grabbed it from her. 'No – I can find my own way.' She passed the servant and rushed off.

Marguerite shook her head reprovingly. 'We should be more careful with our little macabres, Theo. Your wife isn't used to them.'

'Part of the Indian way of life.'

'Granted – but when it's not death it's festival, remember. Which reminds me – I'm getting up a little dinner party . . .'

'Oh, please don't bother. Amelia isn't a social butterfly and . . .'

'She certainly isn't. Takes herself rather too seriously, don't you think? But then, frivolity often comes later. Now lock up carefully,' she instructed the servant as they left.

'Too seriously? You wouldn't have had me marry a flibber-tigibbet, Marguerite?'

'As if you would, dear boy! No, Amelia will do very well for the English wife you decided to acquire. She's practical and has strong nerves – most important for women in India. And I imagine she can speak up for herself if need be?'

'I should say! Her mother complains she expresses far too many opinions for a well-brought-up young lady. But she feels like a raw griffin here at present.'

'All the more reason for giving her the experience of at least one civilised dinner party before you bear her away to the jungles!'

Amelia, contemplating the prospect of the party with slight trepidation, imagined a room full of charming, elegant ladies partnered by suave and witty gentlemen, for she didn't suppose Marguerite knew any lesser mortals. She planned her toilette with extra care and polished a few lively phrases to describe her voyage and first impressions of India, for she didn't wish to appear plain or vapid, for Theo's sake. Unfortunately, the season's intermittent north-easterlies brought heavy rain which, though a blessing for many, gave chills, fevers, etc. to some.

'Oh it's so provoking – now the young Lushingtons are laid low!' Marguerite wailed, reading a chit delivered just before the first guests were due. 'And we're left with only the seasoned old salts who never ail and never say anything new, either.'

'Well, I'm sure it will all seem new to me,' Amelia said, and indeed, when she was conducted into the dining-room on the arm of an elderly gentleman, she was much intrigued by the novelty of the scene. Branched candelabras along the table and oil-lamps on the walls cast flickers of light on the king's pattern cutlery and the several glasses at each place-setting, behind which stood servants clad in differing liveries, for everyone had brought their own to wait on them.

Steaming bowls of soup appeared first and the guests sipped in almost total silence, then stared glumly at an array of platters uncovered to reveal great mounds of roast mutton, pigs and fowls. The damp weather had enlivened nothing but the mosquitoes: people were continually slapping and scratching themselves, the gentlemen noisily, the ladies discreetly, squirming as some bolder invader pricked into crevices that could not be reached with decorum. At the table's corners, servants waved large fans intended to freshen the air, which simply transported insects – flies, moths, winged ants and beetles as well as mosquitoes – more easily from one quarry

33

to the next. Their rythmical flapping was the only sound save for an occasional mutter, the click of plate and glass, and Amelia soon realised the guests were not of the sparkling calibre she had anticipated. Many looked thoroughly *over-seasoned* – by drying winds outside, arid social rituals within, by disease, homesickness and heartbreaks. The women especially made her uneasy; their heavily powdered, wrinkled faces were soured and their glances seemed both envious of her youthful bloom and complacent in the knowledge that it wouldn't last long.

Having eaten only a few hours before, the guests merely picked at the roast meats, then at side-dishes of patties and cutlets which, her neighbour said, were peacock, but Amelia hoped he was joking. Each dish was solemnly passed by each servant to each diner for consideration, however many were refused – a wearisome procedure. Amelia passed the time by imagining servants drawing lots behind the scenes for the richest left-overs. She had set to with more appetite than most, but was only too soon replete, and much relieved when cups of custards and jellies appeared.

As madeira and sweet white wine were poured, the company grew somewhat livelier. Mr Babbage, a corpulent, bald man opposite her, bestirred himself to pass on the latest intelligence from Calcutta – which, as a member of the august Madras Council, he was presumed to have at his fingertips. Lord Auckland, now on an extended tour of the upper provinces, was determined to proceed with his plan of sending troops into Afghanistan, he announced.

'It will be in the press tomorrow: our Bengal regiments are mustering and the G.G. met the Old Lion of the Punjab, Ranjit Singh, in Durbar just the other day. Ourselves and his Sikhs will march on Kabul together . . . So, a toast to our brave army of the Indus!'

The guests drank, echoing his sentiments, save for a retired colonel near Amelia who grumbled that the Bengal regiments always saw the action and why weren't Madras men sent north to show them how to fight? No one replied to this oft-repeated complaint; then Amelia heard her husband's voice.

'And exactly why are we invading Afghanistan, may I ask?'

'A strategically defensive move, my dear young sir. Shah

34

Shuja, our ally, must be restored to the Afghan throne and Dost Muhammad Khan deposed from it. We can't afford a weak and potentially hostile power on that vulnerable frontier where the Russians could take advantage.'

'The Colonel's right, Mr Lang,' puffed Mr Babbage, 'and an alliance with the Old Lion will secure our power as far as the Indus.'

'Well, in my view the campaign will prove extremely expensive and probably calamitous,' Theo retorted coolly.

The colonel stiffened. 'I suppose you favour the upstart Reformists, Mr Lang, who want all our investments spent on teaching the natives to speak and behave like Englishmen instead of on the defence of our hard-won territories?'

'On the contrary, Colonel; I consider the upstart Reformists, as you call them, far too hasty and undiscriminating in their methods and have no wish to see Indians prattling away in tea-party English and attending church on Sundays. But I prefer to see government money spent on the maintenance of peace, not war. You military men see yourselves as so many Alexanders the Great – ambitious to grind the whole of central Asia under your boots.'

Amelia quailed at her husband's temerity, for tempers were plainly rising. She was not of a timid disposition, but the present disputation was beyond her and she looked imploringly at Marguerite, who cut in briskly.

'Oh, how I'd have loved to meet a man who dared to give himself such a title – and in daylight, too! But come, gentlemen, we ladies shall leave you to your smoking and brandy. Only first pray tell me, Mr Babbage, what is the latest report of Lord Auckland's sisters, the Misses Eden? Last I heard they were still at Simla holding fancy fairs with skittle-stalls and shuttlecocks. Are they well? Miss Emily must be tougher than she looks to endure so much upcountry trailing about for months on end.'

'I haven't heard they are ill, ma'am, so they must be well. Miss Emily does not enjoy travelling, however – as she makes abundantly clear every day, I believe.'

Marguerite chuckled. 'She has a delightfully waspish sting in her, does she not? Well, ladies . . .' They rose and Amelia, negotiating between the servants with unusual care, realised she'd never in her life drunk so much wine.

As they repaired their toilettes, Marguerite confided to Amelia that, in the absence of the younger set, she'd cancelled the fiddlers for the dancing. 'Our stiff-jointed old gents simply won't prance about these days, so I fear it will be whist and backgammon again. Deadly lively for you, my dear. I so wish you were staying longer – I'd have arranged a little ball . . .'

Amelia smiled politely; how glad she was to be leaving these rooms filled with over-fed people.

Marguerite stared at her, thin eyebrows raised. 'Ah, you don't give a rap for balls and such as long as you have your precious Theo and baby in a humble bungalow in the jungles, hey?'

Amelia flushed. 'But Tanjore isn't exactly jungles, is it? It's a large market town, Theo says, and I'm used to that at Home, so I might prefer it to Madras.'

Marguerite took her arm. 'There are market towns and market towns, you'll find. You mustn't expect a neat little square with neat little houses and a church and buttercups and daisies and afternoon teas.'

'Of course not! Theo's described it: a famous temple, a fort, the Raja's palace, not much else . . . and a few English to invite for tea.'

'Now who can you have? The Resident, Hubert Wardle – irritable little fellow, I recall. He brought his sick wife here once, they tried all the doctors – ' she waved a dismissive hand ' – useless, one could see it in her face. But there *is* someone rather special – I'll tell you about him later.' She ushered Amelia into the drawing-room, introducing her to the nearest lady.

'Ah, Mrs Babbage, this is Mrs Lang, Theo's wife just arrived from Home. Would you take care of her while I . . .' She swooped off to supervise the setting up of the tables and Amelia looked after her wistfully, wondering how she could prove that she was not the dim-witted hobbledehoy Marguerite seemed to suppose.

36

'And did you have an easy voyage?' Mrs Babbage asked in a weary whisper, patting the seat beside her.

'Yes, thank you. And it was fun crossing the Line with Father Neptune and his Tritons and his Bear who ducked the gentlemen passengers in a canvas pool full of water and . . .' She faltered at the glaze in the eyes of Mrs Babbage, for whom such yarns were only too familiar.

'Ah yes, how amusing. I was looking at the cut of your sleeves, Mrs Lang,' she fingered Amelia's blue silk, 'and the scooping of the neckline. Is that the fashion now? We fall so far behind in these matters and must depend on newcomers to keep us *comme il faut*.'

Amelia laughed. 'I fear I can't help much. My mother's dressmaker made this – good enough for deepest Essex, but whether it would pass muster in Kensington I can't say.'

'What a pity!' Mrs Babbage took her leisurely pick of some candied fruits. 'So you're from Essex, Mrs Lang? But were perhaps in London for the coronation?' Amelia shook her head. 'Hmm. But still you might know – is it true that the poor little Queen nearly dropped the sacred orb because it was so heavy? And rumour has it she's already losing her girlish prettiness?'

'I'm sorry, Mrs Babbage, but I really didn't mix in court circles.'

Mrs Babbage sighed, but decided to persevere. 'And do you have relatives serving in India, Mrs Lang?'

'Just my brother Roland who's with the Company in Peshawar. My two other brothers remain at Home.'

'And were your parents ever here?' Mrs Babbage's habit of ascertaining the background of every new arrival often proved useful to her husband.

'No, never. My father's dead. I was looking after my mother, who is rather an invalid, until my marriage. Now she lives with my elder brother.'

Mrs Babbage comforted herself with another fruit. 'So you won't know much about India yet – but pray don't take your husband's word for everything, from what I heard this evening.'

It sounded like a command and Amelia was nonplussed.

She'd been proud that Theo had declared his unpopular views, but for the moment had only his conviction to go on. Moreover, her head was aching abominably after so much wine, and instead of defending him she slipped away to her bedroom for a while.

By the time Amelia returned, the elderly ladies were flagging, clutching their cashmere shawls round their bony shoulders and sending chits to the card-players saying they wished to leave. She watched in amusement: she'd heard that Anglo-Indians ordered servants to tie shoelaces and fill their tobacco-pipes – and, apparently, carry notes from one room to another. Poor, idle, washed-out creatures! How often the same parting pleasantries had been exchanged among them, and how grateful they seemed for long-familiar presences, even disagreeable ones. 'You're still here and I'm still here and we're surviving,' their veined, spotted hands reassured each other as they prepared to depart.

Mr Babbage, holding her hand too long in his, said genially, 'Well, m'dear Mrs Lang, so pleased to have made your acquaintance. Hope you enjoy Tanjore. Mosquitoes large as snipe down there, I'm told. If they get too much for you, come back to old Madras – you'll always be welcome.'

Amelia smiled politely, standing next to Marguerite who was bestowing cool farewells on her guests as they tottered down the stairs, the men a little addled from drink, the ladies' swollen feet bunched painfully in their tight satin slippers. In truth Marguerite cared little for their company, except for the grim satisfaction of seeing so many well-known and a few once-loved bodies crumbling into decay faster than her own.

But she knew such satisfaction to be short-lived and, as the final guest departed, turned to the young face beside her and moaned, 'Lord love us, what fossils we've all become! Deep buried in the Indian dust and too ancient to move again.'

'But won't some of them retire Home soon?'

'Oh no, we're the rooted remnants. Our children and children's children are here, and how could we bear that wretchedly cold climate with no more than a couple of servants to light our fires?' She twitched irritably at her necklace. 'But did you find anything to amuse you, Mrs Lang?'

'Oh, I thoroughly enjoyed it, and the food was delicious. Yet most people ate next to nothing – I hope the servants have had a good feast in the kitchen?'

'Not a morsel! Khitmagars – the table servants who accompany their masters – are caste, and a single scrap of our unclean food would defile them. So the pariahs come and pick it to the bone – and the pariah dogs get the bones.' She grimaced at Theo as he joined them. 'My dear fellow, for lud's sake teach your little griffin wife something useful instead of filling her head with your historical "jolly palavers".'

Theo smiled at Amelia. 'Marguerite refuses to take Indian history seriously, but you do, don't you?'

'She just pretends – to please you,' Marguerite mocked. 'What she really wants to know is how to set up house here.'

Theo ducked his head obediently. 'I'll do my best, ma'am. But I've never set up a proper house with wife and child before, either.'

'Oh, another pair of babes in the jungles you'll be then and there's no hope for you!' She waved a dismissive hand. 'Wasn't that a dreary affair, Theo? Not even a little prance – which reminds me, you've never seen my grand ballroom, have you? I shut it up after Clifford died . . . But come, both of you, I'll show you a shell of the splendour that was Madras. Lights, boy! And bring a little sweet wine for our sustenance.'

She clapped her hands and servants rushed to her bidding, delighted by the flash of those unpredictable high spirits that once gave them so much food for gossip. Two of them, lamps held aloft, led the way along a passage in the furthest wing, unlocking swing doors that opened into a large, empty hall. Furtive scuffles from its dark recesses suggested the surprised flight of a hundred ghosts.

'Ah – we've disturbed some night revels!' Marguerite took a lamp and ran into the room's centre, swinging it around her. 'One thing India will teach you, Mrs Lang, is that creatures great and small must have their due and, if denied, they'll extract it from you. I like to think of the rats, mice, fleas, cockroaches, ants – and a few scorpions and house-snakes most like – enjoying themselves here just as we humans once did. What frolics we had! Fancy dress balls, the men got up as Russian hussars, Chinese mandarins, Arabian sheikhs . . .' She trailed her fingers along a row of carved, gilded chairs against a wall. 'You know, I've become positively Indian – oblivious to chronology and dust. So I can't remember when it was, but once I brought Captain Gilbert here on just such a night as this after a dinner party. We threw open the shutters and did a little gavotte together – clumping and twirling up and down in the moonlight. Then he flopped on one of these chairs and do you know, it just crumbled away beneath him – puff! Like a chair in a dream. Oh, it was so comical, though he failed to see the joke at first, rubbing his behind and brushing himself down furiously. You know how fastidious he is, Theo?'

'Why no, I've never met him.'

'I suppose not. He's been posted away from Madras for several years. But you'll meet him in Tanjore: he's commanding officer of the Raja's escort.'

'And a friend of yours?'

'Indeed. Also one of the most handsome and intelligent men in the Madras army, though that's not saying a great deal for him! How you'll rub along together I can't say. He's a rather difficult customer.'

'And his wife?' Amelia asked.

'Never married.' Marguerite prodded a chair gently. 'So you see I have a truly insubstantial pageant here. What could be more comforting? Let us drink to it!'

'Have you tried sitting on any of the other chairs?' Theo teased, making as if to do so.

'Oh pray, don't. They won't disintegrate at a touch, but I think another good flop would do the trick.'

'It's the ants, I suppose?' Amelia wished she, too, could find it comical. 'But why don't the chairs collapse by themselves?'

'Ants don't like gilt-lacquer, and that is holding them up.'

Theo drank. 'Ever thought of inviting the people you least

like to a last grand ball, Marguerite? And contrive for them to all sit down at the same moment?'

She chortled. 'Gil had the same idea. So you have a good streak of malice aforethought in common. Stands you in good stead here, Mrs Lang. This isn't a Christian country, remember, and it won't do to be too nice.'

Theo squeezed Amelia's shoulders protectively. 'But she *is* rather nice, by nature. And she'll discover the dark sides soon enough.'

'Well, I don't feel nice at the moment – you make me sound like a simple-minded child!' Amelia shook him off and went to explore the hall.

Its walls were hung with spotted mirrors and tattered hangings; in the dark recesses between the pillars, where rats and scorpions lurked, stood sofas covered in frayed silks. There was a piano at the room's other end, and Marguerite played a tinny tune that sounded dismal enough, but Theo clapped. Both of them seemed to enjoy this eerie setting in a way Amelia couldn't understand. A servant plucked her sleeve and lifted a lamp high to show a grand chandelier overhead, its pendants sparkling like diamonds in the brief radiance. She was staring solemnly upward when Marguerite approached.

Amelia said, 'I'm imagining the splendid balls you held here – light glittering on all this glass, the ladies' jewels . . .'

'Better yet were the masquerades of my earlier days when ladies were scarce as hen's teeth, and newly arrived girls so sought after that some literally danced themselves to death. Dumpy, stumpy creatures with big noses and thick waists who'd have been left to take root in the walls at Home found themselves belles overnight. Dancing began about midnight and they twirled and skipped till dawn, then rushed out, all overheated, to see the sun rise. Next thing you heard they were stone-cold dead of a fever. One friend of mine . . . very pretty . . .' She trailed off, staring into a gloomy corner beyond.

Amelia shivered. 'It's rather late, Mrs Hervey. If you'll excuse me . . .'

'Don't let my sentimental ramblings disturb you, Mrs

Lang. I'm fast falling into decay, held up by the paintwork like my chairs, and I get a trifle morbid sometimes. Let us leave the rats to their revels.'

Amelia felt she hadn't acquitted herself well at the dinner party, having failed either to support her husband or to entertain the elderly ladies. She hadn't enjoyed their society much, either, and was pleased to be moving on. But, though Theo's post 'in the service of the Raja' sounded quite grand to her, it did not rate highly compared to being in the Company's service, and they were obliged to wait several days for a certificate from the postmaster's office confirming that their dak was laid, with stages of the journey, arrival and departure dates meticulously listed.

It was an expensive way of travelling, Theo complained, for one had to hire palanquin bearers in sets of twelve, torch-carriers and men called cowry coolies who bore baskets of luggage slung on poles. In his bachelor days Theo had ridden lightly with one servant and a groom, but Amelia and the child must be comfortable, Marguerite told him, as she filled a travelling box with tins of hams, mock turtle soup, essence of beef and other items she considered necessities, he luxuries.

The day before their departure Theo received a chit, which was not unusual, for these notes of invitation, refusal or gratitude whizzed round town from dawn to dusk in the pouches of messengers, and Marguerite often received up to a dozen a day.

Amelia watched as he opened it.

'Oh – from Gopal Krishnan, who wants to see me "on a particular matter" before I leave.'

'How splendid. I've been hoping to meet him.'

Theo re-read the note. 'Well, he particularly says his wife isn't receiving visitors today.'

'What a shame! But I'll come anyway. He's been a friend of yours for years, hasn't he?'

'But I've only once met his wife.'

'Theo! Honestly? Is he only recently married?'

Theo grinned. 'Lord, no. Gopi was married at sixteen, but foreign men don't mix socially with brahmin wives.'

She puffed. 'But *he* can mix with *me*, surely?'

'But if his wife's not receiving . . .'

'Theo, what does that mean exactly?'

He looked embarrassed. 'Probably she's either fasting or has her monthly period. High-caste women see no one except close female relatives at such times.'

'But that's dreadful . . . Poor shut-up creatures!'

'I don't suppose they regard it so. It's simply Hindu custom.' He went to the writing desk and selected a quill.

'But Theo,' she persisted, 'you want me to like Indians – not regard them merely as servants or ignorant heathen as many Englishwomen do. But how can I like them, if I can't meet them socially?'

'Well . . . look, I'll go first to discuss this "particular matter" and you join us for tea – and bring Rolly. I'll tell Gopi I specially wanted him to see my first-born.'

She turned away, vexed that his closest Indian friend should have no wish to meet her for herself. But brahmins were unused to conversing with foreign ladies, Theo explained, and Mr Krishnan would be ill-at-ease with her, even if he pretended otherwise. So, at precisely the tea-time hour, she and Rolly were ushered into Mr Krishnan's drawing-room, which, though shaded from the outside glare, glittered with glass lamps, mirrors and display cases of foreign ornaments. Gopal, a bony man clad in a simple white cotton garment that contrasted oddly with all this effulgence, bowed slightly, speaking in a rapid sing-song.

'Please to sit down, Madam Lang. And I hope you will be enjoying our lovely country?'

'I'm sure I shall, Mr Krishnan. I was longing to come.'

'And here you are having lovely husband. Very good for lady this fellow, yes? But you are also smelling horrible Black Town stinky-poo? Very shame thing for us, yes?'

Amelia hesitated, knowing something was false, and Theo, laughing uneasily, rescued her.

'Come now, Gopi, she's not been here long enough to appreciate your humble chee-chee talk. Look, here's Roland Theophilus Lang to see you.'

Gopi shook the small plump fist. 'Very 'andsome, Mr Lang,

very 'andsome . . . But I must renounce these silly accents,' he added, in a clipped voice that sounded equally affected.

Amelia smiled gamely. 'I'm most happy to make your acquaintance, Mr Krishnan, in whatever voice you speak. Theo's often mentioned you and your jolly times together in Calcutta.'

'Ah college days, college days, what naughty nights, what idle days! But your husband was a most industrious fellow, Mrs Lang, and it's quite repulsive how many languages he learned.'

'But did you learn nothing at college, Mr Krishnan?'

He flinched. 'Merely a few points of law which I've since put to professional use. But come, some refreshment. Ayah can take baby to the verandah, and for you – China tea which English ladies prefer to our crude native brews.'

'Oh, but I . . .' She stopped, for he was instructing the servant and she would get what he desired.

'Gopi has been making enquiries about Tanjore on my behalf, Amy,' Theo said. 'Raja Sevaji poses something of a problem to the Company, apparently. When they pull the strings he *will* go in the wrong direction.'

'A puppet raja, Mrs Lang,' Gopal explained. 'The Honour-able Company has several and they're usually left to dangle quietly. But Sevaji makes eccentric movements now and then . . .' He angled his arms and shoulders into awkward, mari-onette-like movements, grinning at her disconcertingly.

'Oh yes, I meant to tell you Gopi,' Theo interrupted his display, 'old Babbage was at Marguerite's t'other evening and we had a wrangle over Afghanistan. But later he drew me aside, suggesting I might try to smooth the Raja down and give Resident Wardle a helping hand, quite unofficially of course, hmm hmm . . .'

'Sounds to me as if it's the Raja who might need unofficial help.'

'Precisely.'

There appeared trays of tea and cakes, which servants pressed insistently upon Amelia. Gopal touched nothing, padding about and throwing remarks at them.

'Anyway, from what I hear there'll be plenty of hares to

run with and jackals to hunt with, Theo. But I fear you'll find Tanjore a sleepy hollow after the hectic pleasures of Madras, madam.'

'Oh, I've no worries about that, Mr Krishnan. What with Theo, the baby, a new house – and I intend to learn Tamil and Sanskrit.'

He paused in mid-step, opening his hooded eyes very wide. 'Really? My dear Mrs Lang, you will overheat your brain in our tropic clime. Besides, our vernaculars contain a number of indecorous expressions, I fear, sufficient to persuade most English ladies not to attempt them.'

Amelia challenged his eyes. 'Come, that must be nonsense, if you'll forgive my saying so, Mr Krishnan. Theo has never suggested such a thing, and besides, I'm not "most English ladies".'

There came a bellow from the verandah and she jumped up. 'Oh, that's Rolly. Please excuse me.'

She hurried to comfort the child, wondering why Mr Krishnan seemed so unfriendly towards her. She could not know that her very presence represented a threat to him. Since the turn of the century British women, arriving in increasing numbers, had set up large establishments from which natives, except servants, were rigorously excluded – as had not been the case in earlier days. In general, Gopal regarded them as a swarm of locusts who did nothing but breed and feed on the wealth of India, to which they gave nothing in return. In particular, his friendship with Theo was a purely masculine matter that need not extend to this bold young woman who asked too many questions and expected too much attention.

'Isn't she delightful? Theo asked, as Amelia left. 'I told you – pretty and sweet-natured, but able to speak up for herself, too.'

'Quite charming. Now, to finish our discussion – for ladies' minds are "fickle as dew on tumbling grass" are they not, and politics bores them – I'm also told that Sevaji flounders monstrously in debt. Was there ever raja born who didn't?'

'Oh Lord, and I need a regular salary.'

'Then I advise you to be more importunate than his other

45

creditors, forcing him to – what is your expression – borrow from Peter to pay . . . Theophilus. I must come down soon and suggest how he can raise more money from salt taxes or he'll never afford you.'

Theo grinned. 'That would be 'andsome of you. But doesn't he get an allowance from the Company?'

'Yes, but never enough to cover his debts, duties and self-indulgences – learned at the knee of his royal father, as usual.'

'Surabhoji? Still, he was a grand fellow. Over-indulged me, too, as a child I daresay. He tried to intercede on my behalf when father packed me off Home in disgrace. Couldn't understand all the fuss . . . Why shouldn't a lad of thirteen want a woman? Time I got married in his opinion . . .'

They chuckled but, hearing Amelia's returning step, Gopal changed the tone. 'I don't think I told you, Theo: I may be offered a post in the judiciary; junior, of course.'

'And will you accept?' Theo looked surprised.

'I'm sure I don't know . . .'

He looked uncertain and Amelia, resuming her seat, said, 'And if I might ask, what would your reservations be, Mr Krishnan?'

His look made it plain she should not ask, but he replied politely, 'I studied English law in all good faith several years ago, madam, but without seeing then, as I do now, that the adoption of a European legal system here is part of the British plan to strengthen your rule and weaken our culture. I'm not sure I wish to be a tool of this process.'

She plucked her skirt nervously. 'But would you not agree that some of our laws are more enlightened and humanitarian than yours, and comparatively well codified?'

'To some extent, yes, Mrs Lang, and that is my dilemma. But it is not one that need concern the pretty young wife of my friend. I hope your son is all right?'

'Yes, thank you. But Mr Krishnan, I do wonder . . .' Behind him, Theo shook his head and she sighed. 'Well, never mind. Rolly was a little frightened by all your servants – curious to look at him, I think – and indeed I'm equally curious to see your children.'

'Unfortunately my wife is indisposed today, Mrs Lang, so I'm afraid that is not possible.'

'Oh, what a shame!'

He fell silent. Amelia noticed that the tea things had been cleared away in her absence, and she rose reluctantly.

'Then perhaps we should go, Theo?'

As they drove off, Amelia said irritably, 'Well, I must say I find your friend a little odd, Theo. If he's so attached to his own culture why does he fill his rooms with European knick-knacks?'

'I teased him about that once. He said it was less a contradiction than a perfect symbol of himself – the front aspect Europeanised while the rest goes on as usual, like the parts of his house visitors don't see, still run on traditional brahminical lines.'

'And that won't change? Like his treatment of his wife – and me.'

'He treated you perfectly civilly.'

'But not in the least – friendly.'

'Indian men seldom make friends with women; I told you.' His tone was final and he stared out of the carriage more preoccupied with Gopal's unsettling news about Tanjore than with these social niceties.

Journeys in India invariably began at dawn in order to cover ground before the midday heats, and this, allied to the extensive preparations involved, the uncertainties and hazards of the way, gave an air of drama to every departure. While it was still dark, sets of bearers and cowry coolies jogged into Marguerite's compound, and house servants brought out chests, boxes and baskets filled with the Langs' personal possessions, food, drink and cooking utensils. As first light streaked the sky, Theo helped Amelia into a palanquin.

'There – your first palki! And you can say with the snail *omnia mecum porto* without even having to do the carrying!'

She settled herself and Rolly on the mattress. The inside of the vehicle was indeed like a self-contained shell with canvas-lined walls, sliding-doors, two small windows in front and a shelf below each with a swinging net between, in which she put Rolly's feeding bottle, lozenges, cologne, sewing and writing materials. Outside, the servants and bearers seemed to be quarrelling fiercely, but then came a number of grunts and shuffles, the palki rose unevenly, its carrying-poles came to rest on the bearers' shoulders, and they were off.

The vehicle tipped and jolted like a small craft on a choppy sea as the men got into their stride, but once the city was left behind Amelia began to enjoy herself. From the windows she could see the glistening brown backs of the bearers and, beyond, the flat, reddish, grit track leading across stretches of green land dotted with clusters of palms, mangoes, tamarinds, leaf-thatch houses and people working.

The bearers chanted and called to each other as they jogged along – about the state of the crops, the grazing animals and the people they were carrying. They did not suspect that Theo understood their drift as they speculated whether the baby with his lovely curls was the son of the balding foreigner who must be quite old. The woman was his second or third wife perhaps, for foreigners got through a lot of spouses one way or another – the young men wearing out their first wives with conception and the young women wearing out the wealthy old fellows with too much fucking. Theo grinned to himself; Gopi had a point – perhaps he should teach Amelia only classical languages! But even as he thought this a bearer began a familiar chant he'd have liked her to understand: 'Carry her swiftly, pretty little lady with a curly-haired baby. They're not fat and heavy, so don't drop them in the dust.'

During the hottest part of the day they stopped in a village where a new set of bearers took over and carried them southward until they halted for the night at a choultry – a travellers' resting place. While the cook organised a makeshift kitchen and Theo bargained with the choultry keeper for two hens, Amelia strolled about with Rolly. Gilded by the setting sun, the land was at its most bewitching: doves and pigeons were fluttering in the nearby coconut grove; buffaloes sloshing off the day's dust in a slime-green pool; a boy was leading a string of brown goats towards a distant farm.

The soft, tranquil beauty of this ordinary rural scene filled Amelia with pure joy – at just being there, with the promise of many similar evenings ahead. Yet she also sensed the dark undertow of dread and sadness that flowed in the same Indian channel: little Peter, who lived only long enough to outgrow his rocking-horse; the belles of the Madras balls who danced themselves into early graves; the fateful packet of black-edged letters journeying remorselessly across the ocean towards Lady Munro. She shivered and, clutching Rolly tightly to her, hastened back to the choultry where the fires had been lit and the cook was plucking a stringy hen for supper.

CHAPTER THREE

Three scavenging crows began squabbling over one gobbet of filthy fat. Through the window of his office next to the orderly room in Tanjore barracks, Captain Gilbert watched them, unwillingly, out of boredom. One evening recently old Wardle had regaled him and Reverend Arbuthnot with a titbit about some wretched Moslem woman who'd had her nose cut off for adultery by her husband and was lying in a welter of blood when a doctor happened by. The nose was still on her cheek, and the doctor, handing it to a servant to wash, told the woman he could stitch it back on. But the servant put down the bloody piece of flesh for a moment to get water and a crow flew down and snapped it up for supper. The men had cackled as drily as the crows, but Gilbert couldn't believe even Wardle, who collected gruesome yarns of native doings, could have found it amusing. But it was the custom of Englishmen, gathered in after-dinner solidarity, to remind each other that every bestiality, brutality, defilement had its comical side; as did every death, even if the next one was your own. They had all spent years in India.

The captain removed his gaze to an English hunting print on the opposite wall. It was fly- and mildew-specked, but precariously gummed to its lower edge by an enterprising bazaar tailor was a bright new calendar for the year which began that day: 1839. Before its first month was out, Captain G. Gilbert of the East India Company's Third Light Cavalry would be thirty-nine. 'Over the hill,' he thought, staring at the huntsmen perpetually riding into the grubby distance. 'The nineteenth – *your* century,' his mother used to say significantly, for had she not given it to him and was he not to do something extraordinarily splendid with the gift? She had wanted him to do – what? Rule the country, paint a masterpiece, make a fortune? He'd never discovered, for what she'd most wanted was to keep him near her after his father's death. Her four older sons had gone off early into the world and that was enough, she'd said, having wanted a daughter for the last. So he'd left the home-nest late, flown in the wrong direction, and now, at the start of his fortieth year, was stuck where neither he nor his late mother had ever imagined – in the steamy morass of south India, watching the crows scrabbling in the barrack dust and waiting for the day's routine to begin. As often happened, he was early on duty.

A soldier lurched by, kicking so wildly at the crows that Gilbert realised he was not sober, though it was not yet eight o'clock. Gilbert stood up, straightened his highly-polished waist belt, set his face in familiar lines of constrained anger. The soldier was Gerard Murphy, who would ask what else a true-born Irishman could do on this day but drink to that beloved green homeland where his own mother would be raising a glass . . .

'Cuddy,' Gilbert roared. The lieutenant appeared in the doorway. 'Put that man in the cells. He's drunk.'

'It *is* New Year, sir.'

'Well, his New Year's over.'

'Yessir.'

'Bring the Defaulters' Book, Cuddy.'

Gilbert opened it and added Murphy's name to the three already impounded for the same offence. In New Years gone by, Gilbert had had sternly to renew his self-imposed resolution: no alcohol; no tobacco. But this was no longer necessary for he could scarce endure the reek of either, and took considerable pleasure in the power that healthy sobriety gave him in this sickly, self-indulgent land. Moreover, the man who drank too much gave too much away, and Gil (as his few friends called him) was careful never to do that.

Returning the book, he said, 'I'm to the Resident's office as usual, Lieutenant. If this drunkenness gets out of hand, send for me.'

'Yessir.'

Crossing the barrack square, the captain strolled along the horse-lines, savouring the keenest pleasure India offered him: shine of leather, brass and chestnut flank; smell of beeswax, dry grass, resin, earthy smoke from the gram-boiling shed. Best of all was his sovereignty over these stables which, having been built fifty years before when a much larger British garrison was stationed here, were now unnecessarily extensive, though still kept in spotless, orderly trim at his command. The horse-boy, grooming Gil's Arab after his early-morning gallop, swivelled his eyes in fear as the captain checked the cleanliness of the curry-combs, the strength of every girth and lip-strap, the quality of coconut milk for the tail brushing. As Gil looked up, satisfied, another boy slipped out of the rear stable door. Following quietly, he was just in time to see the boy warn two grass-cutters squatting against the wall beside an array of empty bottles. Or almost empty – for they were tipping the dregs of claret, brandy, porter, arrack and champagne left over from the New Year's Eve festivities into a tin mug from which they drank in turn.

'Ah! Caught you – drunken sots!' Gilbert laughed, as the men tried to hide the evidence. 'And you, too!' he cuffed the boy, shouting for the farrier-major who came running at the sound of his wrath. 'Get rid of these thieving blacks – and the sneak-boy. Never want to see them again. Understand?'

'Yessir.'

Gilbert squared his shoulders and strode off, ready to tackle old Wardle and whatever else the New Year had in store. Perhaps it would be a good one; he would get promoted at last or, better yet, marching orders to the war in Afghanistan, which might have been in central Africa for all the opportunity it gave men stuck here in the south.

'Happy New Year, sir.' Gilbert stepped on the verandah of Hubert Wardle's office near the main entrance to the Big Fort of Tanjore, inside which the Raja's escort was quartered. He grinned, for Wardle looked more than usually at odds with the world – probably another one with New Year's gut-ache.

'Ah – come in, Captain. Bad news . . . oh yes, happy New Year, but bad news.'

'Already?'

'The Raja of Poodocottah has just died.'

Gil placed his forage cap very carefully on a chair and frowned down at it. 'Really? That is . . . inconvenient. His two heirs still being minors.'

'Precisely. There'll be power struggles – internal, interfraternal . . .'

'Internecine,' Gil suggested.

Wardle blinked. 'In short, they'll be at each other's throats. And the Raja wasn't even an old man. Who'd have expected . . .'

'Rajas' lives are frequently curtailed. Any hint of foul play?'

'Apparently not. Diseased liver, they say. He'd been deteriorating for weeks, but nobody told me.'

He glared accusingly at Gil, who shrugged. It wasn't his business to keep this silly old coot informed of what went on at Poo, as it was generally called. The name fitted, for Poo, which adjoined Tanjore district to the south, was the epitome in size and status of a petty State. Though still ruled by the hereditary line of Tondiman rajas, the Company kept it under surveillance, offering advice and loans; and, in due course and season, probably intending to take it over. Whether or not the unexpected death of its raja meant the season was now propitious loomed as a question some bigwig on the Madras Council would soon be posing to the Resident. This, Wardle knew; he also knew he had no notion how to answer it. His mind shied.

'You won't join me in a brandy-pawnee to welcome this auspicious day, Captain?'

'Lime juice, thank you.'

Wardle gave the order. 'Oh, and another morsel of New Year joy – poor old Mayhew's been sent off by the Trichy doctors on a long sea voyage. Last hope for *his* liver apparently, which means we'll be having that cocky young assistant Rundell back here.'

Gil took his cap off the chair and sat down whistling tunelessly. 'Not, as you say, a promising start. So what do you propose to do about Poo?'

'Do? What can I do? Where the devil are those drinks . . . I'll go and . . .'

53

He went out shouting, and Gil, thinking over the news, took automatic critical note of the dust on the desk, the empty inkwell, untrimmed quills.

'Here at last . . .' Wardle returned, swallowing his brandy rapidly. 'They'll all be humbugging each other down there – and me, and anyone else who goes to find out what's what. Then one day there'll be knife in back, poison in cup, and they'll be sending from Madras for me to explain why it happened, who did it and at precisely what hour the crime was committed, Resident, if you please. Not to mention a rap over the knuckles for giving them no advance warning.' He slammed down his glass. 'I'll have to go, of course – offer me condolences. You'd better accompany me with a small escort, Captain.'

'Today, Resident? I really think it most inadvisable. I am, of course under your instructions, but there are at least a dozen cases of drunk and disorderlies in the cells already, and the sepoys have a celebratory extra allowance of arrack. I could send Cuddy with you.'

'And what if there's any trouble at Poo?'

'Mr Wardle, you know as well as I that nothing untoward could possibly be allowed to occur during the funeral observances.'

Wardle squinted suspiciously. 'What's up? You're usually keen enough to go to Poo.'

'Only when I feel my presence isn't specially required here, Resident.'

'Oh well, hell then . . . give me Cuddy. I don't care. Won't make a ha'porth of difference who goes, who don't go, no one's going to find out a dratted thing.'

'Quite.' The captain rose. 'I'll give Cuddy his orders. Four men will suffice, sir?'

As he stepped out on the verandah, Wardle shouted, 'Hang on – I've just remembered – that fellow in the Raja's pay is due any day now. Mr somebody Lang. There's a letter somewhere . . .' He rummaged about. 'Met Lang once – son of that crazy scholar-wallah Bayard. He came rushing down here when his father was dying. About three years ago, I

54

suppose. The father was cremated like a Hindu. Rum old bird. Anyway, you'll have to see these Langs unless His High and Mightiness does something, which is very unlikely . . . especially now, with this Poo business.'

Gilbert took the letter, saluted and left, smiling a little in the knowledge that Wardle's difficulties were partly due to his inadequate grasp of the native lingos, despite which the old coot had managed to bluff his way to his present position. The captain could have told the Resident quite a lot about goings-on at Poo; he was no linguist either, but he had his sources, his secret, secret sources that glittered like a wayward stream below the ordered current of his life.

Wardle, meanwhile, jammed on his hat and was carried the short distance between office and bungalow in a palki escorted by two official bearers granted him for grandeur. Such was his custom on two counts: it didn't do for the natives to see him walking about like a peasant, and he needed to conserve every ounce of his strength, for the Resident had developed an acute sense of his increasing age. This wretched country was to blame of course; time and again he'd seen it carry people off eventually as it had his wife Marjorie, and this year he'd be fifty – a dangerous age for health. His thoughts circled obsessively about Time, dividing and measuring days and weeks, counting months till he could leave India forever – which he would do tomorrow were it not for the cost of educating his sons. He'd seen so many drop just before the Home fence, like poor old Mayhew probably would, though he'd paid scant regard to his health, unlike Wardle.

The only topic that could divert the Resident from the anxiously related ones of Health and Time was his garden. Arriving at his bungalow, he regarded it morosely, for he'd been planning to spend this New Year's Day transplanting the cabbage and broccoli seedlings and the precious white turnips sent specially from Hyderabad, and sorting out the rainy pumpkins from the long-water variety, and planting the love-apples in raised beds and . . . thanks to the dratted Raja of Poo none of this would be done. He gave instructions for the strawberry nets to be mended, the carnations to be watered and his bag to be packed. He left that afternoon, gloomier than ever at the prospect ahead – the jolting tedium of a long palki ride culminating in the noisy mumbo-jumbo of heathen funeral rites.

The court of Tanjore had also to send a suitable representative to Poodocottah, for relations between the two States, though strained in the way of boundary-neighbours, were distantly courteous. Raja Sevaji long debated with his advisers who would best convey that sentiment. It was remembered that, when Sevaji's father had been sent a white umbrella by the Company for carrying in formal procession, the Raja of Poodocottah had received but two silver sticks, and it was important therefore for the Tanjore envoy to represent in his very person the condescension of an umbrella-carrying State towards mere stick-carriers.

Preoccupied thus, the court quite overlooked the arrival of the new tutor-librarian. The Langs jogged into town the next morning unnoticed and unheralded until accosted by an English red-coat who directed them to the barracks. Waiting to greet them was Captain Gilbert – a tall, youthful figure, only the tight creases round mouth and eyes, a small recession of the blonde hairline, suggesting his actual age. They were ushered into his office where the captain curtly told them the recent news, his manner thawing only when Theo mentioned Marguerite Hervey.

'You stayed with her? In that case I'll see what I can do for you. You won't get much attention from the Raja for a while, in the circumstances.'

'Do you know where we are to live, Captain?' Amelia asked.

'In what's rightly called the "Old Bungalow". Built years ago by the Company when we had a larger representation here. The Raja considers it his property now. But it's seen better days, I warn you. One of my men will escort you and I'll send over some supplies later.'

Dwellings left vacant in hot climes are rapidly filled by a multiplicity of animal and vegetable presences, and the Old Bungalow looked ready to collapse entirely under their weight and voracity. In accordance with standard Company pattern, its surrounding verandah led directly into a number of high rooms, their walls supporting a roof which was concealed only by sheets of cloth stretched to form tent-like ceilings. Bathrooms with decaying wooden tubs were attached to some rooms, and all were separated only by archways or half-doors with gaps above and below to facilitate the circulation of what air there was. Behind the main bungalow was a lean-to cookroom with earthen floor and a fire-hole, its walls stained with a patina of wood-smoke, cooking oil and dull red betel juice that looked uncomfortably like dried blood.

Space there was in abundance, but nothing in the way of comfort or decoration distinguished one space from the next, for all shared a similar state of decrepitude. Recent monsoon rains had poured through holes in the tiled and thatched roof and the ceiling cloths were torn, exposing wormy beams festooned with tropical creepers; walls were mildewed, their streaky grey-green enlivened by splotches of rust where pictures had once hung.

Amelia and Theophilus stood together in the centre of the largest room.

'A great deal needs doing, doesn't it?' said she in a small, shaky voice, determined to keep tight hold of the strong nerves with which Marguerite had apparently credited her.

'It's not too good at the moment. I don't suppose the Raja realised its condition.'

'You'll go and see him about it at once, won't you, Theo?'

'Tomorrow, dear. We'll have to manage till then.'

She nodded, pushing aside the vision she'd cherished of a first night in a cosy new home. A number of people, who had appeared from nowhere and followed them from the barracks, stood clustered in the open doorways, staring.

'What *do* they want, Theo?'

'Oh, just curiosity, and some are seeking work. We've already been offered two dhobis, a cook, a house-boy and gardener.'

She looked at them doubtfully. 'Well, we'll have to hire some servants.'

'But these are probably the rag and bobtail. Best to get them from recommendation.'

A grey-haired, spindle-shanked man thrust himself forward, jabbing at his own chest. 'Good recommendation. Mali – garden-man. Work Resident long ago.'

'Which Resident?' asked Theo.

'Long ago,' the man replied.

'Ah – Resident Long-ago.'

The man glared sulkily. 'No. Long ago I work British. Same garden, master.'

'Let's try him, Theo. We must start somewhere.'

Theo nodded. 'All right Long-ago, show me the garden. Let's see what can be done with it.'

The man grinned, roughly pushing a way for Theo through the other spectators. Paths, plots and bushes were webbed with weeds and creepers which the man pulled aside to show irrigation channels leading from the well. The channels were choked with rotted vegetation and the decayed bodies of rats and pariah dogs, while the well itself was a stinking black hole in one corner of the compound.

'All right, Long-ago.' Theo spoke fluently in the man's tongue, much to his surprise. 'You're hired as number one outside man. Choose your own boy and start tomorrow. We'll discuss wages later.'

Long-ago skipped off and Theo, feeling better for having decided something, returned indoors where his wife was trying to communicate with an anxious woman in a frayed purple sari.

'Oh Theo – this is Veena . . . look.'

She handed him a yellowed, much-creased paper dated ten years before; it announced that Resident J. Blackburne of the East India Company had found the bearer to be an honest and reasonably industrious domestic servant.

'Please let's take her. She looks desperate – and I certainly am.'

Theo asked the woman a few questions which she answered in monosyllables; she could be Veena, a thief or a harlot, but she'd have to do for the present.

As the bearers were unloading their baggage, a sepoy arrived with generous supplies from Captain Gilbert, and the sight galvanised everyone into cheerful activity. Two daughters of Veena appeared to help, Long-ago's son was sent for water, and soon a card-table in the main room was set with steaming bowls of curries from the bazaar. After supper, camp-beds were set up in the same room and cloths draped over windows and doors to make it look more cosy – except for the holes in the roof.

Lying in bed, gazing through the holes at the stars in the warm night sky, Amelia felt happy. They were safe in their very own home at last; not quite as she'd imagined it certainly, but things would soon be shipshape. That night she slept as easily as Veena and her daughters and Long-ago and his son in the ramshackle servants' rooms in the compound, for they had secured much-sought-after berths with the rich English and were well content.

The palace of the Raja of Tanjore, to which Theo directed his steps next morning, was situated inside an area of some five hundred acres known as the Fort. Divided by a moat and high walls from the rest of the city, it formed an enclave for the royal and the rich and was dominated by a seven-storey tower that commanded a strategic view of the countryside beyond. During Tanjore's turbulent past, several dynasties – the Cholas, the Pandyas, the Pallavas, the Vijayanagars – came and went and then, in the seventeenth century, came the Mahrattas, who ruled, lost power, and were re-established with British support a century later.

There followed numerous disputes and battles over heirs and boundaries of the kind that went on in many parts of the country until, in 1798, Surabhoji, adopted as heir presumptive by an earlier Mahratta raja, was declared ruler. He, too, was supported by the British, whom he considered his true allies but who left him little to rule, for they controlled most of the former Tanjore kingdom, leaving him in possession only of his Fort and some neighbouring land and paying him a share of the State revenue to keep him quiet. Surabhoji, an enter-prising, intelligent man who'd been educated partly by Euro-pean missionaries, reigned until 1832, when, on his death, his son Sevaji became raja.

Theophilus hadn't been inside the palace since he was a

boy, when Surabhoji still reigned, but he remembered that the iron-hinged main gate used to creak on opening, as it did for him again that morning, its weight having scraped a somewhat deeper hollow in the courtyard stones. Plaster mouldings on the courtyard pillars had crumbled, he noticed; frescoes seemed bleached a little nearer to oblivion; the ancient cannon on the highest wall bore larger scars of rust – but the royal edifice still retained that air of fading but never quite vanished splendour peculiar to its Indian kind.

Theophilus was greeted by the captain of the palace guard and conducted along galleries and passageways where many eyes watched him covertly, for strange foreigners were rare visitors these days. And so, very soon, every elephant- and book-keeper, every drummer and driver, every hunter and cook, every torch, fan and water bearer, stone and firewood cutter, the grandmothers of every tailor, goldsmith and groom, and certainly every wife and widow, collateral relative, astrologer and pensioned retainer within the precincts knew that the scholar whom His Highness had summoned from afar had come unattended to the gate, wearing humble clothes of ordinary cotton. And this was strange, for white men usually came by horseback or palanquin, in tight-buttoned smart uniforms, and made a great fuss about the protocol of the presenting of arms and the firing of guns in salute to their august arrivals. This odd newcomer seemed to expect nothing, and so could not be very important. He was tall, slender and not very old, and the eyes of the dancing girls, who were practising the postures of the swan, the peacock and the restless fish in their special apartments, glittered when they heard this, and they asked if the foreigner was married – but that no one seemed to know.

When Theo had frequented the palace as a child, Sevaji had been a cloistered, pampered princeling, prone to illnesses and tantrums, disliking study and hunting and with a passion for telescopes, astrology and riding elephants – which was all Theo could remember, as he was conducted into Sevaji's adult presence. The audience room was dim and musty-smelling, furnished in antiquated European style, on its walls portraits of former Tanjore princes, descendants of the conquering Mahrattas – stout, proud, round-faced, moustachioed men in embroidered robes and three-cornered, jewel-encrusted hats.

Sevaji was dressed in court style similar to his forebears, but his countenance, already looking middle-aged, seemed but a blurred copy of theirs and his voice, as he gabbled the usual courtesies of greeting, had a querulous tone that was all his own. Often, he glanced distractedly at an older man beside him who'd been introduced as his sirkele, his chief adviser.

When Sevaji paused to gulp a cup of white liquid, the sirkele asked abruptly, 'And is it true, Mr Lang, that your country is now ruled by a young queen – a single woman?'

'Indeed yes, sir. Though no doubt she will soon marry.'

He looked relieved. 'Then you'll have a king?'

'No, sir. He'll be the prince consort and she will still rule by hereditary right.'

'Strange things go on in Europe, Mr Lang.'

Theo smiled. 'They do indeed. But the revered Surabhoji, friend of my late father, found much of interest in its culture – as I trust his royal son may?'

'Ah, but things aren't what they were,' the sirkele replied cryptically, and Sevaji took him up.

'Indeed not. Look what happens nowadays – even the most peace-loving rulers are under threat. The Nabob of Kurnal is in difficulties, I hear – the Company reproaches him for neglect of his people. They'll depose him soon, you'll see, Mr Lang. And now Raja Tondiman has died in Poodocottah, we dare not think what may befall there. Perhaps the Company will march in "to restore peace and order".' He snickered ironically and Theo replied with care.

'Believe me, royal sir, your anxieties concern me, but I've no way of knowing the Company's designs for I'm not in its employ – and right glad of it. But surely the Company's officials wouldn't use the Raja's death as an excuse to . . .'

'Any excuse will suffice if they covet something,' shrilled Sevaji. 'And certain people in Poodocottah might even encourage them. The late Raja's younger brother and his Bengali accomplice, Hemanga Nath Moitra who . . .'

61

'Moitra? Didn't he marry a girl called Rukmini Ayyer who lived here years ago?'

'You are correct, Mr Lang. Hemanga Nath tried to sow his poisonous seeds among us, but we sent him packing.'

'And he and Rukmini went to Poodocottah?' The sirkele nodded.

'And she is alive and well, I hope?'

'As far as I'm aware, Mr Lang. We don't much concern ourselves with the affairs of that court except in times of crisis like the present when the British . . .' The sirkele broke off, frowning at a ruby and gold ring he revolved round his finger. Theo waited for him to continue, but when he did it was on a different tack.

'I wonder how much you recollect of our little domain, Mr Lang? How old would you be when you left for England?'

'Nearing fourteen, sir, and I remember – oh so much! Especially, perhaps, the royal menagerie with its snakes, cassowary birds, cheetahs, tigers . . . Are they still here?'

'Very few, very few,' Sevaji replied. 'My priests tell me it is cruelty to animals, but I still have many elephants – my special joy.'

Theo felt absurdly disappointed; he'd expected not only tigers but also more general signs of majesty.

'All is diminishing,' Sevaji continued, as if picking up Theo's thought. 'And the Company's minions are surely planning to dispossess me of my poor remnants. Yet did not my ancestors entrust the riches of their territories to the British freely? In return for everlasting friendship, protection from enemies and guaranteed solvency? But what do I encounter now, Mr Lang? Why . . .'

The sirkele, struck with a dramatic coughing fit, called loudly for some tea and drank – while Sevaji subsided into cowed silence. Then he put down his cup, fixing Theo with a very keen old eye, and announced the audience was over, for matters of State awaited His Highness's attention.

Theo rose, bowing. 'I'll try to help you, royal prince, in any way I can. But as yet you haven't told me my duties or . . .'

'Later, Mr Lang, this is but a beginning.'

'But there is an urgent matter, Highness. The bungalow

allotted me is in very poor condition. For myself I care not, but for my wife and son . . .'

'Ah yes, you have a son. You must bring him to show me.'

'It will be an honour, sir. But for his well-being the house is . . .'

'It shall be seen to,' cut in the sirkele.

Theo drew his breath for further effort. 'Also the matter of salary, Highness. We haven't really discussed it. The expenses of travelling here were . . .'

'We shall see about it,' said the sirkele firmly.

A servant standing behind Sevaji began to fan him gently and the Raja closed his eyes in enjoyment of the little breeze, while another servant conducted Theophilus out.

The sirkele said sharply, 'You are too hasty, royal sir. You mustn't trust these foreigners. That man may be in the Company's pay – a spy sent to undo us all . . .'

'But I sent for him as a friend. His father . . .'

'Oh sire, what sense of father and son do these foreigners have?'

'But you agreed we should send for him. You wrote the letter.'

'Because he might prove an ally against the Company. But we don't know yet. You leap into trust far too soon, like a hasty boy, royal sir.'

Sevaji remained silent, for he had been accustomed to censure and admonition since childhood and had long learned to let it wash over his unresisting head.

As the main gates creaked shut, Theo hesitated, blinking in the crude glare after the shaded rooms of royalty. Amelia was awaiting his news, but, feeling unequal to telling her how unsatisfactory it was, he wandered instead through the Fort's crowded streets, across the moat bridge and found himself heading for Tanjore's other grand edifice – the Sri Brihadis-vara temple. Its great stone gopuram or tower, its many carvings, were just as he remembered them, for the temple had been well-endowed and well-maintained for centuries. The central courtyard, enclosed by red and white walls, was swept clean and dominated by a colossal statue of the sitting bull, Nandi, its black flanks a-gleam from their daily rub with gingelly oil. According to legend, it was increasing in size every year and would one day outgrow the pillared canopy that gave it shade, but to Theo it looked smaller than when he last saw it in his youth. Worshippers were drifting along the colonnaded passageways towards the inner shrines and sacred tank, and he stood to watch the bright colours pass. Saris of vermilion flecked with gold thread, of limey-green and cloudy purple, sharp lemon, orange and peacock blue threaded with silver; white dhotis of the men, and the priests with oily pates and foreheads marked with the horizontal lines of the god Siva.

His sandals removed, Theo squirmed his toes in the courtyard grit even though they winced at its hot prickle. His heart began to glow with joyous recognition of the boy he once was who, when his father was busy, used to come here and run wild with the temple children, his feet as tough as theirs. Curious, he'd watch the temple servants cleaning torches and repainting wooden festival carts, polishing the ritual brass vessels, pounding sandalwood paste and mending the clothes of the deities. Sometimes the dancing girls had crowded round to tease him, tweaking his nose and his penis, bidding him sniff their musky perfumes and touch the lotus flowers in their oiled hair. Sometimes he'd help the elephant-keeper's boy daub the face and trunk of the temple elephant with vermilion and ochre, and then the keeper would hoist him up beside him on the beast's back and let him ride in lofty glory across this very courtyard.

Remembering such happiness, knowing the same patient services of faith and devotion were still being performed, Theo's anxiety and disappointment fell away. How absurdly English of him to expect any immediate and definite outcome from his first royal audience! He should have known better: the house repairs, his duties, his salary, would all be dealt with in due time – Indian time. He must explain this to his wife so she, too, would be relieved of anxiety!

Happy, he joined the general drift, pausing occasionally to admire frescoes of dancing maidens, bulls, white elephants and celestial beings showering flower petals from the clouds, and to decipher inscriptions on the passage pillars. Here centuries of temple gifts were commemorated: gifts of money towards the blowing of horns at an early hour to herald every festival day, and supplies of cardamon seeds and champaka buds for scenting water presented to the gods on such days; of three cows to provide a temple lamp with butter-oil; of harvest grain to the priests from four cultivators of the soil, and of flowers to garland a deity from four gardeners. As he drew near the inner recesses of this holy place Theo smelled the familiar fragrance of such flowers, of scented water, burning oil, smoky incense and some sweetly-pungent spice used in the baking of coconut-cake offerings, the name of which he couldn't recall.

Sitting on a step leading down to the sacred tank, he watched the women move about in the water, which rippled against their sari-covered breasts 'like the kneading hands of lovers'. It was a simile he'd read somewhere, and he leant his head against a pillar, closing his eyes against the too-delectable sight. Breathing deeply of that particular sweetness, time unfolded backwards as it had not done for many a year, and he was standing in a dim, closed storeroom heaped with sacks of spices and herbs, and his hands were tingling with excitement as they explored the young flesh of the girl whose arms were round his neck. He kneaded her breasts, feeling her nipples tighten, and he reached down greedily, pressing her slender belly, burrowing into the wet warmth between her legs. 'Oh Rukmini,' he whispered, 'oh . . . oh,' and the dark eyes gazing adoringly into his were agonisingly beautiful. He kissed them, her neck and shoulders, shaking, gasping, expelling his boyish lust against her flimsy skirt before he realised what was happening. He clutched her again, burying his face in her hair, inhaling odours of lustrous oils, of sexually-stirred flesh, of spices and herbs and dust.

Until these 'secret games' (as they called them) began in the storeroom, he and Rukmini had been as brother and sister, drawn together by mutual misfortune, for Rukmini had lost both her parents in the same epidemic that killed Theo's mother, Miranda, when he was seven years old. As Rukmini's father had been a collateral relative of the court, she had simply been absorbed as one more female dependant into the women's quarters. However, Raja Surabhoji, influenced by his contact with Westerners, had somewhat unorthodox ideas about the upbringing of females, and court girls of low caste were put to learning skills, such as sewing saddlery, playing the fife, walking on stilts, or passing gold chains up their nostrils and out of their mouths for the entertainment of visitors.

Rukmini, a beautiful child, somewhere between a waif and a lady, was taught European-style dancing, given a basic education and considerable freedom of movement within the palace boundaries. So she sometimes sat beside Theo while his father taught him the classics of European and oriental literature, and sometimes they played together on secluded balconies and stood innocently hand-in-hand watching the Madrassee jugglers and Telegu wrestlers practising their skills, and the water-colourists painting the weird and wonderful creatures in the royal menagerie. More than 500 souls lived in the palace, and it was easy enough for the activities of two shy, lonely children to be frequently overlooked. It was also overlooked that they had reached puberty.

No one was allowed to forget the maturing of the Raja's only son, however, and in 1819 it was arranged for him to marry a young cousin of royal Mahratta blood. He was two years Theo's junior.

Perhaps it was the excited anticipation aroused by these nuptials which encouraged Theo and Rukmini to exchange their childish games with tamarind seeds and counters for the 'secret' ones in the spice-store. Caught up in the timeless enchantment of his first encounter with young female flesh, Theo could still pinpoint with extreme clarity one dreadful afternoon. He and Rukmini were lying in a fumbling, twisting heap across a bag of spice used in the making of coconut-cakes – and the door burst open and his father surged in. He remembered Bayard's harsh clutch on the scruff of his neck as he was marched away, while Rukmini was dragged sobbing to the women's quarters.

They had never set eyes on each other since.

When his anger cooled, Bayard blamed himself more than

his son, for clearly he'd not paid enough attention to the boy's development. So, lest he become quite 'Hinduised' (a term the scholar didn't apply to himself, though others did), Theo was sent straight Home to school.

Just a week before Sevaji's marriage, Theo found himself *en route* for Madras, whence he sailed to England in the care of a missionary's widow. He was utterly bereft of everything that was delightful, exciting and familiar. But he did not forget Rukmini, and for many years he imagined her as a wearer of red flowers, a lotus woman with eyes like a fawn, grown large-bosomed, soft-skinned, a complexion gold as champaka flowers – which, the ancient poets told him, was the most desirable type of all womankind.

Seduced into this warm, voluptuous half-doze, half-day-dream of the past, Theophilus sat for a long while on the temple step, till a slight cooling of the air alerted him to the fading of daylight. He jumped up, wanting to make immediate, passionate love to his wife and then confess the story of his first adolescent exploration of sex, which had been a turning-point in his life, and even more in Rukmini's. For she had been disgraced and was soon carelessly married off to Hemanga Nath Moitra, a court hanger-on fifteen years her senior who'd come from the north with some rare manuscripts for the Raja's library and just stayed on, as people sometimes did.

On the way home Theo pondered how he and Amelia could meet Rukmini again, for there could be no harm in it now. Sauntering up the garden, he heard sounds of extreme distress, and rushed in to find Amelia sitting on the floor of the main room crying and holding Rolly so tightly that he was wailing also and trying to wriggle from her desperate embrace.

'Oh Theo, Theo – here you are at last! Where have you been? I thought something dreadful had happened to you, too. Oh, if only you'd been here!'

'My dearest, what is it? Tell me.' He knelt beside her, gently loosening her grip on the child. Her usually rosy cheeks were white, and she mopped sweat and tears from them as she composed herself.

'I'll try and explain properly, or you'll think I was mad to . . . Well, after you'd gone a sweeping woman appeared who raised a real storm brushing walls and shaking matting and creatures started to crawl about everywhere . . . beetles, cockroaches, centipedes and two scorpions here in this very room.' She shuddered. 'Then Long-ago dragged me to see the dead goat he'd managed to fish out of the well. . . ugh! Oh and then Mrs Arbuthnot, the chaplain's wife, arrived. She invited me to her house to escape the uproar and I wish I'd gone, but I thought you'd be back any minute. So we're both to go for supper tomorrow evening.'

He groaned. 'Oh Lord – a clerical supper! But never mind. Dear, I should have warned you about all these creepy-crawlies.'

'Oh, *they* were nothing. But you see I was afraid Rolly would be stung, so I put him in a little back room out of the way and asked Veena's daughter to mind him. And suddenly she came running to me, screaming. We rushed to the room and . . .' She knuckled her eyes with the horror.

'What was it, Amy?'

'A cobra – he must have been sleeping behind some old water-jars – and there he was, reared up, hissing loudly, hood flaring and ready to strike, wild eyes glittering, and Rolly asleep, almost in his shadow . . .'

'Oh my God . . . Oh my dear. What did you . . .?'

'I just rushed in and snatched Rolly up as the cobra struck at us. He missed the first time and then he came gliding quickly towards us and someone grabbed me, putting me back out of the way, and it was Long-ago with a large stick and he and his son just beat at him so bravely – while he reared and hissed and struck out with his fangs. But between them they managed to kill him. Oh Theo, I just screamed and screamed and so did Rolly! It was like a nightmare, just a nightmare . . .'

He squeezed her shoulders tightly. 'Oh dearest, how very, very brave of you.'

'But I only thought of the child. I kept praying you'd come back – you've been gone all day and I was in such a state . . . But never mind, here we all are safe and thank God for it.'

They held each other close, Theo swamped with guilt, remembering how he'd spent the last few hours.

She rubbed her cheek against his. 'You must have had a good long audience with the Raja, Theo? Are they starting the repairs tomorrow? And what about your salary?'

'It wasn't so very satisfactory, I'm afraid, Amy. First visits here are more in the way of ceremonials.'

'Ceremonials! But it's so urgent, Theo. How can we settle in until everything has been thoroughly cleaned and repaired? Especially after this.'

'I know, dear. But we must be patient – Indian time, remember. No more cobras, I promise you – and a nice, holy supper to look forward to tomorrow!' He kissed her nose and went to reward Long-ago, who had certainly earned himself a permanent position in the household.

Reginald Cuthbert Arbuthnot, chaplain of the small Tanjore garrison, had experienced a trying day, particularly on account of Private Patterson who wanted to marry a Hindu wench because he'd got her pregnant and the child would be heathen else. But the woman refused to become a Christian, saying her family would cast her out – which was probably true, for Hindus were stubborn bigots in religious matters. But the reverend, a good churchman, couldn't solemnise a marriage between a Christian and a heathen, so he'd advised Patterson to cast the temptress from him and return to the arms of the Church. And Patterson had refused, which was especially galling because he had been one of the few regular church attenders. Now, at the sunset hour, Arbuthnot murmured a prayer for Patterson's redemption and turned for solace, as he often did, to the writings of Bishop Reginald Heber of Calcutta.

As he was about to launch into a solo of one of the Bishop's best-known hymns, 'Holy, holy, holy', he heard voices on the front verandah. So instead he combed his hair, pulled his black coat firmly across his sturdy girth and sighed, reluctant to leave his little sanctum, the only room in the house with a full-sized door to barricade him from the prattle and disturbance of the rest. For the Arbuthnots had six children and, though the two eldest were at school in England, the others made their presence very much felt. But now Dora, always the soul of charity, had invited newcomers to supper and he must play his part; he sailed off to greet them, putting a little twinkle in his eye as was his wont with unknown members of the fair sex.

Amelia didn't notice the twinkle, as she was being introduced to eight-year-old Agnes Arbuthnot, her younger sister Ruth and the two-year-old twins, Matthew and John.

'Our budding Evangelists,' Arbuthnot explained.

He ushered them into the parlour, littered with woolly toys, coloured bricks and torn picture books, for Dora was unfortunately incapable of disciplining either the children or servants into tidiness. After preliminary greetings, he poured wine for Theo and himself and they withdrew into the quietest corner.

'And have you yet had the . . . er . . . pleasure of meeting your employer, the Raja, Mr Lang?'

'Yesterday. A short audience only.'

'And may I ask your first impression of him, sir?'

'Oh, he seemed a little unsure of himself, but very pleasant and courteous.'

'Then count yourself fortunate, Mr Lang. For I've received short shrift on the few occasions I've visited the palace – feeling it my duty as a Christian gentleman.'

'I'm sorry to hear that,' Theo replied coolly. 'Of course, I attended in a different capacity, having been summoned here mainly, I think, because our fathers were friends.'

'Ah yes, I recollect Mr Wardle telling me. So your father would have been at court in '26 when our revered Bishop Heber of Calcutta came to Tanjore?'

Theo nodded, recalling a letter from his father describing Heber as an unusually intelligent prelate and well received by Surabhoji, who had a high regard for the Church. Too much regard, according to Bayard, who went on to deplore the effrontery of 'our overweening bishops who entitle themselves "of Calcutta" or "of Madras" as one might say of Winchester or Norwich, when no more than a few hundred souls of the millions who inhabit those Indian cities are professed Christians'.

'And have you read what the good Bishop had to say about his visit here?' Arbuthnot inquired.

'No. I am little acquainted with the writings of clerics.'

'Then you miss a very great deal, Mr Lang, and I shall at once try to remedy . . .' He instructed a servant to fetch the bishop's journals and poured more wine for them both. 'Tanjore was sadly one of the last ports of call on this earth for the Bishop, as you must know. He went from here to Trichy, where he died in the swimming bath of the Residency only hours after delivering a most magnificent sermon in the Fort church. My wife and I arrived there the very next day to find the whole city in a deep state of shock.'

Theo grimaced at the absurdity of this statement, as his father would have done.

'It was my first posting as a junior chaplain. I share his Christian name, and ever since have hoped that a scrap of that divine mantle of wisdom and faith was passed on to me.'

Theo muttered in vague politeness as Arbuthnot, receiving the book, put on his spectacles and began in the tone of a preacher intending to hold the attention of all present.

'The Bishop says that Surabhoji was a man of many parts – you may read the whole for yourself, Mr Lang – with a considerable knowledge of European literature. He was also, and I quote, "a good judge of a horse and a cool, bold and deadly shot at a tiger . . . To finish the portrait of Raja Surabhoji, I should tell you that he is a strong-built and very handsome middle-aged man, with eyes and nose like a fine hawk, and very bushy grey moustachios, generally splendidly dressed but with no effeminacy of ornament, and looking and talking more like a French general officer."'

The chaplain closed the book triumphantly as if he'd written it himself, and the respectful silence was broken by Amelia.

'What was the old Raja really like, Theophilus?'

'Proud and strong-looking – yes. "Eyes like a hawk" sounds rather stern, though.' Theo laughed. 'I remember warm eyes. He was very indulgent towards me.'

'And towards his own son,' Arbuthnot remarked. 'Such a terrible mistake, this pampering of native princes. And so now Tanjore is ruled by a weak degenerate, spoiled by the indulgences of the zenana, the hookah and the betel leaf, and quite under the thumb of scheming advisers and quack astrologer-priests. Are you aware, Mr Lang, that Bishop Heber actually offered to take Prince Sevaji back to Madras to knock some decent English education and discipline into him? And Surabhoji welcomed the idea?'

'Really?' Theo's tone was disbelieving.

'Yes. Really. But then the good Bishop died, and in any case Sevaji's mother wouldn't allow it. Such is the pernicious and primitive power of women-behind-the-screens here.'

'But how can you blame them, Reverend, when they are kept in complete ignorance of the outside world?' Amelia flashed. 'If they received the benefits of education they'd soon see the advantages of it for their sons – and daughters.'

He stared at her without the twinkle before turning to Theo, as if she had not spoken. 'I must warn you that the hold of the priests over Sevaji is so great that he's become something of a religious fanatic – throwing away money on idols enough to furnish thrice over every pagoda in the district.'

'Or, to look at it another way, the Raja is a devout believer who enhances the religion and culture of his own country. For do not all races need places of worship which are kept sacred and beautiful above and beyond the ordinary run?'

Both Arbuthnots stared at him aghast.

Amelia gave a conciliatory laugh. 'But you can hardly expect the Reverend to view it like that, Theophilus.'

'I don't. I'm just putting the "native angle" – for a change.' Theo seldom mixed socially with men of the cloth, and Arbuthnot rose heatedly to his challenge.

'You are actually suggesting, Mr Lang, that Christianity and Hinduism should be weighed in the same balance? That it makes no odds on which religion charity and care should be bestowed?'

'Precisely. I share the views of my father on this issue, you see.'

'Come now, gentlemen,' peaceable Dora tried to intercede, but Reginald glared at her, continuing.

'Ah yes, I heard he was an orientalist of the deepest dye.'

Theo grimaced. 'You make him sound like a criminal, Reverend.'

'Oh, I'm sure my husband didn't mean that!' Dora cut in. 'Your father is still spoken of with respect here, Mr Lang. He exerted a good influence over Raja Surabhoji, as I hope you will over his son . . . which reminds me . . . Are you aware of the shameful practice of selling female orphans or girls from poor families to the court, where they are used for various strange and immoral purposes? Well, I'm endeavouring to open an asylum where they can receive some decent education and training instead. The Raja has not answered our pleas for co-operation so far, but I'm hoping that you, with your fluency in the tongue and the goodwill he bears you . . .'

Theo shrugged awkwardly. 'Mrs Arbuthnot, I fear your hopes are premature. I've only met the Raja once, but on one point at least I agree with your husband – he is surrounded by strong-minded advisers and it won't be easy to persuade him of anything. And my first, selfish, concern is to make him put in hand essential repairs to our rather ramshackle abode.'

Dora pursued this harmless tangent. 'Oh, indeed. I saw it yesterday. Quite disgraceful that the Raja should expect an English lady and her child to spend even a night in such a ruin.'

As Theo considered coming to Sevaji's defence, a voice whined from the door, 'Supper is served, ma'am.'

Amelia turned in surprise, for the accent was familiar to her, and saw a thin young woman with lank, straw-coloured hair looking at her pleadingly.

'I'm Sarah Murphy, ma'am. And if you ever want any help . . .' she whispered, and vanished as Reverend Arbuthnot strode to claim Amelia's arm and lead her to the dining-room.

'And who is Sarah Murphy? She sounds as if she hails from East Anglia, as I do myself.'

'Her parents were originally from Essex, I believe, but she's country-born and married to Gerard Murphy, the worst

73

drunken sot in the garrison. Mrs Arbuthnot, in the goodness of her heart – and time will show you how good her heart is, Mrs Lang – takes in her and her bairns when he's violent, and she helps us on the domestic front.'

'Oh dear – drunkenness is all I've heard about the soldiery so far. Surely this can't be?'

'Well, it's worst at this New Year period, but always common enough, I fear. A wretched vice – but how can you hope for universal sobriety when men are cooped up in dismal barracks with scarcely any instruction, recreation or indeed occupation for months on end?'

He spoke with true feeling, for he'd seen a great deal of the hardship and boredom of the common soldiers' lot in India. Even if their attendance at church was seldom more than an enforced charade, they and their families constituted the flocks given into his care, and he often felt angry on their behalf and did what he could for them.

The meal was the first really appetising one the Langs had enjoyed since leaving Madras, and had a distinctly mellowing effect on the two gentlemen. Immediately after it, Amelia, still haunted by the vision of the cobra, insisted they return home to Rolly, and so the evening ended on an equable note with Arbuthnot counselling in friendly fashion, 'Now take my advice, Mr Lang, and go back to the palace tomorrow to make a proper fuss about those repairs to your bungalow. The fringes of the north-east monsoon are due any day now and you'll be awash indoors and out.'

For Amelia's sake, Theo did return to the palace next morning, only to be told that His Highness had embarked upon certain religious ceremonies in honour of the deceased Raja Tondiman and wasn't to be disturbed for several days. He bowed his head to the inevitable, went to the bazaar and bought some essential pots and a water-filter with his fast-dwindling reserves.

The following day he received a summons to the Resident's office and obeyed reluctantly – but something had to be done and Hubert Wardle, unlike Raja Sevaji, gave at least a semblance of activity, rummaging among papers and giving instructions to his clerk as Theo was shown in. They regarded each other in wary recognition.

'Please accept my belated condolences on Mrs Wardle's death, Resident,' began Theo. 'She was most kind when I was last here – on a sad errand, you'll recall.'

'Ah, thank you, Mr Lang. It is a heavy thing living in an isolated station like this without the support of a dear wife. One craves the softer influences of feminine companionship. I hope to have the pleasure of meeting your wife soon? How is she settling down?'

'Oh well enough, except for a nasty shock the day after we arrived.' Theo explained the cobra and Wardle tutted.

'A disgraceful place to offer you – but typical of the Raja, I fear. Repairs are now in hand, I trust?'

'Well, the sirkele has promised, but things don't happen promptly in Eastern courts, as we know, Resident.'

'And Western patience is sorely tried. Anyway, Mr Lang, I strongly advise you not to pay for repairs yourself and ask for recompense after, or you'll wait till doomsday.'

'Oh I couldn't do that – I don't have the money,' Theo confessed cheerfully.

'Ah,' said Wardle, looking through his papers. 'You probably know I've just returned from Poodocottah?'

'Yes, sir. I gather the situation there is somewhat volatile?'

'Very much so, with at least two factions: the chief Ranee, aided by her adviser, wants to keep hold of the reins till she can pass them to her son, and there's the deceased Raja's younger brother, her own son-in-law and various hangers-on against her. Damned if I could find out . . . Ah, at last.' A boy appeared with brandy-pawnees.

'Your good health, Mr Lang.' He drank, leaned forward to whisper, 'Fact of the matter is, I called you in to ask you to go to Poo for a few days – see how the land really lies. In an unofficial capacity and with your proficiency in the language, you'd find it much easier than I did. And the Company will want to know . . .'

'But I'm not a Company servant, Mr Wardle, and I've no intention of acting as its spy.'

'Heavens – I'm not suggesting that for a moment!' He took

another drink, assessing Theo. 'Let me put it like this. The Raja has left a collection of books – nothing to match the library here, probably just done for the competition; you know how these rajas vie with each other. But no one in Poo has any idea of what the collection's worth, so I mentioned that you – a disinterested scholar – might give a valuation. The Ranee's adviser was delighted, you'll be well paid, and I'll add a generous per diem for your travelling. Now what do you say?'

Theo hesitated. The bait was gilded – and not only with gold.

'You must realise, Resident, that I'm not qualified for either job – valuing books or meddling in politics. I suppose I could sound out the adviser, but as for the Ranee's enemies . . . Here's a thought, though!' He slammed down his glass. 'Isn't there a Bengali, Hemanga Nath Moitra, among them? I knew his wife when I was a child here and perhaps my wife could get an audience with her – for my old times' sake, you might say – and I could tackle the husband.'

'Capital! He's a proper rogue, they say, but certainly in the know.'

'It's only a chance, mind. But if I can take Mrs Lang with me, then I'll take it on. Just for once, you understand.'

'Done! And Captain Gilbert will escort you.'

Theo frowned. 'Why?'

Wardle rang for his clerk. 'Frankly, Mr Lang, it is politic for us to remind Poodocottah sometimes of our neighbouring presence – just to show the flag. So visiting foreigners always have Company escort.' There was more to it than that. Captain Gilbert liked to go to Poo for a change of scene, and Wardle preferred to keep the prickly officer in good humour.

'Would you like a small advance payment, Mr Lang?' he asked, as the clerk appeared. Theo mumbled assent and left a few minutes later with money enough to rejoice Amelia's heart and with a weight of misgiving on his own.

That evening he told Amelia of his childhood friendship with Rukmini Moitra, omitting only its last, dramatic stage. Even as he spoke the wind rose and rain began pouring through the bungalow roof. They slept in tents that night and set off early next morning, accompanied by Captain Gilbert and six sepoys of the Company's Third Light Cavalry Regiment.

CHAPTER FOUR

U pon waking that rainy morning, Captain Gilbert first consulted his bedside book, *The Meditations of Marcus Aurelius*, as was his wont. He'd worked out a system of quick reference to passages that might help him through the day ahead, and most frequently resorted to those under the heading of Tedium and Its Endurance. That morning, however, he chose one relating to 'action of a minor variety': 'Labour not as one who is wretched nor yet as one who would be pitied or admired; but direct thy will to one thing only, to put thyself in motion and check thyself as the social reason requires.' Then he stowed the book in his knapsack with his silver-backed hairbrush and jar of best pomatum, and directed his will to putting everyone concerned in appropriate motion.

Unencumbered, the captain could easily have covered the distance to Poodocottah in a hard day's ride, but with the woman and child at palki-pace he'd planned an overnight halt, which, he explained, would ensure that the court had foreknowledge of their arrival.

'You mean a look-out is kept, Captain?' Amelia asked.

'Yes, people are always on the watch for travellers, but they won't molest us. Indeed the only person to fear meeting on the roads of India is Corporal Forbes, and if you do you're usually in for a longer journey to an unknown destination.' He chuckled.

'Corporal . . . er . . .?'

'Oh, excuse me, madam. It's our military nickname for cholera morbus. Forbes marches up and down the roads between our various stations with great regularity – like a marauding highwayman. But please don't be alarmed – he's lying low for the moment.'

'Oh, I'm not easily alarmed, Captain. And Rolly is quite looking forward to the trip. He's spent so much of his short span on the move that he gets bored and irritable if the world stands still for long.'

'An admirable introduction to life, marm. For indeed the world does not stand still and the "Universe loves nothing so much as to change the things which are and make new things like them."'

'That is a quotation, Captain?'

'From the meditations of the great Aurelius, Mrs Lang.' He bowed and went ahead to join Theophilus.

The two men rode in silence for several miles while Theo wondered how best to lure into conversation one who had the air of preferring solitary travel. He decided to open with an obvious question.

'Have you been stationed in Tanjore long, Captain?'

'Far too long, Mr Lang. The Company penalises those who do a good job by leaving them stuck in it.'

'At least you have an independent command . . .'

'But to what end? I call out my men only to escort through the bazaar a poor-spirited, bedizened young man riding on a painted elephant to the sound of a few trumpets.'

Theo scowled. 'Occasions, I must remind you, that give great pride and pleasure to the local people. So why pour scorn on it?'

'Why? Because it's not a proper task for English soldiers, Mr Lang. And we're only set to it because there are no wars to fight in this soggy south-land and men must be occupied somehow.'

Theo, determined to avoid argument, said, 'As your duties are minimal, I assume your muster is small?'

'Yes, but half could do everything required. The Company likes to keep a respectable presence in Tanjore just in case . . .'

'. . . the opportunity for an easy take-over should suddenly arise?'

Theo's tone was casual, but Gil hesitated before replying, remembering his companion was that *rara avis* – an Englishman in native employ. Gil loathed the Company and most of its works, but still owed it some loyalty.

'The eventuality you mention is most unlikely. The Company adopts such measures only where oppression and misrule are rife, which isn't the case here.'

'Not yet – but perhaps can be so presented by those on the spot for the benefit of those in power at a distance?'

Gilbert shrugged. 'I know nothing of any such schemes, Mr Lang. I am but a simple soldier and do my duty without question.'

Realising he'd presumed too much on a short acquaintance, Theo rode on quietly, enjoying the cool slide of rain on his skin and the rhythmic splash of hooves. 'Looks as if it's clearing ahead,' he ventured at last.

'Often does later in the day.'

'A more bearable climate down here than in Madras, don't you think?'

Gil grunted noncommittally.

'Weren't you stationed at St Thomas's Mount? I believe you met Marguerite Hervey there?'

'Colonel Hervey was my C.O., yes. A fine soldier – served in the Peninsular War under Wellington.'

'And loved larking all his life, according to Marguerite?'

Gil permitted himself a nostalgic grimace. 'Ah – a stickler for sham fights was Clifford Hervey. Three thousand of us in two opposing camps near the race-course: marching and counter-marching, skirmishing to the front and flanks, sneaking up in night attacks, air full of gun-smoke and pumpkins.'

'*Pumpkins?*'

'Hollowed out and filled with combustible bits and pieces instead of cannon balls, but enough to give you a nasty crack. "Boys will be boys," as Marguerite used to say.'

'I was still a boy when my father and I stayed with the Herveys. She seemed – formidable then, and I was rather in awe . . .' He trailed off, realising that only during this recent visit had he begun to understand Marguerite's vulnerability and loneliness. 'Where are all her children? Do you know? She seldom mentions them.'

'The best died young, she says. There's a married daughter

at Home and two sons in Bombay Presidency, but she doesn't approve of the daughters-in-law.'

'She's not easy to please. I very much hoped she'd approve of my wife, but I don't know . . .'

Gil stiffened, refusing to be drawn into these personal byways. There'd been a colonel's daughter when he was stationed in Madras – what *was* her name? Desperate to marry him, but Marguerite hadn't approved of her, either. He remembered a strange occasion when he and Marguerite had danced around her empty ballroom in the moonlight and she'd teased him about the numerous young ladies who'd tried to trap him with their tossing ringlets and sparkling eyes. How could he resist? Wasn't there a single beauty who could melt his stony heart? That colonel's daughter would have been a catch – May, yes, that was her name. But he'd refused her bait and she'd died soon after. Of a broken heart, it was rumoured, but it was just another fever that killed her. Then he'd sat down on a worm-eaten old chair which collapsed, his bottom hitting the floor painfully, and his dress uniform covered with filthy dust. Marguerite had laughed and laughed, forcing him to join in and calling for wine, and they'd frolicked around arm-in-arm summoning for every chair some fool or rogue they'd like to see crashing down with bum in the dust. He could add a few to the list since then, including that pompous ass Hubert Wardle, and he was happily peopling that eerie ballroom with more candidates for the chair-treatment when his companion spoke.

'Is there much contact between Tanjore and Poo in the normal run, Captain?'

'Oh, there's usually something or other going on – disputes over boundaries, water-courses, the usual thing. An earlier Tanjore Resident, Blackburne, exerted quite an influence over the Raja who's just died, introduced him to European literature and so on. So there are residual ties which Wardle likes to maintain.'

'So you go down fairly often, Captain?'

Gil nodded.

'Then I wonder if you're acquainted with Hemanga Nath Moitra, a Bengali? And his wife, Rukmini?'

Gil glanced at him keenly. 'H. N., as he's often called, I've met, yes. But we never mix with the women.'

'I was afraid not. You see, I knew Rukmini Moitra years ago when we were children, and I'm hoping my wife can meet her. Just to find out how she is, convey our regards.' Gil remained silent and Theo had to persist. 'Are the women very cloistered there?'

'No more than is customary.' He laughed unexpectedly. 'Not like the Mussulmans'. Have you heard about the Nawab of Kurnal – who may get the boot soon? Keeps his numerous ladies locked up and half-starved because his real passion is for game-cocks. Decks 'em in gold chains and ankle rings, feeds 'em sweetmeats and has 'em lying in baskets on his bed! His zenana is like a poultry-yard, they say.'

Theo shuddered. 'Well, I'm glad it isn't like *that* at Poo. I was wondering, Captain, if you'd be good enough to facilitate a meeting between Mrs Lang and the Bengali's wife? With your experience of the court . . .'

'Entirely depends on the new dispensation,' Gil cut in. 'You know how it is, when rulers die the earth around moves and resettles – rocks to quicksands, quicksands to rocks.' He spurred his horse. 'Now if you'll excuse me, I've sent the tent-pitchers ahead and I want to see all is in order for your family.'

Theo watched him canter away. 'Simple soldier', indeed! That was just one of the captain's poses; but where the nub of the man lay, Theo couldn't begin to guess.

Captain Gilbert prided himself on his ability to set up a good camp, and when Amelia emerged from her palki at the end of the day's journey she saw a cluster of tents in neat array beside a coconut grove, the nearby ground swept, a night-picket line established and a sepoy with a musket over his shoulder on guard. Gil stepped up to greet her, adorned in the dress-uniform which showed off his fine figure to best advantage. Rolly squirmed in her arms.

'He's longing to crawl about after being shut in for so long, Captain. Is there somewhere I can wash him afterwards?'

'The bathroom tent is behind the dining one, marm, with your tent alongside. Your husband's resting there now.'

'Oh good, thank you.'

She put Rolly down and stretched herself.

'A fine boy, Mrs Lang.'

'Yes – isn't he?'

They watched as he began exploring this delightfully muddy new terrain on all fours, and Amelia felt herself suddenly tongue-tied in the presence of this remote, handsome man, wondering, as many women had before, why he'd never married. Rolly staggered upright, clutching her skirt and reaching for the stuffed monkey she was holding.

'Oh no, Rolly, we don't want monkey Marmaduke covered with mud, too! Just play without him, there's a good boy.'

The child's face puckered ready for howling and the captain drew his sabre from the sabretache at his waist and wheeled it about in the air.

'See Rolly – look at this. Here's a toy that men play with. Perhaps you will one day.' The child watched the metal's gleaming track with fascination.

'Oh, I hope not. I wouldn't want him to be a soldier – saving your presence, Captain.'

'I don't blame you for that, marm. A life of tedium laced with blood. A . . .' He cut himself off. 'Excuse me, I've not yet inspected the kitchen quarters.' He sheathed the weapon, hanging it on the pommel of Theo's horse, tethered close by.

'And I must . . . Can I leave baby here for a few minutes?'

'He'll be all right.' He strode off and Amelia hurried to the 'necessary tent' hidden discreetly in the coconut grove. As she emerged she heard a shout and saw the captain running towards Rolly, who was reaching up towards the fascinating man's toy. As his muddy fingers tugged at the sabretache, Gil scooped him into his arms, laughing.

'Oh no you don't, my fine fellow-me-lad. Not yet awhile.' Rolly screeched in protest and Gil juggled him high in the air, making funny faces till he began to chuckle and wriggle.

'Oh dear . . . I shouldn't have left him,' Amelia panted.

'No harm done,' Gil assured her, a trifle pale for he'd had a sickening vision of that sharp blade falling from its sheath to cleave those bright curls.

'And he's properly messed you up. Oh Rolly! I am sorry, Captain.'

'Think nothing of it, madam. 'Twill give my lazy dhobi some occupation.' He handed the baby to her with a smile and she saw for the first time the face of a happier, gentler man. She didn't then know how rare the sight was and, in the privacy of their tent later, assured Theo that the captain's reputation as a difficult customer was much exaggerated.

Amelia was a natural optimist, and even the next morning's downpour did not dampen her excitement at the prospect of visiting Indian royalty. But Poodocottah was a very small State, its indigo trade was in decline and its palace had seen better days. A number of bedraggled guards armed with staves stood about idly in its main courtyard, which was ankle-deep in mud. The master of the guard greeted them perfunctorily and led the captain away for refreshment, while the Langs were directed along a raised slippery pathway to a pillared reception hall. Here, an elderly, bejewelled man seated on a dais introduced himself in halting English as the Ranee's adviser and, while he and Theo talked, Amelia posed stiffly on an upright chair, trying to ignore the motley group of men staring fixedly at her. They were minor courtiers, Theo told her, but their appearance was far removed from her splendid vision of such gentlemen, which was, admittedly, derived from picture-book representations of Queen Elizabeth's entourage.

After the long-winded courtesies of arrival and refreshment, they were shown to their private bedroom. Theo explained that the Ranee and her sons were still closeted in mourning. The Ranee's sister, Lakshmi, who spoke some English, would therefore entertain her in the zenana while he examined the library and attended a feast with the gentlemen. It was only customary that his programme should be the more interesting, for upper-class Indian women did not mix socially with men and didn't expect foreign ladies to, either.

Zenanas were notorious as hotbeds of gossip and intrigue, and this Amelia could well believe, for the apartment into which she was later shown had an almost palpable atmos-

84

phere of suppressed and cloistered passions. Each wall and alcove was draped in woven cloths of brilliant hues – cochineal, indigo blue, saffron yellow, deep purple – and it was easy to imagine spies lurking behind every arras. Lakshmi, a middle-aged lady in a glossy emerald sari, pressed her plumped, ringed hands to her forehead in traditional greeting and introduced her plump daughters, nieces and cousins one by one.

Her English was little better than Amelia's Tamil, however, and only Rolly's presence saved the occasion from awkward silences of incomprehension. The women stroked and petted him, clapping delightedly as he threshed among silk cushions, tugged at pendant tassels, pearls and beads, basking in their admiration. Then a large silver bowl covered with a velvet cloth was presented to him; it contained a mound of jelly fruits and sweetmeats, and the giggling ladies vied with each other to feed him one sugary morsel after another. They festooned him with their bangles and necklaces, and when he was frightened with too much glitter produced counters of coloured ivory for his entertainment. Occasionally Lakshmi asked Amelia a perfunctory question, but seemed only truly interested in her bonnet, which was passed round for general admiration. The women tugged its ribbons, twirled it like a top, tried it on and generally found it so absurd that Amelia began to regard it so herself.

They were not being deliberately impolite, Amelia told herself, but it was no wonder that Indian men, brought up and cossetted by these women, seemed so conceited and self-indulgent. Yet who could blame the women, whose lives were so empty and restricted? Having diplomatically congratulated Lakshmi on her knowledge of English, she ventured to ask if there was not another lady of the court – Rukmini Moitra – who spoke the foreign tongue, and could she have the pleasure of meeting her? Lakshmi stared fixedly at the curtained recess behind Amelia before confirming that Rukmini did live there, but in a distant room and she'd forgotten her English.

'But I would like to see her anyway,' Amelia persisted. 'She and my husband were childhood friends, you see.'

Lakshmi's eyes closed briefly. 'Perhaps tomorrow,' was all she said.

In the following awkward pause tea and cakes were served and Amelia, nibbling politely, felt increasingly uncomfortable. The air smelled heavily of coconut hair-oil, cloying unguents, cloistered female flesh, and to be polite she'd swallowed too much sugary stuff. She yawned uncontrollably and Rolly, whose mouth was smudged with blobs of green and red jelly, opened it in imitation – and was promptly sick.

'Oh, I knew it was all too much for him!' Amelia jumped up, servants rushed to clean the mess, and the comforting women clustered round the crying child. Eventually Amelia managed to prise him from their clutches and carried him to their bedroom where he fell into deep slumber while she, loosening her stays, dozed on the bed.

She was awakened by some sharp sound that could have been gunfire and lay, heart pounding, in dreadful expectation of riot or murder. Darkness had fallen, the wispy flickering of two oil lamps didn't brighten the room's recesses where, she imagined, a spy was lurking. She strained to identify distant sounds of footsteps and voices – nothing untoward – yet she was oppressed by a sense of strangeness verging on hostility. She longed to summon more light, the comforting presence of her husband, but forced herself to remain quiet, though stiff with tension.

But why should she feel so, she chided herself? Was she not staying in a raja's palace, with silken cushions at her head, jewelled ladies in rich apartments nearby? She'd never been closer to the mysterious East that had inspired her youthful dreams, but its reality frightened, almost sickened her: sickly smells of the zenana, ringed toes squelching in courtyard mud, the shifty eyes of down-at-heel courtiers. I'll never be a good romantic, she thought, cradling her head in her arms and experiencing for the first time since leaving Home a deep longing for the wholesome familiarities of England. It seemed years rather than months since she'd last seen it, and in those months she felt years older.

At length her mood of disenchantment was lifted by Theo's

return with servants carrying trays of food. He hastened to her side.

'Oh, you shouldn't be lying alone in the dark, Amy! I've had such a feast – and this is for you.'

She waved the trays away. 'I couldn't eat another morsel, Theo, and Rolly had sweets stuffed into him till he was sick. He's sleeping it off, poor lamb.'

'You're sure you're all right, then?' He dismissed the servants, loosened his trousers, plopped down beside her. 'Phew! I'm over-stuffed, too. But it was delicious.'

'Greedy! You deserve to be fat as a pig!' She tweaked his nose. 'And did you find out anything?'

'Not a thing,' he yawned. 'Except that everyone is watching everyone else. What about you?'

'I was only with the women.'

'I mean Rukmini. Was she among them?'

'No.' Amelia told him what Lakshmi had said and he groaned.

'"In a distant room", hey? Lakshmi means she and her sister, the Ranee, are on one side in the struggle for power, but the late Raja's brother, who's nicknamed Pussy by the way, is on t'other. Moitra is his ally and known as Pussy's Claws. He was at the feast, a shifty-looking fellow, but it wasn't polite to speak of his wife in masculine company . . . Let's hope Captain Gilbert will put in a good word.'

Amelia went to look at the baby. 'Still sleeping, thank goodness. You can't imagine how they over-fed him.'

'Oh, but I can! The women always do – especially boys. That's probably why Pussy is so fat. I asked him about his name, and apparently when he visited Calcutta with his brother years ago he ate and drank a great deal, then used to curl up in a ball and sleep wherever he happened to be, and some foreigners called him Pussy.'

'Does he mind?'

'Doesn't seem to, but it's hard to guess his feelings. H. N., the Bengali, acts as his eyes, ears and tongue usually. Pussy still prefers to eat, drink and sleep.'

Amelia giggled. 'Good for a nonsense rhyme, isn't it? Let's see – "The corpulent Pussy of Poo, Had ever so much to do.

First he dozed and he dined, Then he dozed and he wined
. . ." You finish it.'

'Hmm . . . hmm. "Then he farted and cried, oh phew,
phew!"'

'Theophilus, really!'

He grinned. 'Come on, let's get into this lovely large bed.'

'In a minute.' She glanced toward an alcove. 'Are you sure
no one's listening?'

He shrugged for answer, and she moved towards the
balcony at the room's other end. He frowned, pulled on his
nightshirt and followed.

'So what about the library?' she whispered.

'A few rarities, nothing exciting. It's only a pretext for me
to spy out the land on the Company's behalf. I'll make a
rough valuation before we go tomorrow, but you must manage
to see Rukmini . . .' He rubbed his temples. 'How I hate this
sort of thing – political intrigue, scheming for power. Why
does it have to go on in a beautiful country like this?' He drew
back the curtain and wandered on to the balcony, leaning
over to look at the moonlight on the paved courtyard and
ornamental pool below. 'For it is beautiful, isn't it, dearest?'
He drew her to him. 'And exactly as I told you India would
be.'

She laid a hand on his shoulder. 'But it isn't *really* like this.'

'Now what do you mean? This is real enough.' He flung
out an arm.

'Well – yes. But it's a kind of dream, too, isn't it? A royal
dream created for the pleasure of rich men only. But I can't
forget what's behind it all – the fear, the squalor, the near-
slavery.'

He clutched his head. 'Oh damn it, Amelia, you sound like
a reforming Evangelical! Why can't you just accept this as it
is now – this night, this . . . us . . . here?' He caught her
hands, fixing her with intense dark eyes. 'Oh my love, I want
so much for you to give yourself up to the spirit of this land
as it is – with all its unredeemable squalor and cruelty, yes,
and beauty and wisdom, also.' He caressed her cheek. 'Don't
tell me I've married a Wilberforce in skirts.'

'Oh Theo, please don't think that I . . .'

He stopped her mouth with kisses, then laughed. 'Why listen – they're even playing sweet music for us.' From a distance came the sudden squeal of pipes, thud of drums and the trumpeting of a wakened elephant. 'There'll be dancing girls . . . Let's to bed, darling.'

Holding her tightly, he led her inside.

The burst of music heralded the arrival of Pussy and his companions in a remote corner of the palace to which Captain Gilbert had resorted hours before, for it was the goal and purpose of all his journeys to Poo. By that stage in the evening he had quite sloughed off Marcus Aurelius's injunctions against imprudence and self-indulgence, which invariably beset him when he first sank among the cushions in H. N. Moitra's apartments, removed his jacket, loosened his collar and prepared for dissipation.

The revelry was pitched especially high on this occasion, for since the Raja's demise the court had been decorously subdued, and Gilbert's arrival made a good excuse for a frolic. These 'frolics' were very special and private; no women of any sort attended them, their temptress roles being played instead by a troupe of boys. The boys' cheeks were plucked smooth, lips red-painted, eyes outlined in black paste, hair shoulder-length, young limbs swathed in rich robes; and they flaunted these charms before the men as seductively as a bevy of dancing girls. Star of the troupe was Josef, a Portuguese half-caste, called a 'chee-chee' by the British, who was endowed with a saucy wit as well as beauty, and who had led the captain many a dance in the past. That evening he was in pliant mood, however, and sat beside Gilbert, rubbing his hands gently and plying him with sugared fruits and juices.

Gil raised his goblet as Pussy ambled up, plonking his satin-clad bulk on a thick mattress. He called for wine, which was brought by a heavily-moustachioed dwarf who sang and capered lewdly about him, pulling up a flounced pink skirt to reveal hairy legs and jewelled ankle-bracelets. Gil watched lazily, aware that this weird ménage was exerting its usual spell – relaxing and exciting him, encouraging him to laugh at all manner of grotesques.

'Your health, Captain,' Pussy raised his goblet. 'You were wise to miss such a dull feast. That Mr Lang is too much the scholar for my taste.'

'And mine,' Gil agreed over-heartily.

'Why has he come?'

Gil shrugged. 'To evaluate the library.'

Hemanga Nath Moitra, taking a chair beside his master, grunted in disbelief. Oiled-flat hair framed his narrow face, his quick eyes; and his small, angular frame was posed tensely even now, though he was as easy in the present company as he could ever be. He gestured for a hookah, then caught hold of his current favourite and began pinching his neck and shoulders hard; the boy, who was dressed in the style of a Gujerati girl, stood stiffly, rolling his eyes fearfully at the squeeze of flesh. Gilbert began stroking Josef's tight young buttocks through his silken skirt while he squirmed and giggled.

'He wanted to know why I'm called a little feline,' Pussy remarked indignantly. 'I thought everyone knew that.'

'Everyone who's anyone does.' Gil, glowing with the sense of warm, secret camaraderie, was happy to feed Pussy's inflated opinion of himself. 'But I wager you don't know *my* real Christian name – hardly anyone does. But I'll tell you privately, now.'

He paused dramatically, but no one seemed much interested except Josef, who prodded his chest, crying, 'Well, what is it, then? Not Gilbert – Gilbert?'

'No, but it begins with "G".'

'Gabriel – you are a holy Christian angel, ha ha!'

Gil shook his fist and laughed.

'No? Then it's Gertrude for certain! Gertrude! Gertrude!'

Gil, roaring in mock anger, jumped on him, wrestling him to the ground where he lay squealing, kicking his legs high. 'Ho ho, Goliath. That is the strong man's name . . .'

Pussy wheezed in mirth and a string of the white curd he was sipping dribbled down his embroidered jacket. He gestured for a servant to wipe him.

'George – that's my bloody silly name,' Gil announced loudly. 'Dull and respectable, mushy like an old uncle. Geeorgie, my mother used to call me.' He got off Josef and returned to his cushion. 'Gilbert – now that has a good martial ring to it, don't you agree?'

Pussy yawned. 'Oh, but George has the regal ring, Captain. Mad King George! Ha! Come you lazy prick-boys, dance before His Royal Highness.'

He gestured to the musicians, who began to pipe a lugubrious air while the troupe of boys bent their supple bodies to its rhythms and Josef, still lying on his stomach, pretended to conduct them with his legs. Gil lolled, looking up into the soft, warm night sky and stars sparkling with an extreme beauty. He accepted another drink, aware of the Bengali's eyes on him. Eventually Moitra would want an answer to the question about Lang's mission; he always wanted answers about Company doings and Gil usually supplied them, because it was Moitra who hired the boys for his own and others' pleasure.

To forestall him, Gil said casually, 'Mr Lang would like his wife to convey greetings to yours tomorrow, H. N. Apparently he knew her years ago in Tanjore. I presume that can be arranged?'

Moitra shrugged. 'I don't see why.'

'Why antagonise him with a refusal? Any English ally is better than an enemy, you always say, and it would predispose him to your side.'

H. N. sucked his hookah. 'My wife is not on my side.'

'What harm? Two women talking.'

H. N. nodded. 'It can be arranged. And why is Mr Lang here?'

'Oh, he's harmless – a scholar and poor as a church mouse, which he might as well get used to as he's in Sevaji's employ. Wardle offered him money to try and find out about "the affairs of Poodocottah" for onward transmission to Madras.'

Pussy chortled. 'Ah, the affairs of Poodocottah! Who knows what they are or soon will be, hey Captain? Even to us, all is veiled in mystery, is it not my wily Bengali?'

'H. N. grinned. 'Yes, master.'

Gil looked at them. They were cooking up something. Or perhaps they simply wanted him to think so; or perhaps they wanted to fool themselves into thinking so? Eventually, probably, someone would feel the point of the knife; Gil hoped it would be 'the other side'.

He yawned, aware that the night's pleasure was fast approaching its peak, and got up, laying his hand along Josef's back. The boy looked up at him with large, kohl-ringed eyes.

'Come,' Gil said, turning to bow to the company. 'You will excuse me, gentlemen. I have matters to accomplish and it's already late.'

Pussy sniggered, drew a ruby signet ring from his finger and tossed it to him. 'Give that to your page for his pains, King George.'

'Thank you, your Highness.' Gil bowed again, surprised and flattered.

'How regal we are tonight,' muttered H. N. sourly as Gil shepherded Josef away.

Soon after Theophilus had been summoned to the library next morning, Amelia also received a summons – to meet Rukmini Moitra. Feeling oddly nervous, she spent a long time arranging her hair and fussing over Rolly before following the servant to the zenana, where Lakshmi awaited her alone. Lakshmi's manner was formal as she bestowed the same compliments as before on Amelia and Rolly; then she turned, saying abruptly, 'Here is Mrs Moitra.'

The woman who appeared between the curtains of an arched entrance was fairly tall and slender, unlike any of the other court ladies, and her face was lovely. Amelia, describing her later to Theo, could say only that, for there was nothing outstandingly beautiful – simply an impression of gentle, oval-shaped sweetness and large eyes shining with pleasurable excitement, which she kept demurely lowered as Lakshmi took charge, saying she would interpret between them. Breaking a shy silence, Rukmini asked if the baby was Theo's. Amelia nodded and Rukmini touched his curls with great tenderness.

'And your children? Where are they?' Amelia asked.

She raised sad eyes, whispering, 'I have none.'

'Oh – I'm so sorry.' Amelia sought to change the subject.

'I think you learned English years ago, with my husband, did you not?'

Rukmini smiled and moved her lips, trying to frame the unfamiliar sounds, then asked for paper and pen. Such items, though not readily to hand in a zenana, were eventually produced and Rukmini wrote a careful note which read, 'I happy to see you. I give greeting. And your husband.'

Amelia nodded encouragement and Rukmini wrote again, while Lakshmi clucked impatiently, for this procedure was not to her liking. The second message was, 'I read English books, but not speak them. Now I have no books. Have you books? Can I speak you again?'

After this Lakshmi crumpled the paper, saying firmly that she would do the interpreting. It was a laborious process and Rukmini, who seemed to understand the general drift, became agitated by Lakshmi's grudging, careless translations. Both women, Amelia gathered, had learned some English from a lady missionary of the Society for Promoting Christian Knowledge in nearby Tranquebar who used to visit them in vain hope of conversion. But this was in some undefined past time, and while the nobility of the court sometimes spoke English with foreign visitors, Rukmini had had no chance to practise the tongue.

At this point Rolly began to fidget impatiently and Lakshmi seized the excuse to end the meeting. Amelia rose in relief, promising to return when she could and send some English books meanwhile. As they said goodbye, Rolly reached out to Rukmini, grinning broadly, and she patted his chubby fist, saying clearly, 'Theophilus little baby.'

Those were her only English words and, as Amelia remarked to Theo when they were leaving Poo a few hours later, it was remarkable she should give such impeccable utterance to his complicated name. They were relieved to be away, but a little haunted by the thought of Rukmini, whom Amelia compared, half jokingly, to a trapped, lonely and beautiful maiden in a grim castle. But for Theo the words held no trace of humour.

* * *

The Langs reached Tanjore at twilight the following day, and were gladdened by the sight of a tidied garden, a mended roof and a lamp in the bungalow window. As they stepped on to the verandah a woman bounded to meet them, throwing out her arms and chanting, 'Thee-off-ilus. Here you are! At last.'

'Durmeen!' He recoiled slightly before submitting to her embrace, and Amelia, too, recoiled – from the swirling hot pink of her European-style skirt, her heavy scent of rosewater, the gestures of possession. Her heart did a quick thump-down, but then steadied as she realised the woman clinging to Theo's arm was certainly over sixty: a stout little body with streaked grey hair in a bun and the spluttering sing-song accent of the half-caste chee-chee.

'And you are Thee-off-ilus's wife?' She grabbed at Amelia, clasping them both to her. 'Has he told you about me? Naughty boy!' She peered up at him, wistful, disappointed.

'Well Durmeen, I . . . er . . .'

'Oh, Thee-off-ilus! And all the years I looked after your poor dear father, now didn't I?'

He sighed; she had always pronounced his unwieldy name like that and it had always irritated him.

'Indeed you did. I'm sorry, Durmeen. I wasn't sure you were . . . er . . .' He disengaged himself, noticing the new coconut matting on the main-room floor and their few bits of furniture set on it in a semblance of homeliness. 'Well, I imagine we have you to thank, Durmeen, for bringing some order out of chaos?'

She plopped into the one basket chair, planting her thick legs down as if forever. 'Yes. You can thank me. I came looking for you but you'd just left for Poodocottah.' She turned to Amelia. 'Theo's father wasn't any good at practical things and I suppose his son's the same. You'll have to manage all that, Mrs Lang, and I'll teach you how.' She snorted. 'Weren't sure I was still alive, Theophilus? And didn't mean to find out, hey? Oh men . . . men . . . ungrateful creatures one and all!'

Theo was crimson. 'Of course I'd have come to see you, Durmeen. We'd only been here a few days and then off to Poo . . .'

'But you didn't tell your wife about me . . . I saw from her face. Well I'll tell you, Mrs Lang. I've known your husband since he was a motherless boy and I came to live with his father. A real gent, Bayard Lang, and such a clever scholar. Oh I mourned when he died! You remember, Theophilus? You arrived just before the end, but I'd been nursing him for weeks. "Don't bother the boy," he kept saying. "He doesn't want to come all this way to see a sick old man." But I sent for you eventually, Theophilus, didn't I?'

'And rightly so, Durmeen.' Theo turned to busy himself with their baggage, hearing his dying father's whisper, 'She's a good, kind woman, my son, and it's hard for a man to live alone in a place like this, you understand me? You'll see she's all right afterwards?' 'Yes, father, I understand; yes, father.' He had flushed then because he'd naively assumed Durmeen was simply the housekeeper of her official designation, and he flushed now because he'd not done much to see her right. He'd given her some of Bayard's things and gone away, putting her out of sight and mind.

'You'll stay to supper of course, Durmeen? Amelia – will you arrange it?'

She nodded, hurrying out in some confusion, leaving him to face the stern glow of Durmeen's protuberant eyes.

'So you've come to work for our Raja, have you, Theophilus? That is not a very elevated post. Your father had high hopes of you. "My son will be a world-wide authority in oriental studies one day," he used to boast. "He mustn't waste his time in a backwater like this." And you did *not*. Yet now you are here! But Tanjore is not a world-wide place, Theophilus.'

He was squirming again, wishing he had visited his father more often, guessing Bayard hadn't pressed him partly for the shame of this half-caste mistress.

'But times have changed since father's day, Durmeen, that's the trouble. No one wants authorities in oriental studies anymore – even world-wide ones! No, English is all the rage now and Indian students are falling over themselves to learn it. They know which pot cooks their rice!' He shrugged dispiritedly. 'I missed the high tide and even father was on its ebb, though he didn't realise it . . . did he, do you think, Durmeen?' He stared at her thick, ageing body, the powder-filled creases in her cheeks. He resented her intimate knowledge of his father – he who'd always maintained a fastidious, detached air that was almost brahminical.

'Oh, he was a happy man, Theophilus. In his library with his books and his Hindu dreams. I never could shake them out of him, though it wasn't for want of trying.' For confirmation she fingered the gold crucifix she always wore round her neck.

And would his wife try to shake them out of *him*, Theo wondered as she came in, murmuring that supper was ready.

'Your little one is asleep? Roland, he is called? About a year old is he not?'

Amelia said tersely, 'You seem to know quite a lot about us Mrs . . . er . . .'

'Durmeen – that does for me. But of course I know about you, and everyone who comes and goes. My son owns the biggest hardware shop in the bazaar and all the gossip buzzes through it.'

'Your son?' Amelia shot an alarmed glance at Theo, and Durmeen burst into hearty laughter.

'Don't worry your head, Mrs Lang. Not Bayard's son. Ooh, I was past that when . . . No, first I married a little Welsh soldier in Madras but he soon died, God rest his soul, and then I married Mr Costa, a man with Portuguese blood like myself. And God rest *his* soul. But we had four children and it's my eldest, Miguel, who keeps the shop. Then came Theo's father . . .' She had ticked the men off on her fingers and gave Bayard the benefit of one, waggling the remaining one coyly to suggest she hadn't necessarily finished yet.

'Oh, I see . . . well . . . dearie me. But you have grand-children, I hope?'

'Oh yes, several, praise be.' She heaved herself upright and waddled towards supper with that proprietorial air Amelia didn't much like. But the woman seemed kind-hearted and obviously Theo wanted to make amends to her.

'Ah, Durmeen,' she inquired pleasantly during the meal,

'now you can tell me something I've often wondered about. Does my husband look like his father?'

Durmeen put down her fork and stared at Theo judiciously. 'Yes and no . . . no and yes. He's taller and thinner and must watch his health. I'll brew my special herb tea for you, Theophilus. You can see he thinks too much – like Bayard who was always thinking – No, I'm wrong! Occasionally he liked to listen to the bazaar gossip.' She looked at them hopefully. 'I don't suppose you've heard much of what's going on yet?'

They shook their heads and Durmeen, delighted to find a new audience, regaled them with a sampling of the latest: that the Raja's Portuguese music master had been discovered playing plaintive love songs to a Mahratta lady of high rank and was doomed to – at least – ignominious dismissal; that the Company intended sending armed soldiers round every village to collect punitive taxes ostensibly for the digging of new wells, but that such schemes were unnecessary anyway because Varanahira, the town's cleverest astrologer, vowed there were springs full of sweet water gushing under three rows of ant-hills just five miles south-east of the Fort, if only people would dig for them. At length, when Amelia began to fade from the effects of the day's long journey, Durmeen rose to leave, accepting thanks for what she'd done and promising to do much more.

On the verandah steps she turned to wag a finger at Theo. 'Mark my words, dear boy – be firm with the young Raja or you'll never squeeze a single anna from him. They tell me he can't hold a candle to his father, who was generous, clever and trustworthy.'

Theo promised to do his best, wondering, as he watched Durmeen leave, whether he didn't hold a candle to *his* father either. Were both he and Sevaji but pale reflections of the last generation, unable either to live up to their parental legacies or strike out new ways for themselves? And had he been misguided to return here and pick up the old threads?

Theo's misgivings about the future increased during the five hours of the next day he spent waiting in the palace ante-

97

room for a summons to Sevaji's presence. It was ridiculous to be upset by such trivial neglect – he of all people, who had often lectured others on the charm and wisdom of the nonchalant Indian attitude towards time. But never before had he been so much at its mercy and that, he humbly admitted to himself, made a difference.

Impatiently he went to look at a picture hung askew on the wall. It depicted Sevaji's wedding procession through Tanjore, with a Company escort of troopers, musicians, torch, fan and pike bearers, and servants behind throwing coins to the multitude from silver treasure chests. It was poorly executed in the European style but still evoked for him the clamour of music, sparkle of ornament, the exciting throb of that festival from which he'd been rudely snatched. It hadn't seemed the least odd to him then that the bridegroom was but twelve years old – for oh, how he had envied him! How he had yearned to marry Rukmini at the same time and so pursue unchecked those explorations begun in the spice-store; for he had long been privy to the smutty male chat of court and bazaar. Well, he had suffered for that early dalliance, but not nearly as severely as Rukmini, and his heart ached as he again remembered Amelia's description of her present lot. He peered intently at the picture, to see if she was among the cluster of veiled women on an overlooking balcony. Of course she wouldn't be!

He resumed his seat irritably, remembering suddenly one of his father's stories about the wedding. Apparently Raja Surabhoji had sent lavish celebratory gifts to a number of Company officials, which they had returned to him in accordance with the Regulations that govern Relationships between Government and Native Princes. 'Stiff-necked old stuffed shirts,' Bayard had grumbled, 'no generosity of spirit, no idea of gaiety and princely festival. Always tit-for-tat-exactly-thating. They're a plague on the land they rule and mind you don't grow up like them, boy.' Well he certainly hadn't, Theo thought, rubbing together the coins Wardle had given him earlier that day. 'For back travel expenses' Wardle had said and winked, for it was a generous sum. Theo had ignored the wink and pocketed the money, for he was in sore need of it.

At that blessed hour when the sun cooled and people revived, Theo was at last summoned to the royal presence. Sevaji was dressed less resplendently than at their first meeting, which Theo took as a friendly sign, but the sirkele was again in attendance and his look was disapproving.

'I trust you had a pleasant journey to Poo?' he murmured after the ritual of greeting.

'Oh . . . er . . . yes, thank you. I was asked to evaluate the late Raja's library, and as His Highness was not receiving visitors and my house was undergoing repairs . . .' Theo trailed off, realising he had lapsed into apology.

'Quite so. The repairs have now been effected?'

'Yes, thank you.'

The sirkele inclined his head, taking full credit.

Theo spoke directly to Sevaji. 'Now I am entirely at your service, Highness, and long to hear what I am to do with your library, which is of infinitely more distinction and value than the nondescript rag and bobtail at Poodocottah.'

Sevaji duly purred. 'Indeed, there is much cataloguing and translating to be done before the worth of my magnificent collection can be estimated, Mr Lang, and I entrust it entirely to your care. No, no,' the Raja flapped his hand tetchily as Theo began to protest, 'I am no scholar – and what messages do the classics bring me? "Kings and heroes are like bubbles in a little stream," and so forth. Ha! But Pundit Dadoo Rao is still in the library and he'll guide you. He is my most faithful servant. Ah yes, now there *is* something I want to show you, Mr Lang. Come, come – now at once.'

He motioned several followers, who formed a little entourage which proceeded across a courtyard through a great, black-pillared hall with a black granite throne in its centre. It was never used, Sevaji said, because it was unlucky.

'In what way?' Theo asked.

'My astrologers tell me so. You've met the Company's cleric, Reverend Arbuthnot? Well, he's visited me – without invitation incidentally – and once had the effrontery to tell me that I was too much influenced by my own astrologers and priests. He even tried to preach his doctrine at me, reminding me of the missionary Swartz who helped my father regain his throne. As if that should be enough to make a Christian of me – a thing my father himself never became.'

'But that's disgraceful! Company chaplains are not missionaries and are expressly forbidden from interfering in the religious beliefs and customs of the native principalities. It's in the statutes.'

'So it might be, but Company officials on the spot will use any stratagem to undermine . . .'

'Here we are, sire.' The sirkele jumped ahead, putting a finger to his lips, as they approached a closed, iron-studded door. 'We proceed quietly where holy men may be at meditation.'

They entered a colonnaded hall; in its centre stood a long table strewn with a number of glistening objects. Shuffling, muttering priests bowed out of the shadows, lamps were lit and hastily held aloft to show that the objects on the table were grouped into a partly-finished replica of a temple, furnished with various statuettes of the Hindu pantheon fashioned in pure gold. Sevaji picked one up, holding it to shine in the lamplight.

'Siva, the moon-crested, Lord of the Hills. Well executed, is it not? Divinity invisibly present – as the perfume in a flower.' He replaced it carefully. 'When the model is finished my architects will use it for the instruction of my master carpenters and masons. And one day my land will be glorified by the full-scale reality. My subjects will travel great distances to worship there.' He clapped his hands. 'Bring the map. See.' He pointed to a dot on the western boundary of his diminished domain. 'There – my priests and astrologers have chosen. Built on that exact place, already sanctified in my heart, this beauteous temple will act as a holy shield against my enemies from every quarter.'

Theo peered. 'Will it be in a village?'

'No, no. The village must go. The people will have to move. The surrounding land will be my private reserve and I shall travel through it very soon, I hope, on the auspicious day of the temple's opening. I shall go before, then my priests and ladies, my Mahratta horsemen, my trumpeters, pipers, drummers shall follow. But on reaching the temple I shall divest myself of these baubles and wearing simple cloth I shall crawl humbly into the presence of the All-Existing.'

His voice had risen excitedly with the conjuration of this scene, but now it suddenly stopped and Theo heard the shuffle of unseen listeners. Were they amused, amazed, awed, he wondered? There was no telling, for the reverence due to royalty stifled them – but from him some response was evidently expected.

'I can see it will be a most magnificent work, your Highness. A noble endeavour and the people will honour you for it.'

Sevaji sighed. 'They are but peasants, Mr Lang. It is greater honour I seek. But I must to my devotions now.' He turned abruptly and the courtiers closed ranks round him so that Theo found himself separated when they stepped into the fading light. As the Raja moved towards an arched entrance Theo sprinted ahead, confronting him on the threshold while the sirkele glared.

'I am sorry, your Highness,' Theo gasped, 'but I simply cannot be dismissed again without some discussion of my duties.'

'You will work under the guidance of Pundit Rao, as was said,' snapped the sirkele.

'But there is your tutoring also, Highness.'

'I will send for you when I require it. My father always wanted me to study English more diligently.' Sevaji looked hunted, as always at the mention of Surabhoji.

'And there is the matter of my salary,' Theo persisted. 'I have a wife and son to support and . . .'

'Oh money, money – I am beset by demands!' Sevaji groaned and slumped against a pillar, signalling a servant to fan him. 'You can see what a costly work I am now engaged in, and that is but one item – there are alms to distribute to the poor, jewels for my palace ladies and gifts for my wise brahmins, the claims of my rapacious sister, expenses for both the mournful and joyous occasions which often occur. Now I must find a new music master who will undoubtedly expect more money than the one who's just been disgraced. And all this without the debts that accumulate and run over from past to present and on into the future like a broken-backed river.'

Again his voice had grown shrill and Theo waited with bowed head until it stopped, as he was learning to do. 'I am truly sorry, your Highness. I will help all I can and your troubles shall become as my own. Yet I must first have the wherewithal to support my family, for my means are scant.'

The sirkele licked his lips. 'That being so, Mr Lang, we find it surprising that you and your family have just enjoyed the expensive luxury of a journey to Poodocottah . . . or perhaps that cost you nothing?'

'The Company paid for it, yes.'

The sirkele glanced meaningfully at his master and Theo floundered on.

'What was I to do? I was forbidden to see His Highness and . . .'

Sevaji signalled limply; a courtier approached and placed a bag in Theo's hands. 'There is money, Mr Lang.'

'Thank you, sire. But this is not the way . . .'

Sevaji had walked into the room and returned, bearing a framed picture. 'And here is a present – a painting done by some old local artist under your father's instruction. Perhaps it is valuable. If you don't want it, you may sell it.'

He moved off, leaving Theo standing with his money and his picture, feeling angry, foolish and confused. He looked round; dusk was falling and he was in an unfamiliar part of the rambling palace. He wandered across a small courtyard followed by a guard with a burning torch. From a wall beyond came the snorts and smells of the royal animals at their evening meal and, stepping through an arch, he found himself on familiar ground again. It was a lofty shed full of ornamental saddlery and ancient equipages: dusty, curtained howdahs, broken-roofed palanquins and a once-handsome barouche with cracked sides and listing from the loss of a wheel.

Taking the torch, he held it close to read the maker's name still visible on an engraved plate: 'Stewart and Co., Edinburgh'. It had been ordered by Surabhoji during one of his spending sprees, but scarcely ever used, and Theo remembered that he and Rukmini used to sit side by side on the leather seats pretending they were riding along Piccadilly – though neither of them had the faintest idea what that grand thoroughfare looked like. But the name's magic fascinated them: 'Peecadeelee'. He could hear her girlish voice chanting it over and over again, he could see her laughing eyes and the sunlight on her lustrous hair. He stared in wonderment at the broken-down vehicle and it struck him more forcibly than ever before that his childhood had indeed been, as Amelia had once told him, extremely strange and odd.

CHAPTER FIVE

Theophilus bought a bottle of French wine from the bazaar
that evening to celebrate the sudden inflow of money and
the first picture they'd ever owned. It depicted a male and
female elephant with trunks entwined as if in embrace; below
were scribbled instructions from a seventeenth-century manu-
script on breeding and caring for these wondrous beasts.
Amelia and Theo hung it on the wall and, with arms entwined
and glasses raised, vowed it should stay in the family for
generations.

For the next week or so Amelia and Durmeen set about
making the bungalow home-like. The latter, determined to
make herself indispensable, haggled remorselessly even with
her shopkeeper son for the best bargains in kettles and
candlesticks. She made sure Amelia purchased good chintz
for cushion covers and calico with fluted silk for the punkahs,
and when a positive bevy of box-wallahs appeared she knew
how to deal with them. Cajoling and praising the charms and
perspicacity of the newly-arrived English lady, each travelling
salesman set his box on the verandah, clapped his hands and
cracked his knuckles before opening the lid and spreading his
wares on a cloth. But this portentous display and its accompanying flattery were wasted on Durmeen, who wouldn't
allow Amelia to pay a quarter anna above the bazaar rate for
their offerings of walnut ketchup, lace cuffs, spotted muslins,
scented envelopes, needles and tin mugs. But just as they
began re-packing their boxes in despair, Durmeen would
instruct Amelia to buy what she wanted. Every evening Theo
returned to another domestic surprise: coloured paper cut
into patterns and stuck round the window edges in lieu of
curtains; a padded footstool made from a finger-drum; old

knives shining new from vigorous application of pipeclay and egg-white.

This nest-building was a delight to them both until the vexed question of servants arose. Theo had told Amelia before the marriage that they would not keep a large domestic staff to enhance their own prestige – as most British in India did. Nor, he said, would they follow the common practice of hiring pariah servants for the dirtiest and lowliest tasks, because this severely curtailed social intercourse with high-caste Indians. At the time Amelia had gladly agreed, and it was thus with some trepidation that she informed her husband one evening that she'd engaged the part-time services of a dhobi and a tailor because their existing servants absolutely refused to deal with their clothes. Theo, perfectly aware of the rigid rules that governed servants' duties, capitulated, adding that on no account should anyone else be hired.

So matters stood until, returning from the palace one evening, Theo found a flushed and agitated wife awaiting him. Catching his arm she dragged him straight to their bedroom.

'Look at these, Theo! Perhaps you'll suggest what I'm to do with them?' With a defiant flourish she removed the lid from a wooden bucket in which her menstrual rags were soaking.

He backed away in distaste. 'But, Amelia, how should I know?'

'The dhobi won't touch them, nor will anyone else. Nor will anyone scour the chamber-pots or take away the rubbish in the back-yard or prepare the dog's food. They are pariah jobs, I'm told.'

He took the lid from her and replaced it. 'But what have you done till now?'

'When we were travelling I threw the soiled rags away. But the cloth is too expensive for that. Only pariahs will wash it – Durmeen agrees.'

He sighed. 'But Amelia, I told you, if we employ pariahs no self-respecting brahmin will enter our house.'

'So who does these jobs for brahmins, then?' She felt

irritable; the lethargic ache of her first day's menstruation was bad enough without this.

'I've no idea. They don't use chamber-pots, of course, and there's a caste of non-pariah menials who might . . .'

She thumped down on the bed. 'Oh Theo, this is ridiculous! What do you expect me to do? Wash them myself like a skivvy? And do the other nasty jobs, too, I suppose? Well I'm not going to! Whatever your principles, we'll have to hire a pariah.'

'But they're filthy creatures who eat putrid flesh and smell foully of toddy and other servants won't eat with them, and when Gopal Krishnan comes to visit, for example . . .'

He trailed off and she too was silent, picking irritably at a thread in her skirt. Outside the dog whined; it hadn't been fed.

She raised her head. 'I suppose they only eat bad meat because they can't afford better. I know, when we hear Gopal is coming I'll send the pariah away till he goes.'

'That's no use. He'll just arrive unannounced one day when he feels like it – that's the Indian way. One can't predict.'

'Well, it's a very inconvenient way. Really, Theo, I simply don't understand your friend Gopal. So well-educated in the European manner yet so tied to caste prejudices that he won't . . .'

'But that's his predicament exactly – the European receiving-room and the rest of the house behind, remember? It takes time – generations . . .'

'And in the meantime there are the practicalities of every-day living.' She wrinkled her nose at the bucket, round which flies were buzzing. 'It's beginning to smell horrible.'

He too smelt it; a dank, female stench. He put his head in his hands to shut it out. The wives of brahmins were closed up in dark rooms during menstruation so as not to contami-nate with their uncleanliness; it *was* rather barbaric, though that hadn't occurred to him before. He regarded her misery. 'All right, Amelia, we'll get a pariah to deal with these necessities when required. I'll arrange it.'

'Thank you.' She picked up the bucket and marched towards the bathroom with it, touching his shoulder in passing. He had to stop himself from flinching. 'Theo, I didn't want a fuss about this – or anything. But there is a great deal you didn't tell me about India.'

'You mean I deceived you?'

'No, no, my dear, you just don't realise or think about many things that matter.'

He looked grim; it was the first time she had openly criticised him so severely. 'Such as?'

'Well . . . er . . . take the matter of servants generally. I've learned quite a lot about Veena now. Durmeen translates for me. She says I should know about the oppression of women under Hinduism.'

Theo groaned. 'She only says that because she's a Catholic. They always stir things up.'

'Well, maybe it's time some things were stirred up to help people like Veena. She's not much older than I, though she looks at least fifty and doesn't even know her age. When she was just a child there was a famine here, apparently, and her parents sold her into the court. They didn't want to, and were reduced to eating roots and boiled tamarind seeds and selling all their cooking pots first. She emphasises that. And in the court some dreadful things happened to her and then she was married to a fat old man before she even reached puberty, and she has had at least two husbands and seven children, most of them are dead – and oh, I can't fathom the whole story of her life. She was amazed that I'd want to know. She can't conceive of her life *having* a story.'

Amelia turned away from Theo's indulgent smile.

'My dear little wife, why is that so dreadful? It's only we Europeans who insist on proper beginnings, middles and ends, a pattern, a progress from cradle to grave. Perhaps it – life – isn't like that at all. Suppose it's a series of circles not even much connected, like silver bangles along an arm – which is why Veena can't put things in order for you. And does it really matter anyway?'

'Oh, you can reduce anything with that, can't you? But yes it *does*. That stinking bucket in the bathroom matters to me just at the moment and what's happened to Veena mattered to her while it was happening. Don't you see – your India is so theoretical, a country full of brahmins who never have to clean up and poets sitting under banyans and warriors going into battle.'

He flushed angrily; it seemed everyone was attacking him these days, even his own wife. 'That's not all I told you! I said there was disease, poverty, ignorance.'

'Yes – but that we needn't try to change any of it because . . .'

He jumped up. 'Oh for heaven's sake stop it! Go out and be a missionary if you want, but don't ask me to support you.'

He rushed out and she heard him thunder across the verandah and down the path, bound, she guessed, for the temple. She sat back on the bed sorrowful and aching, remembering suddenly Marguerite's teasing phrase, 'babes in the jungles'. Marguerite was right; so they were, both of them.

The services of the pariah servant whom Theo hired the next day became ever more essential as the heats increased. Flies swarmed, fruits rotted, smells festered in ditches, rubbish heaps, privies, while plants shrivelled, earth cracked, goats and dogs wilted in the searing land-winds. To keep these at bay, blinds called tatties made from fibrous roots of jungle grasses were hung in every house-opening; when the sun glared its closest from the white sky, Long-ago's son sluiced them down outside with buckets of water to act as a cooling filter. Inside, the bungalow was rather like a large grass hut in which dust-laden air circled sluggishly through a greenish-brown twilight. During the long afternoons, the only sounds were the low croon of the ayah as she tried to lull Rolly to rest, the occasional crunch of a servant's bare foot on dried leaves, the rush and then drip of water down the rustling tatties.

Determined not to succumb totally to the prevailing leth-argy, Amelia sat upright at her desk, clad in flimsiest muslins, hair swept in a top-knot for coolness, struggling with the complexities of Sanskrit and Tamil. Her endeavours were aided and more often confused by her tutor, a bony man with a grubby skull-cap who had a mightily flattering opinion of his own and Amelia's capacities in their respective roles. But Amelia was not deceived for she knew herself an indifferent linguist, and when the going became too monstrously difficult she dismissed him to the verandah and wrote another letter to her friend Joanna instead.

Joanna kept Amelia supplied with copies of her speeches and articles, for she had allied herself to the Chartist cause and was busily expounding her views on social justice for women in the pages of its chief newspaper, *The Northern Star*. 'Fellow countrywomen, we call upon you to actively unite with your menfolk to free us all from political, physical and mental bondage' a recent discourse began, and Amelia dutifully read it to the end, for Joanna still exerted an absentee habit of obedience over her, being several years older and, in both their opinions, much cleverer. Nonetheless, Joanna's influence had waned since Amelia had come to live in this slow-moving south-land where such stirring phrases seemed immeasurably irrelevant. Sometimes, indeed, she felt unequal even to writing letters and dozed into seductive dreams of coolness wherein the splash and run of the water on the tatties merged to the rainswept fields of Essex.

Both Amelia and Rolly suffered the headaches, prickly heat rashes and fevers that beset newcomers in their first hot season. These quite took away appetite and energy, and once in desperation Theo sent to the Fort for Doctor Cauldwell to attend them. He was a bibulous elderly fellow, shunned by most Europeans because he had long ago 'gone native', living in a nearby village with his Indian mistress and their offspring. He was rumoured to drink within twenty-four hours of its arrival the monthly supply of brandy and port intended 'for medical comforts only', and, in its absence, doled out either Dover's powders or large blue pills for the Langs' fevers, Wardle's dyspepsia, Dora Arbuthnot's 'uterine catarrh', and did so with such a shaking hand that Amelia had no more faith in him than in the bazaar herbalist.

The listless rhythms of the hot days were varied only by the arrival of Home letters, which chronicled in graphic detail the various complaints Amelia's mother had suffered for years. Now that Amelia had escaped, mamma's care had devolved upon her two elder brothers – or rather their wives – and there was an insistent note of reproach at this state of affairs. Amelia's father having died when she was seventeen, she had been expected to look after her mother and, in retrospect, realised this was probably why she had remained single until she was twenty-five. Her early suitors, hailing from the locality, had been disparaged by her family as red-necked and uncouth and it was only when, quite unexpect-edly, the manifestly cultured and pale-necked Theophilus pressed his suit that they capitulated, allowing Amelia, who was deeply in love for the first time, to marry the man of her choice.

And, oh, how worthwhile had been the waiting, Amelia sometimes thought as she and Theo sat together on the verandah during the enchanted evening hours. As the breeze cooled and the day darkened, every part of the bungalow was opened as if a besieging army had just retreated from it; plants and animals raised their heads, while from the bazaar came the flare of stall-lights, the rumble of cart-wheels. At about the same hour a beggar with a blind girl came to the garden gate and played gentle music on a conch shell that somehow added to their content.

For the two of them were blessedly happy together, teach-ing, touching, learning to understand each other's heart as if for a long lifetime there. That, indeed, was how Amelia imagined the future – Rolly joined by little brothers and sisters who would play beside them on the verandah while, as Theo's reputation grew, scholars would come to share their knowledge with him. But, for the time being, only Rolly trundled his wheeled rabbit up and down while only she listened to her husband's recent rendering into English of the admirable Sanskrit poet Kalidasu:

> The lotus chain is dazzling white
> As is the slender moon at night.
> Perhaps it was the moon on high
> That joined her horns and left the sky,
> Believing that your lovely arm
> Would, more than heaven, enhance her charm.

At such times, when Theo read aloud or smoked his hookah (whose lulling bubble Amelia had, as Marguerite foretold, learned to love), their ordinary bungalow garden was an enchanted Eastern paradise, lacking, Theo teased, only marble fountains and voluptuous dancing girls.

But he didn't really crave their company for, in the later privacy of their bedroom, he was teaching his wife those moon-guided rituals of Hindu love-making which he'd learned in his youth from high-class prostitutes in Calcutta. Within each lunar month came nights for abstinence, for special pleasuring and squeezing of breasts and nipples, for worshipping of the soft female belly and thighs, nights for nail-marking of the buttocks with the signs of the peacock and tiger, nights for the waiting penis to be tongued and fingered, and others for its plunging into the warm, womanly orifices. Amelia soon learned to anticipate each phase of the moon, feeling her flesh tingle by day with expectancy of that night's pleasuring, excited by its very concentration.

Through the experience of this shared, uninhibited sexuality Amelia began to apppreciate the Hindu carvings that adorned the walls and towers of neighbouring temples – rollicking deities some of them, whose erotic celebrations of the body were, in Theo's opinion, a more positive cause for joy than any of the guilt-ridden austerities of Christianity. But on this point Amelia did not follow him, and continued every Sunday to attend St Peter's Church, where Reverend Arbuthnot reminded his small congregation of the dark powers of heathendom that threatened them on every side in this unregenerate land.

Though lapped in so much happiness, the Langs did not forget Rukmini Moitra and on several occasions Amelia, with Durmeen for interpreter, went to see her, escorted by Captain Gilbert, always willing to go and 'show the flag'. To Amelia these visits were painful duty, for Poodocottah always made her uneasy and her meetings with Rukmini were constrained by the vigilance of the zenana women. But Rukmini's unfeigned delight at their coming, her unspoken longing for more contact and wistful resignation at each departure made the journeys worthwhile. Afterwards, Amelia was wracked with anger and pity at her dismal lot while Theo had another fit of the glooms when she described it to him.

As the heats began to diminish at last, Resident Wardle, long guiltily aware that, though official doyen of the small foreign community, he had not given a dinner party since his wife's death the previous year, was prodded into remedying this by the arrival in Tanjore district of a newcomer – Mrs Catherine Rundell, the assistant collector's wife. Moreover, Nicholas Rundell belonged to the new-fangled, pushy, reforming breed of administrator on whose right side it was politic to keep, and was distantly related to Lord Ellenborough, President of the Board of Control of Indian Affairs.

Wardle had reached his present small eminence partly by taking prudent cognisance of factors such as these; nevertheless, when the date of the party came he wished he'd never embarked upon a project that was so bothersome to manage without Marjorie's help. She had genuinely enjoyed entertaining people, whereas he wasn't looking forward to seeing any of the guests, except Mrs Lang. She was a pleasant, sensible, attractive young woman, and there was something about the way she occasionally glanced at her husband which suggested an enviable sweetness of marital congress between them. Wardle had been celibate since his bereavement which, he thought sourly, was probably good for his health, but he was tired of it. Calling the boy to pick suitable flowers for the table, he went to put on his best pair of black breeches – old-fashioned garments these days he knew, and a sure sign that he hadn't visited a good English tailor for many a year.

The Arbuthnots and Langs arrived at the same time, and all praised his roses which, by dint of much water-drawing and channelling, had survived the worst of the heat. Wardle glowed and, with a flourish, presented Amelia with a choice bloom as he ushered them indoors.

Dora flopped into a chair.

'Well, the south-west monsoon's due any day now and will cheer up your roses even more, Resident.' She liked to bear good tidings even if they were hardly news.

'Ninety-five in the shade at noon, though – much higher than it should be,' Wardle mourned, fussing over the ladies' lime juice and water. 'We've none of us met Mrs Rundell, have we?' He looked round for confirmation. 'From a good army family, I gather. She's just spent the hot season in Bombay with her sister, recuperating from a . . .' he coughed, '. . . a miscarriage. Their previous posting was Bangalore, where she gained quite a reputation as a harpist, I'm told.'

'Oh a harp! I do hope she's brought it here. How I long to hear some proper music instead of these heathenish wails and bangs,' Dora exclaimed.

'Surely even your English-tuned ear can enjoy the subtleties of the Indian sitar, Mrs Arbuthnot?'

'Oh that, Mr Lang. Well yes, but I confess it soon sends me to sleep.'

Theo was about to launch into a comparison of sitar and harp when Mrs Catherine Rundell was ushered in. She was slender, fair and pale; the type of woman who made Amelia want to hide her large hands and feet and apply layers of pearl powder to her cheeks, which still remained obstinately pink. Arbuthnot's eyes glowed: Mrs Rundell would look enchanting with a harp; perhaps he could entice her to play in church sometimes. His wife thought her features too pinched for real beauty, however, and Theo scarcely glanced at her, being more interested in her following spouse. Nicholas Rundell was about his own age, his squarish head topped with flopping fairish hair and his fashionable tightly-cut jacket and nankeen trousers clearly revealing the chunkiness of the flesh beneath. He came in with an air of knowing himself the most important guest, an impression his host reinforced by plying him nervously with frequent brandy-and-pawnee top-ups.

'I notice your garden has benefited greatly from your little home-made irrigation system, Resident,' Rundell said genially. 'Now if we can just extend that principle to the neighbouring countryside we could see some real crop increases within a few years. There's a surveying engineer from Trichy coming soon, did you know? His preliminary report suggests the cheapest and most effective scheme would be to dam the course of the river nearest the city – where the brahmin villages are.'

Theo became attentive. 'Ah, that's probably the source of the bazaar rumour about Company soldiers coming to collect taxes for new wells.'

Nicholas laughed. 'Oh, give the bazaar folk any little twig and they'll get hold of its wrong end! No, the Company's plan is to persuade the Raja himself to make a substantial contribution to the scheme – or deduct it from his annual allowance. What do you think?'

He turned to Wardle, who shrugged. 'He'd scream like a scalded cat at either proposal.'

'And why shouldn't he?' Theo demanded. 'Hasn't the Company robbed him of enough already?'

Nicholas regarded Theo as if from afar; he hadn't liked the look of the fellow's almost Hinduised rig-out from the first, and recalled old Wardle telling him that the father's body had been burned like a native's. 'But Mr Lang, a good irrigation scheme will benefit the Raja's own villages as much as the rest of the district – which is full of his loyal subjects, or so he says. Indeed, I was hoping you, who have ready access to him, might try and awaken his sense of public conscience.'

'Well I'm sorry, Mr Rundell, but I don't see that as part of my function. And in any case the Raja simply doesn't have the funds to spare. He's riddled with debts already.'

'And why is that, Mr Lang? You know as well as I: because he and his royal kind squander their patrimonies on useless fads and flummeries, on jewels and idols and festivals, on women of the seraglio, on jugglers, quack priests, toadies and heaven knows what else.'

'Which, by their own standards, they have a perfect right to do, and as they have done for centuries. What's more, the peasants love them for it – making merry at their festivals and worshipping in the temples they generously endow.'

Arbuthnot, who'd been conversing with the ladies, jerked his head at this, and Amelia felt alarmed – surely Theo wasn't going to be the centre of another quarrel already?

'And do you really consider, Mr Lang, that this absolves the native princes from any contribution towards the betterment of their own people through practical works – of the kind we've been sent here to set up?'

'Oh, let the Company finance your practical works!' Theo glowered. 'It's pillaged this country rotten already. Let some of the greedy yellow-skinned nabobs living in idle luxury on the wealth they've accumulated here pay for them!'

Nicholas prided himself on his ability to keep his temper in public, so he replied as one whose reason was being sorely tried. 'Mr Lang, I don't hold much brief for some of the old Company fortune-hunters, either. But they belong to the past. And the only way to regenerate India now is by more government control, widespread schemes for developing agriculture, health, education. But most of your precious parasite rajas prancing about on their painted elephants aren't going to give a single bauble in such causes, are they Mr Lang? And if they won't voluntarily, then they have to be coerced – or deposed – and that's about it.'

His voice had risen in spite of his resolve and Wardle, who'd been chastising the cook, rushed back spluttering, 'Dinner is now served. Gentlemen, let us cool down, please, and follow the example of the ladies.'

The conversation of the ladies had indeed been as coolly tepid as a garden pool. Amelia had described Theo chasing two bats round their bedroom with a stick one night, but this fell flat, for bats in bedrooms were commonplace. Dora had tried to enthuse them with her plans for a female orphanage, but Catherine had simply started telling them instead about the grandest ball of the season, which had been widely reported in the Bombay papers. It was held in Simla in the G.G.'s honour: brilliant banners and arches of flowers framing the name 'Auckland'; a supper-room hung with exquisite velvet hangings; everyone dancing till dawn – except the Misses Eden who were inclined to be spoilsportish and retire early. This intelligence was conveyed rather grudgingly, for Catherine had been disappointed to find that the handsome Captain Gilbert, whom she'd met on arrival, was not present and so there was no one she need exert herself to entertain. She and Mrs Lang had not found any common ground, and if their husbands were going to disagree, well so be it.

The meal was not up to scratch, alas, Wardle confessed, due to the absence of his dear wife who used to make everything go like clockwork. The other gentlemen were fortunate indeed to have helpmeets at their sides, he added, and how pleasant it was that the accomplished and lovely Mrs Rundell was now of their number. She and Mrs Lang, a lady of similar endowments, would undoubtedly have much in common and it was agreeable to suppose they might be friends, for as dear Marjorie used to say, Tanjore ladies often lacked sufficient occupation and congenial company of their own sex. Of course, he added quickly, he hadn't intended to exclude worthy Mrs Arbuthnot from the charmed circle, but she had so much occupation already, what with her children and the needs of the soldiers' wives. At which point Dora obligingly related some of the latter's recent tribulations, while the other diners champed quietly through the tough mutton, and both the actual and metaphorical temperature of the room moderated to pleasantness. When the gentlemen joined the ladies afterwards, Nicholas made a point of chatting to Amelia, and Theo to Catherine, so that no irreparable breach should occur on this, their first meeting. Wardle, released from the worst strain of the solitary host, drank quietly for a while before allowing himself the pleasure of imparting the hottest news from the north which he'd been saving up.

'You know what came through in the mails yesterday, though it happened nearly three weeks ago – Ranjit Singh, the Old Lion of the Punjab, is dead at last! And no less than four of his wives committed suttee at his funeral – just imagine that!'

The women shuddered, imagining it. 'But suttee is illegal now, surely?' Amelia protested.

'Not where native princes rule the roost, madam – as Ranjit Singh certainly did. And it still goes on in our domains, anyway, especially in Bengal. You can't cancel such entrenched practices with a single stroke of the pen, as I'm sure Mr Lang would agree?'

'Certainly I do and, in a sense, it's a shame the British didn't pick a less difficult and controversial issue to get their legal claws into.'

'But no cause could be worthier, surely?' Dora bridled.

'You know, I'm not convinced of that. Some women throughout history have positively embraced the flames and walked singing to the pyre, certain they'll then be worthy to join their husbands in paradise for as many years as there are hairs on the human body. And who are we to say them nay? Is our faith so firm?'

'Who are we . . . !' exploded the Reverend, but his wife interrupted. 'Hush, dear. You've argued along these lines with Mr Lang already and it does no good to lose your temper.'

And Wardle, wanting to keep peace, also intervened. 'But you must concede that by no means all suttees are voluntary. Y'know I recall old Mayhew describing one he witnessed in Calcutta. Crowds went to watch. The wretched woman, struggling violently, was actually tied face down on her husband's corpse. She fought for life till the flames consumed her and the funeral music drowned her screams.'

'Why didn't Mayhew put a stop to it?' asked Dora.

'Oh, this was in the '20s before the Act of Abolition, and he was a mere junior. The local magistrate could perhaps have intervened but I daresay preferred to turn a blind eye.'

Nicholas seized his advantage. 'Come, Mr Lang, when atrocities like that are committed in the name of religion, you surely can't deny that we live among a barbarous and primitive people in desperate need of humanitarian reform?'

'I don't find it so clear-cut, Mr Rundell,' Theo replied coolly. 'Certainly I don't think suttee should be indefinitely condoned; neither do a number of Hindus who've been influenced by European ideas. It is gruesome and cruel, as are many practices carried out in the name of various faiths. But India is no more barbarous and primitive than Spain at the time of the Inquisition. And we British are wrong to take the law into our own hands. Where religious and cultural matters are concerned, change should come gradually through the participation and consent of the people them-selves – as Munro said.' He would have left it at that, except that Rundell's contemptuous sneer at the name of his hero fired him into a temper of dislike. 'Oh, but I see the sort you are, Mr Rundell. Your aim is to "elevate this country to the superior standards of European culture" almost overnight, isn't it? Everything must change to suit your idea of what is civilised and just and right – because you and your meddling kind know best! Indians must become subject to the laws and standards of the British Empire, which you see as the only good. Well I don't see things in quite the same light and . . .'

Nicholas, taking quick advantage of Theo's momentary diversion to remove a flying insect from his drink, challenged, 'And how do you think we British have attained our present position of supremacy in this country – and in others, Mr Lang? Through the essential superiority and strength of our civilisation – that is how. We, a few thousand Englishmen, hold sway over millions of Indians by force, not of arms, but of moral character based on Christian virtues and humanitarian beliefs. We're not corrupted by bribery. We don't burn widows. And the educated natives respect us for it. Whatever raises our character in their eyes adds to our security and our power; and we are now powerful enough to impose our enlightened concepts of moral justice and social order on the people of this land.'

As he paused for breath he was aware from his wife's raised eyebrows that his tone was too strident, but she gave him no chance to moderate it, saying, with perfectly composed weariness, 'Nicholas, please be quiet and let us go. It's far too hot and late for all this pother, and if I hear another speech from Mr Lang tonight I shall be quite ill. But he'll never stop quarrelling unless you do. I know *his* sort.' She rose, gathering shawl and bag as if nothing were in the least amiss. 'Would your boy call our bearers, Resident? Thank you so much for such a delicious dinner. And how well you have coped with us all single-handed!' She smiled farewell to the Arbuthnots and without a glance at the Langs drifted daintily out.

Nicholas hesitated, glowered, followed her.

After the other guests had departed, Wardle poured himself a last brandy and wandered to the verandah. His damnable indigestion was playing up again and no wonder! Could even tactful Marjorie have wrought harmony from such fractious company? What a confoundedly quarrelsome fellow Lang was – not worthy of his charming wife, who undoubtedly agreed with him only because she *was* his wife. He began to envisage a scene with himself and Amelia in the rose garden, he explaining how wrong-headed her husband was, putting an arm round those pretty pink shoulders, even a kiss perhaps . . . He sighed, swallowing the brandy to fill the emptiness of the solitary host after the guests have gone.

In the days following the Resident's dinner party, Amelia feared they'd never be asked anywhere again, and was thus especially pleased when Mrs Arbuthnot invited her to tea, saying that her husband would be on a day's shoot, and Rolly could play with the twins.

'I fear the Reverend is not very fond of extra little ones about,' she explained apologetically, tousling Rolly's curls. 'I adore them, but it interferes with his work. This afternoon, though, they can have the run of the house, and I've arranged for Sarah Murphy to look after them all so we can have a quiet walk and talk.'

She led Amelia into the parlour strewn with an amazing jumble of objects. 'Please excuse the muddle . . .' She scraped her bushy hair back from her face as if to lessen it. 'Now Matthew, don't play with that. It's Papa's shooting bag. We couldn't find it before he went. He had to take an old sack instead.' She sighed, remembering his irritation. 'Things just lose themselves. Do you find the same Mrs Lang? Anyway, I hope he returns with a "good bag" even if it is in a sack – bazaar meat is so expensive these days.' Rummaging through a drawer she produced her household ledger. 'See, mutton nearly half a rupee more a catty than this time last year.'

Amelia looked. 'You keep careful accounts, Mrs Arbuthnot.'

'I do indeed. My household may be in some disarray but its accounts are always in good order. Even Reginald admits that . . . I thought you might like to see – it's the only way to keep a check on the servants. Unless you're so well placed that a few rupees one way or t'other don't matter?'

'Oh they certainly do!' Amelia grimaced. 'Theo's constantly having to remind the Raja about his salary, and sometimes he gets more – but it's never enough.' She realised they'd just called their husbands by their first names and took it for a sign of mutual friendship.

'Well, then, you'd better follow my example – see.'

Amelia studied the ruled columns showing hourly wages for dhobis, sweepers, goat and dog boys, tailors and grooms.

'And be sure to record occasional expenses: for re-lining tin pots, muslin for straining butter, dog medicine and so on, else the servants will charge for them far too often. And I hope you keep an eye on the milk or 'twill be watered down before you even see it.'

'Dearie me, I have been slapdash.'

Dora patted her arm. 'Never mind, you'll learn, and husbands never bother with such things, do they? As for slapdash – you're a model of prudence compared to that dreadful Myra Blenkinsop. Doesn't sign herself "Blenkinsop" anymore, I notice.'

'Oh? Who was she?'

'My goodness, you don't know? Such a scandal, but just before you came, I suppose. Now let's sit for a minute and . . .' She cleared a space on a chair. 'Oh, there's Agnes's needlework, she was looking everywhere . . . Well Caleb Blenkinsop was a chaplain at Trichy so we knew him and his family well. Myra was always rather flighty – slapdash, as I said. Not at all fitting for a churchman's wife. And do you know, after the birth of their third child she just upped and left the lot of them one day: rode off on a stolen horse to Pondicherry where she had a secret assignation with a French naval officer – and away they sailed. Poor Reginald was most upset – on Caleb's behalf, of course. Said they should have sent a posse to haul her back for a good horse-whipping.'

'And where is she now?'

'In Paris. She actually *wrote* to me.' Dora delved into her capacious bag. 'Says she's having such a jolly time! The impudence of her! Ah, here it is. "It's very pretty and cool and elegant here; trees in blossom along the banks of the Seine and people sitting in the spring sunshine."' She sighed. 'Fancy actually *sitting* in the sun, wouldn't that be grand? It came a month ago, but I shan't reply, of course.' She stuffed the letter, which looked much read, back in her bag.

'And the French officer?'

'Not a word about *him*. Anyway, I shouldn't waste breath on such an immoral creature while there's women with near-beasts for husbands who stick by them and suffer.' She lowered her voice, nodding towards the verandah. 'Poor Sarah Murphy, scarcely a woman herself and with two little ones, and her man spends all his pay on drink and loose native females who should be hounded out of town.'

Amelia sighed. 'But are they really to blame, Mrs Arbuthnot? Durmeen says they usually have no choice: it's prostitution or starve.'

Dora began distractedly popping some children's toys into Reginald's shooting bag. 'I'll just clear up a little and then we'll . . . Yes, yes, Mrs Lang, India is a cruel country for womankind, in my opinion. Now how is that poor lady in Poodocottah whom you visit? Could she read the books I sent?'

'Indeed, yes – and she thanks you most profusely. Her English is improving steadily. And yet, I sometimes wonder, what's the use? She's trapped in that horrible palace forever, I suppose, and I don't know how she can bear it.'

'How indeed? Oh bother, it's full.' Dora swung the bag. 'Now before tea let's go and . . . As for poor Rukmini Moitra we can only pray that your visits and the books will eventually lead her to the support of the one true faith. That's why I'm so anxious to establish my asylum where native girls can understand the truth of Christianity in their hearts, instead of simply using the Bible as a textbook, as some Indians do, I fear. There!' She crammed the bag into a cupboard. 'That's a bit better. We hope one of the old Fort buildings can be used. Now I want you to come and see it – this very minute. We'll go by palki, it's still so muddy.'

Amelia went rather reluctantly, but Dora was not easy to deter and, when they reached the Fort, waxed very enthusiastic about the conversion of a former barracks into dormitories and classrooms.

'Wouldn't it be a splendid work, my dear?' She looked pleadingly at Amelia. 'But we must have the Raja's blessing because this is his land now. The Reverend can't seem to make headway with His Highness, but if your husband could . . .'

'I'm sorry, Mrs Arbuthnot, but I don't think . . . in fact I know he won't help, in this instance. He simply doesn't approve of filling children's heads with little else but the English language and Christian doctrine. And perhaps he's right? Does it not unfit the girls for their future lot in life?'

'But Mrs Lang, what future have they? They've already been abandoned and cast out. If we can bring them to Grace, they will survive – and perhaps act as beacons showing the Way to others. Surely you, a good Christian woman, must agree with that?'

Amelia was embarrassed. 'Yes, well I do, but I'm afraid Theo and I differ in our views on religion.'

Dora laid a hand on her arm. 'My dear, I hardly like to ask, but he isn't, is he . . . a Hindu?'

'Oh no. He frequently goes to temples but not actually to worship. He's really more of a universalist and thinks people should follow their own roads and that no one way has a monopoly of virtue – or wisdom.'

'But you don't subscribe to that, do you, Amelia?' In her agitation Dora forgot their earlier formalities.

'Not really, but it's no use arguing with him about it.' She turned away; some young urchins were running about the Fort tank and teasing a troop of grey monkeys who were frisking in imitation on a wall above. A happy, carefree scene; no, she didn't really agree with Theo, but sometimes she did wonder . . . To change the subject she gestured beyond the tank. 'What's that building? It looks European.'

'That's missionary Swartz's old chapel. Good gracious, haven't you seen it?'

Amelia shook her head and Dora led her towards it at once, thinking it typical of Mr Lang to drag his wife to look at heathen temples with their grotesque, positively indecent carvings, but fail to show her the most famous Christian monument in the city. Reaching the door, they closed it against the following urchins, who'd decided they were of much greater interest than the monkeys. Inside was cool, simple, grey space with a semi-circular recess for the altar at the east end and, in front, a monument to Father Swartz, son of a German brewer.

'It's rather splendid, isn't it? That's Swartz dying on his bed surrounded by sorrowing converts. Raja Surabhoji had it specially made by Flaxman and sent out from Italy.'

She leant against a pillar, enjoying the benediction of its coolness; she came often to this tranquil stone shell for temporary respite from the harassments of her life. She closed her eyes, until the constant multiplicity of Indian sounds fell away and she could imagine a village churchyard, with green grass, one blackbird singing, one evening bell, one Truth . . . She opened her eyes, watching Amelia who was tracing the monumental carving with her fingers. 'How very strange that your husband never brought you here. But he is . . . well, unusual, isn't he? Of course he had a very peculiar childhood, poor man. The Reverend says – but this is confidential, mind? – ' Amelia reassured her and she continued, ' – that his views are rather old-fashioned for one so comparatively young.'

'Really? What does he mean exactly?'

'Well . . . you've promised not to repeat this . . . that his orientalism, his uncritical defence of Indian languages and culture are typical of an earlier generation of Anglo-Indians. They used to hobnob with the natives very freely, too, in . . . well . . . various ways.'

She trailed off and Amelia sighed. 'Oh Dora, it's so difficult sometimes! After all, Theo knows so much more about Indian things than any of us and we've no right, in our ignorance, to call it all heathen balderdash.'

'But as I said before, there's only one Truth, Amelia. You know that in your heart as well as I do. Surely you could just mention my orphans to him?'

'Well all right, but it won't be any use. Perhaps we should go? You promised Sarah we wouldn't be long.'

Waiting Sarah's lips were screwed in anxious irritation. The later she returned, the more she had to pay the ayah who was looking after her own children while she looked after Mrs Arbuthnot's. The difference between these two sums was the only money she could ever save. So as soon as the ladies appeared, she rushed back to the barracks, shrinking past Captain Gilbert who was standing outside the orderly room looking grimmer than usual.

The Murphy's home, just two tin-roofed, white-washed rooms in a row of identical dwellings, was still furnace-hot, for its tiny enclosed verandah faced the sun for most of the day, having been designed to army specifications by an absent engineer. Her clammy little ones, Jack and Rosie, were crowded in a shaded corner while the ayah was waiting as impatiently as she'd just been. Sarah patted the children listlessly, then crossed the back yard and through a hole in the wall to the communal privies that served the whole row. She raised her skirts and plonked down on one of the wooden seats; her urine hissed into the earth-box, disturbing a cloud of flies that went to settle instead on a filthy tin scoop used to cover accumulated faeces with earth from a bucket. The stench from those faeces was sickening, for the scavenger's cart did not come to empty until dusk. She dabbed between her legs with a scrap of paper that she scrutinised hopefully for signs of menstrual blood. There was none. More than two months overdue; no hope now. She rocked miserably to and fro, thinking of what must lie ahead: Gerard would beat her when he knew her condition; then there'd be the weary, unwieldy months; the rough, trembling hands of Doctor Cauldwell; another hungry, unwanted, ailing bundle of flesh trying to survive in that airless room.

'Oh God help me, I wish I were dead,' she moaned. 'I know it's wrong, oh Lord, but I do, that I do.' As she got up, brushed flies and tears from her grubby cheeks and wandered out, she heard the creak of the approaching scavenger's cart. Rosie was wheeling a coloured hoop about in the hot yard-dust, the late sun gilding her pretty brown curls to auburn. Bright-eyed, she ran up to her mother, waving the hoop, begging her to play too. Sarah scooped her up, rubbing her face against her daughter's soft, moist arm and mumbling, 'No, I don't wish that, no I don't.' But as she carried the child indoors she shivered all the same, as if it were too late to recant.

* * *

Sarah's other hope – that her husband would be late home – was granted at least, for Gerard had been summoned to the guardroom, though not in his customary role of miscreant. The previous day, Captain Gilbert had inadvertently overheard Privates Patterson and Cooper discussing him. That their sentiments lacked warmth caused him no surprise; what had fired him to a violent anger akin to fear, however, was their use of his nickname 'Jilly'. He'd half-heard it before and hoped himself mistaken, but this time there was no doubt. The first emotion to equal his anger was regret that, only a few years before, reforming Lord Bentinck had banned the time-honoured punishment of flogging in the Company's army. But that was a crude instrument, and he had lain awake much of the night devising something more subtle that might deter any man from a similar offence.

When Murphy entered the guardroom he saw Patterson and Cooper stripped to the waist, their hands and feet shackled to the wall behind them and, in front, a white-robbed priest cross-legged before a large brass bowl and five tin cups.

'Ah Murphy, over there.'

Gilbert, who stood beside his jemadar (the officer-in-charge of sepoys), motioned him to join three other spectators, summoned because they were prime trouble-makers in the garrison.

'Now let us proceed. Yesterday, in my hearing, the two prisoners used a grossly insulting term to describe their Commanding Officer. When cases of this kind occur – which would have formerly warranted a flogging – C.O.s are now instructed . . .' he read from a paper held in a slightly trembling hand, '. . . "to devise methods of punishing offenders that are as far as possible appropriate to the kind and degree of the act committed".' He looked up, continuing in the same reading voice. 'It seems to me that what is most appropriate for an offence of this nature is an act of purification of the kind commonly performed by natives guilty of impurities of mind, speech, or deed. The act consists of drinking a mixture made up of the five substances emitted from the orifices of the sacred cow – namely milk, curds, ghee, urine and dung.'

There was a stir among the onlookers and Cooper, the younger of the two victims, whimpered, 'Aw gawd . . . no . . .'

'And now we will witness the correct procedure for making this mixture,' Gil continued imperturbably.

The jemadar spoke to the priest, who first held up each cup to display its contents then poured it into the bowl; the dung fell last in a series of sickening plops, and everyone watched in appalled fascination as the priest solemnly stirred the ingredients into a gruesome brown custard. At a command from the jemadar, a sepoy marched forward, saluted and scooped up a cupful.

'And who'd like to taste first? Patterson – as you are the senior?' Gil's voice was jovial, as if he were offering beer. Patterson scowled, but, a veteran who had long ago learned to accept the inevitable, he clenched his fists, opened his mouth and swallowed quickly as the sepoy poured. Beside him Cooper, trembling, sweating and deathly pale, began straining helplessly in his bonds.

'Taken like a man, Patterson,' Gil snapped. 'Now then, Cooper.'

The young man gagged, twisted his head away until the jemadar forced open his mouth for the sepoy to pour. Cooper spat, bawled, retched, and the noxious fluid dribbled down his fair moustache to mess his throat and heaving chest.

Gil's face suddenly closed. 'That will do, jemadar. I think the point has been clearly brought home. Dismiss the men and release the prisoners.'

He strode stiffly out and, in the privacy of his own quarters, stared at his reflection in the mirror. His mouth, set in its grim, straight line, curled into a spasm of self-disgust. He took neither pride nor pleasure in his martinet role, yet he found himself playing it frantically, helplessly, again and again. Tormented by it himself, he seldom felt pity for his victims, but on this occasion he had momentarily glimpsed, in Cooper's frightened, angry pallor, the shadow of another man of similar age lying frightened, angry and dying outside a jungle stockade during the Burmese war, many years before. His name had been Lawrence and he'd been Gil's first, secret love. Gil had given him a ring of finest jade, which Lawrence pretended had come from a beautiful Burmese girl. Two days before he lost his life, Lawrence had lost the ring and had gone into battle with forebodings of disaster. Gil, a witness of his death agonies, had never been able to reveal the extent of his grief, but it was with him yet and, for Lawrence's sake, Cooper had been reprieved.

Gil turned from the mirror and tore up the paper with its punitive instructions from higher command which he had, in fact, invented specially for the occasion, then sat on his bed, head bowed. He was supposed to accompany Wardle to Poo the next day; would it be wise? *Jilly*. How much did the men actually know, or were they only suspicious of his singleness, his singularity? There had been suspicions before but he'd ridden them out; if his frolics at Poo were discovered his career would be ruined, no doubt of that. He snorted. God, he had no more career than a buffalo bound to a treadmill in this southern backwater. He'd carry on as if nothing had happened and the devil take it.

This particular visit to Poo was no mere flag-showing, but was prompted by a confidential letter from the Madras Council concerning rumours of a plot to kill the young Tondiman princes. The Resident was requested to ascertain the veracity of these rumours, and though this was quite beyond his powers, he decided to pay the court a surprise visit. Theo, who might have been a help, refused to accompany him, but mentioned that his wife would welcome another chance to see Rukmini Moitra. To this Wardle agreed gladly, for he was rather partial to Mrs Lang's company.

He did his best to entertain her during the journey with well-worn anecdotes illustrative of the stupidity, indolence and dishonesty of the natives. She, unresponsive to his sallies, commented only that he must find it very trying to live among people whom he held in such low regard and he feelingly agreed, quite missing her under-note of censure. How crass and short he was, she thought; short of stature, of perspicacity, even of humour – compared to her clever and sensitive husband. But she did not betray her thoughts, for Wardle was representative of Company power in Tanjore and her cleverness, unlike Theo's, included a streak of sound practical diplomacy.

Neither she nor the Resident held high hopes of the expedition itself, but in the event felt it rather successful. Wardle was easily persuaded by his unexpectedly cordial reception that the court had, in fact, 'settled down to its usual way of things' as he put in his report, and his 'frank discussions' with all parties had convinced him that the rumours were no more than the usual mischievous gossip. Amelia, for her part, found a Rukmini who had partly overcome her shyness at last, talked more freely and fluently, and laughed with pleasure when Amelia gave her a sketch she'd made of Rolly with his wheeled rabbit. When they parted, Rukmini gave her in return a tasselled silk shawl of the same material as her own which, she explained, was to make them more akin and sister-like. Amelia wore the shawl on her return journey, treasuring this token of Rukmini's affection, both for herself and the pleasure it would give Theophilus.

Amelia was imagining this pleasure when she climbed out of her palki into the bungalow compound, but was immediately distracted by the accumulated heap of household refuse dumped against the wall.

She wrinkled her nose and tried her halting Tamil on Longago, who came to unload the palki. 'Why has this been left here?'

He answered her in English as usual. 'No pariah servant, missus. Master say he go.'

'But why? Is master all right?'

'Yes, missus. He is home.'

Anxious nonetheless, she hastened to the parlour, where she found Theo and Gopal Krishnan lounging on cushions apparently engaged in some amusing disputation, for there was laughter in their faces which faded to dismay at her appearance, like truant schoolboys suddenly confronted by authority. Then Theo came to hug and kiss her, explaining that Gopi had arrived quite by chance a few hours after she'd left, and they'd had to make the best of things in her absence. In fact, they'd clearly been enjoying themselves: eating, smoking and talking till all hours and, to judge by the amount of litter, with no one bothering to clear up after them.

Their shared past had been the main topic – those days of the '20s when Theo had been a student at Fort William College in Calcutta. His earlier years in England had made a dry youth of him: dry-eyed, dry-witted, dry-skinned and dry-sexed, Gopi teased. But then he'd met Gopal and his intellectual set of male friends who had relaxed and warmed him with their easy *badinage*, their guiltless sensuality. A few years after Theo left the college, it was disbanded by order of Lord Bentinck, and now that dandified, aristocratic student life seemed to them both a long-ago golden age, compared to which nothing since had been quite so satisfactory.

Gopal had arrived at the Lang's bungalow with three servants of his own who prepared his food in his own cooking vessels, and had quite taken over the kitchen, instantly dismissing the pariah. During Amelia's five-day absence a more haphazard, desultory, easy-going way of managing things had been created, which seemed to please everyone. But Amelia was not pleased. She immediately set about restoring her hard-won standards of hygiene and tidiness, until Theo teasingly reminded her of the Hindu proverb that much safety lies in disorder, and suggested she listen to Gopi's after-supper reading of Sanskrit verses instead. She obeyed but, failing to understand a word, retired dismally to bed where she lay nauseated by the smell of uncleaned chamber-pots. When she slept, she dreamed that their sweet little home had returned to the neglected, ruinous state in which she'd first seen it.

Next morning, however, her natural optimism returned, and she determined to break through Gopal's brahminical disdain – for was he not the only educated Indian she'd met and her husband's good friend? She could not imagine how unthinkable her resolve was to Gopal who, regarding her friendly overtures as bold and distasteful in the extreme, would have liked to banish her to some remote zenana.

It was the unspoken accumulation of these feelings that prompted him to announce to Theo as lunch was ending that he'd decided to offer support to the Dharma Sabha.

Theo squinted at him. 'Well, I can see your point, old fellow, but it goes against the current grain and won't help your dealings with the Company bigwigs.'

'And I don't intend to guide my life by their stars,' Gopal retorted, while Theo nodded his approval.

'Would someone please explain what the Dharma Sabha is?' Amelia interrupted plaintively, looking at Gopal, who didn't respond.

'Come on, Gopi. Your line of country. As a mere Englishman I couldn't join even if I wanted.'

Gopal turned to her, his tone pompous and distant. 'The Dharma Sabha, madam, is a society formed in Calcutta a few years ago to protest against the passing of new laws by Europeans which interfere in and obstruct our own long-held cultural and religious customs. The most contentious issue being suttee, the burning of widows. The Dharma Sabha considers it our Indian prerogative to decide whether or not the tradition should be abolished. It is not for foreigners to lay down the law in such matters.'

'Hear, hear!' exclaimed Theo, and his wife glared at him.

'But burning alive – surely in the name of common humanity, Mr Krishnan . . .'

Gopal shrugged. 'Humanity is common, Mrs Lang, and commonly disposable. I do not suggest that the custom is to be commended, but it is the principle at stake – and still is, even though suttee has been legally abolished in territories held by the Company.'

She flushed angrily. 'But this is all men's doings, men's principles. Your womenfolk who suffer in the flames and die – what do they feel about it? What say do they have?'

He spread his hands. 'I don't believe women have much say in the making of English laws either, madam. But if you think me cruel and barbarous, let me quote the words of Sir Thomas Munro, your husband's hero: that you British should proceed with caution and as your knowledge "of the manners and customs of the country increases, frame gradually from the existing institutions such a system as may advance the country's prosperity and satisfy its people and . . ."'

'But I'm sure Sir Thomas didn't have suttee in mind, Mr Krishnan!'

'That I can't say for certain, but I know he made a profound study of our cultural and religious beliefs, and may I suggest you do likewise. You will then discover that for a woman the sacrifice of suttee, when performed voluntarily, is the equivalent of the warrior who, in defence of his leader, dies willingly in battle. Both are honoured and glorified for these last virtuous, resolute acts and, I say again, it is not right for foreigners to legislate in the matter.'

His stern tone temporarily quelled her, and Theo patted her shoulder. 'There you are, Amelia! You have much to learn, as you know. And please excuse my wife's temerity, dear fellow. She has an inquiring mind and I am grateful for it.'

Gopal smiled grimly, thanking the gods his wife had no such quality or, if she did, kept it decently hid. The thought of her suggested to him suddenly that it might be pleasant to return home, for the best part of his visit was obviously over. So, after keeping a private appointment later that day, he departed for Madras early the following morning, leaving Amelia piqued and disappointed at her lack of any friendly headway with him. She did not, as a good Indian wife would, rise before dawn to smooth his departure, but lay awake in the half-light listening to the now-familiar sounds of servants and palki-bearers loading and quarrelling. It was a relief that the pariah could now be reinstated and the house return to its normal routine – well, *her* idea of normal, she conceded – as she padded on to the verandah thinking to wave Mr Krishnan farewell.

First light was spreading over the garden like a fan opening' and a fine mist was curling above the nearby water tank. Gopal's closed palki was already jogging away and Theo stood on the path watching it, his posture disconsolate. A wonderfully cool rush of morning air fluttered through her nightgown, exhilarating her skin pleasurably. A year ago when she'd been nearing India's shores, she'd have thought it abominably hot, but one's perspectives changed rapidly and dramatically about all sorts of things – climate being the simplest.

She had seen and heard, felt and learned so much in that first year, and suddenly there on the verandah, watching Theo and, as it were herself from the outside, enjoying the beauty of that fresh dawn, she was seized with a great hunger for the future – for the next year and the next. She longed to know what would happen, to get on quickly with the whole business of living because there must be so much of everything ahead, a grander feast in store than she could possibly imagine. Even Indians, who seemed patiently resigned to a series of continual 'nows', sometimes experienced these same sentiments she remembered, quoting to herself a verse Theo had taught her:

> What's to come tomorrow, let it come today.
> What's to come today, let it come now.
> Lord, white as jasmine,
> Don't give me your 'nows' and 'thens'

A burst of happiness spun through her and she rushed down the steps and along the path calling, 'Oh Theo, Theo, isn't it a beautiful morning?' She threw herself in his arms, twining herself round him, claiming him back as her own.

CHAPTER SIX

The famous library in the palace of Tanjore was furnished in the European style, with gilt-framed portraits of the Mahratta rajas on the walls and, at one end, a number of objects collected by Surabhoji, who'd been given to enthusiasms. These included a crumbling anatomical skeleton, a wooden printing-press, and a pair of bagpipes played by a Highland piper during the Raja's pilgrimage to Benares. Theo sat at a carved kneehole library table made by Hepplewhite and Co. which Surabhoji had bought for Bayard Lang, and he remembered wistfully how his father and the old Raja would sit there for hours reciting snatches of ancient poetry. It seemed like a golden age compared to his own, with everyone nagging about problems of orphans, money and drains.

The library itself was reputed to contain more than thirty thousand items, but no one knew how accurate the estimate was or who had made it. Certainly there were shelves of leather-bound volumes in most of the dead and living European languages, and piles of manuscripts in the Indian vernaculars engraved on bundles of dried palm leaves fastened with pegs at each end and bound between boards. Inscribed on these were histories, poems, laws and legends of the south Indian peoples; their regulations on everything from the dress of dancing girls to the issue of cotton seed for goats; their secret rituals and herbal remedies; their taxes and tithes; their plots and predictions. One of the last, written about 1776, stated that Indians would endure the rule of white foreigners for about 160 years and then be freed to rule themselves.

Theophilus, wandering on to the balcony for a brief respite from his impossible, fascinating task of cataloguing this unwieldy treasure, wondered if that prophecy would prove correct. His thought was prompted by a messenger crossing the courtyard below whose swaggering gait and red belt signified he was one of the Resident's runners, carrying, doubtless, yet another letter for royal consideration. Theo had read them. They implored Sevaji to show conduct more conformable with his 'obligations as a Sovereign Prince'; reprimanded him for presenting accounts 'altogether and wilfully incorrect'; asked for information regarding His Highness's future intentions for his lands and villages.

Wardle, poor old sod, had little else to occupy his time, so it was pointless telling him that the letters were invariably thrown into one of the huge tin trunks containing 'correspondence with the Company' and dating back at least forty years. In any case, and by his own lights, Sevaji was fulfilling his obligations, was keeping correct accounts and felt no need to formulate future intentions.

Returning to his desk, Theo glanced again at the bundle of letters for which he'd asked months ago but which had just been unearthed from one of the trunks. They revealed that the late Raja had indeed been anxious about his son's education and, on his return from pilgrimage, had begged Sir Thomas Munro to provide 'an English gentleman tutor' who would 'guide him in the path of duty and enlarge his mind with the story of mankind'. Theo was saddened to discover how wholehearted had been Surabhoji's faith in the judgement and honesty of the British rulers, and rather chagrined to see that the Reverend Arbuthnot had been correct in claiming Bishop Heber had also been consulted.

He was just re-tying the bundle when the red-belted messenger was shown in, bearing a note from Wardle asking Theo to come to his office. The summons being unusual and urgent, Theo promptly obeyed.

'Ah, Mr Lang. Pray sit down. A brandy-pawnee? Make it two, boy. Bad news I'm afraid.'

Theo sat.

'Another bit of pretty business in Poodocottah,' said Wardle at once. 'The Bengali. H. N. Moitra. Dead. Poisoned apparently.'

'Good God!'

'Probably the chief Ranee and her set behind it, don't you think? There were rumours that her sons were in danger, and she's decided to act first.' He strode about, rubbing his head. 'Where's that brandy? Always the same – you'd think he had to swim to France for it. Damnable thing is, I reported to Madras not long ago that things seemed to have settled down nicely in Poo. They'll have it on record and want to know the whys and wherefores again. I've asked Captain Gilbert to go down, but he won't budge. Not a military matter, he says . . . huh!'

'So you've sent for me to go and . . .'

'Precisely. You know the lingo, Lang, and your wife's friendly with Moitra's wife, isn't she? Ah – at last!' He grabbed a glass, drinking greedily. 'They say she's going to commit suttee, incidentally, and that could be another damned complication.'

Theo choked over his first mouthful. 'Suttee! You mean Rukmini Moitra? But she can't! I mean, it's illegal for a start.'

'Not in States ruled by native princes, as you well know. Rum though, I thought it went on only in the north these days, but the Captain told me the chief Ranee threatened it last year when the Raja died, but was dissuaded on the grounds that the British wouldn't approve and she had to stay alive to protect her sons.'

'Oh yes, there's a southern tradition of it too, among the Vijayanagars for example . . . but the devil with all that. What's to be done?' Theo jumped up.

'Done? Well, the Captain and I have agreed that, as the Company can't legally prevent it, it's better to pretend we know nothing until it's too late.' Glancing at Theo's white face, Wardle realised he'd made another mistake. 'Now, now, no point in getting upset about that, when there's this political palaver to explain. Anyway, some ladies do it voluntarily so they'll go straight to paradise with their husbands.'

'But not her – she couldn't, she hated him. Good God, man – Rukmini to burn alive! Come now, you're the Resident, it mustn't be allowed.'

Wardle called for another brandy, cursing himself for

stupidity. 'Firstly, I'm Resident in Tanjore not Poodocottah, and secondly, the Ranee is the Ranee but this Mrs Moitra is of little account.'

'But she's . . . she was . . .'

'Come now, Mr Lang, let's get back to the main issue. I was wondering – and I'd make it well worth your while – if you'd be prepared to set off for Poo, say, tomorrow evening, after this suttee business is over and done with and . . .'

'What *tomorrow*? Rukmini will burn tomorrow?'

'The hour of dawn, usually. A suttee isn't given much time for reflection, mercifully.'

'I won't have it, Wardle! How can you stand aside knowing this act of barbarism is about to be committed on your doorstep?'

Wardle was getting angry. 'Poodocottah isn't on my door-step, Lang, and the plain fact is that, even if I tried, I probably couldn't prevent it. I've no direct authority there and, as I said to the Captain, I could only go down with an escort as a token expression of the Company's displeasure. But it wouldn't work – you know how the natives are, once they've set their hearts on a spectacle.'

'A *spectacle*!'

'That's how people will regard it, I'll be bound – better than a hanging at Newgate.'

'God's truth, Resident. A veritable Pontius Pilate, aren't you, sir?'

'And I say, sir, you're getting beyond yourself,' Wardle's temper shredded. 'We're not confronted with the crucifixion of our Lord on the cross but the voluntary self-immolation of a wife on her husband's funeral pyre.' He paused, light dawning. 'Why, Mr Lang, I seem to remember your arguing, not long ago in my very dining-room, that the British are wrong-headed and arrogant to interfere with such traditional practices – or does my memory play false?'

Theo shivered. 'No, I fear it doesn't, Resident, and I stand before you corrected, even humiliated. But Rukmini Moitra was the one friend of my childhood and that is my only thought at this moment.'

Wardle handed Theo his glass in a vague gesture of

sympathy. 'Well, well, drink up, 'twill fortify you. There's nothing to be done about it. But with regard to the other matter . . .'

Theo stared at him wildly. 'But there *must* be something . . . well, *we*'ll save her, Amelia and I.'

'Far, far better to leave well alone I do assure you.' Wardle wagged his head sagely.

'Well I won't. And Captain Gilbert must come with us. A show of Company strength . . .'

'And who the deuce are you to order out a Company escort for such an errand?'

'An errand of mercy, Resident. Oh please . . . at least don't forbid it. I'll go to the Captain. He's a man of integrity and I'm sure I can persuade him.'

Wardle barked in disbelief. 'I'd as lief persuade the Tiber to flow upstream, Mr Lang. I tried and failed.' This was a confession, for Wardle was theoretically the senior, but in practice when Captain Gilbert set his face against something he was not to be moved.

'And if you do make a mad rush to Poo, Lang, I want you to report back . . .'

He was addressing a space; Theo, wide white trousers flapping against his long shanks, was already running towards the barracks. Wardle finished his drink for him.

Amelia was sewing when her husband ran in, breathless with the urgency of the news and indignation at the captain, who'd brusquely refused any help.

Their only possible course, Theo explained, was to ride through the night in the forlorn hope of saving Rukmini unaided. Initially, Amelia found the situation almost unbelievable but, when the force of it struck her, was as eager as he to go. She rushed off to leave Rolly in Dora's care.

During her absence Durmeen arrived. She talked to Theo, who then hurried back to the barracks.

Alone in his office, the captain was staring at a map of the north-west territories which had hung there since the army of the Indus, made up of regiments from the Bengal and Bombay

Presidencies, had gone marching towards Afghanistan. Now the British-backed ruler, Shah Shuja, was triumphantly installed in his high fortress, and the Afghan expedition seemed so successful that Lord Auckland had been created an earl for having initiated it, while rumours that the occupying forces were thoroughly enjoying themselves in Kabul filtered back to the disgruntled regiments of the Madras Presidency.

Gil glared at the vast brown sweep of the northern ranges, imagining himself leading a band of armed tribesmen through the mountain passes in search of . . . what? Enemies, savage beasts, new territories to conquer? It hardly mattered – anything to be away from here. Since hearing the news of H. N. Moitra's murder, Gil had been trying to reassure himself that it needn't affect him adversely. He felt no inclination to mourn the sly, unsavoury rogue, but he had been an unfailing procurer of boys, host of those clandestine frolics in Poo that were far too risky to enjoy in Tanjore. Wiser, therefore, to forgo in future the flaunting Josef, those moments of liberating self-abandonment. He thought of the words of his mentor Aurelius, that 'coitus is but the attrition of an ordinary base entrail and excretion of a little vile snivel with a certain kind of convulsion . . .' Nevertheless, there were occasions . . . but now, in his present post and with Moitra dead, he must give them up, that was evident. His tour of duty here was about half over, but his record so far was creditable, his reputation unsullied, and he desperately wanted to leave while the going was good.

He was drafting a letter to his superior in Trichy applying for a transfer when Theo burst in with, 'You are to call out an escort immediately to accompany my wife and me to Poo to prevent this suttee from taking place.'

Gil stared at him coldly. 'But you've already asked me that and I've already refused. Are you mad?'

And certainly Theo did look distraught and dishevelled, though he sat down with an odd air of confidence, saying, 'But you won't refuse me *this* time, Captain.'

'Oh? Has the Resident commanded it? As I told you, I take my orders from him.'

'And those only when it suits you. No, he hasn't. But Captain, I take you for an honourable man and I believe that between us we could save a lady from a dreadful death.'

'I don't care to play the knight-errant,' Gil snapped. 'And if a lady wishes to burn herself, I'm not about to say her nay.'

Theo shouted, 'She does not wish to, that I know.'

'You seem to know a lot about her.'

'I told you – she was my childhood friend.'

Gil ran the quill-feather along his fingertips, beginning to enjoy himself. 'Is that *all*?'

'Confound it, Captain, there's no time for these diversions. But no, not quite all. You see, if it hadn't been for me, she'd have made an honourable marriage to a decent man of her own kind. But with that rogue Bengali she's lived in misery for years and now she's to burn with his corpse – God's teeth, man, in all humanity, help me try and save her. If we leave at once . . .'

Gil shook his head. 'I'm sorry, Mr Lang, but you're not shifting me. It's too tricky – Poo being outside Company jurisdiction.'

'But the court knows suttee is an offence in British eyes and if we could prove Rukmini was being coerced . . . if my wife could manage to see her . . .'

'They'd never allow it.'

'With an armed body of men to support her they would.'

'So – your strategy's worked out, is it? Well, I'm not playing and I advise you and your wife to steer well clear.'

Theo drew a sharp breath. 'That's your last word?'

'It is.'

'Then, as my appeal to your better nature has failed, I shall have to resort to your baser one.'

'What the deuce are you talking about?' Gil said calmly, then bit his knuckles to keep his fist under control.

'About your baser nature, Captain, which you habitually indulge during your visits to Poo. Not to mince words, for there's no time – you're a secret pederast.'

'Mr *Lang* . . .'

'And your favourite boy is Josef. Do you want more details

of your "frolics" – George? Or will you call out your troops this instant?'

There was a short silence. Gil asked, 'And if I refuse . . .?'

'A letter giving full chapter and verse of your – sodomy – will be on its way to your superior officer tomorrow.'

Instinctively Gil covered the draft letter on his desk.

'I didn't think you'd resort to blackmail.'

'You gave me no choice.'

Gil looked down at his desk. 'I'll escort you to Poo.'

'Leaving at once, and your men must be armed.'

'And what guarantee have I that you won't peach on me afterwards?'

'Good Lord, man, I didn't want to press you this far. But I suppose my honour as a gentleman – your might-have-been friend – is your only guarantee.'

'It's very likely this attempt will fail with or without my escort. And you still promise not to tell anyone – ever?'

Theo stood straight, looking at him. 'No one. Ever. Captain.'

As he made for the door, Gil asked, 'But the someone who told you also knows. Who was it, my might-have-been friend?'

Theo hesitated, but his nature veered instinctively towards honesty.

'Durmeen. Josef's family is related to her son's wife. Apparently he often regales them with titbits about the Poo frolics. But come, we're wasting precious time.'

'God rot those bleeding chee-chees,' Gil snarled, then took hold of himself. 'It will mean riding through the night. Can your wife manage it?'

'Can she just! She's not a farmer's daughter for nothing.'

Theo hurried out; the captain stared at the paper before him, thinking of Josef, of what intimacies had been bandied about to amuse the local chee-chees – even the admission of his real name, even, probably, his subsequent giving of the Raja's ring. Gilbert had felt the occasion somewhat significant – a faint re-echoing of that earlier ring-giving in Burma – and he'd implored Josef to guard it carefully. But the boy had teased him, pretending to swallow it, hiding it about his person, tempting Gil to come and struggle for it . . . Gil's cheeks burned as he tore the draft letter into shreds. This was no time to draw upon himself the attention of his superiors.

Amelia found the ride to Poodocottah exhilarating. Not for a long while had she ridden so far and so fast, her body confidently attuned to the beat of the horse's hooves, wishing her stay-at-home brothers could see her – cantering at night through unknown Indian territory. But as they drew near to their destination, the urgency of their mission reminded her that once, when she was young, her nightgown caught fire from a candle and seared her leg. The memory of that agony, the dread that Rukmini would burn alive from head to toe, made her feel sick, and she spurred her horse faster.

On the edge of the town they halted while the men received Gil's orders.

Theo drew Amelia aside. 'We've decided on the plan of action and everything has to depend on you. First, we get our men inside the palace and then demand you see Rukmini to confirm that she is willing to die.'

'And if so, there's nothing to be done?'

'She *isn't* willing. She *can't* be. But you may have to wring the truth from her. The priests will be goading her on – don't argue with them. Just bring her out quickly; take them by surprise. Act as if it were a military attack, the Captain advises . . .'

Gil's voice interrupted them. 'Ready, Mr Lang? Time's getting short.'

They rode quietly through Poodocottah's dark streets, coming to a halt outside the palace gate where surprised guards scrambled sleepily for their weapons. Ignoring them, Gil knocked on the gate with his whip, demanding entrance in the Company's name. The gate creaked open; Gil and Theo rode in alone. Outside, lamps were lit in nearby houses and a small crowd of men gathered to stare at the intruders. The foreign woman on horseback was the main attraction, and they soon decided she was another recent widow brought by her relatives to commit suttee also. Eventually the gate opened and the armed escort pressed inside, forming a solid phalanx in the central courtyard.

Theo hurried to Amelia. 'They've agreed you can see her briefly – after a deal of argument. This girl will conduct you. Oh Amelia, please don't fail!'

'I'll do my best,' she whispered, her throat drying with apprehension as she was led away to the zenana.

Many palace underlings were already astir, for today was to provide the exciting culmination of yesterday's preparations. Wood-cutters, carpenters and labourers had raised a huge funeral pyre topped with a small platform at the burning ghat near the river bank. The processional route between it and the palace had been swept and H. N. Moitra's corpse washed, shaved, anointed with oils and garlanded with flowers in readiness for his last journey along it. His mouth was stuffed with betel leaves and equally dumb were the tongues of those performing these rites, though their heads buzzed with the questions: 'Who did it?' and 'Why?'

As a gentleman of the court, albeit an unpopular one, the Bengali merited a processional guard of honour, so soldiers had polished their accoutrements while court trumpeters had practised their funeral music at full blast, for it must be loud enough to drown the widow's screams – not to mention any last prophecies she might make which, in such fraught circumstances, were bound to be true and probably ominous. Rukmini's maid, Mangalam, had laid out her finest sari, veils and jewellery which she would wear for the procession but which would be stripped from her when she ascended the pyre. And, in anticipation of that dreadful moment, the court ladies had rent the night watches with their wailing laments, gathering round Rukmini in support and sympathy. Most assiduous, too, were the brahmin priests who filled her aching head with murmurings about the transience of earthly joys, the virtue and sanctity attached to the act of suttee, and the paradisian delights awaiting those who committed it. They didn't stress, for she already knew, how joyless her lot in life would be should she cling to it – a childless widow doomed to perpetual acts of mourning and self-abasement, barred like a spectre from all feasts and festive occasions.

These were the alternatives Rukmini faced as she sat

surrounded by the priests and women, staring through an ornamental grille at a patch of chequered night sky beyond. For several hours she had neither turned her eyes from that one sight nor spoken a word. As a suttee, she had eaten nothing since her husband's death, and it was difficult to judge the extent of her awareness.

When Amelia was shown in, many eyes turned on her, glittering with startled anger, but she in the centre continued to stare out and beyond, until Amelia gently spoke.

'Rukmini, I'm here.'

Then Rukmini's eyes came into focus clouded with hopelessness and terror.

'I've come to you as a friend,' Amelia began, speaking clearly and slowly. 'Theophilus and I know you don't truly wish to suffer this terrible death. It is against nature, Rukmini, against all human feeling and you must refuse to do it. Refuse now, this minute, and you shall live.'

Lakshmi, sitting beside Rukmini, took it upon herself to shout a translation of these words to the priests, who began muttering indignantly. Rukmini whispered something and, as Amelia bent close to her, Lakshmi pulled her back roughly. 'Suttee should not be touched by you. She is already purified. A holy sacrifice. That is our custom.'

Amelia stared at her hostile face. 'But she must wish the sacrifice for herself – that is the law. And there's a troop of Company men in the courtyard come to make sure the law is not broken. Send someone to see, if you don't believe me.'

Lakshmi looked astonished, then muttered an order to a servant.

Again Amelia spoke to Rukmini. 'You heard that?'

'But there is no other course for me,' Rukmini said distantly.

'There is – I've come to take you away from here. Truly, there are soldiers outside and no one dare stop us. Please come, Rukmini! Theo can't bear you to suffer this terrible death.'

Rukmini glanced fearfully at the priests who were uttering prayers and exhortations, trying to elbow Amelia aside. But she stood firm, ignoring them.

'You don't want this to happen, do you, Rukmini? You know you don't. You can't. Look at me straight . . . Yes, I can see it in your eyes. Say what is in your eyes, please Rukmini, and I can save you.'

Rukmini whimpered, 'No, I don't, don't want, but . . .'

'There! She has spoken!' Amelia turned to face the priests just as the servant rushed in crying that the courtyard was indeed full of Company soldiers. Seizing the moment, Amelia grabbed Rukmini's wrist and tried to pull her upright. 'Come, dear – now, quickly!'

'But I *cannot*! It is too much, Amelia . . . Please. Wait! I can't go with nothing. What about my clothes, my jewellery?'

It seemed a mundane consideration for the moment and Amelia snapped, 'Tell Mangalam to bundle them together instantly.'

As Mangalam hurried out, Amelia sensed the reassertion of hostility against her. She should have dragged Rukmini away at once – what matter clothes and jewellery? Defiantly, she tightened her grip on the Indian woman's wrist as the priests pressed closer, ordering Lakshmi to translate their anger.

'They ask by what right you, a foreigner, intrude on our religious ceremonies?'

'Tell them I have the right of the law on my side.'

'They say you do not. Poodocottah is not ruled by your British Company. They say you have bullied her to change her mind. Until you came she was ready to make the sacrifice.'

'But I asked her and she said no. Say it again Rukmini – please.' Amelia shook Rukmini's wrist gently, and she whispered a few words in Tamil at which a priest growled sullenly.

'You see? She is not willing and the burning of an unwilling woman is a kind of murder. But Lakshmi, tell them I know they are not murderers, they are educated and civilised men, so why should they want this barbarous act to be committed?'

'It was the wish of her husband,' Lakshmi said. 'He was Bengali and watched his revered mother commit the glorious act in Calcutta years ago. His mother's memory remained sacred to him and his last wish was for his wife to follow in her virtuous path.'

'But Rukmini is not a Bengali . . . Oh Lakshmi, surely you – a tender-hearted woman – could not wish this dreadful agony on another?'

Lakshmi shrugged, looking down at Rukmini who remained crouched on a cushion, head bent, Amelia still holding her drooping hand.

'It has happened before many times – and what is the purpose of this woman's life now? She has no husband, no children. Why so much fuss about one wretched, barren female?'

'In the eyes of our Christian God all humans are of equal value, and are worth saving for His sake.'

As Amelia rapped out this well-learned litany, Rukmini raised her head and spoke clearly in English.

'You hear, Lakshmi? "Equal in the sight of God," as the lady missionary told us. I thought of it often – in those long years of serving and obeying a vile man of evil habits, as if he were a superior being.'

She rose, staring with tremulous defiance at the priests, who seemed about to close in on her.

'Come Rukmini – *now!*' Amelia pulled her towards the doorway just as Mangalam returned with two bundles. For an indecisive minute no one moved, then the priests, the women and the guards at the entrance fell back to let them pass.

Mangalam led the way along dark passages and stairs to the edge of the main courtyard where the Company's escort sat silent on their steeds, weapons glinting in the flare of several torches.

Amelia released her hold on Rukmini. 'Follow me by yourself. Don't hesitate.' Rukmini did hesitate; then, drawing her veil tightly over her head, prepared to follow.

The main courtyards of Indian palaces are large; Amelia was to say later that the largest in the country was the one they crossed that night, she tensely aware of countless watching eyes, behind her the slide of footsteps which she prayed would not falter, the clank of unseen weapons, the distant wail of the zenana women. Then Theo was at her side.

He held out his arms. Rukmini cowered.

Theo fell back, understanding. He turned to his wife. 'I've hired a palki.'

As she was helped into the vehicle, Rukmini's control broke and she fell forward half-fainting on to the cushions, Mangalam crawling in beside her with the bundles.

Theo hurried up with a brandy flask. 'Here, make her drink this. Tell her it's foreign medicine.'

Amelia pressed the neck of the flask against Rukmini's mouth, forcing her to drink. She spluttered, swallowed, choked, swallowed again and later was to say that the sting of that fiery liquid on her tongue was like the burn of returning life instead of death. Never before had a drop of alcohol passed her lips; never before had anything tasted so intensely desirable.

First light spread across the eastern sky as they rode through the town and past groups of men moving towards the river.

'They're in for a disappointment,' Gil chuckled to Amelia. 'Funerals are everyday, but a suttee would have been an event.'

She shuddered. 'But at what cost! Oh Captain, I want to thank you most profoundly for all you've done. Quite honestly, I don't think I'd have succeeded without the support of your escort outside, making the Company's displeasure very plain.' She beamed such sincere, innocent gratitude at him that he was caught speechless. 'I thought Theo would prevail upon you,' she rushed on. 'I told him you're not nearly as black as you're sometimes painted – if you'll forgive my saying so.'

He coughed into his hand, concealing a laugh. 'Madam, I thank you for your gratitude, but it may be misjudged. Let me warn you never to assume you have fathomed the degrees of blackness in a man's heart.'

He rode on ahead, pleased to leave her puzzled and also to be safely away from Poodocottah without, as it were, his past catching up on him. He'd been a reckless fool and, as he

stared ahead into the blue clarity of morning, felt exhilarated
by the hope of the pure life he would lead henceforward.

Theo, riding further ahead, was even more exultant. As he
watched the early light flooding over the fields, he murmured
rapturously the words of the Persian poet,

'"Out of the chaos of the black, there arises silently,
imperceptibly, irresistibly the glorious, the blushing, the
beautiful, the amber-clouded, opal-shredded, amethyst-
bedappled Dawn. Oh Dawn how I do love thee! For is not all
sweetness collected in the heifer, the Red One of the Dawn."'

CHAPTER SEVEN

Theophilus stood on the library balcony staring down into the courtyard. It was but forty-eight hours since he'd seen the Resident's red-belted messenger arrive with his summons, but it seemed immeasurably longer. During that interval he'd been thrown by the scruff of the neck into an urgent emotional dimension that he didn't usually inhabit. The fate from which he'd helped to rescue Rukmini was of a kind honoured by ancient Hindu religious tradition, and he winced now, remembering his earlier pronouncements on the subject. At the time they'd seemed perfectly sound, but he'd been deceiving himself for they had been purely theoretical, untried by any direct experience. And he hid his shamed laughter, knowing all the arguments he'd ever adduced on the subject had proved totally irrelevant compared with the passionate fervor that had carried him forward.

He paced about in a kind of wonderment that he had gone about it with such a fierce directness, but he regretted nothing, indeed felt himself better able to understand some aspects of human behaviour that had formerly mystified him. Years ago, in Calcutta, one of his friends, a peaceable enough fellow usually, had unhesitatingly killed a man in a duel over an Italian actress; another had been imprisoned for embezzlement even though he'd been a pillar of the Church. To Theo, such frailties and contradictions had seemed beyond comprehension, but yesterday he had blackmailed, threatened, would have killed to save Rukmini's life. So that was how it happened; he felt older and wiser, but more vulnerable and apprehensive – an emotional combination that was new to him.

Realising from his clerk's covert grin that he, and probably

148

the whole city, knew what had happened, he sat at his desk and pretended to occupy himself with some translations of Hindu proverbs. One leapt at him from the page: 'I have put my head into the mortar; no use dreading the sound of the pestle.' He was still contemplating that when a summons came from the Raja. He obeyed, in dread of the pestle's imminent thud.

But Sevaji's attention was seldom drawn to the latest gossip and was now fixed on the just-completed model of his new temple. Shutters in the colonnaded hall had been pulled back to let sunshine glow on the painted and golden miniatures of walls, galleries, courtyards, gopurams and deities reposing in their niches. Courtiers stood round the table expressing fulsome admiration which Sevaji, seated at its head, was graciously accepting. Theo went to pay his respects.

'It is most beautiful, sire.'

'Ah – there you are, Mr Lang. Yes, my craftsmen have done well and today we celebrate our pride and pleasure in the work. The site for the temple itself has been cleared and closed off and now the architects and builders can begin. Soon I shall visit the holy place, the priests will bless it and I shall plant a pot of seed in the earth so the temple may grow strong and straight. It will be another joyous occasion and I shall require your presence, Mr Lang.'

'I shall be most happy.' Theo bowed.

Fruits and cakes were circulating and the architects were flower-garlanded with as much flattering ceremony as if the actual building was already finished. One of them seized Theo's arm and propelled him round the table, pointing out how every detail had been thought of – even to a store for processional fly-whisks and umbrellas, and a hut for the elephant-keeper's boy. Theo murmured appropriate praise, but his pleasure in the creation was alloyed by an undertow of misgiving. Curse people like Nicholas Rundell and Dora Arbuthnot, with their self-righteous talk of drains and orphans and other worthier causes into which Sevaji's resources should be channelled! Feeling confused and tired, he left as soon as he decently could and hurried home in hope of actually seeing Rukmini.

* * *

149

But on that day and for a considerable time, Rukmini remained a veiled and withdrawn presence in his household. Her narrow escape from death had deeply harrowed her and, although she'd desperately wanted to live, she now suffered pangs of guilt and shame. During the hours following her husband's death she'd fought to prepare herself for the most extreme suffering but, in the event, had suffered nothing. It was a gulf her mind and body could scarcely bridge, and she sometimes held a finger close to a lighted candle as a reminder of what agonies need not, after all, be endured. From childhood she'd been schooled to obedience and self-abnegation, and that she had both prompted and participated in this defiant act of self-rescue seemed unbelievable. To Lakshmi's last scornful question, 'Why so much fuss about one wretched, barren female?' she had no certain answer.

And there was another uncertainty that plagued her, of a more shadowy, sinister kind that she scarcely dared admit to herself. For had she not devoutly wished that H. N. would die? And had she not voiced that wish more than once to Mangalam and other trusted intimates who shared her loathing of him? It was by no means inconceivable that they, acting in secret and in good faith, had made her wish come true. For there was a puzzle about her husband's death. Immediately afterwards, rumours began circulating that those most likely to have caused it seemed genuinely surprised and mystified. For the heated rivalry between the two court factions had already cooled, and H. N. posed little threat. Rukmini, removed from all contact with the court, had no way of knowing whether the mystery had been solved, but in the dark, lonely hours she brooded on poison and on the narrow-faced man whose baleful eyes probed her dreams.

Nor were Rukmini's daylight hours easy, for she found herself in very different circumstances from the sheltered, pampered women's quarters that had been both prison and protection for many years. Now, feeling vulnerable and anxious, like a long-caged creature deprived of its familiar bars, she converted the Lang's guest-room into her private refuge. Its ever-shaded atmosphere smelt of hair-oil and sandalwood, its only sound the quiet padding about of devoted Mangalam. When Amelia and Durmeen came to visit this little zenana, they would chat lightly, hoping to draw Rukmini out, but she responded only in mumbled, empty courtesies. At length, wearying of this, Amelia tried a more direct approach.

'Rukmini,' she began firmly, 'what were you thinking about when I saw you in the palace on that dreadful night? Perhaps it would help to tell us about it?'

Rukmini focused her distant eyes and spoke in a quick whisper. 'Thinking? I don't know exactly. It seemed as if I'd sat there for long days and nights staring at the piece of sky I could see through the grille. I was thinking – yes, I remember – how beautiful it was, knowing I shouldn't see another night fall. But that was what I'd come to want – not to see or feel ever again. I couldn't believe everything the priests told me about the joys of paradise, but it was only the time *before* death that terrified me. I had screamed and cried and fought and argued with them before you arrived, but they had fixed me with their glittering eyes and worn me down. I hadn't been allowed to eat or drink from the hour of my husband's death and I was feeling as empty as an old, thrown-away pot. Then they gave me a little liquid to calm me, they said, and it did. I couldn't quite imagine the flames after that and lost all feeling – which was a blessing.'

'Probably a drug,' Durmeen said. 'But it would have worn off soon enough.'

'But didn't any of the women plead for your life?' Amelia asked.

'Oh, they sympathised and wept and wailed, but they were afraid of the priests' power and I was of no particular account to them. And I was born at a very unlucky moment, you see – an astrologer told my father so, and I kept thinking there was no point in trying to resist the influence of the stars. And worst of all was being the Bengali's widow, which everyone held against me.' She paused and then plunged on, wanting at last to tell everything. 'He was a vile man. I shared his bed for a while when we first married, but I could tell he loathed me.'

'Don't be silly, Rukmini, of course he didn't.'

She turned away, embarrassed, muttering, 'But he *did*. He . . . he preferred boys, you see.'

'Boys? You mean to . . . Oh my dear, how very horrible! But that's called sodomy, isn't it?' Amelia turned to Durmeen for confirmation, having never uttered the word before.

Durmeen nodded.

'My husband made me pregnant once,' Rukmini continued, 'but I lost the baby – a boy. And from then on he would have nothing to do with me. People despised him for that and for his filthy habits, and I was dishonoured also. And they still blamed me for being childless – because I'd killed a snake in a former life, the old women used to say.'

'But it was all so unfair!' Amelia protested.

'Well, in this country a woman's position depends entirely on her husband and her sons, you know. With such a husband and no sons I was seldom allowed to take part in festivals or family celebrations. But don't imagine all the women of the court were so unhappy, Amelia. I didn't fit in, you see. I used to climb to an upper tower sometimes and look out over the paddies and wish – oh, so desperately – that I was a humble peasant woman, who could work in the fields and go to the wells and bazaars . . . And any peasant would have made a better husband than H. N. Moitra!'

Amelia, close to sympathetic tears, said, 'But at least that's all in the past now, Rukmini, and you can go wherever you choose. Why don't you come to the bazaar with me tomorrow?'

But that was a mistake; Rukmini stared at her in alarm, then lay down and pulled a quilt over her head, shutting out the awful prospect of so much empty liberty.

'Let's leave her,' Durmeen whispered, continuing as they went out, 'I don't suppose she can accept that she's not suffering the full penalties of widowhood. In the palace she'd have had that lovely hair shaved off, you know, and never be allowed to wear pretty clothes or jewels, nor even look at another man. It's a cruel code for womenfolk, this Hinduism. I used to say as much to Bayard, but he wouldn't think of it from that point of view.'

'Nor did Theo, till recently.'

'Oh, that's typical men's way, isn't it? Lots of high-flown theories that blow straight out of the window in practice when someone you really care for is involved!'

Amelia was rather startled. 'I suppose so – though I don't know. I mean, Theo only knew her as a childhood friend.'

'Of course – just a manner of speaking.' Durmeen pursed her lips; she knew from Bayard exactly what had once passed between Theo and Rukmini, and had resolved neither to mention nor forget it.

Mindful of this, Durmeen was content for Rukmini to remain in her self-created zenana, but to the Langs it seemed unnatural. Theo was constantly tantalised by Rukmini's unseen proximity, and Amelia was rather affronted and disappointed that, after all their efforts, she seemed to prefer a cloistered solitude. So, gently but firmly, they eventually persuaded Rukmini to participate in the everyday life of the household, though it was long before she could be induced actually to share a meal with Theo. On the first occasion, Amelia had almost to pull her into the dining-room.

'Oh come, Rukmini – he won't bite you!' She was half-laughing.

Theo stood at the table's head and they exchanged the traditional Indian style of greeting.

'Now you are really with us. Welcome to our humble table, Rukmini Moitra. I am so happy to see you here. I didn't imagine I ever would.' He spoke in her native tongue to put her at ease and she replied, eyes lowered.

'And I didn't hope to see you anywhere – ever again.'

'But come – you must look at me in the European way. See – I am a balding old man now!'

'And I a wrinkled old woman!'

They smiled at each other in denial of their words, although, in truth, each was rather shocked by the other's appearance.

'So let us sit and eat. For this is your home now and our ways must be your ways.'

Theo gestured to a chair, but she stood behind it, saying in a formal whisper, 'First, I must thank you from my heart's depth, Mr Lang, for what you have done. I am eternally in your debt, and your wife's, also.'

He shrugged awkwardly. 'Oh, it's nothing. I am still Theophilus, as I always was. Now, please be seated. I have bought wine to celebrate the occasion though I doubt I can persuade you to take even a sip?'

She shuddered at the very idea, but tried to eat, relieved no knife or fork had been laid for her. Both she and Theo found themselves tongue-tied at first, leaving Amelia to liven up proceedings.

'Now tell me – when was it exactly that you two last saw each other?' she questioned gaily, and their eyes met in an instant of collusion.

'Just before I went to England,' Theo replied, 'and before Sevaji's wedding. Was it a grand festival, Rukmini?'

'I . . . I think so. I didn't see much of it. I . . . I wasn't very well,' she faltered, which he recognised as an euphemism for 'in disgrace'. 'But it went on for days and nights – music and dancing and fireworks and the bridegroom riding about the streets resplendent in his robes and jewels.'

Theo chuckled. 'Ah, His Highness always loves a show!'

'And now you work for him. What is he like as a grown man, a ruler?'

'Grown man? Well, in his fashion, I suppose. But he has none of his father's curiosity or willpower. He is very traditional and religious in his thinking – but this may be because he is persuaded into it. He is a pliable branch and not happy I fear – pushed this way and that by ambitious, unscrupulous people, including Company officials. I feel sad for him. He is a victim of – well, history I suppose.'

Amelia, who'd been trying to follow their Tamil, asked, 'A victim of what, did you say?'

'History, dear.'

She wrinkled her nose. 'But aren't we all?'

'A nice philosophical point. But perhaps men like Sevaji who have power thrust upon them are more so than most. He should have been a private man – a brahmin astrologer would suit him excellently. Then he could keep changing his mind in accordance with whatever the stars foretold each day and not be accused of vacillation and weakness as he constantly is.'

They laughed and Rukmini, feeling easier, was emboldened to ask about the years Theo had spent in England and Calcutta. He answered willingly enough but asked nothing in return, for he rightly conjectured that she had no joyous tales to tell.

Indeed, Rukmini was so unaccustomed to positive joy that the several occasions for it in her new life took her by surprise. She and Amelia spent many pleasurable afternoons in mutual language teaching, and sometimes Rolly joined in, proudly showing off his knowledge of both English and Tamil. Rukmini soon grew fond of the child, and he took to her in a way he never had to Durmeen, who rather frightened him. When the half-Portuguese woman cuddled him, her ample body smelt overpoweringly of sickly rosewater; her mouth, when she kissed him, was an almost toothless hole; and he could see the darker streaks in her cheeks where her thick white powder had cracked in the heat. It was as if she wore a mask, and he imagined that one day she might rip it off and reveal a bulbous devil-face beneath. Rukmini, by contrast, was cool, olive, slender, all-of-a-piece, and he soon discovered ways of playing one doting lady off against the other. Then there was his ayah to command, his mother to love and, much admired, Rolly took to strutting about with his toy sword, bellowing orders.

'You're getting above yourself, Master Rolly,' his mother smiled one morning, returning from a visit to Doctor Cauldwell. 'But in a few months you'll have a little brother or sister to take you down a peg or two. Isn't that exciting?'

Rolly's face puckered doubtfully, but everyone else welcomed the prospect of another child. To Rukmini especially, Rolly's solitary state seemed positively unnatural and the Langs' house quiet, humble and stark compared to the zenana at Poodocottah, full of the noise of children, women and servants laughing and scolding, their bangles and anklets in a constant jangle.

Deprived of all this familiar Indian bustle, Rukmini was delighted when her married cousin, Parvati, renewed contact with her. She used often to visit Parvati's house in the Big Fort, where some of the minor ladies of the court gathered for tea and gossip. Parvati's widowed sister-in-law, Belveena, was she with whom the Portuguese bandmaster had fallen so wildly and inappropriately in love. He was stout and middle-aged, Parvati told Rukmini, giggling at the memory, and it had been a rare treat to see him below their balcony at all hours serenading his love with flute, violin, pipe or even bugle – for he was a versatile musician. Belveena had been almost won over when he was suddenly sent packing and wished now she had succumbed sooner, for, though still young and pretty, she'd have no other chance of a man.

Condemned to desolate widowhood, Belveena became obsessively, sulkily devout, and Rukmini sometimes accompanied her to the Fort temple, though she found little consolation there. Nor could she expect it, Belveena told her spitefully, for neither her appearance nor her behaviour befitted a proper widow, and no wonder the sharp-eyed priests seemed to curse her very existence. Veiling her unshaven head from them in shame, guilt and fear, Rukmini protested she could not conform to the orthodox rituals while living in a European household. It would have made everyone most uncomfortable, and what a fright she'd have looked to Theo bereft of her hair and jewels – though that consideration she admitted to herself only in the empty nights, along with other unworthy, troubling thoughts.

Thus estranged from her native faith, Rukmini eventually accepted Amelia's invitation to accompany her to St Peter's Church, where she sat unobtrusively near the door with the air of one poised for instant flight. The Reverend Arbuthnot soon spied her, however, and caustically remarked to his wife that, if Mr Lang had known he was snatching a possible Christian convert from the flames, he might have left her to burn. But Dora, reprimanding him for his lack of charity, saw Theo's action as proof of being less 'irredeemably Hinduised' than she'd feared, and warned her spouse that to taunt him on the subject of his inconsistencies might only redirect his sympathies to that native idolatry from which he might yet be saved. So Arbuthnot, who frequently took his wife's advice without admitting it, denied himself the pleasure of reminding Theo of his earlier pronouncements on the subject of suttee and related customs.

So, too, did Hubert Wardle, for whom the spectacle of a man failing to practise his theories was not in the least surprising – indeed, it further justified his own lifelong practice of avoiding theory altogether. And the report of the affair that he dispatched to the Madras bigwigs skated quickly over the matter of Moitra's inexplicable murder but brought fully to their attention the no small share of credit due to himself and Captain Gilbert for saving the poor widow from a barbarous death. For this he received commendation and a sum of money for expenses, which he put away in an envelope marked 'Mr Lang'. He felt sure Theo would soon find himself in debt again, and the money would come in handy for services he would then render to the Residency. It seemed a fair enough bargain.

Counting himself fortunate thus far, Theo was puzzled to hear nothing sarcastic from Nicholas Rundell, until a chit arrived from his wife explaining that they had been in Trichy where, after 'much false hoping and fussing' her pregnancy had been confirmed. Would the Langs come to dine next week in celebration of her news? And would Mrs Lang come early, so they could enjoy a little feminine gossip first? Theo favoured refusal, claiming that Rundell only wanted to grind his tongue in the dust of his earlier arguments, but Amelia overruled him. The invitation was an olive branch it would be churlish to refuse, and besides, she looked forward to reminding Catherine Rundell she was not the only English-woman in Tanjore capable of pregnancy.

As Amelia approached the Rundell's verandah on the appointed day, Sarah Murphy darted out and grabbed her arm.

'There you are, ma'am. A word with you, please. She's asleep.' She jerked her head housewards.

'Oh Sarah, I do hope you're keeping well? I hear you're expecting another little one?'

Sarah's narrow face twisted sulkily. 'That's the trouble,

ma'am. However am I to manage? Murphy gives me nothing – except more babies.'

Amelia put an arm on her bony shoulder. 'Sarah dear, I'm so sorry. Can't your parents help you?'

'Pa's dead and Ma's gone home. *She's* happy now at least, living in a little cottage in Finchingfield with her sister.'

'Why, that's quite near my family at Thaxted.'

'Is it? I know nothing of it, ma'am, being born here. But I'd love to see the cool green countryside Ma used to tell me about.'

'You will one day Sarah, I'm sure.'

Sarah squinted at her dubiously. 'Well, what I wanted to ask, ma'am, was, if you've any lace or silk stockings that wants mending or cuffs and collars for starching? I use arrowroot, ma'am, which is much better than rice-water. The natives ruin your fine stuffs, but I'm ever so good and careful. I learned young, doing it for the officers' wives at Pa's old station.'

Amelia bit her lip. 'But, Sarah, I don't really have . . .'

'Ooh, I know you don't flounce about in a lot of finery like her in there – and she pays me next to nothing. But that dhobi of yours is a rogue. He hires out your best dresses to the chee-chee girls to wear for an evening. Did you know that? So why don't you let me keep them nice and proper? Just to earn an extra bit now there's another bairn on the way.'

'Is that really true? Oh dear, Sarah! But the baby's your husband's responsibility – he must be made to pay.'

'Oh, him!' she snorted furiously, twisting her faded apron in her hands as if it were her spouse's neck. 'He's back in solitary – so violent drunk they had to carry him there in a strait-jacket. What's the use of a man like that, I ask you?'

'Is that you, Mrs Lang?' Catherine's clear, high tone reached them.

Sarah clutched imploringly at Amelia; she smelled of sweat, babies and stale curry.

'Well, you can have my dresses, Sarah. Come and see me in a few days.'

'Tomorrow, ma'am. I'll come tomorrow.'

She shrank away and Amelia, removing her bonnet, went into the parlour.

Catherine was posed on the *chaise-longue*. 'Ah, Mrs Lang, good afternoon. Do sit down. Did I hear you talking to someone?'

'Sarah Murphy, yes.'

'Oh, she's a perfect pest that girl – always whining. But good with the goffering iron, I'll give her that. She's pregnant again, as you see. Yet she can scarcely feed the two she has.'

'But I don't suppose it's her fault.'

'Well it's absurd all the same, and I've been trying so hard to have a baby. I've had two miscarriages already and must be very careful. So excuse me for not moving.'

Amelia smiled. 'And Doctor Cauldwell confirmed my pregnancy the other week. So that makes three of us in the same boat!'

'Oh, I wouldn't want to share a boat with Sarah – phew!' Catherine held her nose. 'But are you really? Well . . . congratulations. My son will be just a wee bit older than yours, then – what fun!'

'But I'd prefer a daughter this time.'

'Would you really? Not such a good playmate for my boy. You see, Nicholas says the Indians believe that if the future parents keep talking about the baby as a boy, then it will be. So we do.'

'I wonder if the same applies to girls?'

'Ah, tea at last. Put it there and pour, boy. Girls? I don't suppose any Indian ever tried it!'

'In which case,' Amelia pointed out, 'if their theory worked, no girls would ever be born!'

Catherine looked vexed. 'I suppose not – so perhaps they do want daughters occasionally, but they certainly don't rate females very highly . . . Talking of that, we managed to lure Captain Gilbert to dinner the other night. Do you see much of him?'

'I'm afraid not. He's avoided us entirely since our expedition to Poo. I can't think why.'

'Well he keeps to himself, doesn't he? So lonely – the life of a barracks bachelor. I asked him more or less straight out if

159

he held such a low opinion of our sex that none could ever suit him. He hinted at an early lost love. What a waste of a handsome man, isn't it? He's off to Madras on local leave. I twitted him that it was to find a wife at last, but Nicholas thinks he's going to tackle the top brass for another posting. Well, I only hope he doesn't get it! His replacement would probably be married and army wives are so dreadfully low toss – always screeching with laughter and drinking and flirting with every man in sight, except their own, of course!'

In her pause for breath, Amelia asked, 'I suppose you saw a lot of them in Bangalore?'

'I should say – far too much. Still it was fun there: dances, parties and picnics always going on and the number of auction sales, you wouldn't believe. People always moving on or dying or something. We picked up some good furniture bargains but it was far too expensive to cart them here – and we couldn't even bring our little buggy. So now we're reduced to stuffy old palkis and local furniture – just cobbled together. Look at those chairs – they crack in the heat till they fall apart.'

'Perhaps if you kept them well oiled,' Amelia murmured.

Catherine, however, wasn't listening; she hadn't conversed with anyone except Nicholas for days, and he always refused to listen to her 'domestic tittle-tattle'. 'We did bring that folding what-not, thank goodness, so we have somewhere for display.'

Its shelves were neatly arrayed with ornaments – bronze figurines, family miniatures, marble heads with a Grecian look.

'It's all very cosy,' Amelia reassured her, including in her praise the primrose-washed walls, hung with watercolours of the English landscape and a grand print of 'The *Wellington* off the Dover Coast', the pert chintz frills of the punkah and the floral border of the Axminster carpet. The whole was indeed a tribute to three generations of English women who had learned the tricks of creating and preserving a 'little bit of Home' in this inimical country and climate.

'And we did bring our good silver,' Catherine rattled on. 'It doesn't show to much advantage here and there's no one

. . .' she was about to say 'worth bringing it out for' but that sounded impolite, if true.

'Oh yes, Durmeen suggested I tell you that it's known about in the bazaar and you should guard it carefully.'

'Oh, we've had long experience of keeping the light-fingered natives at bay! Durmeen, you say? That chee-chee woman? You're very kind to her, Mrs Lang. What with her and the Hindu suttee you must feel a bit overcrowded?'

She peeped at Amelia, who held her gaze calmly. 'On the contrary, Mrs Rundell, I'm grateful for the company, and shall be more so in the next few months when I'm less active.'

'Well, well – we must go to the Trichy military hospital together a month ahead of our confinements, at least. Trichy may be a hole but not such a *deep* one as this! And I've actually found a native tailor there who can make up decent bonnets. You must keep spare ribbons for them wrapped in flannel against the monsoon mildew by the way, did you know? And . . .'

Amelia, battered but determined, made her one point. 'I don't think I'll be going to Trichy, Mrs Rundell. It's much more expensive and . . .'

'Oh lud, you mustn't trust yourself to that drunken old bungler, Cauldwell. He nearly let poor Sarah die last time and she's living in dread of the next.'

'Perhaps *she* should go to Trichy, then.'

'Imagine her husband bothering to arrange such a thing! No, she'll have to take her chance here, but we ladies must certainly go. We'll be company for each other, too. Trichy is full of army wives and there's no one with much conversation. I'll speak to your husband about it, shall I? Where can the men have got to?'

As Catherine went to the verandah to look for them, Amelia inhaled a distinct whiff of camphor and realised Catherine was wearing one of her best lace-trimmed gowns, usually kept in store. She herself was clad in short-sleeved muslin – in keeping with her own makeshift-seeming parlour. But what did that matter? she chided herself, remembering the recent letter from Joanna, who was now in Manchester helping destitute girls. Severe Joanna trusted Amelia was not squandering her time and money on idle frivolities and luxuries in the manner of Anglo-Indian women. Amelia shifted uncomfortably, pricked by the scorn with which Joanna would regard Mrs Rundell – who at that moment returned, clapping her hands.

'The masters are coming at last! Bring the glasses, boy, on the *silver* tray.' She resumed her seat, patting her hair in place. 'He *will* use the painted tin trays because they don't need cleaning. But they're so dreadfully vulgar, aren't they?'

'I use wooden ones – quite cheap in the bazaar.'

'And you can be sure they'll collapse with more than two cups on them! Ah gentlemen, here you are – Mr Lang,' she extended her hand.

Theophilus acknowledged her stonily. It was clear to the women their menfolk had again been at cross-purposes, which Catherine, at least, had anticipated and warned her husband against. Nevertheless, Nicholas had insisted on showing Theo the plans for the irrigation scheme drawn up by the army surveyor from Trichy.

'Here – see,' Nicholas had spread the plan on his office table. 'More water must be directed to the river Cauvery from this branch here. As things are, these villages suffer terribly from either drought or floods because the river is silted up at its head. Then there must be a bridge at this crossing where ferries get stuck in the dry season and swamped in the wet. Those little islands in the middle are infested with alligators, and many a meal of ferry-passenger they've enjoyed, apparently!' Theo muttered vague approval. 'But we'll also need to dam the main current near the city – here.'

'Isn't that the Raja's territory? Couldn't it be further downstream?'

'No. River's wider, more expensive. And it will benefit his brahmin villages, too – where half the water-courses are choked because no one oversees the cleaning of them.'

Theo stared at the plan with its shaded areas and coloured markers, remembering a very different scheme he'd recently seen in the palace, marked with painted towers and golden deities. Both were intended for exactly the same spot. The idea amused him and he chuckled.

Nicholas scowled. 'What's so funny?'

'Oh nothing – nothing at all.'

'Well, there *is* something funny going on! The Raja has had some land cleared there, very near the dam site. And now this road's being shut here, which will be our way of access. The villagers refuse to talk – they're scared stiff of the Raja's men. Do you know anything about it? Does Sevaji know of our plan?'

'Well I haven't told him, if that's what you're implying,' Theo replied coldly. 'Didn't know of it myself till now.'

'It's rumoured he plans to build another crazy pagoda.'

Theo stared out of the window. So, let them fight it out between them – the inroads of modern progress versus the status quo of traditional religion. Like two gladiators, one armed with a surveyor's chain and a musket, the other with a lingam and . . . a garland of flowers! A pretty conceit; he saw it clearly, for his mind had an allegorical bent.

'Well?' Nicholas challenged, sure he'd hit the nail.

Theo turned on him fiercely. 'I've told you before, Rundell, I'm not your spy. Wardle's supposed to be the channel of communication between the Company and the Raja. Let him find out what's going on.'

'You know Wardle's a confounded old muddlehead and can't get a word of sense out of H.R.H. Good Lord, man, we're trying to help the people. Proper irrigation will improve crop yields; build a bridge and the alligators won't chew 'em up, and you . . .'

'Personally, I'm not against any of that, Mr Rundell, but I refuse to become involved. You've chosen a bad spot for your dam, though, I'll tell you that much and that only.'

Nicholas hissed in annoyance and began rolling up the plan. 'Confound it, Lang, but you're an odd one. I've never known a fellow so critical of his own kind and country – one of the greatest in the world – and what it's trying to achieve for the benefit of mankind. But you seem to have no concept of our imperial responsibilities. I must say, I sometimes wonder if you are a proper Englishman at all.'

'So do I, Mr Rundell, so do I. Certainly I'm not the kind who believes high-flown phrases about the benefit of mankind and imperial responsibilities. I follow, rather, the opinion of the late-lamented Munro who pointed out, and I quote, "we British regard every country as ignorant and uncivilised whose state of improvement does not approximate to our own even though it should be higher than our own was at no very distant period". We can afford our present arrogance only because we have money and power.' He gave Nicholas a bland smile. 'May I suggest we go? Your wife is expecting us for supper.'

'Dinner,' Rundell growled, stuffing the plan in his desk drawer.

Theo watched. 'By the by, Rundell, I shan't say a word about your irrigation scheme but it's bound to reach Sevaji's ears soon – his spies are sharper than you may think.'

'Dinner' was indeed the word for the lavish meal that awaited them, for Catherine had to keep her servants up to scratch somehow, or they'd quite forget how to prepare for a really important occasion. So the table was covered with best damask, the glass and cutlery fresh-polished and shining in the candlelight, which also showed to advantage Catherine's low-necked gown. Both food and wine were excellent, for Catherine prided herself on her training of cooks as Nicholas on his judgement of claret. Determinedly steering clear of provoking subjects, Catherine led them into a discussion of names for their expected offspring. Their son was to be Victor Horatius – the latter a family name, but one could hardly saddle a child with it alone, she explained.

'And if it's a girl?' Theo inquired innocently.

Catherine lowered her voice so the servants shouldn't hear. 'Oh, we don't expect – well, if it should be, probably Anna Catherine.'

'Our daughter will be Elizabeth Miranda,' announced Amelia, 'after my grandmother and Theo's mother.'

'And if it's a boy?' teased Catherine.

'Bayard,' replied Theo. 'I've a growing admiration for my father and only wish I'd told him so while he was still alive.'

'Ah, that so often happens with parents and children, doesn't it?' Catherine agreed. 'What a shame he isn't still here to enjoy his declining years in your home!'

'Well, yes and no. My family he would have loved, but how he'd have hated what's going on in the country generally.'

Catherine looked puzzled.

'My father was, as you know, an oriental scholar, madam, with a great love of Indian culture, and I sometimes think it was as well he died just before Macaulay's infamous Minute on Education appeared. For what is the result? The languages my father loved and taught are completely discounted as useless and dead – they've even been labelled "barbarous". While English is touted in every school and college.'

'My dear sir,' Nicholas broke in, 'surely even you must see that English is the language of the future – of science, of rationality, of progress? Yet you orientalists want to bar Indians access to it – a sure way of keeping them in a backward condition.'

Theo flushed angrily. 'No, I don't want to bar them from anything, nor do I want them to neglect all they now have. But this wholesale and indiscriminate thrusting of English language and learning upon them will have long-term consequences. There will soon grow up a generation of educated natives who will know more about Europe and its ways than their own country. Then they'll feel dispossessed and discontented. Will that be good, I ask you?'

Nicholas poured himself more claret; it was too good to waste on Lang, who was so Hinduised it was a wonder he drank alcohol at all.

'So you are against progressive changes being introduced here, are you, Mr Lang?' he said nastily. 'Not even – just for example – the legal abolition of suttee?'

'I know what you're going to say, Mr Rundell, and yes, I was proved wrong there, I confess freely, but it doesn't follow that I want to see every Hindu temple become a church or every native school an English seminary, or this country ruled entirely by the English statute book. I still maintain that reforms on the scale you desire must be carried out gradually and with careful respect for the basic Indian way of life.'

As Nicholas paused, wondering whether to agree a truce, his wife sighed in exasperation, for the mother-of-pearl dessert knives had not been brought out and the mango fool was definitely below par.

'I hope you're enjoying the fool – it's rather the cook's speciality?' She beamed; her mother had taught her this way of dealing with culinary failure.

'It's very nice, thank you,' Amelia replied, condemning herself to eating every morsel of the sour mess.

'Needs more sugar,' growled Nicholas, reaching for the caster, as then they all did.

But at least, Catherine thought, it had deflected the men from their tiresome wrangling. Before they could begin again she declared that pregnant women should not dwell on such serious matters but be diverted by music and poetry for the sake of their unborn, and she therefore proposed to play the harp for her own and Amelia's benefit – and the men must endure it, whether they would or no. Two servants carried her magnificent Evard harp into the parlour, reverently removed its quilted cover, lifted it from its tin-lined wooden case.

Catherine stroked the strings. 'They snap so often in this climate. I'm always having to send to Calcutta for more.'

'Costs a small fortune, that thing!' Nicholas grumbled.

'Oh, Nicholas, you know you love to hear me play.' She arranged herself on the stool and Theo thought vindictively: Ho-ho, my angelic and golden madam, you chose the harp to show yourself off to best advantage, did you!

But in this Theophilus was mistaken, for the moment Catherine began she forgot to pose and played the instrument with skill and love. Amelia, pleasantly surprised, closed her eyes and drifted with the music through the rural scenes of her youth. She settled upon a memory of Mr Grint's wife who had also played the harp, but badly. Mr Grint, the organist of Thaxted church, always wore black and had long white hands. He played the organ most beautifully and Amelia had fallen earnestly in love with him when she was thirteen years old. On the occasions of his wife's several pregnancies, Amelia prayed she'd die in childbirth so Mr Grint could marry her.

But in due course her longings were displaced by ruddier, younger gentlemen who flirted and danced in the manner of their kind. When Mr Grint was middle-aged his wife did suddenly die and, at twenty-two, Amelia again suffered the excited attraction of a thirteen-year-old. He came courting her with surprising alacrity (as if he'd always known), murmuring Latin love lyrics and playing to her on the organ after choir practice – until the day he fell and broke his ankle in the icy churchyard. The older spinsters of the parish were all attention and sympathy; but Amelia, watching him hobble into the church on a stick, saw an ageing man, soon destined for arthritis and allied infirmities. Prudently she withdrew, leaving the field open for one Miss Rackstraw who married him within the twelvemonth.

The music ceased and Amelia opened her eyes, a surge of happiness flooding through her because she was here in strange and lovely Tanjore with dear Theophilus beside her, instead of in dull Thaxted nursing elderly Mr Grint!

They all clapped enthusiastically, begging Catherine to continue, and she was happy to oblige.

The liquid notes flowed into a back room where Sarah Murphy was slumped exhausted on a chair, waiting for the iron to re-heat. She, too, closed her eyes and imagined an England she knew only through picture books and her parents' stories. Oh, if only she could have taken her children there, so they could romp in apple orchards and hayfields as had her mother when young! Gerard had returned from duty in a particularly foul temper yesterday because, at the monthly inspection, several tent-canvases had been gnawed by rats, and he'd been held responsible. He had hit Sarah, which wasn't unusual; but frightened Rosie had run away unnoticed and been carried home later by Captain Gilbert, who had found her playing with the horse-boys in the stables. Her hair and pinny covered with chaff and dust, her grubby arms round his neck, she was riding him like a horse and he, to Sarah's amazement, was actually laughing.

Oh, how carefree and rosy-cheeked she and the children could be in that sweet, green English countryside which the notes of the harp conjured for her. She dreamed it was being played by an accomplished lady in the stately drawing-room of a country house. And that, when she, Sarah, had finished ironing in the servants' quarters, she'd walk home through a large park with lawns and trees, beside golden cornfields, to a pretty thatched cottage where Jack and Rosie would be waiting with their father – a kindly, hardworking countryman who'd hug her to him, saying in that easy drawl her parents used, 'There yew are at las', gul. They shouldna' work yew so late in the big house.'

The music stopped and Sarah opened her eyes. 'They shouldn't work me so hard and late,' she muttered, thumping the iron furiously over Nicholas's shirt as the realities of the squalid barracks, her brutal husband, her unwanted pregnancy overtook her.

CHAPTER EIGHT

'One, two, three – blow!' Rolly puffed his cheeks, blew long and seriously till the birthday candles were out. Dora and her children, Rukmini, Durmeen and Amelia clapped.

'Well done, dearie.'

Amelia cut the cake while Rolly strutted about with his wooden sabre and shield. They were unexpected presents from Captain Gilbert, but their martial effect had been somewhat vitiated by the servants, who had daubed his forehead and palms with powdered sandalwood in honour of the day and adorned him with flowers and coloured beads that clashed comically with his martial accoutrements.

'And next year you'll have a little brother or sister to share your birthday party, young man.' Dora tweaked his hair and he raised his face to hers.

'He can ride on my rabbit 'cos I'll be riding on a big horse by then.'

Durmeen chuckled, trying to cuddle him. 'Oh funny boy, he'll still be too little for that!'

He evaded her, running behind her skirts and laughing. 'Ever so little – little like a bean, little like a mouse, little like a . . . him?' He waved a toy soldier at her.

'No, no, Rolly, much larger than that, but smaller than you because he'll be less than a year old and you'll be four.'

Rolly frowned. 'Where's he being old now, then? How big is he being now?'

The women laughed; Rolly flushed angrily and Ruth Arbuthnot, a prim child in starched gingham, said, 'You mustn't ask things like that, Rolly. It's a secret. He isn't being anywhere yet. He's with God.'

'He's not, he's not. 'Cos how do they know . . .?'

'Now here's your cake, Rolly dear.' Amelia held him still. 'And let's talk of baby as a girl, shall we? You'd like a little sister, wouldn't you?'

'Yes please,' he said solemnly. ''Cos she'll be littler, won't she? Girls are littler than boys.'

'Not if they're born first,' sang out Ruth. 'I'm much bigger than you, Roland Lang, and you can't catch me!' She pranced away to the verandah and he pounded after.

'Now, Rolly, come back and eat . . .' Durmeen readied herself for pursuit.

'Oh, leave him be,' Amelia smiled. 'He's over-excited. He can eat the cake later.'

'Well, as I was saying, Rukmini,' Dora continued an earlier thread, 'our first four orphans are now in the asylum, even though it isn't finished and the Raja isn't very pleased. Now can I persuade you to come along and teach them a little basic English? You are bilingual and . . .'

'Oh, but I'm not. No, no, my English is very bad,' Rukmini protested.

'But my poor orphans know nothing – except their country vernaculars, which I find very hard to comprehend. But if you could just interpret for me sometimes when they get distressed and I can't understand why, it would be a fine, fine work.' She munched some cake, then persisted. 'The Madras Auxiliary Bible Society has promised to send me a Tamil translation of *Pilgrim's Progress*.'

Durmeen sniffed in loud disapproval of those orphans having their heads stuffed with Protestant doctrines of sin and duty, being made to feel guilty about wearing bangles and flowers. No wonder they got 'distressed', poor things! But no one paid attention to her and she helped herself to more cake, feeling left out, as she often did since Rukmini had joined the household. And now here was Mrs Arbuthnot trying to press her into the service of the Anglicans; but Durmeen could have told her that Rukmini was still a haughty brahmin lady underneath, and her refusal stemmed less from inadequate English than a reluctance to mix with the lower castes. If she becomes a Christian convert, she'll want her own cup to sip the sacrament, I'll warrant, Durmeen thought, drinking her tea and wagging her head sagely, as she usually did when she agreed with herself.

Amelia, fearing Dora might again try to enlist her in these worthy endeavours, slipped away to her bedroom and, as she dabbed her brow with cologne, heard a louder uproar than usual from the children on the verandah. It came from Rolly, Matthew and John who'd been building a fort with some new birthday bricks until Matthew suddenly kicked it down. Rolly flew at him furiously, John sided with his brother. When Durmeen rushed to investigate, the scene was a tangle of fighting boy and Rolly's lip was bleeding. She scooped him up.

'There, there, Rolly, my own little love. Don't cry, Auntie Durmeen will bathe it better. And you two should be ashamed of yourselves – on his birthday!'

Agitated by Durmeen's stifling embrace, Rolly bawled the more.

'Whatever's the matter?' Dora's tone was weary.

'Rolly's got a little cut. Don't trouble yourself,' Durmeen answered, jiggling the child. 'There, there, little fellow!'

'A cut?' Rukmini appeared on the verandah and Rolly held out his arms to her.

'Auntie Rukee!' he squawked. 'Want Auntie Rukee!'

Durmeen gripped him tighter. 'Silly boy! Auntie Durmeen will look after you.'

He thrust out a fist, pushing away her mask-like face. 'Go away! Auntie Rukee!'

As Rukmini came up and Rolly squirmed to free himself, the women's eyes met above his head in mutual hostility. Then Durmeen dumped him on the floor.

'All right – go to her. Poor old Auntie Durmeen's not good enough for you anymore, is she, Rolly? But you shouldn't trust yourself to a troublemaker, child.'

'And what do you mean by that?' Rukmini's eyes opened very wide and glittered.

'Never mind – we'll see. Go and bathe that cut, it's bleeding.' Durmeen trundled off to find her shawl, for, she decided, the party was over and hadn't been much of a success.

* * *

171

Amelia, on the other hand, felt the party had been quite satisfactory, though she was rather worried at its cost when she next added up her household accounts. This she usually did on a Sunday, which was, Theo teased, her day of reckoning with both God and Mammon.

'Ingredients for the birthday cake were rather costly.' She handed him the ledger. 'And we had custards, macaroons, one sponge cake each spread with strawberry jam . . . Well, Rolly's so fond of it.'

Theo shrugged. 'I told you not to encourage the taste in him.'

'But only once a year! Anyway, it's not just the party, we have more people in the house all the time. Rukmini and Mangalam with their special vegetarian food.'

'Cheaper than meat.'

'Yes – but separate.'

'Well, for a Hindu eating meat is like burying the dead in your stomach. Perhaps we should all be vegetarian when you think of it like that.'

She glowered. 'Rolly needs building up with meat, in my opinion. And soon there'll be another mouth to feed. The long and the short is, Theo, you can see for yourself, my allowance simply won't stretch to everything.'

He pretended to examine the 'miscellaneous column', made up precisely as Dora had taught her, to show the exact cost of a new fire-fan for the kitchen, a yard of brown holland for repairing the punkah, a foot-tub for Rukmini, a wheeled cart with bricks for Rolly's birthday, Sarah Murphy's wage for ironing cuffs, tobacco for Theo's hookah, two dresses for Amelia . . .

She peeped over his shoulder. 'I simply had to have the dresses, Theo. My ordinary ones wouldn't fit anymore.'

He stroked her cheek. 'My dear, of course you did! I could give up the hookah, I suppose . . . But no, something must be done.'

'Then speak to the Raja. He knows you have a growing family to support. You must pin him down.'

'Huh! Like trying to pin down a grasshopper, as Wardle

says, and at the moment he's in full flight with this temple-building, and running into greater debt.'

'Well, Theophilus, so are we.'

He kissed her forehead. 'You mustn't worry. It isn't good for you. Here – take this for now.' He dug out a few coins. 'And I promise to do something before the next bills fall due.'

He wandered to the verandah cupboard and took out stoppered bottles containing chopped tobacco, molasses, aromatic spices, herbs and musk; in a copper bowl he blended them in the proportions that pleased him till his tobacco cake, called a chillum, was ready to smoke. Then he asked Long-ago's son to bring his silver-mounted hookah, its snake and flask of water, and a ball of hot charcoal to light the chillum. He relaxed in a basket chair, feeling guilty at his indulgence, but convincing himself it was a necessary aid to a proper consideration of the options open to him. In fact, he had only one. He hadn't told his wife, but he'd already tackled the Raja unsuccessfully on the subject of a salary increase, and that left Resident Wardle. Resisting the temptation to light another chillum and postpone the whole matter, he put on his hat and sauntered off to the Residency bungalow.

It was February, a time when Wardle was happiest in his garden. China roses, plumbago and oleanders bloomed, figs, melons and pomegranates promised well, and he was just digging up some ginger roots for the cook to grind into his daily medicinal brew.

'Ah, Lang! Not too beastly hot yet, is it? Come in, come in. Fine ginger this year. Would your good wife like some for her condition? She's keeping well, I trust?'

'Splendidly, thank you.' Theo closed the gate.

'Good, good. Here's a root, with my compliments. Boy, wash this for Mrs Lang – oh, and some figs. Women have a fancy for them at such times, didn't Shakespeare say something to that effect? And boy – two brandy-pawnees on the verandah.'

'You're very kind, thank you.'

Wardle ushered his guest to a seat. 'You know I was thinking about your good wife this afternoon. I've lost all faith in doddering old Cauldwell. Make up your own medicine

– does much more good than his infernal blue pills. I don't think she should trust herself to him for her confinement. Mrs Rundell's going to Trichy and I advise you to send your wife, too.'

'Honestly? Well, Mrs Rundell did mention . . . but Amelia feels sure it will be plain sailing like the first and, well, the expense of Trichy would be fairly considerable.'

Wardle smiled broadly. 'But you can't take that into account if there's any risk.'

'Good Lord no, of course not.' Theo was fervent. 'I'll talk to her again, tell her what you say . . .'

They settled down, sipped drinks, Wardle rambled on about the state of his crops, and, seeing Theo waiting for an opening, eventually asked, 'Anything particular I can do for you, Mr Lang? Always ready to help a fellow citizen, as you know.'

Humbug, thought Theo, smiling. 'Well, Resident, I have an idea we could perhaps be of some small assistance to each other.'

'Really?' Wardle's eyebrows indicated immense astonishment.

'Yes, really. I believe I'm correct in thinking you've unsuccessfully sought an audience with H.R.H. several times recently? So I wondered if I might – well – act as intermediary between you, facilitate matters?' He trailed off, averting his eyes.

'Ah yes, I see. Well I might as well confess that relations between the Raja and myself are increasingly strained. So, in short, Mr Lang, I'd be delighted to accept your kind offer. It is, though . . . er . . . something of a *volte face* for you, is it not? Nothing wrong in that, my dear fellow. Indeed I seem to remember another occasion not so long ago when . . .'

'Yes, Mr Wardle, the point has been made – and taken. I'd make a poor diplomat: I'm far too impatient and so, to come straight to the point, my *volte face*, as you call it, is dictated by financial stringency and doesn't come free.'

'Quite so,' Wardle nodded happily; the envelope marked with Theo's name had weighed on his conscience occasionally and he'd gladly dispense its contents. 'That can certainly be arranged, and quite generously, I assure you. And, as we're coming straight to points, let me tell you that the Raja has absolutely refused to see me until his confounded pagoda is built – a year, at least. I've not yet informed Madras of this.' He tipped his glass and called for refills. 'The Council has directed me to inform His Highness that if he proceeds with his nonsensical plan – nonsensical both on account of location and cost – they may consider removing that site and the nearby villages from his jurisdiction.'

'You mean the Company will use it as an excuse to seize more land?'

Wardle spread his hands. 'It's most unfortunate that Sevaji's astrologers should select as auspicious the very place where the irrigation channels and dam are to be built. So much for astrology, say I!'

'Ah – but perhaps a period of conflict was predicted, in which case they're merely fulfilling their own prophecies.'

Wardle frowned at Theo's flippancy, holding his glass to the light. 'Good brandy, isn't it? The Company thrives on conflict, and the Raja should be advised of that now in the hope of avoiding it, for his own sake. That is what you can do for me, Mr Lang.'

Theo drank; the brandy was indeed good. 'I suppose it's useless to point out to you, Resident, or to the Company in general, that the man you are dealing with belongs to the proud Mahratta dynasty? He, in common with most heredi-tary rulers of his kind, regards the whole issue quite differ-ently. *You* see Sevaji "squandering money on pagodas and idols" instead of taking measures to improve the lot of his peasants. But *he* sees the resources he owns as his to dispose of as he wishes. His subjects expect nothing else from him – indeed they applaud his devotion in building this temple. That is how matters have been arranged here for centuries between rulers and ruled, Mr Wardle, and it won't change overnight.'

Wardle swirled the liquid in his glass. 'You may be right. In fact, I've been in India long enough to know that, up to a point, you are. But it makes not a ha'porth of difference.

Company men like Nicholas Rundell call the tune now, and what would they say to your line of argument?'

Theo chanted, 'We are on the side of reformation and irrigation and righteousness. The wicked who dare stand in our path shall be punished and overwhelmed.'

'Pre–cisely – and of that His Highness should at least be warned. He won't listen to me – but you may have some influence over him?'

Theo shook his head. 'Not really, but I'll try. And you'll have to pay me something whether I succeed or no.'

Wardle went to his desk and, returning, handed Theo a sum of money.

'You trust me? I could pocket this and not say a word.'

'I take you for an honourable man, sir. Let us drink to that.'

They did so, relaxing to contemplate the garden flowers that appeared even more beautiful in the softening haze of sunset and brandy. Wardle sighed, awash with mellow melancholy.

'As I was saying just now, Lang, I've been in this country long enough – far too long, indeed. Came out as a young Company employee in 1808, hoping to make a quick fortune in outside trading. I'd have preferred my father's business at Home, but there was a slump – Napoleonic wars and so forth. Had to learn the native lingos, of course, and suddenly found myself collecting taxes and sitting in judgement instead of making that fortune and clearing out – which was all I wanted. Never understood what went wrong . . .' He topped up their glasses. 'Never really understood the lingos – nor the wallahs who speak them, come to that. Just floundered along, that's what I've done, and that's how I view this country, Mr Lang – a great sticky morass of monsoon mud that you keep wading through, praying to get Home before it sucks you under for good.'

Theo chuckled. 'Seas of treacle, hey?'

'Hmm? Oh that – Macaulay's minute. Well, it had its points.'

'Points made out of bigotry and ignorance, Resident.' But Theo had no stomach for argument just then and added in conciliation, 'Still – it must be wretched for you feeling as you do – especially without your wife. Can't you just resign and go?'

'Would have years ago, dear boy, but for the children. Marjorie and I had six. Two died in infancy and one aged seven – little Jessica – the sweetest smile she had, I can see it yet. Cholera. Here, might as well polish off the bottle. Corporal Forbes is on the march again, bye the bye, and heading south. So Captain Gilbert wrote the other day. He's on his way back from Madras via Trichy and taking his good time . . . Well, as I was saying, once the youngest son is off my hands, I'm Homeward bound.' He stared sombrely at his companion. 'Family responsibilities – they dictate your life, Mr Lang, you'll find that out.'

Theo laughed sharply. 'I *am* finding it out, Resident. That's why I came and that's why I must go. Amelia will be waiting for supper.'

He rose and Wardle searched about fussily. 'Ah well, a wife is a wonderful support for all that, is she not? Here we are – the ginger and figs, with my compliments to her. And I'll expect a little report from you in due course, Mr Lang.'

Theophilus had intended going straight home, but the jolly hum of the evening bazaar convinced him he should buy his wife a present, now he was again in funds. He strolled along the narrow alleys between stalls selling beads, rice, pyramids of dark blue and rose kapiti powder, ropes and sandals, toy animals, yellow saffron root, boxes of woven leaves, onions, garlands of pith for the temple; groups of men were chatting outside the barbers', children jostling round piles of amber and green jelly-sweets. How fortunate that the pall of Christian Sunday didn't reach here, he thought, feeling his brandy-raised spirits lift even higher as he sniffed the usual bazaar odours of baked dust, decayed fruit, coconut oil, crushed flowers and spices. And how strange that hundreds of Englishmen like Hubert Wardle could spend most of their lives here and still yearn only for grey Home. He was tempted first by a coral necklace, but when he reached the Gujerati weavers' stalls he became certain that what his wife would prefer was a sari.

'Look, dearest, a present for you!' He floated into the parlour holding out a silky length of crimson flecked with silver thread. 'Come – stand up and try it on.'

She stared at his flushed face. 'Theo, wherever have you been? It's quite late – and what's the matter?'

'Nothing at all. I went to see old Wardle, then I bought this sari for you in the bazaar. Stand up, I say! I know how to put it on.'

'But Theo, what are you thinking of? I don't want a sari and you've no money to spare for one.'

He giggled foolishly. 'But I have, for I'm now appointed unofficial intermediary', he pronounced that very carefully, 'between His Highness Sevaji, Raja, and his other Highness, Resident Hubert Wardle.' He dragged her to her feet, trying to drape the silk over her dress.

'I know what's the matter with you – Wardle's brandy! I can smell it! Oh, Theo, please stop – it's not like you to get tipsy.'

'And why can't I be not like me sometimes? Why can't you be less like you? It's so boring!' As he spoke he fumbled and pulled the material around her body, increasingly irritated because it would not hang properly. He wanted miraculously to transform Amelia into the lithesome sari-clad beauty of his imaginings.

'Oh for lud's sake, Theo – of course I can't wear this, especially in my present condition. You'd better give it to Rukmini. It'll suit her better and *she* doesn't bore you, apparently!'

He stepped back, the silk slipping to the floor. 'You mustn't say that!' His tone was thick and distressed. 'I bought it for you, not Rukmini, no, not for her. And I'm sorry. I didn't mean that about being boring. I just wanted you to be lovely in red silk instead of this humble muslin you always wear because I can't afford better.' Looking ready to cry, he handed her the rest of the money. 'See – that's for you, too. From Wardle, for carrying his messages. He's a silly old coot but I felt quite sorry for him today. Oh lor', he sent you some figs and ginger – I must have left them at the sari stall.'

'Oh Theo, really – now those I would have liked! Much more acceptable than *your* idea of a present, I must say.'

'Oh so sensible Amelia . . . come on.' He tried to undo the ties on her dress. 'Let me just take this off, then the sari might fit and then we could go to bed and . . .'

She pushed him away fiercely. 'Theophilus, I'm not wearing that sari, especially while I'm pregnant. And, if you think I'm too sensible, *I* think you're behaving remarkably like a silly old coot, so there!'

He swayed, caught between desire, irritation and disappointment, then marched off to the bedroom. He felt the onset of a headache.

Amelia picked up the material, frowning as she examined its fine weave. Until now, she'd never consciously thought that her husband – so devoted, so sensually attuned to her – might find a dark-skinned native attractive, any more than she could imagine being attracted to one herself. Yet, if the suspicion hadn't been lurking in her mind, why had she spoken as she had? She shrugged and stuffed the material in a cupboard, attributing her suspicion to the general feeling of malaise that was afflicting her during this second pregnancy.

Amelia Lang's malaise was due to over-activity – at least that was the considered opinion of Catherine Rundell, who had decided the safest course was to do absolutely nothing. Every afternoon was spent reclining on her *chaise-longue* in the greenish twilight of her shaded parlour, straining to read a novel she scarce had the strength to hold. Her latest acquisition, *Delicate Dilemmas*, did not warrant the effort and the book slipped from her sticky grasp.

She moaned, dabbling the freed hand in a basin of water beside her, then holding her arm aloft to let the tepid drops slide towards her moist armpit. Her muslin sleeve fell back to reveal a milk-pale arm and she stroked it with her other hand; how well-moulded and smooth it was, how perfect were her pink-shell fingernails! Fondly, she patted her hair, long brushed and perfectly plaited by the ayah that morning, and then reached for the embroidered handkerchief a box-wallah had just tempted her into buying. Nicholas would complain again that she was forever spending money on trifles, but what on earth else was she to do? She dabbed her damp arm with it, pondering the awfulness of living as a woman inside a dirty-brown skin. She'd heard that Indian men secretly desired the flesh of white ladies, indeed she'd sensed as much sometimes in their heavy, dark eyes. She shivered deliciously at the thought of their useless, caged lust, wondering if the handsome young horse-keeper now dozing in the stable like an animal among animals was dreaming of her fair, unobtainable body. She became aware of the throbbing hot silence and called, 'You there – wake up!'

There was a snort and shuffle from the other side of the grass tatties, then came the sweet sound of water sluicing down them, so that the scorching wind blew through coolly – well, as coolly as the hot breeze of an English August. Catherine closed her eyes. 'Imagine waterfalls tumbling over rocks in green valleys,' her mother used to instruct when she and her sister tossed and cried, tormented by prickly-heat rashes. Complacently, she smoothed her muslin dress over her swollen belly; she knew already how to rear a baby in India. Not like that silly little Sarah Murphy who was due to produce her next any day now. Honestly, it would be a mercy if the baby didn't survive, for she'd soon have Sarah back whining and begging even more desperately. She must dispense with her services; the girl was nothing but a wretched dawdle these days.

Steps sounded on the verandah. 'Catherine! Are you there?'

'Mrs Lang, er . . . Amelia.' Catherine decided to accept the sudden intimacy. 'Yes – do come in.'

Amelia looked flustered: pregnancy didn't suit her; it exaggerated her ruddy country complexion. Catherine raised her head.

'Boy, tea – quick. Pray sit down . . . Amelia. What an afternoon to venture out!'

'Oh, I *had* to tell someone.' Amelia sank into a chair mopping her cheeks.

'Whatever's happened?'

'It's poor Sarah Murphy, she died in labour. Dora Arbuthnot came to tell me. Something went wrong – the baby died too. That clumsy old fool of a doctor!' She mopped her eyes as well. 'Oh, it's so very sad – such a poor little fish! Not quite twenty-one, and she kept saying how frightened she was. Oh dear . . .'

'Oh dear . . .' Catherine echoed, quickly beginning to un-think what she'd been thinking a few minutes before. 'Yes, how very sad. I am sorry. *Water*, boy!' She paused, listening for the familiar sluice.

'Whatever will happen to poor Jack and Rosie, with that drunken brute of a father?'

Catherine clucked soothingly. 'Here's tea. Drink up and forget it, dear. People of that sort always manage somehow.'

Amelia blinked. 'But I feel so awful about it, don't you?'

'Well, of course, but it's not good for us to get upset in our condition. Especially over something we can do nothing about.'

Amelia swallowed tea hard to dissolve a lump in her throat, wishing she hadn't come. 'The funeral's tomorrow. It's diffi-cult to get flowers at this season, isn't it?'

'Oh, there's always the eternal marigold.'

'Shall you come?'

'No, I don't think so. Ladies aren't expected to attend funerals – mercifully.'

'Well, I'm going. It's only right in a small community like this.'

Catherine hesitated. Considering her recent train of thought, it might be as well to manifest her sorrow plain. 'Poor Sarah! So good with the ironing, too. All right, I'll come – as long as it's before the heat of the day.'

'Nine in the morning, Dora said.'

It was indeed still relatively cool when the small group of mourners came out of St Peter's Church after the funeral service. Gerard Murphy, dragging red-eyed Jack by the arm, followed the coffin to its place of interment while Dora Arbuthnot kept Rosie beside her.

Rosie was chuckling helplessly, pointing at the squirrels flicking their tails on the old gravestones and scampering in the dust-laden trees. A boy, hoping for free grazing, herded a few goats into the far gate and Arbuthnot rushed over tombs to chase him off – an absurd figure, black-stockinged legs leaping below his surplice, holding on to his broad-brimmed hat. Rosie, seeing him, chuckled even more and Amelia glanced at her compassionately. Considering her wretched little life, she looked surprisingly bonny, with an inbuilt sturdy cheeriness that must have come from her East Anglian forebears.

Dora patted her head. 'I hate to think of this one left to the mercy of that man and his heathen woman.'

'Won't the army do anything for her?'

Both Dora and Amelia eyed Captain Gilbert, who'd returned to Tanjore the previous evening.

'Let's hope so. He seldom misses funerals,' Dora added. 'Seems rather to enjoy them.'

And so it appeared, for the captain had a distinct glint of merriment in his blue eyes. It was true that funerals often provided him with a certain macabre amusement (so many normal, healthy-seeming young men dying before the ageing reprobates), but on this occasion his thoughts were far away with Major William Taylor whom he'd recently met in Madras. An ordinary name for a most unusual officer – witty, well-read, pleasantly cynical and secretly one of his own kind. They had got on famously, and Bill had promised to approach a certain 'sympathetic fellow in a higher place' to secure a Madras posting for Gil in due course. Meanwhile Bill had advised him to steer clear of frolics of the Poo sort and get himself a wife. 'Best cover there is, old fellow. I've been married for years. Wife and daughter at Home. Unfortunately their health can't stand this climate.' He pulled a face. 'Leaves me free and above suspicion here.'

Gil came to attention, realising his positive grin at the preposterous idea of marriage was hardly appropriate to the occasion. He composed his features, gazing solemnly at the scene by the grave.

Amelia followed his look, murmuring to Dora, 'Such a sad, sad life! Sarah so longed to go to England. We talked about it – her mother comes from my part of Essex. But she never saw a thatched cottage or a cornfield, after all.' She shivered with distress and fear, for the scene suddenly looked very ominous and the weight of the child within her turned to menace. This graveyard is swollen with deaths like my belly, she thought, aware she was sweating profusely. The warm morning sky and the larking squirrels were of an intense beauty that terrified her with the thought she might soon share Sarah's fate and lose sight of them forever. Catherine Rundell, clinging to her husband's arm, was a prey to similar forebodings and the two women caught each other's eyes and looked away, seeing their own fears reflected.

As the mourners dispersed, Theo went to speak to Nicholas and then came over to his wife. 'Mrs Rundell is soon going to Trichy in preparation for her confinement,' he reported. 'Captain Gilbert has agreed to send an escort with her – I've said you'll go too, Amelia.'

'Oh,' she smiled in relief. 'Yes, all right, Theo, if you think it best.'

He patted her shoulder. 'Well it is, isn't it, dear? Obviously.'

The only question remaining was whether Rolly should accompany his mother, but when he developed a slight fever Amelia (who since the funeral was prey to numerous fears) decided against his travelling. Rukmini assured her that she and the ayah could manage perfectly well, while Durmeen vigorously asserted that her little boy was not to be left entirely in the care of natives. And so, on the day Amelia and Catherine set out for Trichy, Durmeen arrived and took over the running of the household – a move that wasn't only to do with Rolly.

Since Rukmini's arrival, Durmeen had gradually transferred most of her considerable allegiance from Theo to his wife, and was watchful of Amelia's interests. It did not escape her notice that, after Amelia's departure, Rukmini took to washing her lustrous hair every day and drying it over fragrant smoke wafting from an iron pot filled with live charcoal and scented herbs. Nor did she fail to observe that the poetry Theo sometimes read aloud after supper was more than usually lyrical and that, on such occasions, Rukmini's eyes shone with especially warm brilliance. And so she seldom relaxed her vigilance – except that, on Sundays, she attended the Catholic church and then went to visit her sons.

'How I used to hate Sundays when I lived in England,' Theo remarked to Rukmini, sitting to his food on his return from the palace about a fortnight after Amelia had gone. She hovered about offering dishes, finding it too uncomfortable to eat with him alone.

'Did you? Why?'

'So deadly solemn and Christian – putting on best clothes, going to church, and some of the boys seeing their relations, whereas I hadn't any.'

'You were lonely?'

'Yes – terribly.'

She nodded, fully understanding loneliness, but said, 'Well, I was grateful to the Christians who visited Poodocottah. At least they bothered about women like myself.'

He mumbled vaguely; Rukmini's growing interest in Christianity displeased him, though he hesitated to say so.

'Nothing much else ever happened there,' she added defensively.

'There must have been lots of palace festivals and so on.'

'But the Raja's mother loathed me because I was married to H. N. and I wasn't allowed to take much part.'

'Raja Tondiman's mother? Never heard of her!'

Rukmini smiled. 'Haven't you? She's ancient as the rocks under the sea, withered as a nut in a dark cave, and hasn't left her bed for years. But she's still there – the "power behind the screens", as they say.'

'Amazing, the secrets and intrigues of the old courts! I wonder if the Company knows of her existence?'

'Probably not. But I think she was behind Moitra's death. At least I hope she was.'

'Do you? But why?'

'Well, who poisoned him is still a mystery as far as I know. And far better the "old mother" than . . .' she trailed off.

'Than who, Rukmini?'

'Oh Theo,' she clasped her hands tightly to her forehead, 'I wonder and wonder about it! I desperately wanted him to die. I know I did. I even told my faithful servants so – several times when he was particularly loathsome. And perhaps one of them . . . Mangalam even . . . The thought frightens me . . . I can't forget it.'

'Oh nonsense! It was a political murder, the court was seething with intrigue.'

'But if so, why hasn't there been any revenge killing? Why has nothing else happened?'

'Come, Rukmini, don't worry yourself. The "old mother" was bound to be behind it, as you said. And we should be grateful to her . . . shouldn't we?'

She didn't reply; clearing plates, bringing fruit.

'Are you grateful, Rukmini? To be here, away from that dreary life? You don't say much.'

She looked at him directly and he saw how beautiful were the eyes she usually kept demurely lowered. 'I've spent so many years not saying much, Theophilus, that I've lost the habit of talking. I marvel to remember how playful and noisy I was when we were children together. I must seem very old and dull to you now.'

'Oh no, Rukmini! Of course you aren't. You are still . . . well . . . the girl I once knew.'

She shook her head. 'Not really, Theophilus. I am an emptied shell, but I am happier here than I was at Poodocottah, yes – thank you.'

He began peeling an orange, thinking of her life and how cruelly and unwittingly he had blighted it. She was well over thirty now, but as she moved into shadows beyond the lamplight he could recall very clearly what it was about her that had first fired his boyish lust. Having borne no children, she was still slim as a girl, her eyes still offered those warm, shy, hopeful glances to which he had once innocently responded. He arranged orange segments on his plate.

'But you must find *me* older and duller, Rukmini – because I am!'

Unexpectedly, she laughed. 'Ooh, I had a shock, yes, when I first saw how bald you are, but now I don't notice it. And you are still curly-haired young Theophilus in many ways, are you not? And how can you be dull with all your cleverness and education?'

'Come, Rukmini, I'm a family man with responsibilities and don't feel young anymore.' He began to eat the orange, murmuring, half to himself, 'I wish I did – just at the moment – young and carefree.'

She went to peep through the blinds. 'Durmeen will be back soon. Yes, you have a very sweet family, Theophilus – your wife, your son, another child coming.'

He nodded in solemn agreement. 'But I've often wanted to say, Rukmini, how very sorry I am for what happened long ago. It made such a sad difference to your life – but I wasn't to know that. I hope you haven't blamed me in your heart?'

She turned quickly. 'Oh no, no – of course not, Theophilus. We were two innocents then.'

'But not now.'

'No, not now.'

He got up and went to put a hand on her shoulder, feeling her shiver, turning her towards him. 'And part of me has always wanted you . . . always, always. When I thought you were about to burn to death I lost all reason because I wanted so much to see you alive. Don't we – almost – owe it to each other? Now?'

Her eyes widened. 'Owe it? Oh no, no. We owe it to dear Amelia not to . . . want.'

'But I can't not want. Even though I love my dear wife truly, I also love you and I do want, I can't help it.' He drew her close, brushing her cheeks with his lips, pressing his hands into the soft flesh of her waist, feeling her summon the strength to resist.

'No, Theophilus, please. It's so very wrong. You mustn't tempt us, please don't.'

'But you do want, too, don't you? he murmured triumphantly, raising her chin with his hand, forcing her to look at him. 'Admit you do, Rukmini, even if that is the end of it. Tell me, please.'

Her eyes moistened. 'Yes, Theophilus, I have to want – still. There has been no other man to love in my life, so how can I not?'

'Oh dear, dear Rukmini!' He held her tightly till she pushed his hands away.

'Let me go, please. Durmeen will come.' He shook his head, trying to nuzzle her again. 'Please, Theophilus!'

He released her and she hurried away; he was still munching the last of the orange when Durmeen came plodding up the path, complaining of the heat and bringing a bazaar toy for Rolly. Rukmini didn't reappear for the rest of the evening and Theo behaved with over-careful normality, like a half-drunk pretending to be completely sober. He listened with seeming attention to Durmeen's tales of her grandchildren, smoked his hookah, bade solicitous goodnight to his son who slept in a room adjoining his own. Then he looked at a book, the words '*she does want, she does*' drumming across every page, and he beguiled the time until Durmeen retired by translating them into as many languages as he could. He soon went to his own bed and lay tossing in the hot dark, beset with lust, guilt, tenderness, shame, excitement. 'A running river is all legs, A burning fire is mouths all over, A blowing breeze is all hands.' The verse dinned through his mind and, though actually from a religious poem in Sanskrit, seemed to him, then, passionately secular. Just once, he told himself, just once – to seal the promise that was made long ago.

He crept along the passage to her room, went in quietly, whispering her name, knowing she would be wakeful. And so at long last he moved over her in love, sure she would not resist him, and in hushed, cautious silence, the making of love went on between them until, near dawn, they slept exhausted in each other's arms.

Until they were awakened by a loud voice outside.

'Theophilus, leave your paramour this instant before your son and the servants wake up.'

In the manner of her kind, Durmeen always spoke in thick, sing-song fashion, which her rage accentuated so the term 'paramour' was charged with spluttering venom. She'd had plenty of time to choose it with care, having come to investigate Rolly's continued whimpering during the night and discovered Theo's empty bed.

The lovers lay entwined for a few last sweet moments till Theo whispered, 'Dear one, I must go.'

Rukmini shuddered. 'Oh Theo, what shall we do?'

They heard Long-ago's son shuffling past outside on the way to the well; dawn had broken. He kissed her deep and long, filled with sadness and renewing desire. 'We'll talk this evening. Try to sleep now.'

'But Theophilus, it's no good. It's wrong, wrong.' Her eyes filled with tears.

'I know, dear one, I know.' He reached for his nightshirt and crept back to his own bed as the first water of the day appeared over the rim of the well.

Durmeen waited until mid-morning, when Theo had gone to the palace and the cook to the bazaar, Veena had swept the verandah and the ayah had taken Rolly to play with the Arbuthnot boys. Then she told Mangalam that her mistress was to come to her. Mangalam bridled at the peremptory tone, but did as she was bid and, to her surprise, Rukmini obeyed the summons promptly. Durmeen sat bolt upright in Amelia's usual chair.

'You are to leave this house today, Rukmini Moitra, and go to live with Parvati in the Fort.'

Rukmini was taken by surprise; normally she would never have endured such high-handedness from a mere half-caste, but she'd betrayed her own dignity, her own self-esteem, and stood a convicted culprit.

'Please, Durmeen, I beg you not to tell Amelia – I am already so ashamed, you needn't make me more so. Oh, don't tell her, please!'

'And if I don't, will you leave today?'

Rukmini stared at her, then lowered her eyes and bowed her head in acquiescence.

'You're no better than a whore!' Durmeen announced triumphantly. 'Fornicating with the husband of the woman who saved you from the flames of suttee! Why did we all do so much to rescue you, I kept asking myself last night – you, a heartless, treacherous whore!'

'You know that's a lie!' Rukmini flared. 'I'm none of those

things. I'm a frail woman who has loved only one man since we were children together, and when he came to me last night – yes, he to me, not I to him – I was too weak a vessel to resist what I had secretly wanted for so long. Yes, I have wronged Amelia deeply and so has Theophilus. Why don't you blame him, too? Oh, but I know why – because a woman is a melon, is she not? And whether the knife falls on the melon or the melon on the knife, she is the sufferer. But you, too, are a woman with woman's longings and weaknesses, and you should show a little mercy and understanding.'

Durmeen quivered; she was enjoying judging Rukmini harshly, not only for this sinful act, but for her brahminical disdain, her capturing of Rolly's affection, her very presence in the house – interloper and usurper of Durmeen's own earlier role. She was not disposed to remember those extenuating tugs of the flesh to which she also had once been susceptible.

'I think,' she said stonily, 'that you have sinned in the eyes of God as well as man. As for Theophilus, he has behaved weakly and foolishly as a boy. But you know as well as I that men remain boys in their hearts and loins and it is women who keep their heads and stuff their ears with the cotton of decency when they are tempted. He and you have both wronged Amelia.'

She got up and waved her arms in increasing fury. 'Now go – shoo! And I tell you, Rukmini Moitra, I shall watch you and Theophilus like a lizard on the wall watches flies, and if fornication is ever committed between you again, I shall find it out and I shall tell poor Amelia, whatever the cost to her. And why don't I tell her *now*? Because I love her, that's why, and she is worth a lakh of rupees compared to you both and, oh, how deeply wounded she would be to return home with her new-born babe only to learn what filthy shameful deeds had been committed in her absence! For her sake I keep quiet – you can tell Theo so. You can tell him everything I have said in a letter and you can write it here and now before you go and I will give it him this evening.'

Against this well-planned assault Rukmini, still benumbed by the night's passion, had no defence. Her lowered gaze fell on a picture-book of Rolly's, and her heart sank further with the thought of missing him. But she said only, 'I shall ask Mangalam to pack my belongings and you can tell Rolly I have gone away. That will please *you*, won't it? Though not him!'

Drawing her veil over her head she walked slowly out.

Durmeen watched her go, her plump, ringed hands clenched in triumphant vindication. Never before in her life had she been able to humble a proud brahmin.

Theo, returning that evening in a state of guilty anxiety, found the house unusually quiet and Rukmini's letter on the table. His first reaction to it was profound relief; Durmeen's draconian measures had provided a solution. It was by no means congenial, but what solution could have been a happy one? Exhausted and depressed, he picked at his supper, not looking up when Durmeen eventually appeared.

'I saw Mrs Arbuthnot today,' she began. 'She asked me to tell you that Mrs Rundell has had a son.'

'Oh good – just as she wanted. Now let's hope we are granted a daughter.'

Durmeen sniffed. '*Amelia* certainly deserves what *she* wants.' He continued eating. 'You've read that letter?' He nodded. 'Well?'

He put down his fork. 'I've behaved disgracefully, Durmeen, and I'm most grateful to you for promising to keep this unfortunate episode a secret from my wife, whom I love dearly.'

She waggled her head. 'But it is never to happen again . . .'

'It won't.' He picked up his fork, but she lingered, thirsting for greater drama.

'Now that Rukmini has left, I want to move into her room. It's more comfortable than mine.'

'Please do as you wish.'

Realising he was not to be goaded further, she stamped out. He pushed aside his food and roamed about, restless despite his exhaustion. Searching in a cupboard for some light reading to distract his thoughts, he came upon the unworn crimson sari. He fingered its rich sheen under the lamplight and sighed with sick understanding. Then he took it back to the bazaar and exchanged it for a length of best printed cambric to make Amelia a morning dress.

That was Theo's only ostensible act of contrition during the next two weeks – which were not pleasurable for anyone. Rolly threw tantrums at the disappearance of his Auntie Rukee (from whom no word was heard); Durmeen ran the household with an air of high-handed self-righteousness that ruffled the servants; Theo, beset with guilty terror that he would be somehow punished for his faithlessness, waited in a state of irritable anxiety for news from Trichy. At last it came: Amelia had been safely delivered of a daughter.

CHAPTER NINE

Amelia, Catherine and their new-born returned together to the outskirts of Tanjore, where they parted in mutual relief. Catherine wanted only to devote her full attention to baby Victor, while Amelia was bored of hearing that his development was already outstripping Elizabeth's by far more than the actual slight difference in their ages. On the journey Catherine had regaled her companion with received lore on the subject of wet-nurses or amahs, a touchy, pernickety breed apparently, but indispensable. They had to be constantly supplied with rice-cakes and sago to increase their milk flow, hot baths, coconut oil for massage; and, if not carefully supervised, they chewed garlic and chillies (spoiling the taste of their milk) and fed their own babies by stealth. Amelia, disquieted by this, secretly decided to continue nursing Elizabeth herself, at less trouble and less cost.

Overjoyed to be safely home, Amelia accepted without question that Rukmini had gone to stay with her cousin in the Fort because of continuing friction with Durmeen; indeed, she was somewhat relieved because it meant less drain on the household expenses. Pretty baby Elizabeth was the focus of everyone's adoration; Theo brought the best flowers from the palace gardens to adorn her cradle; the servants cuddled and petted her, crooned rhymes and called her 'little Missy'; the box-wallah dangled coloured beads and ribbons before her eyes; and Rolly wanted her to ride his rabbit at once because he was too big for it.

In such happy accord the days flowed by, until interrupted by a letter from Marguerite Hervey: Gopal Krishnan having been summoned to Tanjore by the Raja's adviser, she'd taken the opportunity to accompany him. 'By the time you receive this we'll be almost upon you,' she wrote, 'so don't bother about a thing. Gopal will stay at the palace and I can plant my palki in your garden and sleep inside like a snail in its shell.' Disregarding this last, Amelia made what preparations she could before their visitors arrived two days later.

Gopal, Theo thought, looked exactly as he had for years past and probably would for years to come, but Marguerite had definitely aged. Her slenderness was reducing to the gaunt, and a deep weariness had settled behind her eyes.

'Oh, this country travelling is so infernally uncomfortable and tedious! A palki is but a moving coffin, and I've vowed that once I get back to Madras I'll never again venture further than a carriage can take me. But here I am, my dear Amelia.' Marguerite surveyed the guest bedroom and called to her laden bearers, 'Put everything in here. Pray don't be alarmed, Amelia, I'm not descending on you for a twelve-month, but I was never able to travel light. When we marched with the regiment it didn't seem to matter how much one carried about.'

'Can I help at all?' Amelia hovered.

'No thank you. I'll just dab off the top layer of dust.' She went to the washstand and inspected her face. 'Well, well, life among the Hottentots is even dirtier, I'm told. But tell me, how are you, my dear? And the precious little new-born I had to come and see? Theo wrote that you'd settled well into this jungle life.'

'Yes, I have, thank you.'

'Paid no attention to my forebodings, hey? Quite right. And it's a *good* marriage, I saw it instantly in your face.' She chuckled with a hint of salacity that made Amelia blush. 'There, there – just as it should be. Now if you'll excuse my dire dishevellment, I'd adore to sit comfortably beside a nice cup of tea before unpacking.'

Approaching the verandah, they heard Theo's protesting tones. 'Oh come now, Gopi, that's not true. I'm delighted to have you as my guest for as long as you don't prate about the inconsistencies of your host's past behaviour. His piteous inability – proved in all too public a spectacle – to fit his theories to his practice. I've heard more than enough on that score from that arrogant prig Rundell without *you* . . .'

Marguerite drifted in and sank into a chair. 'Oh dear, oh dear, Gopi! Now there's a fine tease denied us! And I had a store of merry quips ready. If I promise to make you laugh, Theo . . .?'

'It's no laughing matter, madam.'

Gopal signalled with his eyebrows at Marguerite, who nodded.

'Then I shall be the soul of tact and forebearance, Theophilus. Shall I regale you with the outrageous price of Madras oranges or the latest gossip from Afghanistan?'

Gopal rose. 'Pray excuse me from both, madam, for I was about to leave. The Raja will know of my arrival by now, and I mustn't offend him by lingering here. You'll come to the palace soon?' he reminded Theo, who escorted him to the door while Marguerite sipped the welcome tea.

'Now. Yes, please tell us what's going on in Afghanistan.' Theo drew up a chair. 'The papers seem to find the subject unworthy of attention recently.'

'Government doesn't want attention drawn, dear boy. But Babbage tells me there's considerable unrest among the Afghan tribes and our occupation is costing a pretty penny.'

'So are our forces there being reduced?'

'Far too much, people say. And General Elphinstone's left in military command – a sick old man who has to take orders from political wallahs hundreds of miles away. Rather an ominous picture. But the Misses Eden are flipping about in Calcutta as usual and entertained the exiled Afghan chiefs in great style on the Queen's birthday. Marble halls packed with princes and princelings, the very punkahs scented with attah of roses – silks and sweetmeats, bands and bunting! So perhaps there's nothing amiss after all . . . I don't know, or even much care.'

'More tea?' Amelia offered.

'Please, dear. I seem to get so stupidly fretting over little matters these days that I've no time for the larger ones.'

Theo grinned affectionately. 'But it's *not* worrying that

keeps you young, I remember you saying – advice I try to follow.'

She dabbed her face with a cologne-drenched handkerchief, wrinkled her nose at it. 'Faugh! how I loathe Indian dust these days – and it never used to bother me. You see, I'm getting old because I do worry, mainly about my beloved ramshackle house. When I go, my sons will simply sell it off from a distance – lock, stock and barrel. And the old place will be pulled down because it's on valuable land. I positively shudder these days when I read the auctioneers' notices, knowing that soon it will be my pickle pots and footstools and toasting-forks under the hammer. I'm leaving you my books, by the way – so be sure and get some decent shelves made when you hear I'm sinking.'

'Oh Marguerite, don't talk like that, please!'

'My dear boy, I'm only being realistic. I've been a resolute evergreen for quite long enough and it's time I drooped a little into the sere and yellow. But what's to become of Spring's Gardens, I ask you? They don't build like that nowadays – no sense of style anymore. Our Anglo-Indian newcomers are sober and frugal men: administrators, mission-aries, dentists . . . good for the soul and the teeth, I suppose. But enough of them on my first day here! Now . . . I'm simply longing to see your baby. Come, bring her to me, please!' She held out her arms towards Amelia.

'She's with the ayah. I'll go and fetch her.'

Marguerite sat back, eyeing Theo purposefully.

'*Now*, I promise not to tease, Theophilus, but there's a thing I will know. The lady you rescued from the flames is called Rukmini, isn't she? And the name seemed to ring a tiny bell – ting-a-ling?' She swung a hand to her ear.

'However did you know that?'

'Ah, but didn't your father bring you straight to us in Madras after your disgraceful conduct in a palace cupboard? Poor you – like a nervous, skinny little rabbit.' She laughed. 'And how do you find Rukmini these days?'

He evaded her eyes. 'She's well . . . older, of course.'

He put a finger to his lips as Rolly charged in, followed by his mother.

'Oh my! What a grown-up soldier-boy with his sabre and shield!'

Amelia tussled his hair proudly. 'His favourite toys. A birthday present from Captain Gilbert.'

'Ah, the grim Captain! I hope you've found a friend there?'

'We scarcely see him, I'm afraid. We've invited him, but he always makes excuses.'

'Prefers to keep to himself, it seems,' Theo added, rising.

'What a shame! And he can be such good company. I'll have to see what I can do. But where is the baby?'

'She's sleeping soundly. Ayah will bring her soon.'

'Then I shall content myself with General Roland. Are you off to the palace, Theo?'

'If you'll excuse me – Gopi asked me to dine with him.'

Marguerite leaned forward eagerly as soon as Theo had gone. 'Now Amelia, I'm agog to hear everything about the escapade at Poodocottah. It was reported in our press at the time, but not in any detail. And you did more than anyone to save the Hindu lady, I believe?'

'Well, I wouldn't say that,' Amelia began modestly, but was pleased nevertheless to describe her part, for which she'd never received much credit.

As she finished, Marguerite clapped her hands. 'A magnificent tale my dear! And where is Mrs Moitra now?'

'She stayed here at first, but . . . Rolly's very fond of his Auntie Rukee, isn't he?' The boy nodded politely and rushed off to the garden. 'She and Durmeen didn't rub along,' Amelia explained.

'Ah, of course not. Bayard's chee-chee was only a bit of Vepery bait when she was a girl – not suitable company for a well-born brahmin lady.'

'A bit of what?'

'A thing of the past, but when full-blooded white women were scarce, swarms of half-castes settled round the military station at Vepery near Madras and decked their daughters in frills and flounces. And many a susceptible soldier-boy was hooked on the bait of their flashing eyes and oily curls. Among them, Durmeen's first husband. But your average chee-chee does go off rather quickly and run to such fat! I was always a leetle shocked at Theo's father, I must confess, but he was a good man in many ways . . .'

'How I wish I'd known him,' Amelia began, as the ayah came in with the baby and Marguerite held out her arms.

'Oh, how utterly delicious! Lovely dark hair like Theo's. Bayard's granddaughter, just think of it.' She rocked and cuddled her. 'Elizabeth: a right royal appellation! I suppose we shall have a crop of Victorias next? Too modern for my taste – Elizabeth we're used to. Has she been baptised?'

'No, there's a pother about it. Catherine Rundell and I thought we'd have a joint christening at St Peter's, but Theo doesn't attend, as you know, and says he'd prefer a Hindu naming ceremony.'

'Oh fiddle-de-dee! Of course she must be baptised. But why not both?' She held the chortling child aloft. 'Yes, you shall have them both Eliza–liza–bet. We'll have a tamasha – a festival, you know. Baptism in the church first then a naming ceremony here, and we'll invite English and Tamils and even chee-chees. Theo will agree to that, I'll warrant!'

Elizabeth's grand naming tamasha was fixed for the following Sunday, which gave Marguerite something to 'go at' and renewed her flagging zest. Considering the assortment of guests, she decreed there should be places for 'mutually agreed separations'. Swings for the children were put up in the back compound, alcoholic drinks would be served on the back verandah only, and in the front garden a makeshift pandal – a canopy of leaves and branches supported on pillars and screened with grass blinds – was created for the cloistering of the Indian women. As for eating, Marguerite prophesied that the English – especially the clerical ones – would be thoroughly piggish while the brahmins, in the pink of their Hindu politeness, would pick disdainfully at a few seeds and nuts.

Amelia giggled. 'Oh, but I do wish they weren't quite so pernickety! It makes one feel quite unclean, doesn't it?'

'That is their intention, but don't let it disturb you.' She beamed at Amelia. 'But I'm sure you can cope with them. Indeed, you're doing splendidly all round, my dear. Settling in, taking the sundry surprises of India in your stride, and not giving in to Theo's occasional Hindu excesses.'

Amelia glowed, glad that her growing assurance was recognised, especially by Marguerite, whom she found less awesome and more likeable than at their first encounter.

One of the constants of Indian life was the predictability of the sun, which shone to order that Sunday on the marigold garlands wreathed round the pandal and through the windows of St Peter's on to the heads of the new-born, who were respectively christened Elizabeth Miranda and Victor Horatius. In a short address, Reginald Arbuthnot expressed his satisfaction that the two babes were now safely within the shelter of the Christian Church, which he likened to an all-embracing banyan tree, its branches forever taking fresh root in the native soil to produce vigorous new growth. Neither baby cried; their fathers did not quarrel; their mothers wore new bonnets. Dora Arbuthnot played Bishop Heber's stirring hymn, 'Brightest and Best of the Sons of the Morning', and then everyone sauntered towards the Lang's bungalow.

Long, long afterwards, Amelia was to remember the occasion as a bright skein linking disparate people together in celebration of birth. And it was thus fitting that the adults were outnumbered by the children: from the Fort came librarian Pundit Rao's many grandchildren, and Parvati with her husband Sannasi and their offspring; Durmeen's seven grandchildren were there and the brood of Arbuthnots, with Jack and Rosie Murphy.

'How many children are here? How many?' Rolly kept asking, but it was like trying to count a swirl of goldfish in a pond. Stately in the seclusion of the pandal sat elderly Mrs Pundit Rao with her two married daughters and also Parvati, but the widows Rukmini and Belveena, although invited, did not appear. It was not a fitting occasion for them, Parvati explained, but would say no more. Nor could she be persuaded to mingle with the other guests in the parlour where Elizabeth held court. The baby's cot was festooned with gifts – tiny carved toys, lotus flowers, sweets, ribbons and highly-coloured pictures of the Hindu deities. Late in the afternoon a modified version of the Hindu naming ceremony was performed: Theo, seated in a chair with his daughter in his arms, traced on a large bowl of rice the day of her birth, her heavenly constellation and her name, which he then called out three times.

'Elizabeth,' the word was repeated in approving whispers by the guests, who were then served with vast quantities of vegetable and meat curries, rice-cakes, curds, chutneys, banana custards, guava jellies and sago puddings. Rollie, too excited to eat, dragged Rosie to his father, who was still holding the infant.

'Look, Rosie, that's my new sister. Her name is Elizabeth,' he announced proudly, and Theo held the baby for Rosie to kiss. Amelia, coming upon them, felt a surge of joy that was close to tears and longed to sketch the scene, for the moment seemed very precious and worthy of record.

'And see who's come after all to grace our proceedings.' Marguerite's light tone interrupted her emotion and she turned to see Captain Gilbert, looking rather correct and formal amid the jolly throng.

'Why, good afternoon, Captain, and welcome!' Theo handed the baby to her ayah, and the captain jerked a bow.

'Good afternoon, Mr Lang. I've just called to convey my congratulations and bring a little present for the new-born.'

Amelia took it from him. 'Thank you indeed, Captain. Shall I look? But how very beautiful!' On a square of blue silk lay a thin gold bracelet. 'This is much too kind! Do put it on her!' She held out the baby's wrist and he fastened the bracelet round it gently and seriously.

'She'll say thank you one day!' Amelia smiled. 'And now please stay and enjoy our little feast.'

'No thank you, Mrs Lang. Lieutenant Cuddy has brought his wife, recently arrived from England, and she's so delighted to find herself in company at last that I've promised to take his duty at the barracks.'

'Then you must come and dine soon, Captain,' Theo said, accompanying him to the verandah.

'You are most kind, sir, but I'm already greatly in your debt,' muttered Gil in an ashamed manner that surprised

Theo, for to betray the captain's secret was so unthinkable that he deserved no gratitude for its keeping.

'Think no more on't, for I certainly do not,' he replied, and was seeking further words of reassurance when Marguerite called from her chair in the shade.

'Come hither, my skulk-in-the-mud officer, I insist. Leaving already, are you? To be sure, I've never known you quite so elusive. What *is* the matter?'

Gil grimaced. 'Age, I think, madam. I feel myself too old for jollity, especially just now, holding the hand of a new-born babe.'

'I wonder you dare talk so in my presence.' She slapped his sleeve. 'Am I not an ancient crone and yet can summon a little friskiness for an occasion like this?'

'You were always the younger of us, Marguerite, even when I was a scant-bearded youth!'

She tossed her head. 'Why, you make me sound like a witless fool, sir!'

'No, madam, I mean that you have more zest for living, that's all.'

'Then sit you down and explain why you are so unzested at your tender age.' She indicated a chair, but he shook his head.

'No, I'm taking Cuddy's duty.' He leaned over her, whispering, 'But – strictly in confidence, mind – I'm optimistic of a Madras posting within the sixmonth. When I get there I promise to be friskier. It's this hole makes me leaden.'

'Oh, grand tidings, Gil! There's a dire shortage of kindred spirits in Madras these days.'

They clasped hands and he hurried off, leaving her sunk in a chair, her last reserves of friskiness draining away as she watched the sun set in its habitual abundance of purple, pink and gold.

Servants came round with flaring torches to light lamps, and one inadvertently set fire to the dried leaves of the pandal, instead. The women fled outside screeching like a flock of exotic birds as buckets of water were fetched to extinguish the flames. After the disturbance, Parvati realised she'd lost a valuable earring and set children and servants to hunt for it.

Meanwhile Arbuthnot, Rundell and Wardle, who'd been sipping steadily from a hidden cache of brandy, began launching into stentorian choruses of 'Where'ere you Walk' and 'The Maid of the Mill', watched by round-eyed, giggling children. Such ale-house merriment did not appeal to Dora and Catherine who, upbraiding their spouses for making a spectacle, eventually whisked them off homewards.

Hubert Wardle, wishing he had a wife to return him to the path of sobriety, slumped on the verandah steps sipping the rest of the brandy alone, while Gopal Krishnan, seeing the youngsters deprived of entertainment, started telling them Tamil folk tales. Wardle listened, morosely aware of how little of that language he truly understood, and this reminded him of something he'd been trying to forget all day, so he went to seek out Theophilus Lang, who was conversing with Sannasi.

'A word in your ear, if you please.' He pulled Theo's sleeve.

'What – now?' Theo frowned.

'It's rather urgent.'

Theo excused himself and followed the Resident, whose state of semi-inebriation convinced him that a spy lurked behind every bush, and so he led Theo to the garden's furthest hedge.

'Here – have a drink.' He held out the bottle, but Theo shook his head. Wardle snorted. 'Remarkable how many people were merry on only tea and tamarind water today. Wish I knew the trick! Well, anyway, Lang, the point is – there's been an affray.'

'An affray?' The unexpected word jolted Theo like that earlier word, 'paramour'.

'Yes. Peasants living near the site of the Raja's new pagoda have been forbidden to gather firewood or graze cattle thereabouts – or even to use the nearby road to the markets. They were harassed and turned back, so they created a bit of trouble – and who can blame them? But in retaliation a posse of the Raja's soldiers cudgelled a number of them mightily a couple of days ago. Rundell's just got wind of it. Happened on the disputed boundary land, but some of the victims live in Company territory and a strong complaint has to be lodged – a very strong complaint . . .' He wagged a finger at Theo, drained the bottle, stared at its emptiness unbelievingly and tossed it into the hedge.

'You could sell that in the bazaar.'

'Oh confound it – hardly to the point. Point is – very strong complaint has to be lodged personally. By me.'

'But Sevaji won't see you.'

'Precisely. So you've got to get me an audience, Lang, and come to interpret. Can't pretend I understand everything that's said, and my official interpreter's a snake in the grass. It's a serious matter. Weighty report to the bigwigs called for. Can't have this sort of thing – who does H.R.H. think he is?'

'He's a Raja; they're his subjects. If they cause trouble he has 'em cudgelled over the head. Simple . . .'

Wardle peered at him. 'Who's side are you on?'

'Neither, if I can help it.'

'Well you can't help it. You're a British subject and – look, Lang, be a decent fellow!'

'Decent be hanged! If Sevaji finds out I'm in the pay of the Company . . .'

'But you're not. Still . . .' Wardle nudged him, the brandy having dissolved his small store of subtlety, 'Still, I imagine this little spree will cost a pretty penny, hey?'

Theo snorted and turned on his heel.

'I'll make it worth your while,' Wardle shouted after him, then stood for a few minutes trapped in that melancholy spot beyond the lights and the laughter, thinking of an icy comment in a recent letter from Madras to the effect that the only reason for maintaining a Resident in Tanjore these days 'seemed to be to further inflate the Raja's sense of his own dignity'. He groaned, and as he moved towards his palki thought he heard a rustle in the hedge behind – probably a beggar after that bottle.

The rest of the guests were now making their protracted farewells and, when the last had departed, Amelia began to organise the clearing up, while Theo strolled on the verandah munching a coconut bun.

'I'm still here, my good fellow.' Gopal's voice came from a basket chair. 'Too comfortable to move. That was a most successful tamasha.'

'And so say I! The sort of thing that should happen more often. Did you notice that the Rundells were quite affronted to see so many "natives" at first, and old Pundit Rao to see the chee-chees? Then they all settled down and enjoyed themselves. And, as old Wardle commented, 'twas good to see so many perfectly sober people perfectly happy – with the honourable exception of himself, of course. By the way, there's been a bit of bother . . .'

He related Wardle's news and Gopal tutted. 'Could be serious. Just the kind of excuse the Company might use to seize the rest of that land for the irrigation scheme. I've been looking through the palace accounts – hopeless mess. Sevaji wants advice on how to silence his numerous creditors legally. I also came upon some recent letters from the Resident – Sevaji doesn't pay them enough heed. There are ominous phrases about H.R.H.'s unsatisfactory behaviour which could, and I quote, "lead to the necessity of our adopting some decided measures for the protection of your own subjects". And now, if his soldiers are actually cudgelling aforesaid subjects . . .'

'Nothing new about that,' Theo grunted.

'Quite so – gone on for centuries. Just depends if the Company wants to make capital out of it at this particular time. And that we don't know, so we might as well let matters take their inscrutable course. Reminds me of one of Napoleon's maxims I happened upon recently: "In the eyes of empire builders, men are not men but instruments."'

'Quite so. Here, hang on a minute.' Theo went to fetch his cheroot box. 'Have one? Amelia asks to be excused. She's very tired. Look – Parvati's precious earring's been found. Such a pother she made about it. I'll return it myself sometime, might be a chance to . . .' He paused to light a cheroot. 'Rukmini didn't come and I was hoping so much that she would. I can't stop worrying about her. A tamasha is too festive an occasion for her to attend, I suppose. A widow's lot is a damnable one.'

He sat down sighing, absently dangling the jewelled earring in the lamplight, while Gopal assessed him before saying quietly, 'Well, if I hadn't stepped in it would still be far worse.'

Theo stared. 'You? What the deuce have you to do with it?'

'I gather H. N. Moitra was poisoned by a person or persons still unknown?'

'Yes. Poo court being the proverbial nest of vipers, several people were suspected. Rukmini thinks the late Raja's old mother was behind it.'

'Hmm. Just so and just as I planned.' Gopal sat back, regarding his fingertips smugly. 'In the unusual circumstances I'll partake of a cheroot. Thank you.' He rose, took one, lit it, then halted before Theo. 'Do you promise me, Theophilus Lang, that you will never repeat what I think I simply must tell you?'

Theo blinked at his changed tone. 'Well, that depends, Gopal Krishnan, but . . .'

'I know I shouldn't, but I simply can't resist,' Gopal rushed on. 'It's just too delicious and I've been so very clever and you, of all people, should know the truth.'

'Well, tell me then, man, I'm all agog.'

Gopal resumed his seat. 'I shall begin at the beginning, long, long ago when you were still a dry youth in that dreadful English school and I was at the Hindu College in Calcutta. We hadn't met. You've heard of that half-caste poet and philosopher, Derozie?'

'Of course – leader of the New Bengali Movement, died young.'

'He and his Hindu friends were marvellous modern – down with ancient custom and tradition, down with all the stupid brahminical taboos of our forefathers. So they ate beef steaks, drank French wine, whored with the white trash of the city. H. N. the Bengali was of their number for a while.' He paused. 'Can't you guess now?'

'Guess what?'

'That I was another.'

'You! Oh-oh, that's very rich Gopi, and I love you the more for it.'

Gopal's mouth twisted sourly. 'Well I've never loved myself

for it. I want to rinse out my insides with the five cleansing fluids whenever I remember. But the past, you know, has a nasty habit of growing a long tail which twists round sometimes and stings a man in his present posterior, which is what happened when I last visited you here. H. N. came to see me secretly. He was threatening to write to the papers and the law council, "feeling it his duty to report that a respected member of Dharma Sabha had in Calcutta long ago" – you can guess his tone. An unmitigated scoundrel, but not a very accomplished blackmailer because he forgot the golden rule – never try blackmail if you've got more enemies than friends.'

'My God! You mean it was *you* who . . .?' Theo was round-eyed with amazement and a kind of admiration.

'So I arranged for that particular stinging tail to be cut off.' Gopal chopped the air with his slim brown hand.

'Phew – Gopi! You! That's . . . that's . . . I don't know what to say. But what made H. N. do it?'

'Simply money. He was always desperately short of funds to pay for his filthy pederastic pleasures. You knew about them? And boys come more expensive than girls. Anyway . . . it's all worked out as I hoped – except I didn't imagine a certain gallant white knight would rush to rescue his widow and then arrange a cosy little *ménage à trois*; isn't that how the French put it?'

Theo jumped up angrily. 'It was nothing of the kind. Now stop it!'

Gopal peeped at him over his fingertips. 'Can you look me straight in the eye and swear by all the gods that you have never sampled the flesh of the body in question?'

Theo sagged. 'No, confound it, I can't. Just one night. And now she's banished from this house because Durmeen discovered us and Amelia must never suspect and – oh, it's such a damnable mess! I know she feels as guilty as I do, but I can't even see her, give her any comfort . . .' He paused. 'H. N! She felt guilty about him, too – had a crazy notion that she was somehow responsible for his death . . . Well, at least I can set her mind at rest on that score now.'

Gopal rose to confront him. 'No! It's a secret – you promised.'

'Not quite. I said it depended.'

They glared at each other. Gopal blew vigorously on his cheroot, then stubbed it out. 'Filthy weed! And what about my peace of mind if she knows?'

'But Gopi, I feel so responsible for all her miseries. I – who've always loved her in a way, ever since we were children.'

'Ho-ho. So the tail of the past stung you, too?'

Theo grimaced. 'I thought of her often today, wishing she were among us. What joy is left for her in life?'

'Very little. You should have let the tail burn itself off, don't you think?' Gopal was casually sauntering to the door.

'No, I do not. Damn it, Gopal, don't be so heartless!' Theo put the lost earring in his pocket. 'I'll walk back to the Fort with you.'

Gopal turned on the verandah step. 'You're not to tell her – I trusted you.'

'And I'd trust *her* with anything – my life or yours. Come.'

They walked the short distance to the Fort in silence, Gopal knowing it useless to pursue the matter further. The palace gates were already locked for the night, and while Gopal was bribing the guards to let him in, Theo slipped away in the direction of Parvati's house. Its gates, too, were locked, but lights still shone from the balconies. The gatekeeper answered Theo's knock and he was shown into a small reception room while a servant went in search of Sannasi. Theo stood, rocking from toes to heels, rolling the earring nervously between his hands. Then he crept to the doorway and nearly bumped into a servant bearing tea.

'The master asks you to wait. He will attend you soon.'

'Where is Mrs Moitra?'

'She? Why . . . in the widows' quarters . . .' He gestured vaguely down a dim passage.

Theo accepted the tea and pretended to drink until the servant left, then he quickly padded off down the passage. He was in the same kind of impulsive ferment as when he'd heard of Rukmini's intended suttee; nothing mattered except his desperate need to see her again. The passage curved and darkened and he proceeded more cautiously, but nevertheless nearly fell over a large bundle of clothes that lay across the way. It emitted a girlish shriek and he stepped back.

The disturbed servant stared up at him in horror and a voice from the curtained doorway ahead called, 'What is the matter?'

The curtain was drawn aside and a woman clad all in white stood there, holding a flickering oil-lamp above her head. Its rays shone on her bald, bony skull, leaving the large hollows of her eyes in shadow; she was like a ghost, the very similitude of death.

'Oh no! Rukmini!' he gasped.

'Theophilus!' With her free hand she tugged at the shawl round her shoulders.

'Oh my dear, my dear!' He stumbled towards her but she drew back.

'Theophilus, whatever are you doing here? In our quarters – at night!' Handing the lamp to the servant, she drew the shawl close over her shaven head with thin, trembling, ringless fingers.

'I hoped you'd come to our tamasha today. I wanted to see you so much – find out how you are.'

'Well, you see', she said, 'how I am. I could not come.'

'But Rukmini, it is dreadful. I am so terribly sorry. Please tell me – what can I do for you?' He longed to touch her in comfort, but she had about her now the untouchability of the social outcast.

'There is nothing you can do.' Her tone was flat and he bowed his head in despair.

'Well, there is just one thing I came to tell you, to ease your mind a little. You were in no way responsible for your husband's death.'

She started. 'Are you sure?'

'I am honour bound not to say who it was, but I swear by all the love we've ever shared between us, Rukmini, that the deed had nothing whatever to do with you.'

She looked in his face and smiled. 'I believe you. Thank you. Now all you can do for me is go – at once, this instant. If you are discovered here it will be I who suffer.'

He groaned. 'As always . . . as always. Oh Rukmini, can

207

you ever forgive me for . . .?' He swayed, desperate to kneel at her feet, kiss her saint-like robe, when a voice called in the distance.

'Go!' She retreated fearfully, holding up her arms against him. He hesitated, then, hearing a second call, turned and ran back along the passage. As it curved he looked back. She was standing as he'd first seen her – white, bald, still, aged. He shuddered and fled.

Sannasi was waiting at the door of the reception room, and scowling. Theophilus produced the earring, mumbling that he'd gone to present it to Parvati as a surprise but had lost his way in the dark. Probably Sannasi didn't believe him, but was sufficiently mollified by the sight of the jewel to let it pass. After the exchange of a few cool politenesses, Theo departed.

The city was asleep. Moonlight silvered palace and temple roofs, carved balconies, winding waters, rustling palm leaves. Theo's heart raged against the beauty of it – the passive, changeless beauty of India that endured, unsullied by the suffering of the millions whose lives were cut off and blighted there. He thought of Rukmini's hair as he'd last seen it, fanned long, black, lustrous across the pillow of their lovemaking.

CHAPTER TEN

M arguerite and Gopal departed for Madras two days
after the tamasha, leaving the Langs to put the house
and garden to rights and count the cost. Though a comparatively modest celebration, the tamasha, in the manner of its
Indian kind, had somehow exceeded its budget and landed
them back in debt. Theophilus fumed and prevaricated but
eventually had to concede that the easiest source of ready
money was Resident Wardle, on whose behalf he again
approached the Raja. Fortunately, Sevaji was in buoyant
mood after an auspicious blessing of the new temple's foun-
dations, and agreed to grant the British official an audience.

On the appointed day Wardle, determined to impress His
Highness with the dignity of his office, rode into the palace
courtyard on an elephant – a quaint, plump, buttoned-up
little figure bolt upright in a gilded howdah, preceded by four
sepoys and two drummers, led, Theo noticed from the library
balcony, by Lieutenant Cuddy rather than Captain Gilbert.
A few ragged guards presented arms, a gun fired a single
salute and the elephant halted, swaying lugubriously from
side to side, its ears and housings flapping as the ladder was
placed for Wardle's descent. When he was halfway down, the
animal listed alarmingly to starboard while the Resident
clung on, his feet on different rungs, looking as if about to
burst his old-fashioned breeches. Theo laughed aloud, Cuddy
looked up and winked, and the drummers grinned as they
beat their instruments.

Landed safely, Wardle was greeted by the sirkele, and
strutted into the palace followed by a red-belted messenger
carrying a rolled document which, Theo guessed, was the
irrigation plan. Shortly after, Theo was summoned to the

audience hall where an already-classic scenario of British–Indian relations was in progress. Sevaji, glittering in royal array, his three-cornered turban particularly laden with pearls, sat, ringed by courtiers, on a raised dais under a canopy beside a sunken courtyard where, at more festive times, wrestlers fought and acrobats tumbled. Confronting him sat Wardle, cocked hat on knees, attended by his escort. The irrigation plan and a sketch of the new temple were spread on a low table between them. The benevolent mood in which Sevaji had granted the audience had not extended to the holding of it, and he was scowling before Wardle had stumbled through the preliminary courtesies of greeting and gratitude. Theo was offered a chair beside the Resident, which he shifted to a more neutral position before taking on the task of explaining to Sevaji the Resident's displeasure at the recent affray.

'It is but a nothing,' Sevaji waved a jewelled hand. 'The peasants know that land is now a sacred preserve for my temple. They trespassed on it and were punished – none even killed.'

'But your Highness . . .'

Sevaji glared at Wardle and cut in, 'I know why you are making a big disturbance over this nothing, Resident. It is but an excuse to try and deprive me of my remaining territory so you can complete your water scheme. Put it somewhere else, I tell you! On the land your Company has already seized from my ancestors.'

'It will be for the benefit of your own subjects, sire.'

'Will it? Will it?' Sevaji clenched his fist. 'What about the water-carriers who will be deprived of a livelihood and the peasants who will be furious if new channels are cut across the ancient divisions of their fields? But when my magnificent temple is built they will crowd round it in wonder and happiness and thank me from their hearts' core for the beauty of it.'

Wardle ground his teeth. 'But let me show you, sire.' He grabbed the plan and pointed. 'If a dam is built here, the seasonal rains can be diverted towards crops here and here in the dry season.'

Sevaji looked and bellowed, '*Not there*! My temple is to stand *just there*!'

The silence of stalemate fell on them. Tea and stale cakes were served to the visitors; their hosts did not partake.

Wardle swallowed a crumb, tried to change tactics. 'Your father, who had a sense of great respect and gratitude towards the British, frequently took our advice and help. Can you not see the wisdom of following his good example, your Highness?'

'Ha! Respect and gratitude – why should I? For your own ends, you British helped him regain his throne which he'd lost by trickery. That is all.' He banged his fist on its arm. 'Now the throne is mine by rightful inheritance – no thanks to you! And in return for their support the British took away my father's realm, his wealth and his power, saying you would be allies of Tanjore forever. But now see! You want to grab my last shreds of land and lie to me as you do it! But I know your ways! The men of your greedy Company march about our country deposing rajas and nawabs under some pretext or other. And now you have designs on me.'

Wardle kept shaking his head emphatically, trying to interrupt, but Sevaji was in full spate.

'My duty is to support and perpetuate the ancient grandeur of my Mahratta forefathers – so it is written in the old texts. And so I try to do with the few resources left me. I perform the duties of a sovereign, support my royal establishment, maintain the water-system within this Fort, build temples to the glory of Siva – you tell me none of this is good enough! You want more, always more from me and I have no more to give . . .'

'Your Highness,' Wardle managed to break in, nudging Theo into his role as interpreter. 'We don't want more! We want you to manage *well* what you have. But your treasury is in chaos, you constantly borrow from one to pay off another, your servants cry for their rightful wages while your favourites flaunt your gifts of jewels, and now you are pouring money into yet another temple, and closing the land about it, dispossessing your own subjects. Shouldn't a sovereign rule with justice and reason and mercy? Yet I hear your men are now seizing the very salt which the peasants bring from the coastal pans, to make bricks for that pagoda of yours!'

Sevaji banged both fists on his chair. 'It is *my* salt, *my* bricks, *my* temple.'

They were back in the same place. Wardle pushed his tray away, shaking his head sorrowfully. 'And this is what you wish me to report to the Company's grand Council in Madras, your Highness?'

'Report what you like and let them do their worst. For worse is yet to come. That is foretold by my astrologers. With cunning, you divide and rule us. Do you think I don't understand all this?' He rose to his feet and snorted. 'I do. I understand everything, Mr wily Resident, and I *will build my temple*.' He took a deep breath, turning to a courtier. 'Please see these gentlemen out.'

Wardle turned. 'Confound it, Mr Lang, see if you can prevail upon him a little. It may be our last chance. Speak to him personally . . .'

Theo began softly. 'Your Highness, I sympathise most deeply with your position but speaking as your friend I . . .'

Sevaji turned his glare full on him. 'You should stay in your library, Mr Lang. You are no friend of mine. You are in the pay of Mr Company Resident, that I know. I have my loyal servants who have pricked up their ears behind doors and *hedges* and I know I can't trust you in the manner my father trusted yours. Times have changed, Mr Lang, and perhaps such trust is, in any case, no longer possible.'

Theo bowed and silently followed Hubert Wardle out.

'You might as well ride back with me.' Wardle gestured to the elephant and Theo dispiritedly complied. 'There must have been someone listening at our tamasha,' he remarked, as the elephant got into its ponderous stride.

'Thought I heard a movement in the hedge after you left,' Wardle tutted. 'Treacherous bunch! Simply can't trust 'em you know, Lang.'

'And doesn't your Company use spies to find out who its friends are? But you never look at the other side, do you, Resident? Now if you'd just conceded *something* to Sevaji's point of view today, we might have got on a better footing.

The man is not simply a religious fanatic – he's frightened of losing the remains of his authority, and that would be a grave personal disgrace. Can't you see that? Why don't you show him some respect and sympathy?'

'And where would that get me? Pleading with the bigwigs for one petty raja wouldn't change the outcome one scrap. March of progress, they call it. This country has to be made more solvent, that's government orders. I'm just a tool for carrying them out.'

Theo sighed, depressed and temporarily defeated by War- dle's cynical realism. As they approached the Residency office, he remarked, 'You know, when Sevaji was ranting on, I was suddenly reminded of King Lear when his daughters tell him he has no more need for such pomp and circumstance. "Oh reason not the need; our basest beggars are in the poorest thing superfluous."'

'Ha!' Wardle barked appreciatively. 'And look what hap- pened to poor old Lear! At least your Sevaji is unlikely to end up on a blasted heath with only a Fool for company. He'll still have his courtiers, his women and jewels even if we do remove him from Tanjore – and I ain't sure we will. Well, let's get down – a confounded tricky business. You go first and hold the ladder, Lang, this elephant-wallah seems to think I can shin about like a monkey.'

In his report to the Madras bigwigs, Wardle duly stated that he'd made no headway with the Raja and the outlook for future harmony was unpromising; nevertheless he felt he should persevere (for he didn't want to be sent to some even thornier post at this stage). While he waited anxiously for some response to this, sultry October arrived and the skies, dissolving sometimes from clear blue to pewter grey, presaged the onset of the north-east monsoon.

Captain Gilbert, partial to John Keats' poetry in his mellower moments, murmured to himself as he had before at such times, 'Season of chills and sodden mildewness'. But that autumn brought a far worse scourge than mere mildew, as indeed he'd feared, for he knew of its earlier advance upon military stations to the north. So he was neither especially surprised nor alarmed when Doctor Cauldwell arrived at his office one morning carrying a piece of paper in his shaking hand.

'It's here: three sepoys down.' He read them out, for he could never remember native names five minutes together.

Gil made a note. 'Two Hindus, one Moslem.'

'What does it matter?'

The captain grinned. 'Different funeral rites.'

'Confound it, man, they're not dead yet. I'm doing my best, ain't I?'

'Out with the cholera pills, hey Doc? Extract of opium powder and cayenne pepper are the basic ingredients, I believe? Or will it be your famous cholera tincture – laudanum and spirit of camphor? Or both?'

Cauldwell plopped into a chair. 'Both – and don't sound so damnably cheerful.'

'Not cheerful, Doctor, just philosophical. "Our life is reaped like a ripe ear of corn, One is yet standing and another is down," etc. Having survived twice when old Corporal Forbes was on his rounds, I think I'm well salted.'

'Well I hope you're right, Captain. Did your regiment keep on the move?'

'Under canvas – yes. Till we out-ran him, I suppose. Can't do that here, of course.'

'Started in the lal bazaar. It's a filthy place.' He meant the regimental brothel of native prostitutes, and Gil wondered fleetingly if his lack of interest in women was why he'd never caught the disease.

'You've isolated the sick?'

'Of course.'

'Is it in the city generally?'

'Bound to be – and the palace, I'll warrant.' Cauldwell took out his brandy flask, swigging deeply; he'd seen too many cholera epidemics and dreaded the days ahead. 'Hoped it was just dysentery, but no. That first fellow on the list is shrivelling and sinking fast. He'll be gone before nightfall.'

And sure enough, as the pink-gold sunset light glowed on the tiled barrack roof and scuffed barrack grit, ashen-faced Lieutenant Cuddy came to report the first death, and not only that – two other families in the native lines were stricken. Gil ordered immediate burial to reduce the spread of infection, and decided he should confer with the Resident.

As he rode through the Tanjore streets where everything seemed as usual, he puzzled, as had many before him, on the mystery of a disease so terrifying in its unpredictability. Certainly it often started in a town's dirtiest bazaars, but hundreds succumbed who'd never been near such hell-holes. Clerics suggested it was the Lord's punishment for over-indulgence in food and drink – but if so, men like the old doc would be long gone. Perhaps, as some medical experts suggested, the disease was airborne; but if so, why was it possible to march away from it, as his regiment had?

Gil vividly recalled his terror on that occasion, when half the muster had died and a mad recklessness infected the remainder. Some drank themselves into a stupor every night; others, like Gil, went riding for miles through the dark, feeling highwayman Forbes at their heels. Returning from one such expedition, Gil had come upon three fellow officers standing on the mess-tent dining table, goblets raised and roaring in unison:

> Who dreads to the dust returning?
> Who shrinks from the sable shore?
> Where the high and haughty yearning
> Of the soul shall sting no more.
> No, stand to your glasses steady
> The world is a pack of lies.
> A cup for the dead already
> Hurrah for the next who dies!

Their blustering bravado had not helped; by the end of that week none was left to shout 'hurrah'. But the captain had survived. Why? As he dismounted at Wardle's gate, his ponderings were interrupted by a drum roll and musket-fire from the barracks. He stood to attention for a moment and muttered, ' "Consider *thyself* to be dead and to have completed thy life up to the present time and live according to nature the remainder which is allowed thee." '

Wardle came down the path, a hand cocked to his ear. 'Do I guess aright?'

Gil nodded. 'You've heard?'

'Yes. It's come. And you were praying, Captain?'

Gil grinned. 'In a manner of speaking.'

'I shall now inform the other British residents officially,' Wardle announced. 'The children should be kept indoors.'

'And told to breathe as little atmosphere as possible, Resident?'

'It's no jesting matter, Captain.'

'I'm well aware of that, sir, though past experience of such outbreaks leads me to believe one can do little but keep cheerful and take comfort from the ancient philosophers.'

'Well, I shall stick to my bottle! It's seen me through before now. You won't join me, I suppose?'

The captain declined, and Wardle went to fortify himself for his unpleasant errand.

Medieval plagues must have felt like this, Amelia thought later that evening, as she and Theo, their hands clasped tight, looked down in silent dread on their sleeping children. Acting on Wardle's instructions she kept them inside for the next three days, but Theo went to the palace as usual, saying he was as safe there as anywhere else. Confined to their homes, Dora, Catherine and Amelia sent each other reassuring notes, but Dora's note of the third evening brought no reassurance: Lieutenant Cuddy had succumbed – the first European to die. Elizabeth tossed and moaned fretfully throughout that night, and Amelia watched over her in agonised anxiety. As heavy, lacklustre dawn broke, they both slept at last, and by the time Amelia roused herself Theo was finishing breakfast.

'Are you feeling all right?' His tone was concerned.

'Just tired.' She yawned and stretched, her white muslin robe and washed-out complexion giving her the look of illness.

'How is she?'

'Sleeping peacefully, thank goodness.'

'I might as well go, then. Nothing I can do here, is there?'

'Not really. Poor Clara Cuddy. They were married less than a year. I'll visit her later.'

'But we'll be all right,' he reassured her.

'How can you be so certain?'

'Oh, I just feel it in my bones – my well-seasoned Indian bones.'

'But mine and the children's aren't!'

He came to kiss her, pushing back her limp hair. 'You'll be all right – because of me. Just stay here with the children, dearest, and don't go to the barracks where the contagion's raging.'

'But poor Clara!'

'The women there will see to her.'

Amelia nodded listlessly. Depressed and limp, she sat down at the breakfast table, and was still there an hour later when Durmeen arrived, her gray hair plastered tight to her skull in the dank heat. She plumped down.

'Horrible sort of day – if only it would rain.'

'Tea?'

'Please, dear.' Durmeen glanced at her and away again.

'Is there more bad news?' Amelia steadied herself against it.

'I'm afraid so. They suspect Dora has it.'

'Dora! Oh no – I must go to her!' Amelia jumped up. 'Has the doctor seen her?'

'He's there now. I just talked to the servants. And you're not to go, Amelia, in case of infection. You must think first of your own little ones.'

'But Dora . . .'

'She'll understand. She wouldn't want you to take any risk.'

'Oh, this is terrible, terrible! We're so helpless.' Even as she spoke, an ominous presentiment of grief fell on her bent shoulders like a shroud she longed vainly to shake off.

'Her husband is with her.' Durmeen's words, meant to comfort, sounded doom-laden.

They sipped fresh tea; on the verandah Rolly pushed his wooden cart up and down, the creak of its wheels grinding through Amelia's head.

'Thank goodness the boy hasn't been to play there recently,' Durmeen said, putting down her cup and mopping

217

her face. 'I'll go and enquire about Dora and come back later. Try and brighten up, dear, for the children's sake.'

Durmeen patted her hand and went to kiss Rolly before leaving. Amelia dressed slowly, then wandered to look at Elizabeth still cradled in sleep. She stroked the downy head; hovering about it, in her mind's eye, was highwayman Corporal Forbes: black cloak, black broad-brimmed hat framing an empty-socketed skull. Elizabeth whimpered, and as Amelia bent over her, she heard a step and turned. Theo was leaning against the door-arch, his face ashen, his eyes wide and frightened.

'Theo! What's the matter?'

'I don't feel very well,' he croaked. 'Nothing to worry about.'

He hurried to the bathroom and she heard him retching violently.

'Theo – Theo, I'm sending for Doctor Cauldwell,' she shouted.

'Yes.'

So he knew it was serious; her insides seemed to plummet at his one word and she hurried to instruct Long-ago to fetch the doctor and Durmeen. The latter came at once, but Doctor Cauldwell, hurrying from one sick-bed to another with his nostrums (tartar emetic, camphor, opium, sulphate of quinine, laudanum), keeping himself more or less upright on draughts of undiluted brandy, did not reach the Langs' until late afternoon. In that short space it seemed as if all Theo's vital juices had drained from him. He had vomited up every remedy Amelia and Durmeen had pressed on him, had filled pots with watery, greenish stools and become so weak he could scarce raise the stone-weight of his head from the pillow. He did manage it when the doctor entered, but Cauldwell's face offered no reassurance.

'Ah, Mr Lang – now let me see . . .' He dug in his bag.

'It's cholera, isn't it?' Theo gasped.

'Hmm – looks very like, but we'll pull you through. Three men in the barracks are over the worst now, they'll survive. So you must follow their good example, Mr Lang, hey?'

'But what's to be done, Doctor?' Amelia begged, clutching Theo's icy hand.

'I'll try bleeding him, Mrs Lang. And here are the pills – dosage on bottle. Now go and heat some water, put into bottles, wrap them in cloth, apply to spine and legs, apply mustard poultices to keep blood circulating.' The exhausted man had repeated these instructions so often in the past few days they had become a meaningless incantation. Equally mechanically, he jotted down the usual notes: blood dark and thick; pulse low; respiration oppressed.

He rose, 'Well, well – just follow my suggestions, Mrs Lang. Massage, pills, not much fluid. I'll be back later.'

She followed him out. 'But Doctor . . . is he . . . will he?'

'We don't know, Mrs Lang. We can only hope for the best.'

Just as dusk fell they heard a roll of muffled drums and firing of several rounds of musketry from the barracks. Amelia jumped nervously.

'Oh – whatever's that?'

Durmeen sighed. ''Twill be for Lieutenant Cuddy, dear.'

'Cuddy, oh yes, poor Cuddy. He was so young.' She wanted desperately to weep, but mustn't let Theo see her doing so.

'There, there.' Durmeen patted her hand and went to fetch a lamp. Its flickering light revealed more clearly the livid hue of Theo's skin, his bluish nails, the inward-collapse of his cheeks and mouth.

Amelia stared in growing terror. 'Oh Theo, Theo dearest, can you hear me? You can't just . . .' She choked into a handkerchief. 'Die', she was about to say; but he could; people did.

His eyes focused vaguely towards her, filled with fear and anguish, and he rasped, 'Amelia, dear Amelia. I do love you.'

'And I love, I love you – oh my dearest only one, rally your forces, please, please.' She clutched his arms, desperately rubbing his skinny, restless legs, kissing his shrivelled lips despite the rancid smell of his labouring breath. He tried to smile at her, a ghastly grimace.

'I'll be all right, Amelia . . . If I can just sleep . . .' His dilated pupils roved beyond her and his eyes closed.

Gently Durmeen loosened her grip on him. 'There, there,

dear. Go and see how the children are. I'll call you if he wakes.'

Durmeen sat on, alone with Theo in the gloom, gently wiping perspiration from his forehead. As she fetched a fresh cloth, Theo suddenly shot bolt upright, staring before him.

'She's coming!' he shrieked. 'See – see her!'

So convincing was his cry that Durmeen, too, stared into the dim, empty door-space.

'No, Theo, no . . . there's no one.'

She reached for his hand but he shook her off, pointing in front of him.

'See, there – all in white! And without . . . without . . . her lovely hair!' He fell back on the pillow moaning.

'Shush!' Durmeen commanded. 'Shush! That traitor woman's not here. Not here, I say! Now quiet . . . quiet, my poor soul.' She pressed the cloth over his working mouth, wiping away his muttering and his sobs.

Later that night, which seemed to become in itself a kind of death, Doctor Cauldwell returned and counted Theo's faltering pulse, drew more of his thick, sluggish blood, felt his drying skin, gave him mercury pills to stimulate the action of the internal organs and tried to evade Amelia's question. But she caught up with him on the step.

'Doctor, you must tell me – is he going to live?' Her voice sounded steady.

'I have grave fears, Mrs Lang, but the next few hours will be crucial. I'll come back soon.'

'And Mrs Arbuthnot?'

'She died an hour ago.'

Amelia leaned against the verandah post, weak from lack of food and sleep, wondering without fear if she, too, was succumbing to the plague. If she ate something and vomited she would know. In the kitchen she found some rice and pickles which she forced down her dry throat; the food made a cold lump inside her, but stayed. She stood for a while, summoning courage to return to that agonising scene; all was silent save for an intermittent sound from the water-filter on the kitchen verandah. She went to stare at it: two earthenware pots were supported one above the other in a wooden frame.

The top one, layered with gravel and sand, had been recently filled, and water was seeping steadily through the layers and small holes in its base down through smaller holes in the second pot into a large water-jug on the floor.

Moonlight gave each drop a crystal sparkle as it fell, followed by the tiny splash of it in the dark jar. The sound was like a clock ticking away the short remainder of Theo's life. She reached to catch a few drops in her palm as if to suspend the process, looking at them intently. And such a stinging surge of relief swept over her that she gasped in amazed horror at herself. It was not she dying; she wasn't going to die. Until that moment and since the nightmare began, his death had been hers, too. But in that moment it was his alone; they were separated; forever. She would see water for years yet – sparkling in moonlight, spraying over rocks, laving her hands – and she accepted her fate, her fortune, in a mixed intensity of guilt, anguish, relief and love.

'Oh Theophilus,' she murmured, 'Theophilus, I would gladly die instead of you this minute, but I cannot. I am going to live.'

She rubbed her wet hand over her forehead and returned to the sickroom. She had not been long away but Theo's breath was still more laboured, cheeks and eyes sunken further back into his skull. In less than twenty-four hours he had aged some forty years. She knelt by the bed, clutching his clammy, shrivelled hands.

'Oh God, please God in Heaven, don't let him die. Please God, I love him so much, please.'

Just once more, Theophilus opened eyes that looked far beyond her, his blue lips moved in a hiss. 'No time . . . no time . . .'

After that his breath came in increasingly protracted gasps as he fell into a coma and died, just before dawn.

CHAPTER ELEVEN

Theophilus Lang and Dora Arbuthnot shared a funeral at sunset and were buried near each other in St Peter's churchyard. The brevity of the interval between death and burial seemed to Amelia an added cruelty, but such was the custom, especially when cholera raged. Resident Wardle conducted the service, while Reginald Arbuthnot stood in one front pew with his offspring and Amelia with Rolly and Durmeen occupied the other. Captain Gilbert and Nicholas Rundell were the only other English present, but the back pews were full of Christian converts, Dora's orphans and representatives from the palace. As the service began, a woman heavily veiled in white slipped into a pew just inside the door, and disappeared before it ended.

Dry of eye and lip, Amelia mouthed the appropriate words, and only when she walked outside and saw a squirrel sitting on the pillar of a tomb gilded rose in the dying light did she give way to tears. She remembered Sarah Murphy's funeral with its attendant squirrels, Rosie chuckling at them, her own spasm of irrational fear and, worst of all, as if it was only yesterday – and indeed it wasn't so very long ago – her husband coming to tell her she should go to Trichy for her confinement. She saw the warm concern in his eyes, heard his very words inside her head, and an anguished horror that was like a nauseous illness broke over her at the full realisation that she would never again see those eyes, hear that voice.

She joined Reginald Arbuthnot beside the open graves.

'Thy will be done,' he was muttering in choked tones, 'Thy will be done.' He glanced at her, red-eyed, as if seeking comfort but she could find nothing to say. From what seemed a long way off she heard Rolly crying, Durmeen comforting him, and then Captain Gilbert and Hubert Wardle came to escort her home.

The sad occasion had revived Wardle's own sense of loss, for Marjorie was buried in the same churchyard, and he could find nothing to say. Gil, distancing himself carefully from the emotion of the present, speculated again on the mystery of cholera. One could surmise that Lieutenant Cuddy had succumbed because of the sinister highwayman's reputation for killing off the most terrified first. But Theo and Dora had conspicuously lacked fear, so he tried to recall what experiences they'd recently shared. All three had visited the palace where the disease was rampant, but so had others who still seemed in good health. There was no sense in it, he thought, as he opened Amelia's gate and looked on her white, young, stricken face framed by a black bonnet.

'Madam, try to look at it this way: "Death is cessation from the impressions of the senses, the tyranny of the passions, the errors of the mind and the servitude of the body," so says Marcus Aurelius.'

She listened eyes lowered, then murmured, 'Thank you, Captain,' and went past him into the bungalow.

Collapsing in a chair, Amelia waited for Durmeen to bring an infusion of herbal tea; the familiar surroundings seemed unfamiliar and lacking in substance; the state of death, as the captain had just described it, infinitely desirable. Durmeen's plump hand shook as she handed the tea, and Amelia remembered how she had once used her fingers to count off her dead men – one, two, three. Marguerite had done the same, and Amelia had found it quite comical at the time. Now she wondered if they had once endured what she was enduring, and how they had survived so strongly. Shortly after drinking the tea, which tasted as bitter as her grief, Amelia fell into a deep slumber and Durmeen, gently removing her bonnet and shoes, left her to enjoy the temporary release the special brew had induced.

Amelia woke with a sharp shudder; she had been dreaming that she and Theo were alone together in some sunny, happy place, and the pain of the truth seeped through her body like a grievous wound opening, cutting her into two parts. She rose, surprised she could walk normally; it was dark and silent, for everyone had crept to bed without disturbing her. Peering at the clock, she saw it was just after eleven; so many weary hours before dawn – and she was now wide awake. She wandered to the verandah; from the direction of the bazaar came the continuous beat of music and voices raised in unison. This was so unusual at that time of night that she banged her forehead to make sure she wasn't still dreaming. Deciding she was indeed inhabiting reality, and longing for a diversion from its pain, she set off towards the sounds.

The bazaar stalls were boarded up and the noise came from a central space where goats and oxen were usually herded. Shrouding her head in her shawl, Amelia crept close till she could discern, by the flicker of a few oil-lamps, what was happening. Knots of silent people stood watching a circle of women who were dancing slowly round, each with a brass bowl which she raised above her head and lowered in time to a monotonous wail, augmented by several men with drums and pipes. She was astonished to see that the women were clad only in long skirts, with bare breasts and feet, and in the circle's centre five older women, naked except for a kind of loin-cloth, were working themselves into a frenzy. They twirled and twisted, kicked their legs high, beat their hands above their heads and shrieked, slapped their thighs, breasts and buttocks, while the chant of the circling women rose to screaming pitch and the music banged and shrilled at full blast.

As the pace quickened, the women flung water from the bowls at the air and each other, and the whole eerie scene seemed to explode into a storm of fury, despair, supplication, sorrow. Amelia found she was sobbing loudly, as were many of the bystanders, caught up in the tide of communal grief. Her concealing shawl slipped off as she threw back her head and raised her arms, glaring up into the clouded night, shaking her fists, imploring and groaning with the rest. For as long as the music lasted she felt a blessed release from the burden of her pain, as if she were sharing it with everyone else; but then it ceased abruptly, and the women drifted into stillness and silence.

People nearby began staring at her and muttering, their eyes glinting in the darkness. Amelia retrieved her shawl from the ground, feeling suddenly terrified; she saw herself utterly alone in this whole vast continent packed with a dark, alien race whose ways were incomprehensible to her, whose good-will, in this hour of her need, she scarcely even deserved and certainly couldn't count on. Without Theo – as interpreter, protector, mentor, lover, friend – she felt absolutely abandoned and petrified with fear. Men, their expressions more curious than hostile, began to press closer. One of them shouted at her and she gave a loud shriek. Suddenly, a familiar face pushed through the throng: it was Veena. As Amelia half-fell towards her, Veena rushed to her support, chivvying the men away. There followed much babble and bustle and shouted explanations, until a litter arrived to carry her back to the bungalow.

There, too, all was upset, for her absence had been discovered and Long-ago was about to go in search of her. Preparing more tea, Durmeen explained that what Amelia had witnessed was a traditional dance performed in hope of driving away the cholera.

'Only a primitive peasant ritual,' she added. 'Even the brahmins scorn that sort of thing, but the ignorant people still do it.'

'I thought it rather beautiful and strange and was quite carried away, until I got frightened, which was silly of me. Anyway, Durmeen, let us pray their dancing has the desired effect.'

Perhaps it did, or perhaps it was the monsoon rains that began in earnest the next day, flushing out the fetid ditches and tanks that supplied the town's water. At any rate the worst of the epidemic was over within a week, and cruel Corporal Forbes had marched off as unpredictably as he'd arrived, leaving victims dead or suffering, survivors grateful or heart-broken. But heart-broken Amelia had no time or strength to devote to her own recovery, for first Elizabeth and then Rolly were stricken with a 'monsoon fever' that could prove as fatal as cholera, especially to the young. She tended them fiercely and tirelessly, her nagging terror of further loss accentuated by the news that Catherine's baby Victor had died of fever after a two-day illness.

For Amelia the ensuing days and weeks were meaningless stretches of time during which the children cried, shivered and sweated; Dr Cauldwell and Durmeen came and went with their potions and comforts; and the rains fell. Mildew spawned behind pictures, under matting, over shoes and books; mosquitoes whined, winged ants blundered into every drink, frogs frisked across the verandah, scorpions sidled through crevices and fleas multiplied everywhere. When the doors and windows were opened for coolness, bats and green, noxious-smelling bugs flew indoors. Outside, bedraggled hens and monkeys huddled by the wall; rivers and tanks over-flowed, the huts of the poorest dissolved back to their original earth.

The Old Bungalow did not quite dissolve but its roof sprang several leaks, its drains became streams, its verandah steps were often awash. One morning a messenger sloshed up these steps bringing a small quantity of coins in a bag and a letter from Raja Sevaji expressing his 'oceans of sorrow' at Theo's death. The money was to facilitate Amelia's journey Home; clearly no more would be forthcoming. Hubert Wardle also brought some money – which he'd apparently owed Theo for 'services rendered'. When not tending the sick children, Amelia wrote letters to relatives and friends describing the circumstances of Theo's sudden illness and death. The very repetition of that doleful tale seemed to dull the edge of her pain, which worsened when she finished and surveyed the emptiness around her.

As the children began to gain strength at last, she, enfeebled by exhaustion, anxiety and grief, succumbed to the same fever and lay for days in a semi-conscious delirium, followed by a state of such physical weakness she could scarce hold the spoonfuls of sustenance offered by Durmeen, who nursed her devotedly. Throughout this dreary time Amelia felt she was groping alone along a long, dark, damp tunnel without the assurance of any light at its end; and yet eventually light literally came, as the rains moderated and the lush garden sparkled in intermittent sunshine. And one bright morning the box-wallah arrived on the verandah bringing tinned York hams, fancy biscuits and crystallised fruits which he'd specially ordered from Madras for the foreigners' Christmas festival.

The prospect filled Amelia with dismay, but she made of it a rallying point and, after the Christmas service in St Peter's, provided a meal for the remnants of the town's foreign community. Hubert Wardle brought his best claret, Reginald Arbuthnot brought his own children and Sarah Murphy's, Captain Gilbert brought Clara Cuddy, who was pregnant. The Rundells were absent, for Catherine had fallen into a state of nervous hysteria after her baby's death and was still in the Trichy hospital. Apart from Clara's tendency to dab her eyes in a corner, everyone bore up well: Reginald and Gil organised games for the children; Wardle produced a fiddle and played a few carols rather badly; Amelia stretched her mouth into the requisite number of smiles. Only when everyone had gone did she allow her face to droop as she wandered on to the verandah, remembering not only the few Christmases spent with Theo, but the distant festivities of her youth. She seldom felt homesick, but that night she longed for snowy fields, log fires and holly boughs, picturing herself returned to such familiar sights by the next year's turning.

On New Year's day Amelia resolved to put the tears of heart-sickness behind her. First, she would put flowers on Theo's grave (which she'd not yet summoned strength to do), and then decide her course of future action. The churchyard was verdant again, the squirrels frisking among shiny-leaved trees, a few goats illicitly chewing weeds by the wall. Reluctant to face the finality of her husband's tomb, Amelia lingered, pausing to read the stone of one Lilian Bradlaugh, 'Relict of Judge Cornelius Bradlaugh' who had died while in the district fifteen years before. 'Relict' – she shuddered; was she no more than that? A pathetic, left-over remnant from the life of Theophilus Lang?

She tossed her head in defiance and walked on, pausing again beside a large, newly-carved stone angel that looked down on the small remains of Victor Horatius Rundell, aged four months and five days. Taking a flower from her bunch, she laid it on the slab. Poor, poor Catherine, how ridiculously proud she'd been that her Victor was older than Elizabeth; now, already, Elizabeth was older than he would ever be. Theo's stone was as simple as he'd have wished, and she was relieved to see the inscription had been carved correctly. Would she, who had always been the junior, know years of maturity denied him? The very thought of it was wearisome and she sighed deeply, but yet saw in her mind's eye the clear water dripping from the kitchen filter and acknowledged she had no wish to join the beloved dead beneath the alien sod.

A discreet cough sounded behind her. She turned. 'Why Reverend . . .'

'Ah, Mrs Lang. We are both on the same sad mission this New Year's day, I see.'

He, too, had brought flowers which he placed reverently on his wife's grave, then clasped his hands and closed his eyes in prayer. Amelia began to sidle away, but his voice detained her.

'Oh please don't go, Mrs Lang. This is most opportune. Indeed, I had formed the decision to come and visit you this afternoon and now we are met here – survivors who, from this day forward, must begin to look to the future, must we not?'

'I'm trying to, Reverend, though the future, what I can see of it, looks very uncertain.'

'Ah, Mrs Lang, but God has his reasons and he will guide you. You have but to put your trust in him and present uncertainties will eventually resolve into a new and shining Way. Come – I have a bottle of madeira in my study for a quiet celebration of the New Year. Let us drink a glass together to restore our spirits.'

Amelia had no wish for his company, but the madeira was a temptation and his hand was already under her elbow steering her relentlessly towards his bungalow. Its earlier disorder was now compounded into near chaos, and its thick atmosphere smelt of stale meals and not very clean children. Wan, wispy Agnes in a dirty smock threw herself into Amelia's arms as they entered.

'Oh you have come, Mrs Lang! Papa said he was going to . . .'

'Shush, child! Not another word,' Arbuthnot barked. 'Mrs Lang and I are going to partake of a little wine. Please leave us in peace this instant.'

'Yes, papa, of course, papa.' She fled from his scowl, knuckling her eyes as she went.

'Oh poor Agnes! You shouldn't shout at her so, Reverend. She's trying hard to manage.'

'I know, I know, and I'm sorry. It's just too much for me – for Agnes and all of us. Four helpless, motherless children – my heart bleeds for them, Mrs Lang.'

Kicking aside the toys that littered the passage he ushered her into his study. 'My only haven – 'Twas ever so and even more now.' He fussed over her, took her bonnet, offered a cushion for her back, poured wine, complaining the while of the sorry state of the household. 'I can't manage the servants, you see, whereas Dora had such a way with them . . . but come, let us drink to a happier New Year!'

She drank. 'It could scarcely be worse than the last, could it?'

'No indeed.' He brooded over his glass. 'Dora was, as you know, a very good, Christian woman, Mrs Lang.'

'She was, Reverend.' Amelia felt the need to make a point. 'And Theophilus was a very good man. Not entirely in the Christian mould, but in his own dear way.'

'Hmm. Yes, of course. And so now we are bereft of our worthy partners – me of a wife and mother, you of a husband and breadwinner. I trust the Raja has been of some pecuniary assistance to you?'

'Not much, and I cannot hope for more from him.'

'I feared as much. And so – if you'll excuse my asking – you must be finding the times rather difficult?'

'Yes I am, Reverend. I've written to my brother in Peshawar for some pecuniary assistance, as you put it. And once this arrives we shall be leaving Tanjore.'

'Oh, but alack the day! I'd heard it rumoured and it would be another sad loss to our dwindling community. Some more wine?'

He attended assiduously to their glasses. 'Yet you have proved yourself admirably suited to our strange Indian life, Mrs Lang. You have adapted well to the climate, shown yourself an excellent housekeeper and mother to your children – children who must sorely miss the guiding hand of a father, as mine the loving care of a mother.'

He glowed at her, paced softly to the window and looked out. She stared at his fat back that bulged against the seams of his black broadcloth coat. He turned, grabbed his glass and drained it again. As he did so, she saw his shining glance fasten on her bosom, and understood. She began to rise, but he made a positive jump at her, pressing his hands on her shoulders to keep her seated.

'Ah, Mrs Lang, you mustn't go yet! You really mustn't. I ... well ... can you not guess what I have in mind for us? What a right and worthy solution it would be for our own troubles and those of our respective offspring? Do you not feel a deep sense of Christian duty urging you – as it does me?' He breathed deeply, kneading his strong, plump fingers into her shoulders. 'Come, Amelia ... You say nothing? Then I must ask outright ... Will you do me the honour of becoming my wife?'

She squirmed from under his grip and stood up, glaring at him. 'No Reverend Arbuthnot, indeed I will not. And to tell the truth I can scarce believe that you, a man of the cloth, should even begin to contemplate such an idea, when our spouses – at whose graves we met just now – are so lately laid to rest.'

He clasped his hands, keeping the warmth of her flesh between them.

'Mrs Lang, I know this to be a little precipitate and I do not propose an immediate union. But your intention of leaving Tanjore soon prompted me to speak. If we could come to some understanding now, you need not go and your mind could be at rest for the future.'

'At rest, you say ...' she began, but he overrode her with his sonorous tones.

'You speak of the short interval since our mutual bereavement, and it is true. But I am certain my dear Dora would, in these sorry circumstances, want me to . . .'

'Well Theophilus certainly would *not* want me to. He'd be horrified. Indeed it would be a betrayal of his memory, all he stood for. Don't you recall how deeply you and he disagreed over matters of religion and principle? How could you ask . . .?'

'But my disagreements were solely with him, Mrs Lang. You remained a steadfast churchgoer, I was happy to see. Idolatry never tempted you as I fear it did him.'

'You may call it idolatry, I call it Hinduism, Reverend. That much at least I've learned.' She was increasingly angry. 'But my own opinions don't interest you a single jot, do they? I don't suppose you gave them a thought! Enough for you, isn't it, that I fulfil certain essential qualifications – good mother and housekeeper, a reasonably young Christian woman.' She snorted indignantly. 'Why, there are probably hundreds who would suit you admirably. I just happen to be the nearest. Isn't that so?'

'My dear Mrs Lang – no, no, of course not. Why, I have always held you in very high regard, more than that – of feeling. But it seemed indelicate to . . .'

She cut in again. 'Well in any case, Reverend, I'm not looking for the nearest widower, and were I ever to remarry, which is most unlikely, it would be to a man possessing qualities similar to my dear husband. I won't pain you by enumerating them, but must say I see few of them in you. Now, if I could have my bonnet, please?'

He hesitated, affronted, still incredulous. 'My dear, dear Mrs Lang, I fear I've annoyed you. I've not expressed myself well, I can see that now. I spoke too much of Christian duty in general, not enough of my feeling towards you in particular, as one who . . .' She whisked her bonnet off the rack and made for the door, which he scurried to open. 'Oh Mrs Lang, pray don't be offended. I sprang this on you too fast. Think the matter over at least.'

Staring at him, she realised he hadn't truly listened to half that she'd said, it being so out of tune with his own opinion of himself. She wanted to slap his face; instead she rushed out, almost colliding with Agnes and Ruth who'd been lingering in the passage, anticipating her emergence on their father's arm. She shuddered at the thought – of that arm and the fleshy clerical body attached to it and the smelly disorder of the house he wanted her to put to rights for him. So great was her distaste that she started to run, and nearly tripped over Rosie Murphy who was struggling to carry a jug of water up the garden path.

'Rosie, dear! How are you? Here – let me. It's far too heavy for you.' The child looked up at her, brown eyes shining hopefully. 'Do you live here now, Rosie?'

She shook her head and stuck a dirty thumb in her mouth. Amelia sighed, trying to smooth her tangled hair.

'What are you doing here, then?'

Rosie removed her thumb and whispered, 'I help Agnes.'

'Oh dear! I don't think at your age . . .' She looked back towards the bungalow, wanting to intercede but dreading another encounter with the reverend. 'You must come and play with Rolly soon.'

'Oh yes, please, please.' The child clung to her skirt as Agnes's shrill tones came from the verandah.

'Rosie, where are you? Where's that water?'

Rosie shivered, holding tight to Amelia.

'Oh *really*!' Amelia picked up the jug and carried it to the verandah. 'Here you are, Agnes. It's much too heavy for Rosie to carry, you know.'

Agnes came out, staring at her with small, angry, miserable eyes.

'It's none of your business, Mrs Lang, if I may say so. *We* do what we can for Rosie. *You* do nothing to help any of us.'

'Well, I . . .' Amelia reddened, surprised into anger, and was about to spring to her own defence when she saw Reverend Arbuthnot enter the room behind. 'You must come to tea soon, Rosie,' she gasped and fled towards the safety of her own bungalow.

In Amelia's absence that day Hubert Wardle had called to leave a New Year gift of fruit and flowers and a note saying he would come again soon. He did so the following Sunday afternoon, just as she'd finished the dispiriting task, one she'd recently neglected, of trying to balance the household accounts. The reckoning was worse than she feared: Theo had left little except books; the funds from the Resident and the Raja had long since gone; and she discovered that debts with local tradespeople were accumulating. She could barely afford their day-to-day existence, much less the considerable extra expense of travelling, and it was too soon for a reply from her brother in Peshawar. Marguerite had sent a warm letter of condolence suggesting she and the children stay with her in Madras – but how were they to get there? Marguerite herself would help, but Amelia hated to worry one who described herself as 'a sick old woman with scarce enough strength to paint my wrinkled cheeks anymore'. As if death itself were not terrible enough without these attendant difficulties, brooded Amelia, who was sitting at her desk, fists clenched over the closed ledger, when Hubert Wardle was shown in. He was carrying a parcel and an oblong box.

'My dear Mrs Lang. How are you? Well on the way to recovery, I hope? And the children?'

'We are all gaining strength, thank you, Resident.'

'Good. Good. I've brought this for your little one.' He tapped the box. 'Shall I show you?' He placed it carefully on the desk and opened it with significant tenderness to reveal a painted plaster doll. ''Twill need some new clothes, I fear. It's lain there for several years. Belonged to my heart's treasure – my daughter Jessica. And now it will belong to your Elizabeth.'

'That's most kind of you, Mr Wardle. But are you sure you wish to part with it?' Amelia murmured politely, fingering the doll's moth-eaten and grubby gauze dress.

'Yes, yes. Why, maybe I'll have the pleasure of seeing your daughter playing with it one day.' He pointed to the parcel. 'The very first figs from my garden. On my way here I was thinking – it seems hardly possible that less than a year ago, I gave some to poor Mr Lang to give to you.'

She turned aside, remembering all too clearly that she'd never received them because he'd left them in the bazaar and bought a sari instead and she'd scolded him for it . . . Dear Theo, so impulsive and generous! Her lip quivered; Wardle sat down, loosened his neckcloth a little.

'There, there, Mrs Lang. Such memories are melancholy indeed. I remember feeling the same about poor Marjorie. But we who are left must carry on as best we may, even though the road is often lonely.'

He seemed to relish not only opening wounds but pouring in salt, she thought irritably.

'Some tea, Mr Wardle?'

'Thank you kindly.'

As she summoned Veena, he got up and marched about the room bracing his back and shoulders and expanding his chest in the way of a short man convincing himself he was tall.

'I've just come from Captain Gilbert, bye the bye. His posting to Madras has just come through and he'll be leaving us very shortly.'

'Oh really? I didn't know – what a shame!' She sighed, for she thought of the captain as a distant ally.

'Well, perhaps his successor will be a married man, which would be to the good. And what about your own future plans, Mrs Lang? Have you begun to consider, may I ask? Are you longing to shake our pervasive Indian dust from your feet or would you prefer to stay?'

'I scarcely know what I want, Mr Wardle.' She sighed again, moistening a handkerchief and beginning absentmind-edly to clean the doll's face. How could she, when all she wanted just then was to be as unconscious of the world as a doll in a box? 'In any case, it's more a case of what's practical and possible in the circumstances.'

'Quite so.' He cleared his throat. 'There'll be the question of money. Your husband not being a Company man, you are not eligible for any help from the Widows' Funds and I cannot imagine the Raja has been generous? He has gone quite mad – simply pouring rupees into that pagoda of his.'

'No, he hasn't been much help. I've written to my brother in the north but . . . Ah tea, Veena, thank you.'

'I hope your brother isn't in Afghanistan, Mrs Lang? The

news from there is most disquieting – tribes increasingly restive and our holding in Kabul not as secure as it should be, I fear.'

'He's at Peshawar near the border. I suppose if there were trouble he might be sent in.'

Wardle took a cup, prowling up and down with it. 'Well, let us hope for the best. In these difficult times women need the protection and support of men, do they not? As men need the sympathy and companionship of a good woman. I'm sure you agree?' He seemed bent on pointing out the extent of her loss; she pursed her lips, continuing to polish the doll. 'So you're not settled on going Home?' he persisted.

'No. I may, but I've grown to love India in spite of everything.'

She rubbed more vigorously, thinking that her love of the country had grown through and with Theo's; alone, she hardly knew how she felt about it. But whatever her feelings she had no wish to share them with the Resident, and his questions were quite getting on her nerves. She rubbed the doll's nose very hard and it suddenly crumbled away under her fingers.

'Oh dear . . . I've . . .' He rushed to look. 'Oh, I am so sorry!'

'It doesn't matter,' he said heavily, making it plain that it did. 'I suppose it had begun to decay underneath.' He propped the doll against the box and the sight of the ugly hole in its face became the last straw in a thoroughly miserable afternoon; she began dabbing her eyes with the dirty handkerchief.

He put his arm round her waist. 'There, there, Mrs Lang – Amelia, if I may. Please don't upset yourself. It's only a doll and I know how feelings overcome you when you're alone. You need companionship and support – as I said, as I do myself. And that is why I have come to you Amelia – to ask you . . .' He was gibbering now, excited by the feel of her waist which he was squeezing convulsively, seeming unaware of her efforts to disengage. 'I've often thought warmly of you in the past, most warmly . . . but then of course you were married. Now we are both widowed and alone – ask you to become my wedded wife.' He got it out just as she managed to free herself and retreat, putting the desk between them.

'Marry you, Mr Wardle!' She doubted she'd heard aright.

'Yes, Mrs Lang – Amelia – marry me.' He drew himself up. 'Oh, I realise there is some slight difference in our ages, but that can be no objection surely when the man is the older, and it means I am in a position to offer you and your children considerable financial security for the future.'

She gasped, caught between tears and laughter as he continued.

'In three or four years when my youngest son's education is complete we can go Home at last and enjoy a happy and comfortable retirement together, Amelia. And in the meantime whenever you feel ready to . . .'

Laughter won. 'Retire, Mr Wardle! Me! But I shall only be in my middle thirties.'

'And I in the middle fifties dear, so . . .'

'So you think I should forfeit the intervening twenty years to your care and needs, do you? In the interests of financial security?' He blinked reproachfully at her mirth. 'Yes, I have to laugh – or cry. But of one thing I am certain, Mr Wardle – I will not marry you. So now please go, and take your doll with you. It's even more hideous now I've broken its nose, I'm afraid, but it was only a little bribe, wasn't it?'

She pushed the box at him.

'Mrs Lang! You are not yourself! Don't you realise what an opportunity you are rejecting in such cavalier fashion? Why I'm sure your husband, for whom I had considerable regard, you know, despite his freakish opinions, would counsel you to think over my proposal most carefully, for he always had your best interests at heart.'

She tossed her head. 'And you have only your own interests at heart, Resident, as did Reverend Arbuthnot who also proposed to me a few days ago and also met with refusal. As for Theo, I don't know how he'd weigh the two of you in the balance, but I'm quite sure he'd be horrified at the idea of my marrying either.'

Wardle had gone very red. 'Well well . . . two refusals, hey? A self-willed woman are you, Mrs Lang? And a most ungrateful one, if I may say so – to spurn offers of support and devotion from such worthy gentlemen. You are scarce in a position to be so proud, but we shall have to wait and see how you manage alone, then, won't we?' He picked up the box, slamming the lid down on the doll and breaking off one of its arms in the process. It fell to the floor but, disinclined to compromise the dignity of his exit by bending over, he stamped out.

She picked up the severed limb, cradling it in her hand and stroking it as if it were a living creature. 'Ah, worthy gentlemen ... worthy gentlemen. How shall we manage without them, hey dollie? Well, we'll see what we can do, won't we dollie?'

She shuddered, for the pathetic limb seemed to represent to her all the vulnerability, fragility and pathos of her present female condition. She flung it from her in defiant disgust, took a deep breath, straightened her back and solemnly began to inspect the parlour for articles that she could sell to raise immediate cash. She was reluctantly contemplating the picture of the two elephants when Durmeen returned from her usual visit to her sons.

'Ah, dearie – there you are. Is anything wrong?'

Amelia smiled, but painfully, for she'd been thinking of the occasion of that picture's hanging – she and Theo with arms entwined lovingly, like the elephants' trunks. 'Oh, I was just wondering how much this picture is worth.'

Durmeen tutted. 'Come now – that was to be a family heirloom.'

'But times change.' Her tone was brittle.

'Ah me, they, they do indeed. You've had someone to tea?' She glanced at the table.

'Resident Wardle.'

'Did he bring those?' She indicated the parcel of produce with a smirk.

'He did.'

'And?'

'And he proposed to me – as you evidently suspect.'

'And?'

'And I sent him away with a flea in his ear.'

'But was that wise, Amelia? He is, after all, a fairly senior Company man and . . .'

Amelia flung her hand at the picture. 'And I'd sell that and the clothes off my back before I'd wed such a silly old coot, so there!'

Durmeen waggled her head. 'Now, now, don't get so upset. Remember the old adage: "A wise woman marries first for love, second for money and third for companionship."'

'How cynical and depressing you are! Just because you . . .'

'And many another woman, Amelia. What choice is there for us, I ask you? Still if you won't, you won't, and you'll have to go Home and I'll never see you nor funny little fellow Rolly again.'

Amelia went to touch her bent shoulders. 'I'm sorry, Durmeen. You've been so very kind. But I refuse to marry either of those two "worthy gents" just to stay in India. And there's no one else is there? Except', she grinned roguishly, 'Captain Gilbert?'

Durmeen sniffed. 'Oh, *he's* no use!'

'What do you mean?' Durmeen didn't reply. 'He's posted to Madras and will be leaving soon, the Resident said.'

'And good riddance, say I.'

'But why do you dislike him so?'

Still without replying, Durmeen called Veena to clear the table.

From his office window Captain Gilbert watched the crows picking at the dust with unwonted pleasure; in just a week from now he would never again have to contemplate their odious scavenging. There would be other crows, of course, for they were an integral part of the Indian landscape, but none, surely, so filthy ugly as the crows of the Tanjore barracks. Madras crows would be sleek, comical and cosmopolitan by comparison – or that is how they'd appear to him in that state of intimacy with Bill Taylor which he joyously anticipated. All the omens were favourable at last, and the Aurelian text he meant now to live up to was, 'This time that is present, bestow thou upon thyself.'

An orderly appeared. 'Mrs Lang to see you, sir.'

'Really? Well, show her in.' He rose as she entered, noting that she'd quite lost her colour and taken on the wan, strained, fatigued look of the resident Englishwoman. 'Pray sit down, Mrs Lang. May I order tea?'

'Thank you, Captain.' She removed her black bonnet, laid it on her lap, pulled its ribbons nervously.

'Shall I?' He extended his hand, but she clung to it.

'No, it's all right, thank you.'

He resumed his seat and waited; it was evident she'd come with a purpose she found difficult to explain. 'Quite pleasant weather at present.'

'I suppose it is, yes.' She looked at him. 'I hear you're leaving for Madras soon, Captain?'

'In a week, madam. And you want me to perform some commission for you? I should be most happy.'

'No, not that, more than that . . .' She retreated from the enormity of it. 'Captain, may I speak to you frankly?' He nodded, intrigued. 'You see, I'm in a very difficult position. First and foremost I'm desperately short of money. I'm sure I needn't explain why, it must be obvious. I've written to a relative for help, but can't hope to hear from him for a while, and soon the heats will again be upon us. And I don't quite know how to manage in the meantime. Also, I'm terribly worried about Rolly's health – he's listless, often feverish, and I dread to think of the effect on his constitution of a long journey during the hottest season. I feel I simply must get away before then. Marguerite Hervey would like us to stay with her in Madras, but the cost of transporting ourselves and our possessions thither by private palkis is, as you know, considerable. So I was just hoping that . . . maybe you could take us with you in your entourage much more cheaply?'

She'd come out with the last in a rush, but he was already shaking his head.

'I'm sorry, Mrs Lang, but that is not possible. Such travelling privileges are only permitted to the families of military men or Company officials and, in any case, my orders are to go first to Trichy and join up with a small contingent for the rest of the journey.'

The orderly came in with tea and cakes. The captain

watched her face sag. He recalled how he'd swung Roland Lang up high on that journey to Poo, the evening light on his chuckling, grubby, healthy little face. The child's father, his might-have-been friend, had kept his word and never told a soul of their pact over the suttee affair – not even his wife obviously, or she'd have had a lever on him now.

He sighed. 'I'd be only too pleased to help, Mrs Lang, but regulations are very strict on this. It's just possible the Resident could pull strings on your behalf.'

'Oh him! He certainly won't lift a finger.'

Gil raised his eyebrows; she wound her bonnet ribbons tight round her fingers.

'I may as well confess – there's another reason that I'm desperate to get away. They've both proposed to me – he and the Reverend Arbuthnot – and I've refused them both and now they're sulking and it's all extremely uncomfortable.'

'The devil they have! Excuse me, madam.' He actually giggled. 'And bravo to you, say I!' It hadn't occurred to him that she was now an eligible lady. 'But don't you find it rather flattering?'

'Not in the least. Those worthy gentlemen regard me rather as one of those second- or third-hand sideboards you see in people's homes – ordinary but useful, and as someone has gone to the expense and trouble of bringing it to these remote parts it might as well be used again.'

'You do yourself an injustice, Mrs Lang,' he muttered, again remembering her resemblance to that colonel's daughter he'd once been expected to marry. Then he thwacked the desk with his open hand. 'I have it, Mrs Lang – but how shall I put it to you?' He strolled to the window. The crows were still scavenging; he could imagine how ardently she longed to leave this godforsaken hole. She nibbled a cake, watching him hopefully and he rewarded her with a broad, collusive smile. 'I suggest you and I play a little game – a little joke at the Company's expense which it can easily afford. Let us arrange an "engagement of convenience". We will pretend that *I* have proposed to you and you have accepted, and as my affianced you, your children and baggage can be transported to Madras for practically nothing and in great safety. How does that take you?'

'But it's marvellous! Oh thank you, Captain!'

Her eyes shone with positively alarming enthusiasm and he added hastily, 'When we reach Madras we will, of course, discover ourselves mutually incompatible and the arrangement will be dissolved.' He lowered his eyes, embarrassed. 'You need have no fear I might use the situation to take . . . ha . . . any liberties.'

'No, of course not, Captain. It's most kind of you, indeed.'

'But let me impress one thing upon you, Mrs Lang – the fact that our engagement is a pretence must be kept a total secret from absolutely everyone. Walls have ears and discovery would, at the least, cost me my chances of promotion.'

'Oh, I promise. No one shall know, no one.' She longed to take his hand to seal the bargain, but he was a man one couldn't spontaneously touch.

'I shall send to my superior officer in Trichy today, asking for permission. There'll be no difficulty. You can be ready within a week?'

'Oh yes.' She jumped up eagerly.

'But wait – there should be some sort of token.' He took a key from his desk drawer, opened a wall cupboard behind him and produced a battered tin box of the type in which military men usually kept their personal mementoes – locks of hair, battle trophies, love letters, lucky charms, family miniatures. Gil's box wasn't full despite his years in India, but it did contain one item of value. 'Rings are unlucky in my experience, but you can wear this.' He held up a gold bracelet. 'It belonged to my mother.' He came to fasten it on her wrist.

'Oh Captain – but I feel I should provide my own token in the circumstances.'

He burst out laughing. 'Not at all! And how I'd love to see the faces of the worthy gentlemen when you show them this!'

She chortled. 'Oh *them*! Of course they will concede immediate defeat. Why, you have solved everything for me, Captain, and how can I thank you?'

He escorted her to the door, saying, 'I'll call on you in a

day or so for appearances' sake and send a couple of men to help with your packing.'

He bowed to her very formally and she went out, pausing on the square to secure her bonnet strings, the bracelet glinting in the strong light. Watching from the window, Gil noticed that glint, and only then remembered the counsel of his new-found friend Bill Taylc. that a wife was the best 'cover' one could possibly acquire.

CHAPTER TWELVE

Amelia hurried through the bungalow garden, still breathless with surprise at this turn of events.

'Come and sit, dearie, you look hot!' called Durmeen from the verandah. 'Well – and what had the grand Captain to say? Not much, I'll be bound.'

Amelia giggled. 'On the contrary – Phew, yes, I'm hot.' She sat down, mopping her face. 'Well ... I'll have to explain, I suppose.' She removed her bonnet, called for a drink, began deliberately to finger the bracelet, avoiding Durmeen's curious gaze. In her excitement, she hadn't considered how to handle her new secret.

'What a pretty bracelet! I don't remember seeing it before,' Durmeen remarked obligingly.

'Er ... no, you haven't. Well – it's rather difficult. As you know, I went to ask if we could join him for the journey to Madras, but he said it was quite against all military regulations.' She paused, sipped tamarind water. 'Well ... then, after a bit, most unexpectedly I must say, he suggested that we ... he and I ...' she peeped nervously into the silence, '... we should become engaged. As his fiancée, I can travel to Madras with the children for practically nothing ... That's not the only reason, of course. Please don't imagine that. But it probably made the Captain declare himself now.'

Durmeen's face, which had a natural tendency towards convexity, looked about to explode. 'No! I can't believe it! Captain Gilbert proposed to you?'

Amelia nodded, gulping her drink.

'And you accepted him?'

'Well, er ... yes in a manner of speaking. It will be a prolonged engagement in the circumstances.' She held up her wrist. 'This was his mother's. He gave it me as a pledge. He considers rings to be unlucky,' she finished lamely, avoiding Durmeen's horrified gaze.

'But it's unbelievable – and quite dreadful!' Durmeen waggled her head violently.

'But why dreadful? Durmeen, I'm surprised at you! You actually encouraged me to accept one or other of the "worthy widowers". And Captain Gilbert is far more eligible and attractive than either of them, you must admit. So what is dreadful?'

Durmeen got up, waddled to the verandah rail, peered over. 'I wonder where Rolly is?'

'The ayah's taken him for a walk, hasn't she?'

'Yes.'

'Then that's where he is . . . So?'

Durmeen rubbed her moist forehead and mumbled, 'Men can change . . . I suppose.'

'Change what, exactly?'

'Hmmm. Well, he's been a bachelor for many years, hasn't he? It would mean a great change for him to take on a wife and two children, and it mightn't suit him.'

'Indeed not,' Amelia agreed eagerly. 'Nor me – and we're both free to change our minds at any time. Nothing is to be in the least hurried – except leaving Tanjore. I must be ready to go a week from today.'

Durmeen's eyes enlarged with sorrow. 'Oh no! Not so soon! You – and the children – in a week!'

'Come, come, please don't look so sad.' Amelia felt like weeping herself. 'It's supposed to be an occasion for happiness.'

'Was the Captain happy about it?' Durmeen's tone was disbelieving.

'He was very . . . correct. He realises I'm still in mourning for Theo. But, as he's leaving, the matter couldn't wait.'

'Extraordinary! Of course he's always been very fond of Rolly.'

Amelia suddenly lost her temper. She jumped up. 'Well, you are a fine one, I must say! He's not marrying Rolly. I suppose you think it strange that such a very eligible bachelor should choose an ordinary widow like me!'

Thoughtfully Durmeen smoothed a cushion, then plumped down on it with a great sigh. The strains and sorrows of the past few months had taken their toll and she was feeling old and tired. Her inclusion in the Lang household had given her status as well as pleasure, but with Theo's death that was all over. She fingered the gold cross at her throat. 'One can never tell in such matters,' she muttered. 'The Lord giveth and the Lord taketh away.' She had her own sons, her grandchildren; her life before the Langs came had not been unhappy. Matters would have to take their course. She closed her eyes on the present troubles, her head sank back and she fell into a warm doze. She was awakened by the slide of a nearby foot; a woman, robed and veiled in white, stood looking down at her.

Durmeen blinked. 'Why . . . who? Oh, it's you, Mrs Moitra. A proper widow now, are we? What are you doing here?'

'I've come to see Amelia. When I came earlier you sent me away saying she was ill and would see no one. Now I hear she is better, and I *will* see her.'

Ponderously, Durmeen rubbed her eyes. 'Why?'

'Perhaps I can help her?'

'She doesn't need your help. She is leaving Tanjore next week – forever. With Captain Gilbert, to whom she's just become engaged.'

It gave Durmeen considerable satisfaction to pass on that bad news.

Rukmini gasped. 'Leaving – forever? Engaged – to *him*? I don't believe it!'

'Then go and ask her.' Durmeen rose slowly, shaking herself. 'It's a bad business, but none of yours, for all that.'

'But *him*! Why, he's a . . . You know what he is, don't you?'

'A sodomist.'

'Yes . . . and how *could* she? So soon after . . . oh Amelia!' Rukmini leaned against the rail, her lips working in pain.

'She must get away from here – and he's her best chance.'

'Doesn't she know?'

'Of course not. Let sleeping jackals lie.'

'No, I won't. It's too terrible. I was married to a sodomist, and I shall tell her what I know about the handsome Captain.'

Durmeen fixed her with large, hard eyes.

'If you do, I shall tell her what *I* know about the pretty Indian friend she rescued from the flames.'

Rukmini drew her veil more tightly round her face in a gesture of defeat, and was silent. The two women stared at each other and Durmeen thought how plain and old Rukmini looked now, bereft of her lustrous hair, her bright saris and jewels, the joy that used to shine in her eyes.

'At least', Rukmini began in a harsh whisper, 'I loved him. I truly, truly loved him – all my life. I will not betray him as Amelia has. Let her marry her sodomist, then! I shall always be faithful to Theophilus.'

She turned and walked slowly away, down the verandah steps, along the garden path, pausing now and then to stroke a leaf or a petal, singularly unhurried. At the gate she turned to look back at the bungalow; Durmeen couldn't see her expression, but her posture was proud. Then, with that disdainful brahminical gesture Durmeen had always loathed, she summoned a waiting servant to open the door of her palki. She climbed in and was carried away.

Amelia's last days in Tanjore were not agreeable, for the children, the servants and herself were harassed and upset by the rapid dismantling of the household. Only an unexpected visit from Reverend Arbuthnot brought a little light relief. The reverend was ever one to persevere despite adversity, or so he told himself, and came carrying flowers to renew his suit. Shocked and affronted was he to learn from Amelia's own lips that Captain Gilbert – who could, after all, have had his pick from a positive bevy of desirable ladies – had chosen she on whom his own intentions were fixed. Stiffly, unconvincingly, he wished her well, hinted that her refusal to accept him and his brood showed a lamentable lack of Christian dutifulness, and departed, leaving the flowers on the table. She picked them up, whispering into the soft petals, 'Thank you, Captain.'

Arbuthnot was thwarted but not otherwise touched, for his

thoughts soon circled back, as they did so often, to that maddeningly lovely temptress Myra Blenkinsop, after whom he had desperately and hopelessly lusted for years. Oh, to have had her here, now he was a free man again! To have chastised her severely with words, perhaps even with corrective blows, for her wicked immoralities, and eventually in the fullness of his Christian mercy to have enfolded her to himself as his lawful wedded wife! But Myra had fled far beyond his reach, warm in the seductive Mediterranean sun with that scoundrel Frenchman and the devil knew how many other men. Sweeping through his disordered home, he slammed his study door and poured himself a large glass of wine, muttering, 'Damn women, damn all women!' Principally he cursed the fugitive Myra, but directed his glare towards the Old Bungalow where Amelia, her brief triumph over, had returned to the dreary business of packing.

Durmeen's son had arranged an auction of her household goods, so she had quickly to decide what should go into it. She could not part with the elephant picture, though it might be valuable, nor Rolly's rabbit on wheels which seemed such a part of their happy bungalow life . . . but what about Theo's hookah? She was unprepared for the intensity of her emotion when she looked at it – the empty water-flask, the silver-filigree chillum box, the long pliant tube with its agate mouthpiece. Its sweetly distinctive aroma still hung about it, as did the presence of its user – reading, talking, versifying or just smoking during those peaceful tropical evenings on the verandah.

She stroked the cool agate, understanding now what Dora had meant about her husband being old-fashioned. Theo, akin to his father in temperament, had harked back to the past century while living in the very different present. Had he lived, he might have attained unity, but he was still fragmented and uncertain when he died. And Amelia knew that, in the future, it would seem very strange to her children that their father had been in the habit of smoking this odd contraption and she of listening with pleasure to its dreamy bubble.

She took up the flask and was wrapping it in protective cloth when Durmeen appeared in the doorway.

'You might help!' Amelia turned irritably. 'It's a wretchedly awkward shape.'

Gently, Durmeen took it from her. 'I'll do it, Amelia. Come and sit down a minute. I've some news.'

Amelia jumped, instantly frightened by her tone. 'What is it? Not the Captain . . .?'

'No, no, don't worry.'

Amelia stared into her face. 'But it's bad.'

'Well it's . . . I don't know. Depends how you look at it . . . in a way.' She paused, then blurted, 'Rukmini is dead.'

'Rukmini . . . dead? Oh no, she can't be . . . But how? Why?'

'She took poison the night before last and her body was discovered at dawn. It's being hushed up, but the story's circulating in the bazaar. My son just heard it.'

'But it's terrible . . . terrible. I can't believe it! Suicide . . . Rukmini, poor, poor Rukmini . . .' Amelia's voice broke, the grief that was always near the surface these days flowed in a tearful flood.

'There, there, dear.' Durmeen patted her head. 'I knew you'd weep for her, but you needn't, you mustn't. She was a high-caste brahmin, remember, widowed and childless – and she simply followed her own way in the end.'

Amelia raised her head. 'She's committed suttee, hasn't she? To spite us? Theo and me.' She twisted her fingers in her lap. 'And why now? So long after her husband's death? Do you think, deep down, she hoped for paradise after all? Was that it?'

Durmeen waggled her head in sudden rage, realising with whom Rukmini hoped to share paradise.

'Probably she simply felt that nothing could make her life better. And there *was* nothing you know, Amelia.' She stopped, hearing Rolly's footsteps.

He dashed in waving his wooden shield. 'I want to take this. It's a bit broke but . . .' He glared mutinously at his mother; he'd seen far too many tears recently. 'What's the matter, mamma?'

Amelia glanced warningly at Durmeen and wiped her eyes. 'Nothing, Rolly dear. I was a little upset, but I'm all right now. Yes, you take it. Let's see if we can find a little box for it, shall we?' She shepherded him towards the store-room.

'And what about the hookah?' Durmeen called.

'I'm taking that too. Could you pack it carefully please?'

Durmeen picked up the snakey tube, stroking its mouth-piece in her turn, thinking of Theophilus, Rukmini and their long-secret passion. Fervently she prayed that Theophilus's soul was safe in some Christian heaven a million miles from the paradise of the Hindus, for she was beset by a horrid suspicion – that Rukmini Moitra had wrested a final victory from defeat.

Before dawn, three days later, army bearers supervised by a sepoy arrived to load Amelia's baggage on to bullock carts. She'd made her farewells the evening before, and only the wailing servants were awake to help settle the children in the palkis and wave goodbye. Amelia turned to look at the Old Bungalow for the last time, imagining the creepers climbing back along walls and through windows, insects and animals taking up residence again, perhaps another cobra slithering into the shelter of a back room to coil there undisturbed for – who knew how long? Such incursions and abandonments were a common enough feature of Anglo-Indian life and did not distress her unduly; what wrung her heart much more was the vision she carried away of Theo's grave in St Peter's churchyard under the dusty trees where the squirrels played.

Captain Gilbert, who liked to cut a bit of a dash, wore full-dress uniform to make his departure: blue jacket with braided cuffs and collar, trousers with three-quarter-inch-wide silver lace down the outer seams; a leather belt with silk-lined leather pouch attached; shining sabre, spurs on his ankle boots, the ensemble topped with a roman-style helmet of plated scales with horse-hair mane. Amelia watched as he rode grandly to the Fort gate between two lines of soldiers at attention and saluted the officer who was taking his place. Orders were barked, a gun fired and the captain, without a glance in her direction, briskly led his small troop of accompanying soldiers out of Tanjore, with Amelia, the children and the baggage-carts following humbly in his wake.

They travelled to Trichy along a flat, well-beaten road from which the famous fort and temple built atop a massive rocky outcrop were visible long before they arrived. Gil, whose behaviour towards Amelia was courteously considerate, lent her a military handbook which informed her that the city had been the scene of fierce fighting between British and French before its eventual capture by the former. The conquerors' network of law enforcement and revenue collection was now well-established, and recent 'Important Events' there included the drowning of Bishop Reginald Heber and the assassination in the Protestant church of the ex-Nabob of Kurnal. One of the largest stations in the Presidency, Trichy boasted a cricket-ground, race-course, theatre, racquet-court and was also renowned, Gil told her, for the quality of its cheroots, the availability of cheap arrack from Colombo and the mischievousness of its numerous monkeys who swarmed about the cantonments and pinched balls from under the noses of the games' players. The cantonments, which they reached after dark, lay at the foot of the fort, and Amelia was immediately conducted to the officers' guest quarters for the night.

With no experience of the recondite rules of military etiquette, Amelia was quite at a loss about what to do the following morning after she and the children had breakfasted. But her arrival had been carefully noted by the wife of the garrison's commander, Mrs Matthew-Fayne, who, after due consideration, selected Mrs Cedric Farrell to call upon her. Mrs Farrell's husband, his sprightly little spouse explained, was the closest in age, rank and years of service to Captain Gilbert – and happened to be her second husband, to boot.

'And Cedric hadn't been married before either,' Mrs Farrell confided to Amelia, 'though he is years older than me. Scared stiff of women he always said, till I came along and cured him. And you can't imagine, dear Amelia – I may call you that, mayn't I? – we of equal military rank don't stand on that kind of ceremony nearly so much as the highty-tighty civilians. And you may call me Ninette. Funny name, isn't it?

Antoinette really, there's a French strain in our family, but Cedric found it too much of a mouthful. "Your mouth's always full of food," I told him, "that's why you've no room for my name." I could make him laugh, you see, and we were soon engaged. My first husband had been killed in a riding accident a few months before – well, if a lady doesn't remarry she'll soon be off Home in a widow's cap and gown, won't she? So I quite understand your position – but in any case, Captain Gilbert is such a dashing fellow, isn't he? So remote and mysterious! Mrs Rundell mentioned him when she was here, but she couldn't keep her mind on anything for five minutes together, poor soul. Utterly broken down by her baby's death.'

'Oh dear, I heard she was still unwell.'

'Worse than that – you should have heard her screams at night. She quite took against you, by the way – as if it was your fault that your baby lived and hers didn't.'

'And where is she now?'

'Her husband's taken her back to Bombay. We hear he's distantly related to the new G.G., Lord Ellenborough, who's about to arrive. So Mr Rundell will probably land nicely on his feet. Well, as I was saying, what with Mrs Rundell's remarks and all, you can't imagine how curious we've been about you – the first lady to capture the affections of quite the handsomest bachelor captain in the Presidency! And not for want of others trying, I do assure you!'

Amelia, ever more embarrassed, murmured that perhaps the captain wasn't as stony-hearted as he appeared and that her late husband had rather liked him.

Ninette laughed. 'What a blessing! Makes you feel easier, you know. My first, dear Andrew, couldn't abide Cedric. "Farrell the barrel" he called him, and he is, but one can't always be so particular second time round, though of course in *your* case . . . Anyway, dear Amelia, I've really come just to welcome you to our regiment and find out how long you're staying?'

'That depends on the Captain's orders. He thinks about two weeks.'

'Splendid! Quite a long stay by our standards – we're

always on the move, no sooner set our goods and chattels in one hot and dirty cantonment than we get marching orders to the next. So – you and the Captain will be here on Saturday, and I'm to give you a special invitation to our picnic at Annandale.'

'Oh thank you – Rolly loves picnics.'

Ninette squealed with mirth. 'Oh my dear, no! Not that kind of picnic. It's of the very *adult* moonlight variety. Let me explain. We leave after the heat of the day and eat a late lunch when we get there. Then we snooze and gossip and the men go off to shoot at a few nothings, and when the moon finally comes out we drink champagne and flirt and play and eat some more and ride back through the dark countryside. It's such fun! We go across the plain over there – to a mere hillock with a valley only wide enough for two spread tablecloths, and a smelly old tank with a few crumbling idols about it. It's our apology for the real Annandale, you see. You've heard that name, haven't you? The beautiful green valley in Simla where the Misses Eden held their *fêtes-champêtre* and the ladies and gentlemen of the Governor's entourage reclined beneath the deodars, played battledore – and other sorts of games, I'll be bound. But you must come – you and your handsome fiancé.'

She rolled her lively eyes and wouldn't take no for an answer, so Amelia finally said she'd go if the captain wished. Given time, she and Gil might have concocted a credible excuse, but Ninette immediately sent the captain word that his betrothed was pining to go a-picnicking and he had perforce to accompany her.

Trichy's Annandale may have lacked natural grandeur, but preparations to picnic there were almost on a Simla scale of luxuriousness. The six gentlemen and four ladies who rode off on the appointed afternoon had been preceded by twice their number of servants and bearers. The gentlemen rode ahead to organise things and by the time the ladies arrived everything that could conceivably be required for ten people to eat a meal outdoors was set in readiness.

Ninette reined her horse. 'See, Amelia! We may not be with

their high and mightinesses in the Himalayas but don't you find this a rather pretty sight?'

And yes, it was: starched white cloths spread in the shade of coconut palms and covered with earthenware dishes, glasses, silver, and cruets ranged round a centrepiece of cold roast fowls adorned with tropical fruits and flowers. Turbanned, uniformed servants stood at attention ready to serve as the military gentlemen bowed at the ladies and helped them dismount. At least, five of them did; Gil went fussing off to tether and water the horses and came to join the feast later, drinking the Queen's health, as proposed by Major Tripp, the senior officer present, in limejuice instead of claret. The wine flowed freely, the food was delicious, and Amelia was soon lulled into a temporary respite of pleasurable ease. Captain Gilbert, always uneasy at social gatherings, was particularly so in the present case, and soon absented himself again to tend a slightly lamed horse, at which a sandy-haired officer came and sat by Amelia, introducing himself as Captain Thorold Hillington, engineer.

'And you've just come from Tanjore, I believe, Mrs Lang? I was in the district for a time surveying for the new irrigation scheme.'

'Oh really, Captain? I heard much about it when my husband was alive – but nothing recently. What is happening with it?'

'Oh, we're getting on well enough.' He kept popping dark berries in his mouth one after another. 'We're going to build three huge tanks that can be filled with monsoonal flood-water from the river. The peasants will come from afar to marvel at their size.'

'I trust they'll also be able to marvel at the temple Raja Sevaji is building?'

Hillington chuckled, threw a berry in the air and caught it on his tongue. 'Ah – but they cannot have everything! That pagoda has been abandoned because the Company has taken over the land it was to stand on.'

Amelia gave a protesting cry.

'My dear Mrs Lang, surely you don't share the eccentric views of your late husband in this matter – about which I heard from the Assistant-Collector? The people of the district already have temples enough for every conceivable act of devotion. Now they'll also have water for their summer rice crop. You must surely see the sense of that?'

Amelia turned away her head. 'Simply as you put it – yes, of course. But I think, at bottom, it is more complicated. Tell me, Captain, how did the Company get that land?'

'There was some sort of affray a while ago. A circuit judge was sent to hold a trial and prove that the Raja had ordered his men to bully peasants off the land and was therefore unfit to wield authority over them. Simple.'

'And he is to be deposed for *that*?'

'Oh no, nothing so drastic – yet.' He grinned. 'He still has his palace, the Fort and a few nearby villages.'

'And that's all?'

'Quite enough for a Lord of Misrule like His Highness, madam.'

Captain Hillington swallowed the last berry and rose, for Ninette was signalling him with her bright eyes. He'd intended to tease her by flirting with the newcomer, but clearly Mrs Lang was not to be trifled with; she and Captain Gilbert would seem to deserve each other. Amelia sipped more wine, very conscious of her mourning apparel, of being at variance with the spirit of the company. She was still sitting alone when Gil came up the slope, summoned by a call to tea. He sat beside her, pleased by her detachment.

'In thus wise officers of the Company's armies pass the weary years,' he whispered. 'I suppose you've not attended this sort of thing before?'

She shook her head.

'Then count thyself fortunate.'

The cloths were now spread with cakes and jellies; the junior officers amused themselves by flicking bits of cork at each other; Ninette's high laugh rose often from the shade where she sat with Captain Hillington; Major Tripp and his lady were snoozing, propped against separate tree trunks.

Eventually Ninette, tiring of the surveyor's humdrum chat, swivelled her gaze to Gil and Amelia, querying loudly, 'Well – are you sitting there fixing the happy day?'

Amelia choked on a crumb. 'Oh dear me – of course not. Much too soon. It was only because the Captain was leaving Tanjore that we ... that I ...' She floundered and Gil coughed. 'That wasn't the reason, of course, but anyway we've not made any further plans yet.'

Ninette giggled. 'Oh but she's blushing, Captain! Too soon, you say? But I've known widows – and more widowers forsooth – who've remarried well within the twelvemonth. One has to seize the day in this deadly country, you know.'

'Well I certainly wouldn't dream of ...' Amelia began but Ninette interrupted.

'So you'll wear your mourning garb the year round, Mrs Lang, will you? Early October last, wasn't it, when your husband ...' She counted on her fingers. 'So, say about seven months more to make it seemly, hey Captain? Ah well, they do say prospect is better than possession, not that ...'

She broke off, for Gil had risen abruptly. 'And they do say, madam, only fools mistake impertinence for wit. Shall we take a little exercise, gentlemen?'

In embarrassed silence the men grabbed their belts and rifles and went scrambling down the slope, eager to take a few pot-shots at the parakeets and pigeons that winged towards the city around sunset.

'Oh dear me, now I've offended your fiancé – though it was only a tease to be sure, Mrs Lang.'

Amelia inclined her head and walked away to compose herself. She looked across the plain: high on its rocky hill Trichy fort glowed russet and mauve in the evening light like some idealised painting of an exotic Eastern land; birds came wheeling across the sky and she heard the occasional crack of the men's rifles. It only increased her despondency to imagine how happy she might have felt at this moment if she and the captain had been truly and lovingly engaged. Her surroundings were as perfectly arranged as in a romantic story and were just as much of a fictional façade behind which ached her grief, her unspoken anguish over the conversation just passed. How could people who had loved each other and lived together forget so soon? she thought, resting her cheek against a tree. In the distance a flock of parakeets suddenly swooped low as if on reconnaissance and, following their path, Amelia discerned a solitary figure riding across the open ground. She watched with increasing interest for he seemed in a great hurry.

'There's someone coming at full gallop,' she called back. 'Looks like an officer.'

'Oh lud – it's probably Cedric,' groaned Ninette, who had no wish to share the approaching moonlight with a mere husband. She joined Amelia. 'Not Cedric, anyway – too thin.'

The officers, having also seen the rider's approach, came up the slope to train their field-glasses on him. 'Who the deuce is it?'

'It's young Brandon,' announced Major Tripp at last. 'And he's waving like a madman.'

Minutes later Lieutenant Brandon cantered up, drawing rein in front of the picnic remains, his horse snorting breathlessly as he dismounted.

'An urgent despatch, sir.' He saluted. 'Terrible news, I'm afraid. Just come by flying seal from Madras. The C.O. thought you should have it straightway. Shall I read it out, sir? Nothing confidential – indeed, we must be some of the last people in the entire continent to hear it.'

'Yes, yes, come on then, man!'

Brandon's hand shook as he peered over the paper in the gathering dusk and read, 'It is with profound regret that we have to inform you of an insurrection of the Afghan tribes in and around Kabul at the end of December last. On January 6th our garrison in Kabul was forced to retreat from its cantonments, having guaranteed assurance of safe escort to Peshawar. The trust was betrayed and our forces were repeatedly and savagely attacked by Afghans in the mountain passes. Our losses were extremely heavy; it is estimated that up to 3,000 men, women and children were killed. On January 13th, a single survivor, Doctor W. Brydon rode into Jalalabad with news of this terrible disaster. Forces are now mustering on the frontier to relieve our garrisons still holding the forts of Jalalabad, Ghaznie and Kandahar.'

He stopped; no one moved or spoke, then Ninette uttered a

loud shriek. 'My brother, my little brother Francis was in Kabul with the 5th Light Cavalry.'

Mrs Tripp rushed to console her. The men lit a lamp and passed the paper round for each to read. Then a fine fury began to surge among them: they stalked about muttering oaths; Major Tripp buttoned up his jacket, jammed on his forage cap, roared an order, and they went dashing for their horses, trampling morsels of fowl and fruit under their boots as if these were treacherous Afghans.

Amelia retrieved a glass and poured the lieutenant some wine. 'My brother's in Peshawar. He'll be all right, I hope?'

'Oh yes – no trouble there.'

As he drank she saw his hand still trembling.

'I felt strange as I watched you riding here across the plain. There was something ominous about you. What was the name of the survivor?'

'Doctor Brydon.'

'And you're Brandon . . . Well!'

He handed her the empty glass and within minutes the men had gone, leaving the women and servants to salvage what they could and follow.

Only Ninette's sobs broke the silence of the dark ride back, during which Amelia tried to recall the details of the argument over the Afghan question that had occurred during her very first dinner party in Madras. Theophilus had been the only one to express disagreement with British policy. 'And by what right are we fighting in Afghanistan at all? The campaign will prove very costly and perhaps calamitous.' She could hear his defiant tones now; but no one had agreed and even she had doubted, for the weight of older and presumably more experienced opinion had been set against him. But he'd always viewed British strategies in India from a slight distance and so, she realised, had sometimes seen things more clearly. But this was no use to her now and she urged on her horse, wishing she could ride through the night and never see these Trichy military folk again.

They were, of course, all agog at the news, wanting to gallop to Madras on the instant to hear the latest intelligence from the north and be within closer range of any call to active duty, while Captain Gilbert managed to convince his commanding officer that he at least should set off at once with his contingent, in case such a call came. Unfortunately for Amelia, Ninette Farrell also convinced him that she should travel with them in the hope of hearing her brother's fate.

The next morning preparations got underway for the movement of fifty men and an equal number of camp followers. The journey was expected to take about two weeks. Hackeries were laden with sacks of rice, salted fish, betel nuts, curry stuffs, water-skins, bellows, kegs of arrack and rum, farriers' and cartwrights' tools, muskets, medical supplies, brine tubs, writers' documents – and this without the paraphenalia for the preparing of food, the daily ablutions, the sleeping under canvas. Gil was truly in his element – barking orders, checking lists, making sure every load was well-balanced, every horse well-shod, every man sober. At length he pronounced all in order and the procession of horses, bullocks, carts, litters, palkis and people trundled out of the Trichy cantonment, down the rocky hillside and headed north, while those remaining wondered enviously if they were bound for battle and glory.

Marching with the military was a novel experience for Amelia, but most of those over the age of five were quite used to it and soon shook down into a routine. The wake-up bugle roused them soon after dawn and it was up at once; tent pegs had to be loosened within five minutes, tents down by the second bugle call. A breakfast halt was made about nine o'clock, followed by another three or four hours' travelling; then camp was struck for the night. The hot-baked afternoons were for sleeping in the tents, the cool evenings for strolling about the camp, chatting, shooting game for the pot. Suppers, prepared by the army cooks, were abundant feasts eaten outside the tents by candlelight – a romantic time, Ninette sighed, thinking it strange that Captain Gilbert paid so little heed to his affianced.

But his attention was fixed on quite different goals, for he had persuaded himself that orders were waiting in Madras for him and his men to march north to join the so-called

'Army of Retribution'. Solitary in his tent at night, he indulged again those youthful fantasies of campaigning on the wild mountain frontiers and doing battle with the Afghans who had slaughtered his countrymen. He cared nothing for the rights or wrongs of the case, yearning only for a chance to prove himself in action after years of tedious peace. So he pushed the company forward as hard as he could, with little thought for the fiction of his engagement – capable and cool as ever, upset only by argument or delay.

Amelia, for her part, was equally anxious to arrive, particularly because Rolly was again assailed by bouts of fever. The doctor prescribed a tincture that induced him to sleep during the day, but at night he was wakeful, and disturbed his mother and sister with his whimpering and tossing in the stuffy discomfort of the tent. Throughout one especially wretched night the children didn't sleep till almost dawn, when Amelia, desperate for fresh air, crept outside past the slumbering guard. Detached and a little light-headed from fatigue, she wandered across an open stretch of ground and through a coconut grove, stopping at its furthest edge.

Ahead of her was a small village and, as the eastern sky paled and cocks began to crow, women came out of their houses to light the cooking fires, collect water. This rhythmic tranquillity of existence she had grown to accept and love without even realising it. Yet surely England was Home, wasn't it? She paced up and down, glancing occasionally at the rural scene, the waving palms, the morning sky, reluctantly admitting to herself that Home was beginning to seem to her, as it had to Theo, a chill, lacklustre, unwelcoming land. She leaned her head against a trunk, imagining the commonplace, restricted life that inevitably awaited her there as a widow with two children, even while watching the beloved familiarity of the village scene unfolding before her eyes.

Familiar certainly, but not truly understood and with little more meaning for her than a picture in a geography book, for she'd not learned much about the actual lives of the people during her stay here. She'd been so stupidly busy with ordinary matters – running a household, having a baby, caring for the family – just the sort of thing she'd have done in England. Imagining years of Indian discovery ahead, she'd felt no sense of urgency; but now, suddenly, she was to leave it all behind, probably forever – the women at the well, the boys with the goats, the whole everyday life of the country still no more than a picture book.

How could she bear to do that? She straightened, lifted her head, and in that moment was resolved. She would not go Home; somehow she and the children would survive here; she would earn money of her own; it could be done; other women had done it. She would stay in India – she and Theophilus still under the same warm, bright, welcoming sky. A great wave of relief and exhilaration flooded her and she laughed aloud in the first surge of pure joy she'd known since his death. The sun was gaining strength every minute and she strolled back towards the camp, thinking over the implications of her decision and seeing, as she emerged from the grove, the captain coming to meet her. She stepped out, eager to tell him of her resolve, when she realised he was shouting.

'Amelia – come on . . . hurry up!' He ran to her. 'Where the devil have you been? Didn't you hear the bugle? You've had the whole camp in uproar.' He took her by the shoulders and shook her. 'The men were striking tents when Mrs Farrell announced you weren't in yours.' An orderly had been sent to his tent in search of her, which made him doubly furious.

'Oh I'm most dreadfully sorry, Captain! I just came out to "eat the morning air" and fell to thinking and . . .'

'Well, thanks to you our day's march is behind schedule. This is a military camp, not a picnic. You'd better hurry.' He turned on his heel and strode back so fast she had to run to keep up with him.

It was only a lovers' tiff, Ninette said. Military men were prone to tetchiness at the best of times and, she added sagely, the captain probably found it easier to keep out of her way as he couldn't yet be intimately in it. Amelia kept her own counsel, wishing only to finish the journey without more fuss.

Within two days' march of the Presidency capital, they pitched camp near an abandoned hill-fort, the scene of heavy fighting during the Mahratta wars. A grim, desolate place, it was reputed to be haunted by the ghosts of both the Mahratta chiefs and a drummer-boy from an English cavalry regiment who'd died there. The boy's entire estate had apparently consisted of two pairs of white pantaloons, and sometimes he prowled about the ruined battlements after dark, drumming fiercely, his pantaloons shining in the moonlight. As if that wasn't bad enough, the moat round the fort was infested with very real alligators. A soldier, climbing up a rope into the barracks with a bottle of smuggled arrack once, had lost his footing, fallen in the water and been devoured by them. The smell of arrack had haunted the moat ever since. The alligators were said to be greediest for human blood when the smell was at its strongest.

Amelia took a little walk as far as the moat, where several alligators were indeed basking on the mud-banks in the late afternoon sun. She sniffed and, emboldened by the lack of alcohol on the air, stood a few minutes on the fort bridge looking towards the nearby camp. She had left Rolly dozing, but suddenly he appeared, holding Captain Gilbert's hand. The captain produced a ball and began playing with the boy and she could hear her son's squeals of laughter, which gladdened her because he'd been very low-spirited since his father's death. She started towards them, pondering the captain's fondness for Rolly, Rolly's need for a father, and Gil's character which remained such a puzzle to her.

'Thank you for routing him out,' she called as Gil approached to retrieve the ball. 'He needs more exercise.'

Gil threw the ball to the boy. 'Yes, he's growing fast. I suppose he'll be about ready for school by the time you reach Home?'

The words cut sharply across her line of thought.

'The fact is, Captain, I don't intend to go Home. I've decided to try and find a way of staying on in India.'

'Staying? Really?' He stared at her. 'That won't be very easy – alone, with two young children.'

She met his gaze calmly. 'Not easy, perhaps, but possible – and much more exciting.'

He smiled, saying with impulsive, genuine warmth, 'Then I'm delighted, and please count on me to help where I can.

261

Except, of course . . .' He paused, looking at her more keenly. A pleasant, sensible, attractive woman; of the type he'd certainly have chosen to marry if . . . He traced a pattern in the dry earth with his boot, the pause between them lengthening into embarrassment.

The next morning, Ninette vowed she'd been too terrified to sleep a wink because of the sound of drum-beats from the fort, and Captain Gilbert came to announce he and a fellow officer were riding on ahead to Madras – he'd arranged for Amelia to be escorted directly to Spring's Gardens on her arrival. He then bade her farewell with such preoccupied haste that Ninette decided she was probably better off with roly-poly, warm old Cedric after all.

Amelia, the two children, two sepoys, two palkis and a cart-load of baggage reached Spring's Gardens in a straggling, dusty procession during the hottest part of the next day. The house was closed tight as if against a blizzard; its walls and shutters even more cracked and blistered from the onslaughts of sun and rain; its parched garden empty of servants and animals. For a dreadful moment Amelia feared Marguerite was dead, the place sold, but the sepoy's knocks conjured a servant and they were taken in.

The mistress of the house was still alive, Dashwood explained, but his mournful tone suggested this was something of a miracle, for she'd been confined to her sick-bed for the past month. She was not to be disturbed when sleeping, but had left instructions for them to be made welcome and comfortable. Aged servants, roused from their siestas, stacked the baggage in the hall, brought tea, exclaimed over the growth of Rolly and the beauty of the baby, whom Kamba, the old ayah, cradled in her arms as she'd once cradled the boy. Dashwood himself solemnly conducted Amelia to that same bedroom into which she'd first walked after the long voyage out. She stood in the entrance looking round; it was just the same, but totally, terribly different. She slipped off her shoes, drew back the green-gauze mosquito-netting and fell upon the bed, which seemed enormously large and empty. She lay there exhausted, miserably beset by the crowding difficulties of the future, the lost joys of the past.

CHAPTER THIRTEEN

O n hearing of their arrival, Marguerite rallied her forces – hairdresser, nurse, personal maid – so that Amelia was shown into the presence of a still-elegant figure propped against the pillows, wearing a lavender-lace night-gown, smelling of cologne, the large blue eyes sparkling with sympathy.

'My dear,' the bony hands held hers, 'I am so desperately sorry. I wrote and told you so and I can say no more. Now I am entirely at your service. I want to help in every way possible. Sit beside me, dear, and tell me everything – anything you wish. And let us have chocolate to drink.'

Amelia sniffed. 'Thank you, Marguerite. I've been longing to see you. Don't worry, I'm not about to cry. I made a New Year resolution. But how are you? Are you really ill?'

'Ah – nothing serious, my dear, just Natural Decay. And I, too, made a resolution – we are not going to discuss it. No,' she raised a hand, 'I insist. There is no more boring subject on earth than the pains and penuries of old age. I think I've managed not to bore people too dreadfully for over seventy years and I don't want to start now. Kamba tells me Elizabeth is blooming and Rolly amazingly tall and you . . .' she put a finger under Amelia's chin for a closer inspection, 'You will do, do very well in the circumstances. We must plump you up a bit and put some country pink back in your cheeks before you go Home.'

'But I'm not going Home – not for a long while anyway.' Amelia's cheeks reddened, though not with returned health. 'Of course you don't know . . .' She could not explain the looming complication.

Marguerite clapped her hands in a familiarly gleeful

manner. 'But that's splendid and just as I secretly hoped! You and the children can stay here as long as you like and I shall be only too delighted.'

'And *I* was secretly hoping you'd say that. But, oh dear, I don't know how to put it . . . or if I need to, or . . .' She wrinkled her nose agitatedly, not meeting Marguerite's puzzled look. If only she'd straightened matters out with the captain. 'We three and all our baggage came up from Tanjore with Captain Gilbert, you see, and it cost me scarcely anything.'

'How clever of the good Captain! How did he manage to arrange it? Regulations are usually very strict.'

She gulped. 'Well, it was only possible because the Captain and I are, in a manner of speaking, engaged.'

Marguerite put a hand to her throat. 'Engaged! Captain Gil – to you!'

'Oh, people are always astonished.' Amelia was stabbed with irritation. 'And indeed why should he choose an ordinary widow like me when he could take the pick of the belles?'

'Pray don't underestimate yourself, Amelia. He is showing excellent judgement. But . . . Ah, here's the chocolate.'

They drank; Amelia noticing Marguerite's difficulty in holding her cup steady; Marguerite noticing that Amelia wasn't behaving with her usual directness.

'Well, well – you and the handsome Captain!'

'He gave me this – it was his mother's – as a kind of pledge.'

'Show me.' Marguerite examined the bracelet, murmuring, 'Good carat,' as if she'd expected a fake. She kept gentle hold of Amelia's wrist. 'But I must talk to him.'

'Oh I wish you would! You know him much better than I do.'

Marguerite chortled. 'Not so well as I thought, it seems!' She looked at Amelia sharply. 'And how do you feel about this?'

'Oh, I . . . really don't know . . . it's much too soon.' She took Marguerite's cup. 'Please let us say no more about it until the Captain comes – though lud knows when that will be. He thinks of nothing but marching off to fight the Afghans.'

'Single-handed, of course – just like him! But I doubt he'll have a chance. The whole Madras army is chafing at the same bit. Such a wretchedly tragic business and so unnecessary.'

'Do you remember that dinner party when Theo said the Afghan campaign would prove an expensive mistake and your guests howled him down?'

'I do indeed. Poor Theophilus! So perceptive in some ways – and a teeny bit obtuse in others.' She saw Amelia's lips tremble. 'You should have been here a couple of weeks ago when the ship bringing our new G.G., Lord Ellenborough, anchored in the roadstead. He'd been at sea for weeks so knew nothing of the Kabul disaster. When the news was signalled to him from the fort flagstaff they say he went turkey red-and-purple and stormed about swearing, calling Lord Auckland a damn'd fool and vowing personally to slit the throats of at least a hundred Afghans. They expected him to shout "My kingdom for a horse!" and go galloping over the waves on an instant, in such a fine martial frenzy was he. He's said to be a military-minded man so I daresay he'll muster a strong force of retribution to do the throat-slitting for him.'

'It sounds very cruel and bloodthirsty. Yet I suppose if Theo had been killed there . . .'

'Exactly so. My first husband, Roger, was killed in the Third Mysore War, leaving me with two young children – just like you. And given the chance I'd gladly have marched with an army of retribution and throttled Tippu Sultan with my bare hands.'

Amelia peeped at her shyly. 'And how did you get on – by yourself?'

'I didn't, my dear, not for long. Eligible women were scarce as hens' teeth then and I was positively besieged with offers. So after a while I chose Humphrey Perks the lawyer – rich, elderly and widowed. Quite deliberately chose him for those very qualities.' She snorted. 'But it wasn't very wise. He'd entailed most of his money on the children of his earlier marriage and was "perky" enough to father two more on me before he died.'

'Perhaps you should have married for love?'

'Bless me, no! Women have to be practical in such circumstances; romance is a luxury only men can afford. In any case, far better a second-rate husband than the perpetual widowhood of the poor Hindu ladies.'

'Oh Marguerite – I forgot to tell you! The last tragedy, just before I left – Rukmini Moitra committed suicide.'

'Did she now? Well . . . well. Bless my soul!'

Amelia said, 'But you don't seem in the least upset – just like Durmeen. I was horrified and think of her often. How she enjoyed living with us . . . playing with Rolly. So many of the good people seem to have died – poor young Sarah Murphy, Dora Arbuthnot, my dearest and best Theo . . . and then Rukmini.'

'Come now, Amelia! You really mustn't suggest to one in my antiquated state that all the *good* die young. And Rukmini – perhaps it was for the best? We don't know. She was Indian and we are Europeans. There's much we'll never understand about each other.'

She leaned against the pillows, a hand to her throat. 'Would you please call the nurse as you leave, dear?' She waved an imperious hand. 'And I must ask that neither you nor the children come to my room till I send for you. You've seen quite enough disagreeables of this kind recently.'

Amelia left. It was true that she'd had more than enough of sickness and death and yearned for the reviving springs of laughter and happiness as a parched wanderer for water in the desert.

Amelia was not, therefore, particularly charmed by the sight of her first visitor the next morning: not Gil (as she'd hoped) but Ninette Farrell, her head-to-toe black relieved only by a big white handkerchief held in readiness for tears. She sank into a chair, raising her eyes heavenwards. 'You will guess my news by these mourning weeds, Amelia. He – my dearest brother, Francis, but twenty-three years old – was among the 3,000 slain by the Afghans.'

'Oh dear, oh, how awful for you. I'm most dreadfully sorry.' Amelia patted her shoulder awkwardly, finding Ninette's grief too dramatically perfect. 'It's very sad. Does he leave a widow and children?'

'No – no one to perpetuate his *joie de vivre* – a carefree and handsome bachelor, which makes it even worse.'

'Well . . . in some ways. May I offer tea?'

'Thank you. I can't stop dwelling on his horrible fate, Amelia. Hundreds died of cold during the retreat, you know, and, as they left Kabul, saw the flames burning down the cantonments. Fire behind; ahead icy mountain passes and Afghan knives. Can you imagine the terror of it? Some of our women are still prisoners – Lady Sale, wife of 'Fighting Bob Sale', for one. I keep wondering what fates await them.' She clenched her hands in her lap and brooded; Amelia sought the right words of comfort; tea came and they sipped mournfully.

'They say Lord Ellenborough is getting things under control, at least,' Ninette remarked. 'So much more the sort of man we need. And good riddance to that weak-kneed Lord Auckland and his spinster sisters, say I!'

'Well, I never saw them.'

'No more did I. But my friend Mrs Lightfoot in Calcutta has a friend married to a high-up civilian who saw them often. She says the elder Miss Eden is a Whiggish and waspish creature.'

'Well, it can't have been pleasant – trailing across India and back with hundreds of camp-followers.'

'Thousands, my dear – and where the hardship? Why, they travelled in the style of the great Mogul emperors and even their little dog had its elephant to ride! Well . . .' she rose. 'I must get on my rounds. I can't seem to settle anywhere five minutes together. We shall surely meet again. I propose to nurse my grief here for a time, now I'm out of Cedric's clutches.' Her eyes betrayed a sparkle. 'And how is Captain Gilbert?'

'I've not seen him since I arrived, but am expecting him at any time.'

'Ah – then I must let you prepare yourself for his call.' Her critical glance at Amelia's morning muslin suggested it was not up to the occasion and Amelia, anxious to be rid of her, agreed she should change.

For want of better employment she did so, but in vain, for the captain did not appear until the following morning, when she was again clad in simple muslin. He seemed in excellent spirits, greeting her with the brilliant gallantry that used to dazzle Catherine Rundell. His jauntiness made her uneasy and she divined a similar sentiment in him.

'I'm so glad you've come,' she began, when they were alone. 'I've been in such a predicament about our little charade. You made me promise to tell no one and I have not, but we forgot Marguerite. She's not easily hoodwinked and I didn't enjoy doing so. I assume we can now tell all and laugh about it together?'

'Ah . . . well . . . hmm.' He paced around with uncharacteristic nervousness. 'About that – you see, Amelia,' he turned to give her another brilliant smile akin to a salute, 'I wondered about letting things be for a while? See how we feel in a few months, a year even . . .' He trailed off and she was nonplussed. The pause lengthened into embarrassment. 'You see, I was wondering if, at some future date, we might perhaps wish to make more rather than less of our little charade . . .?'

She looked up but he didn't meet her eyes.

Bill Taylor had made it sound easy enough to arrange – a non-committal half-proposal from which he could still withdraw if 'the going got rough'. But if it didn't and Amelia was willing, the advantages were considerable, and Bill had bawdily described how fellows like themselves could occasionally rise to their conjugal duties. Most amusing at the time, but Amelia's candid, totally unsuspicious gaze made him uneasy.

'This is something of a surprise, Captain,' she was saying evenly. 'You've been most kind already and I do hope you're not moved to this by pity? I couldn't bear that, and besides there's no need. I've just received some funds by flying seal from my brother in Peshawar, but he can't leave because the relieving forces for Afghanistan are mustering there.'

'Lucky dog! At least he's somewhere near the scene of action.'

'Quite near enough, in my opinion. But, as I was saying . . .'

'Madam, I assure you my proposal, indefinite and imprecise though it be, has nothing of pity in it.' He seemed to hesitate about going down on a knee, but remained standing, fingering his sword belt.

'Then let us wait, Captain. As I told you in Tanjore, it's far too soon for me to consider any other attachment. But I should say frankly that I like and trust you and I suppose it's conceivable I might feel more – in course of time.'

He gave another brilliant smile. 'And I like and trust you, Amelia, indeed I do. So shall we leave the arrangement for the time being, unsure whether we are deceiving the world or not?'

'Oh, I care not about the world, but Marguerite, a good friend of us both, deserves . . .'

At that moment a servant entered, handing the captain a chit. 'Talk of the devil! Marguerite insists on seeing me alone this minute. I can but tremble and obey.'

He bowed and left her. She wandered about restlessly, blowing the dust off ornaments, trying to analyse honestly what she felt. Captain Gilbert was undoubtedly an attractive suitor and marriage to him would resolve much: the question of long-term financial support for herself and the children, her wish to stay in India, even perhaps, eventually, her terrible sense of loss. The lot of an officer's wife did not strike her as enviable, but she felt optimistically capable of surviving it, as Marguerite had.

Rolly came in, dragging Kamba by the hand.

'Where's the Captain? Dashwood said he was here. I want him to play with me.'

'He's with Aunt, dearie. I don't think he has time to play today. Another day, perhaps.'

Rolly tutted disbelievingly and ran on to the balcony to watch the monkeys swinging in the trees. Amelia fetched the letters from her Home-staying brothers and re-read them for confirmation of her first impressions. Having expressed the conventional condolences at her bereavement, they went on to bemoan their own situations. Times were getting harder in the countryside, corn prices were falling, rural workers unemployed and even gentlemen farmers like themselves feeling the pinch. Clearly the prospect of a widowed sister and her children to support did not delight them: the elder mentioned a cottage on his ground that could be fitted up for her; the younger suggested she might stay in India for a while 'to see if anything turned up'. He meant another husband, of course; to him it was the only conceivable possibility. She sighed as she put the letters away, wondering about Captain Gilbert and what he and Marguerite were discussing so long and privily.

'I say – he's just riding away!' called Rolly indignantly. 'That's not fair!'

'Really?' She joined him on the balcony in time to see the captain take up his horse's reins and trot speedily down the drive without a backward glance. 'Never mind, Rolly. He'll come back.'

Amelia spent that afternoon with her son, her lips reading to him, her mind full of conjectures about what had passed between Marguerite and her 'fiancé'.

At last she was summoned to the presence of that ancient, flimsy body, carefully propped up as before, and Amelia marvelled that it could still inspire a little awe.

'Ah, my dear, pray sit down. I have slept – such a blessing! I hope you are managing to entertain yourself?'

'Oh yes, I'm teaching Rolly the alphabet.'

'Capital!' She sipped water, casting a shrewd eye. 'You're not upset, I hope?'

'Why no – should I be?'

'Absolutely not.'

'You mean because the Captain disappeared without speaking to me again? And you knew he would?'

'I guessed so, yes. Men are cowards in such matters – braver in the battlefield than the boudoir, as they say.' She closed her eyes, her head falling back against the pillow. 'I've not much time left, unfortunately, Amelia. No, I'm not seeking sympathy – I've had more than most and what I've

270

frittered away is my own fault. I merely explain that I've no time for games, the tippy-toe toings and froings, the misunderstandings, misalliances, leaps back and forth in the dark that are so fascinating between men and women. Years ago I'd have let this little situation linger on a while, but not now – and besides, it's not fair on you.'

Amelia smiled. 'You're talking in riddles, Marguerite.'

She snapped her eyes open. 'The Captain asked you to maintain the pretence of your engagement for a while, I believe?'

'Oh, I'm so glad he told you it was a pretence – though he's now suggested . . .'

'Yes, I know.' She closed her eyes again, but spoke with firm distinctness. 'But you see, he mustn't be allowed to marry you – or any woman – because he secretly prefers boys.'

'Boys! Captain Gilbert! He . . . what?'

Marguerite's weary eyes reopened. 'You do know what I mean, Amelia?'

'I . . . er . . . yes. I've heard of a case before – from Rukmini Moitra. About her husband.'

'Men like that have to conceal it, of course, and Gil has managed to, with his good looks and deceitful flirtations. But he wasn't to deceive you, and I told him so. We'd never actually spoken about it openly before but he confessed at once. Such a waste of a fine man – and oh, the foolish hearts he broke years ago, when he was a gold-laced young spark! There was May, a colonel's daughter. "May be or maybe not," he used to joke . . . Wicked boy!' She chuckled hoarsely. 'But I wouldn't let him use you as a cover. It would be too cruel.'

Amelia felt hot. 'I've made rather a fool of myself, I suppose – imagining he might honestly prefer me to others.'

Marguerite reached to grip Amelia's hand. 'But he does, you see! That's why he helped you to get here with this little pretence. He spoke most warmly of you and hopes you can still be friends – and that you'll keep his precious secret?'

'Why, of course I will. He's been kind and considerate in many ways.'

'Then that's an end on't.' She sighed in relief, definitely closing the subject. 'So now let us move to the balcony, my dear, and "eat the evening air" and sip a little wine.'

As the nurse helped her up, Amelia considered the implications of this revelation. She thought of H. N. Moitra of Poo and how Gil always used to vanish there; she made some connections, others she would never make, which was as well for her peace of mind.

Marguerite settled in a long reclining chair with a hood of wicker and gauze to shade her from sun and insects; it was, she said, just like a cot in which she could indulge her second childhood. A servant brought sweet white wine and biscuits on a silver tray and Marguerite raised a trembling glass to the sunsets of India. 'May you enjoy as many of them as I have, my dear!'

They drank. Amelia wandered to the balustrade and looked over. 'Did you sell your animals? I don't see a single one.'

'No, I didn't, and I was told they died. But I'll warrant they *were* sold. My old servants are faithful and honest but their sons are a different tribe who say to themselves, "Let's grab what we can before the old crone dies and we're thrown out on the streets." And that's the trouble. Some of them, like Dashwood, know no other home. They watch me fading away and fear for the future. So how can I blame them if they cheat and have no heart for the work anymore? You must have noticed how neglected things are?'

Amelia nodded. 'The garden's overgrown and there's a lot of dust and rubbish lying about. But it could easily be taken in hand. Shall I try?'

'Oh would you, Amelia? 'Twould be such a relief. Servants are like children, you know – they need overseeing and chivvying and a little praise!'

'Then let me do it! Dora Arbuthnot taught me quite a lot in that line – and how to keep household accounts, too.'

'Then I shall instruct them first thing tomorrow that you are the mistress in charge. Wonderful! A little more wine for a toast, Amelia!'

They drank together again, thinking it a very pleasant

arrangement, fearing it would be short-lived. Marguerite was the first to break the companionable silence.

'But you mustn't immure yourself in Spring's Gardens, my dear. You should gad about occasionally, and Mr Babbage would be only too pleased to escort you.'

'Mr Babbage – that fat old man at my first dinner party who pontificated about the glories of the Afghan campaign?'

'Not so *very* old, and you made quite an impression on him.'

'But I was such a griffin then, I hardly spoke!'

She chuckled. 'That's probably what he liked. He thinks you'd make a good listener for his pontifications. He always complained that Emmeline, his wife, talked too much. She's dead, you see.'

'Great heavens! Do you mean he thinks of me as . . .' she trailed off in disgust.

'I imagine he has matrimony in mind, yes. And, if so, you should consider it. There's a lot of competition for husbands these days. Shiploads of Kabul widows – and Babbage will soon be snapped up. A man of some consequence, still on the Council, with a fair portion of this world's goods. Moreover he eats and drinks far too much and I wouldn't give his liver more than three years at most!'

Amelia gulped her wine. 'Marguerite, what an absolutely odious idea! You're just as bad as everyone else. Well, I'll tell you now – I've already had two proposals, from the Reverend Arbuthnot who wanted a stepmother for his wretched children and Hubert Wardle who wanted a companion for his lonely old age, and then Captain Gilbert who wanted me as a cover for his revolting pederasty . . . No, don't try to excuse him! It's true!' She was very red, poured herself more wine and glared at Marguerite. 'And now you dare to suggest Babbage! He and I using each other for our own purposes. That's all marriage seems to be for most people. But I refused all of them – so perhaps I should be burned to death like a bit of leftover rubbish, in the way of poor Hindu widows? That's what society – even English society – would like to do with us, isn't it? No one ever thought about me, myself, apart from Theophilus, did they? Arbuthnot and Wardle loathed his opinions but they didn't care a fig whether I shared them or not – I had no mind of my own, I was only his wife and mother of his children – to

you, to Gil, to everyone. So now I'm a widow and I'm nothing –
until I become someone else's wife, which is all you can think of
for me.' She slammed down her glass. 'Well I'm simply not
marrying any of these selfish, pompous men! I'll find a way of
being by myself – you'll see!'

Marguerite had begun clapping her hands gently, eyes
shining. 'Bravo, oh bravo, Amelia! I've thought such thoughts
myself sometimes, but not when I was as young as you, not
when I married old Humphrey Perks. But you are braver and
I applaud you . . . Pour us more wine!'

Amelia did so, continuing more quietly. 'Joanna, my
dearest friend in England, used to talk about a married
woman as being but a slave to her husband, who has control
by right of contract over her labour, her property and her
body. I didn't pay much heed when I was happily married to
Theo but now I begin to understand. In her last letter, Joanna
quotes one of the Owenites who compared a widow to one
"who haunts her husband and becomes only half-solidified
when he is no more". Take care not to become less than you
have been, Amelia, she warns, just when you have the
opportunity to be so much more.'

'Now don't get carried away by this woman's extremes,
Amelia. One can be very happy as a wife, and you know it. On
the other hand, I agree that you shouldn't have to marry just to
survive, and certainly my years with H. Perks Esquire were not
agreeable. So we shan't marry you off to Babbage after all!'

'Nor to anyone else unless I choose to,' Amelia laughed.
'There must be something else I can do?'

Marguerite pulled her spectacles down over her nose,
saying gruffly, 'You can become a lady missionary!'

'No, not I! But I can teach, and I want first to learn more
Tamil.'

'Then I know just the person – Clifford's old teacher, the
book-keeper's father who still dwells in a dark corner somewhere nearby. He'd be delighted and it would cost very little.'

The next day a new regime began in Spring's Gardens.
Armed with keys to every store-room, Amelia doled out daily

portions of supplies, supervised the cleaning of glass, china-ware, lamps, the weeding of paths, the mending of punkah frills and pillow-slips. During the midday heats everyone snoozed, then Amelia had her language lesson, and in the blessed cool of sunset Marguerite lay in her long thin cot on the balcony next to Elizabeth in her little tubby one, enjoying their mutual childishness, as Marguerite put it. Occasionally Captain Gilbert, who hadn't received the longed-for call to active duty, called on them. On his first visit Amelia handed him back the bracelet, which he took, he said, only because it was his mother's. His tone was clipped with embarrassment and she was unable to look at him directly, seeing him in such a different light. But on his second call he brought her an almost identical bracelet as a token of continuing friendship and a pony, on which he began teaching Rolly to ride, so after that his visits became highlights of the boy's life and a pleasure for everyone.

Their only other callers were wizened ladies inquiring tremulously after Marguerite's health, until one morning Gopal Krishnan unexpectedly appeared, asking to see Amelia. He'd earlier sent a letter of condolence couched in terms that seemed to her so flowery and contrived she couldn't believe it genuine – and she'd not expected to hear again. But there he stood in the morning-room, youthful-looking as ever, handing her an object wrapped in purple cloth. 'Ah, Mrs Lang, good morning. A small memento. How are you and your children?'

She replied appropriately, removing the cloth to reveal a box of wrought-silver inlay and the words, 'In Memoriam: Theophilus Lang' engraved on the lid.

'Oh Mr Krishnan – how beautiful! And so very thoughtful of you!' She opened it. 'I shall have to find something appropriate to keep inside.'

He shrugged modestly. 'Scissors, thimbles, perhaps?'

'Oh, it's much too grand for such workaday objects! Will you take tea? Coffee?'

'Nothing, thank you.'

'You'll find Marguerite failing, I fear.'

'Alas, so I've heard. But you and the children will be a

comfort to her.' He turned as Marguerite tottered in on her nurse's arm. 'My dear lady! How are you?'

'My dear fellow! Dying on my feet, as you see. But we don't discuss my health. Suffice it that you appreciate the effort it cost me to move my skeleton this far before noon.'

'Madam, I am deeply honoured.'

'Well sit you down,' she snapped. 'And tell me what goes on in your spider's web world.'

'Spider's web, madam? You flatter me, for that is a beauteous fabric – a creation in which its creator resides like a deity.'

'Oh fie on your poetry, Krishnan! No, my spider is akin to you lawyers – well-fed and wily creatures who bind and blind us in the legal tangles you create, and we must pay for.'

Gopal raised his eyebrows. 'But what would you have us do? "Wherever law ends, tyranny begins," so saith your John Locke.'

'Tush! Men will have tyranny within or without the law. But tell me, how goes your campaign against the new tyranny of the reformists and Evangelicals bringing their compulsory brightness and light to the benighted Indians? Is there not a branch of your Dharma Sabha in Madras, now? And are you not a leading member?'

Gopal looked embarrassed. 'Yes and no, no and yes. It's a lost battle. You British will have your way with us – for the time being.'

'But Mr Krishnan,' Amelia asked, 'isn't it possible for Indians to accept gradually what is good from Europe and reject what does not suit?'

His hooded eyes showed his customary disapproval of her boldness. 'Would that it were, Mrs Lang. But you British are always in a hurry . . . however fast your horse gallops, you spur it on; however fast your bearers run, you call them lazy dogs. And so you will not permit any gradualness in adapting us to your new age.'

Marguerite, drumming her fingers on the chair-arm, inter-rupted. 'You've evaded my question, Gopi. Are you active in the Dharma Sabha?'

'Yes, when I hear of the terrible things going on in the

European colleges – our brahmin young dissecting human bodies to discover how they're put together – Faugh! But no – because I don't truly believe in its power to resist the present current of history.'

'So you will swim with the tide?'

He fluttered his long fingers at her. 'I wriggle a little, then I am carried along and relinquish the struggle. For is there not constant flux, constant renewal, and is not everything forever going wrong and catastrophe happening and we see it is what was intended all along?'

'Ho-ho, listen to the wise brahminical fellow! That is why Indians keep being conquered and surviving their conquerors, Amelia.'

But Amelia saw he was rather piqued by that and said soothingly, 'But to an extent Theo would have agreed with Mr Krishnan.'

'And would have worried himself into a veritable spider's web of contradictions too! It has occurred to me recently, Mrs Lang, that Theophilus, for all his good intentions, sometimes took we poor Indians and our beliefs rather too seriously. Whereas we are often quite simple and frivolous you see – a pat of butter on the nose of the right god at the right moment, a banana for the temple elephant, and we are in good marching trim for the next life. But Theophilus saw complexities where there were none – seeking a perfect, logical theorem of Hindu thought in our misty speculations, our "seas of treacle and butter", as Macaulay put it.'

They were puzzled; even Marguerite could not decide whether or not he was teasing, and he pressed his advantage.

'Take our petty Raja of Tanjore. Now dear Theophilus fretted abominably over his likely fate. But I do not. He just happens to be where he is at the wrong historical moment and the likes of him have no chance against your enthusiasts of progress. I was reminded of your poor King Richard.' He jumped up and declaimed, '"For within the hollow crown that rounds the mortal temples of a king, Keeps death his court and there the antic sits, Scoffing his state and grinning at his pomp . . ." and so on. And now I'll leave, for I see Marguerite is weary of my voice.'

Amelia accompanied him to the hall, where she thanked him again for his gift.

'I shall like to think it is being admired in some English country drawing-room,' he replied graciously.

'Then I must disappoint you, Mr Krishnan, because I don't intend to leave India for a long time.'

'Really? And why not, may I ask?'

'Because, like Theophilus, I've grown to love it.'

'But most English ladies long to go Home.'

'But I'm not "most English ladies". I think I pointed that out to you when first we met, and perhaps that's why Theophilus married me.'

'Perhaps so . . . Well, in any event, I wish you well and good-day, madam,' he muttered, thinking as he went that if such were the case, poor old Theophilus had again made life unnecessarily complicated for himself.

During the peaceful interlude that followed Gopal's visit, Amelia felt herself gaining strength of body and mind. She wrote questioning letters to Joanna about the theories of reformers like Mary Wollstonecraft and Robert Owen in which her friend had earlier failed to interest her. And she asked Joanna what she thought she should do next – though she was edging towards her own decision on that score. So occupied and thoughtful was she that she seldom left Spring's Gardens save for an occasional evening drive along the esplanade with the children. It was on one of these that she saw ahead a group of English women standing beside an open carriage. Amid the soft pinks, creams, blues and ochres of the evening scene they stood out like a flock of carrion crows, for they were all clad in deepest black. Though recognising unwilling kinship with them, she was driving past when she glimpsed a familiar face and asked to stop.

'It is – isn't it? Mrs Green? Constance Green?'

The pale, black-bordered face surveyed her. 'Why – and it's Mrs Lang, from the *Minerva*. And you, too, have been bereaved?'

Amelia nodded. 'Cholera – yes. And you – the several of you?'

Constance Green heaved a deep sigh. 'We have become known as the Kabul widows, alas. Our husbands slaughtered by the treacherous Afghans.'

'Oh dear, I'm so sorry.'

'And I – for you.'

They regarded each other. 'It seems a long time since we landed here, doesn't it?' Amelia ventured.

'It does indeed. A lifetime.' Mrs Green sighed again. 'We boarded the *Protector* in Calcutta and have just called here for provisioning before setting sail for Home. Are you joining our ship?'

'No. I'm staying here.'

'Staying! In this loathsome, filthy country that kills Europeans off by the hundreds – men, women and children – and ruins the constitutions of any who survive!'

Amelia nodded. 'I've grown very fond of India, you see.'

The other women gasped in amazement, and one said, 'Some*one* in India she's grown very fond of, more like!'

Amelia turned on her. 'No, I'm staying alone, by my own choice. I feel I can be more use here. So goodbye, Mrs Green. I hope you and your companions have a safe voyage.'

She jumped back into the carriage just as Rolly was trying to escape from it. 'No, Rolly dear – we'll get out for a walk further on. You don't want to meet all those black ladies.'

In the early hours of one morning, soon after the *Protector* set sail for Home with its melancholy cargo, Amelia was wakened by a gentle voice at her bedside. It was Marguerite's nurse and her tale was brief: her patient was dead. It had been an easy death and, as the doctor said, they were not to mourn, for Marguerite had been suffering from incurable growths and was already on heavy doses of laudanum.

The whole household did mourn, nevertheless, as did the citizens of Madras, well-seasoned as they were against death's inroads. Most of the mourners who gathered at St Andrew's Church for the funeral were male, and this, thought Amelia, would have pleased the deceased, who had ever relished the attendance of gentlemen despite her somewhat jaundiced view of their capacities. Indeed the entire occasion, conducted according to her specific instructions, would have given her much satisfaction. The coffin, covered with a pall of best European black cloth, supported by six bearers (short Mr Babbage seeming to take the heaviest burden), was carried to the accompaniment of the late Clifford Hervey's regimental band playing the Death March.

Marguerite had requested that a funeral banquet be served in the Pantheon Assembly Rooms, where her 'mourners could enliven proceedings with copious draughts of free champagne'. Nevertheless, the atmosphere was sombre at first but, as the draughts flowed, tongues loosened. The elderly ones recalled with increasing hilarity the long heyday of Marguerite. At least one duel had been fought over her, it transpired; moreover, she had once arrived at a masquerade ball as Queen Titania in a sequin-covered palki borne by four suitors dressed as hobgoblins, and during one of her widowhoods had nearly landed a very rich lord of the realm. But why, they asked each other with brightening eyes, had she not married the victor of the duel? And were they genuine sequins or just silver paper? And had the rich lord really sent her passionate love-letters from every port when he was bundled off Home by an aristocratic uncle in Calcutta? Amelia, unobtrusive beside a pillar, listened in astonishment until she saw Mr Babbage bearing down on her, when she sidled away to Captain Gilbert.

'What wonderful stories I've been hearing about the dear departed!' she smiled at him.

'Me too! I didn't know the half. How we shall miss her!'

'Indeed we shall! And Captain, may I be practical for a moment? I need to find economical lodgings for myself and the children at once. Would you have any suggestions?'

He stiffened. 'Oh . . . er. . . I'm afraid not, Amelia. I don't know the city very well.'

'You see, I don't want to cause any embarrassment for Marguerite's family.'

'But no one will expect you to move immediately.'

He changed the subject dismissively, making it clear she wasn't to presume too far on his goodwill. 'A piece of news from Tanjore about Gerard Murphy – you remember him?

Part of the barracks burned down the other week. Such mysterious fires are not uncommon – usually started by someone in the pay of the natives who get the contracts for rebuilding. Anyway Murphy, in his usual state of befuddlement, didn't get out in time and died in the flames.'

'Oh heavens! And the children?'

'Perfectly all right . . . staying with Arbuthnot at the time. The Reverend, bye the bye, is rumoured to be in vigorous pursuit of a Danish missionary lady from Tranquebar.'

Amelia smiled. 'Well, I wish her joy of him. But what will happen to the poor mites?'

'Jack will go to the regimental orphanage and I daresay they'll make a drummer-boy out of him.'

'And Rosie?'

He shrugged. 'I suppose there's somewhere for girls, I really can't say. Perhaps the Danish lady will take her on.'

'Poor little scrap – there must be a lot in her position, one way and another.'

Clearly this did not interest him either, and they lapsed into silence. Darkness was falling and the mourners, having ridden high on a champagne-tide of nostalgia, were slipping back into bleary-eyed reality.

'I'm going,' Amelia whispered. 'It's getting melancholy again and I prefer to be sad alone.'

'I quite agree.' He escorted her to the door, ignoring several curious glances and a loud remark from one gentleman about the propriety of a lady and an officer who were 'first affianced, then dis-affianced' going off into the darkness together. Outside, Gil handed her into the carriage, assuring her of his willingness to help her and the children in any way possible, and she responded politely, not believing a word.

Spring's Gardens seemed enormously empty that night, its servants creeping about forlornly like strays already dispossessed. Amelia slept fitfully, disturbed by thoughts of the morrow's various heavinesses. She rose late and was still summoning strength for the first ordeal of explaining to Rolly that his dear Aunt Marguerite had not only gone away but, like his father, was not coming back, when she was handed a calling card from Mr J. Jarrett, the family lawyer. Hastily, she dressed, thinking that deaths and their subsequent rituals occurred with more rapidity in India than elsewhere, as if to compensate for the slow pace of its life.

'Ah, Mrs Lang, good morning.' Large, avuncular Mr Jarrett rose to greet her in the drawing-room. 'I trust you will forgive my calling so soon, but I thought in the circumstances . . .'

'Oh I quite understand, Mr Jarrett, you will have much to arrange. Let me say at once that I intend to look for lodgings for myself and the children this very day.'

He took a chair. 'Well now . . . let us see.' From a capacious bag he produced a portentous parchment document. 'Mrs Hervey's Last Will and Testament, Mrs Lang. Signed by her and witnessed in the presence of myself, her physician, and Captain George Gilbert.'

'George! So that's what the "G" stood for! He never would say and no wonder! It doesn't suit him.'

He frowned at her irrelevance. 'Yes, George. Now – would you like me to read the will in its full legal terminology or may I summarise what concerns you?'

His words suggested a narrow limit of her mental powers, but she was in no mood to quibble. 'Please summarise anything I should hear, Mr Jarrett. It's a matter for her family really, isn't it? I was only her friend.'

'That would be the common assumption, but in this case . . . in this particular case . . .', he savoured every word, 'the entire will concerns you most profoundly. Because, the long and short of it is, Mrs Hervey has left Spring's Gardens and practically everything it contains, except for certain bequests, to you. What do you think of that?'

Amelia gasped, almost horrified. 'To me? No, that can't be true! But . . . but why?'

'When she executed this new will about a month ago, she insisted that the doctor be present to testify she was perfectly *compos mentis*, as indeed to all intents and purposes she was. I pointed out to her that to bequeath almost her entire estate outside her family was somewhat irregular, not with any prejudice against you personally, Mrs Lang, but I felt it my duty as her family lawyer so to do. But she said she'd often acted irregularly in the past and never regretted it and that this was probably her last chance to do so.'

He recalled with a sigh the final flicker of that famous sparkle. 'Only the duller regularities of her later days did she occasionally regret – or so she claimed. As to the reasons for this change of heart, they seem sound enough: her three surviving children are all very comfortably placed and she's left some money to them and to her grandchildren. The sons in Bombay wouldn't be able to move here and her married daughter is happily settled at Home. But Mrs Hervey loved Spring's Gardens dearly and hated to think of it being sold off lock, stock and barrel. Her last words on the subject were that she believed you to possess sufficient resources and strength of character to keep the house and its staff going – somehow.' He glanced at her dubiously. 'I warn you that you've inherited a mixed blessing, Mrs Lang. Spring's Gardens is in a dilapidated condition and many of its servants could be similarly described. But she left only a modest sum for immediate upkeep until "you find your own way forward", as she put it.'

'Oh Marguerite, dear, dear Marguerite! If only I could thank her this minute . . .' Tears welled in Amelia's eyes and she pressed her clenched hands in her lap. 'Oh what a tribute she has paid me, Mr Jarrett! This whole house – all of it.' She looked round in amazement.

'Mrs Hervey did say you'd expressed a strong desire to remain in India. I hope she was not mistaken in that?'

'Oh certainly I want to stay – and now she has made it altogether possible! Oh Mr Jarrett, it's hard for you, a man, to understand the magnitude – the magnificence – of this gift. And now somehow I must prove myself worthy of her trust.' She stood up, her face shining with just the qualities Marguerite had attributed to her.

'You will, of course, need to think matters over most carefully, Mrs Lang, and there are several gentlemen – myself for one – who will be only too happy to offer our professional advice and friendly help. I'm sure you won't do anything precipitate without consulting some of us first, for women are not well suited to deal with financial and property matters. Perhaps I may begin by suggesting that you . . .'

She grinned suddenly as the realisation dawned that she did not have to listen to him, she didn't even have to suffer his presence in this, her house, a moment longer than she wanted.

'Thank you, Mr Jarrett. Naturally I shall be glad to avail myself of your professional services in due course. But first I'd like to take stock, for this has come as a most tremendous surprise to me. I never for an instant dreamed that dear Marguerite . . .' She checked herself, unwilling to betray more of her emotion. 'So if you wouldn't mind leaving now?'

He rose reluctantly, for he'd had much advice at the ready. 'I think the servants should be told at once, Mrs Lang. It would ease their minds.'

'Yes, of course. Kindly tell Dashwood and the word will spread like wildfire. Say also that I intend to keep everyone on – at least for the time being. Thank you.'

He paused at the door, still holding the precious document. 'I had thought we might peruse this together, Mrs Lang?'

She held out her hand. 'Ah yes. But I'd like to look at it myself first and I will then consult you, Mr Jarrett. Thank you.' He blinked resentfully as he handed it over, for he'd imagined her quite broken down at the enormity of this sudden responsibility and only too ready to place everything in his capable hands. Perhaps, he thought, as he went to find Dashwood, she was indeed of the calibre Marguerite had supposed; oddly, that possibility had not before occurred to him.

Amelia first wandered round the drawing-room in a daze, then sat down and read the will in its entirety. The king's pattern silver and most of Marguerite's jewellery were to go to her daughter in England; to the Bombay sons and daughters-in-law went a telescope, two pairs of stuffed birds, two pinchbeck rings, two diamond pins, two Greek statuettes, two dress swords, a gold spy-glass and (which seemed rather pointed) a copy of Buchard's *Advice to Mothers* to be shared between them. At the end she read Captain Gilbert's signature and smiled, realising why he'd evaded her plea for help the previous day and that she could count on him after all.

She rang the handbell and Dashwood appeared instantly, bowing very low and expressing effusive loyalty to the new mistress of Spring's Gardens. Outside, other head servants waited with similar pledges, and smiling Kamba placed a garland of marigolds round her neck. She thanked them in some embarrassment and they urged her gently forward, determined to conduct her on a tour of her new domain. So a solemn little procession was formed, she at its head holding Rolly by the hand, then Dashwood and Kamba with Elizabeth in her arms, followed by the cook, the head groom and gardener.

They ushered her into each room as if she were a total stranger, opening drawers and cupboards, taking books and ornaments from shelves for her to inspect, and pointing out certain items she'd not noticed before: ten mildewed volumes of the *Spectator*, a trunk full of faded satin and gauze ballgowns still smelling of lavender water, and, in Marguerite's writing-desk drawer, a battle ribbon from the war against Tippu Sultan and a duelling pistol inlaid with mother-of-pearl. Outside, her attention was drawn to empty kennels, stables, hen coops and a shed full of tent-poles, rat-bitten saddlery, bullock whips, picnic baskets and candelabra-like branches of iron spikes for carrying lighted flambeaux. They seemed so genuinely pleased and proud she'd inherited all this that she felt obliged to keep exclaiming with pleasure as if at a series of presents. At last, Dashwood announced the tour over and that luncheon would soon be served.

Amelia nodded. 'Thank you, Dashwood. Now I'm just going to take a peep at the old ballroom, which we've overlooked. No – there's no need for you to come, thank you.' Exerting her authority for the first time, Amelia asked a servant to light her a lamp and set off alone along the dim passage to the furthest wing. That ballroom had rather awed and frightened her on her first visit; now it belonged to her she wanted to chase its shadows away.

Tiptoeing to the middle of the floor, she held the lamp aloft, peering into dim recesses where the few sun rays that slanted through the closed shutters couldn't penetrate. All was silent, for at this midday hour even the busiest ants were resting. Two more of the gilded chairs had crumbled of their own accord, leaving little piles of debris. Amelia thumped the seat of one still standing and sure enough it began to disintegrate, rocking as if with laughter as it collapsed and sending out clouds of dust.

She sneezed violently and the sound reverberated round the room, seeming to waken echoes from the past – men with powdered wigs and snuff-boxes sneezing, gasping and laughing as another energetic gavotte ended, the skirts of their bright and breathless ladies rustling as they took to the floor yet again. Amelia stood listening, half-trammelled in the webs of the past, as Theophilus had always been. What would he have made of this marvellous gift? But that train of thought led nowhere, for if he'd lived, she would not have received it. Now she had to make her own plans; he couldn't be her guide. She sighed, seeing his grave in her mind's eye – the dusty trees, trespassing goats, lively squirrels, and Rosie Murphy chuckling at the little creatures on the day of her mother's funeral.

Poor little Rosie! Of course – she would take her in and look after her; that was one decision made at least. But were there not many girls in India like Rosie, and would there not be hundreds more in the future as white men arrived in increasing numbers? Amelia began to pace up and down purposefully, fingering and assessing the threadbare hangings and sagging sofas, her grand idea crystallising as she did so. She would open a board school for orphaned and abandoned girls, both European and half-caste, here in this very house, and she would bully the military and medical authorities into supporting it. For, as Marguerite used to complain, was not the country filling up with every sort of 'do-gooder' eager to remedy the injustices of the past? But she would not allow her school to be controlled by them, especially not by missionaries who were already causing dissension. Her school would be secular and practically adapted to the country. Her pupils would learn both Tamil and English, Hindu doctrine and

Christian, Asian history and European; they would learn to weave, embroider, play the piano and sitar, to ... oh, it would be wonderful what they would learn, what she, with the right help, could teach them!

So excited and inspired was she by all this that she wanted to shout from the rooftops like a prophetess. She rushed to the shutters, wrestling with the rusty bolts and dragging them open – one, two, three. Brilliant daylight and hot breezes poured into the cloistered room, disturbing its slumbering inhabitants who began to squeak and patter and slither and crunch about in panic. But she was no longer afraid of them, nor of anything in the world just then. She watched the sunlight sparkling on the central chandelier that was swinging in the breeze like a great cornucopia of jewels. It must be quite valuable; she would sell it and with the proceeds buy her first desks, benches, slates. In her imagination the room was already repeopled with little girls studying at those desks, learning ways to survive.